CONVERSATIONS WHILE TRAVELING THE CIRCLE

A NOVEL BY

A.C. ETHERIDGE

This book is a work of fiction. Any resemblance to actual events or persons, living or dead, is entirely coincidental.

"Conversations While Traveling the Circle," by A.C. Etheridge. ISBN 978-1-60264-278-2 (soft) ISBN 978-1-60264-280-5 (ebook.)

Published 2008 by Virtualbookworm.com Publishing Inc., P.O. Box 9949, College Station, TX 77842, US.

Manufactured in the United States of America.

Author's Note

This book is a work of fiction, a novel not intended to portray any person who actually inhabits or has inhabited this planet. Although all of the actors and speakers whose deeds and words I recount in this novel are entirely products of my imagination, I have placed my fictional characters in real places, involved them in actual historic events, and allowed them to make references to renowned Americans as a vehicle to accomplish what I strived to do in this novel. And that is to tell the story of how the culture of the American West and events of the last half of the twentieth century and the beginning years of the twenty-first century shaped the lives of people living in an apprehensive time.

While I have tried to be true to history and geography in the actual events and places that I have used to move the story along, I realize it is quite possible that some keen readers may find factual inaccuracies. After doing a reasonable amount of extensive research, I reminded myself that I was writing a novel, not a work of journalism or history, and I should not let facts bog down my tale. So, dear reader, if you find an inaccuracy, forgive me. I hope you still enjoy the story.

The person to whom I dedicate this novel is not a creature of my imagination but my life partner, a caring parent whom any child would want to have as a mother, a lover who should engender envy of me by all men, one of the most intelligent people I have ever met, and a consummate professional in the numerous endeavors she has undertaken. Thank you, Joyce, for putting up with me all of these years as I work through my personal "bucket list."

Chapter 1
A Portentous Night in Tijuana

I first met those three boys in a dark Tijuana alley.

I suppose I should say, "Those three young men." I should call them men because they were Marines -- old enough to defend the country and old enough to go across the border and engage in activities they wouldn't dare tell their mothers, great aunts, and old maid teachers about.

When I first saw them, they were in the alley relieving themselves of a night's load of Mexican beers while comparing the young women each had given fifteen dollars to do what young men want done to them as often as they can scrape up either the money or nerve to ask.

I was John Clarence "Flash" Golden, a has-been singing cowboy whose movie career had ended with the advent of television. By 1962 when I met Buck, Jordan, and Norman in that alley, I didn't go to Tijuana for the same reasons they did. I went down there to inconspicuously have a few beers with an old friend.

Now before I go any farther in this tale, I probably should explain that I'm talking in the omniscient first person. Yes, I know some of you who read a lot of books are probably thinking there can't be an omniscient first person. Those of you who don't read many books probably don't know or give a damn about what omniscient means. But you got a hold of this book somehow, so I'll assume you are a reader and probably were told by some English lit teacher at some point in your schooling that omniscience comes through the third-person voice. Most of the time that's right, but not always. Bear with me, and about halfway through this tale, you'll understand what I'm talking about.

In the meantime, I hope you find these pages worth reading, listening in on the conversations of my younger friends as they grew older while traveling along this circle of life. Now, back to my story about the night I met Buck Leherifen, Jordan Robech, and Norman Victor.

Norman, who was sitting on a wooden crate smoking a cigarette, said, "My girl didn't have tits as big as your girls, but I think she was better looking. But yours were pretty too."

He made that assessment in an almost analytic voice as the three young Marines prepared to walk back toward the border to San Diego. Their plan was the usual routine -- find a cheap hotel and sleep off their debauchery before returning to Camp Pendleton on Sunday.

As Norman stood up, he said, "Mexican women are really pretty, especially when they are young."

"Most women are pretty when they are young," I said.

Startled, the three young Marines looked toward the back of the alley and saw my silhouette, the darkened outline of a man in a cowboy hat zipping up his jeans.

Jordan said, "I didn't see the sign, but this must be the Tijuana public men's room."

"Every Tijuana alley is the public men's room. And you can bet they are cleaner than the ones in the cantinas," I said. "What are you boys doing out here, just having a smoke? I assume you've been inside sampling the pleasures of this idyllic town."

Buck said, "Mister, your voice sounds familiar, but I don't suppose I know you since I doubt that you are in the Marine Corps, and I don't know anybody else on the West Coast, and I doubt that you came all the way from Texas because it's a lot closer to go to Juarez, Acuna, or some other Mexican border town."

"Well, I was in the Marine Corps once, and I did come all the way from Texas, but that was about twenty years ago," I said as I walked toward them and slowly lit a cigarette. I guess the lighter flame lingered and illuminated my face because Buck almost screamed.

"You – you look like Flash Golden. Are you Flash Golden?"

Norman scoffed. "Flash Golden – the man we used to watch at the Saturday afternoon movies? Can't be. We wouldn't be in a Tijuana alley with a famous movie star."

"Fraid so, boys. But I doubt many people would say I'm famous or a movie star. Flash Golden has gone into another phase of his life. You boys don't go to the Saturday afternoon movies anymore. You grew up, and now you spend your Saturday afternoons in bars and whorehouses, and the kids who are the age you used to be watch television."

"But if they still showed your movies on Saturday afternoon, I'll bet we would all go see them. Of course we probably would go to the bar after we got out of the movie," Jordan said.

Norman giggled and said, "Yeah, and Flash Golden didn't hang out in bars. We had to go to Randolph Scott or John Wayne movies to see cowboy heroes hang out in saloons."

"Maybe that's the key – saloon scenes. Duke and Randy are still making movies. Me, I'm just picking my guitar and writing a few songs. So are all you boys from Texas?"

"No sir," Norman said. "I'm from Iowa."

"Iowa's a good place to be from, too. My friend, Duke Wayne, was born in Iowa."

"Yes sir. Everybody in Iowa knows John Wayne is from Iowa. He's probably the most famous Iowan ever."

"I don't know about that. Herbert Hoover was born in Iowa, too," Jordan said.

"Aw, John Wayne's a lot more famous than him," Norman said.

"Your friend's right," I said. "How many people do you think would recognize the ex-president? I'll bet just about everybody around here, especially you Marines, would recognize John Wayne if he showed up down here in Tijuana. Of course, Herbert Hoover is close to ninety now, so I doubt he would be down here drinking and carrying on like you boys. But I guess a man who got elected president of the United States wouldn't be carousing and carrying on and getting blow jobs from young women, no matter even if he were a lot younger than Herbert Hoover, would he?

"I guess I should explain to you boys that I didn't come here to carouse and get blow jobs. Not recently anyway. I came down here to have a few drinks with an old cameraman buddy of mine. But he couldn't stay long because his wife's mad at him. I know this place offers opportunities for healthy normal young men like yourselves to get some relief from celibacy, but me, I have a good woman friend, so as I said, I'm down here just for a little relaxation. And I think I've relaxed enough, so I'll be heading back north...."

A young woman interrupted my departure speech as she stumbled into me. Chasing her into the alley was a man who stopped and then took a cautious step forward.

The woman-girl gripped my arm and pleaded. "Please help me. Please don't let him cut me!"

The pursuing man muttered a Spanish curse word while staring with hatred at the woman-girl.

"Senors, this woman is no good. She is a thief who took money from a young sailor's wallet while he was taking his pleasure, a pleasure for which he had already paid her. This is none of your affair. I will take care of the woman."

The woman-girl gripped my arm even harder and said, "No, please, I am not a thief."

"If you are not a thief, why did you give me only ten American dollars when the sailor said he paid fifteen dollars for you? Zorra, I will make it so a man will not even pay five pesos for you."

The man took a step closer to the woman-girl, who at this point was crying. "Please, no, don't let him cut me."

The man with a knife said, "Cortar, zorra. These Yankees are down here like the rest to drink cerveza and fuck putas like you."

I put my body in front of the woman-girl and said, "Hold it, feller. You're not going to do any harm to this young woman as long as she is with us."

The man with a knife snarled, "Oh, no, gringo. So are you going to pay me what this woman stole from me and your fellow Americano?"

"Yes. If it will get you out of this alley and away from this girl, here's a twenty-dollar bill."

The pimp took the money with a smirk. As he walked out of the alley, the woman-girl's tears grew larger.

"It's okay, girl. He's gone," I said.

"Si. He's gone, but where will I go? I cannot go back. He will cut me, and even if he does not, what will I do? I have no money. I have nothing. I have no family. I became a prostitute after my father left and I could not beg enough coins from the touristas to help feed by mother and my baby brother. Then they became ill, and now they are dead too, and I am all alone."

As the woman-girl continued to cry and cling to me I finally looked down at her and said, "Oh, hell, come on, girl. I guess the only right thing to do is to give all four of you young people a ride out of here. I know a better place across the border to get another beer."

Chapter 2
Baja Angeles

We walked to my Chevy Impala. After I tipped the boys who had guarded it, I opened the trunk and took out a blanket and a leather jacket.

"Okay," I said. "Here's how we are going to get all of us past the border boys without having to make the girl get in the trunk."

I told Jordan to get in the shotgun seat up front with me and took my hat and put it on the woman-girl's head after stuffing her hair into it and draping the leather jacket over her shoulders. I positioned her between Norman and Buck in the backseat and placed the blanket around the woman-girl.

"Now, young lady, and by the way what is your name?"

The woman-girl looked up at me and said "Angelina. Angelina Perdidos."

"Well, Angelina, my little lost angel, you keep my hat over your pretty face and the leather jacket over your upper feminine features and the blanket over your equally attractive lower feminine parts and make those Customs boys think you are just a another drunken Marine. If you can do that,

I think we can get you away from the miserable life that you've been leading."

Slumped over in the back seat almost hidden by Norman and Buck, Angelina caused no curiosity at the border, and we were waved through after assuring the Customs guards we were just another carload of American revelers on that early summer night.

I drove through San Diego and up Highway 101 to a Mexican food café and bar near San Clemente, the first city north of the Camp Pendleton Marine Corps Base. It was about 1 a.m. when I led the four young people through the doors of the Baja Angeles. There were no other customers, and Ray, the bartender, was pouring bloody mary and margarita mixes from gallon bottles into smaller mix bottles. He looked up as we came through the door.

"Buenos noches, Ramon. You can pull that bottle of five-dollar Scotch out again and keep filling those Chivas Regal bottles. I've been drinking so many years that it doesn't matter to me, and these young people ain't been drinking long enough to know the difference. Besides, we're not going to tell anybody."

"Flash, you know I'm not doing that. It's illegal. I'm just putting the mixes in bottles small enough to pour from."

"Just kidding, amigo. I know you're honest as the day is long. Course it's been dark for several hours now."

Dear reader, I know these jokes are decrepit, but if we don't keep reciting them, the new generations will think they are fresh and somebody will make a million dollars because people will think he or she came up with them in his or her own mind. But, hey, why should I begrudge somebody making money because people haven't read historic humor or watched old movies of people like Bob Hope and Bud Abbot and Lou Costello.

So back to the story I'm trying to tell. I promise I'll try to control myself with the asides.

"We'd probably never get caught if I did substitute the rotgut for the good stuff because most of the people who come in here couldn't tell the difference between kerosene and Courvoisier," Ray said.

"Ain't that the truth," I said. "Hell, most of 'em can't pronounce Courvoisier. And they go by the common sense rule that it all will make you drunk, or at least feel better for a little while. After all, ain't that why we drink? But we didn't come here to get drunk or even philosophize about it. Do you think you could rustle up some food?"

"You'll have to talk to Arlene. I think she just cleaned the griddle."

Arlene, the owner of Baja Angeles and my dear lady friend, heard us and came from the kitchen.

"Flash, why can't you eat your dinner when you're supposed to. I'll fix you some food, but I should make you clean the griddle again," she said.

"I can do that. Done it many times. Buck, Norman, Jordan, and Angelina, this gracious and beautiful lady is Arlene Bearclaw, and the fellow behind the bar is Ramon -- or Ray -- Garcia.

"Arlene and Ray, these fellers are Buck Leherifen, Norman Victor, and Jordan Robech, three of the nation's finest – United States Marines. And this beautiful young woman is Angelina Perdidos. How these fine young people got hooked up with a drugstore cowboy like me is a story too long to tell here, so we'll save it for another time."

After everyone had acknowledged the introductions, Arlene picked up menus, pointed to a table, and told us to sit down.

"We don't need menus, sweet lady," I said. "Five of your famous green chile cheeseburgers will take care of our hunger and make us look forward to the rest of tonight and tomorrow. And, uh, if you're so inclined, some French fries would go nicely with those burgers."

"I can do that. We haven't drained the fryer, but are you sure your friends want chiles on their burgers? You know some people aren't accustomed to chiles."

"Arlene, darling, you're from New Mexico. You know green chiles are a subject of evangelism. People who haven't tried them need to for the good of their souls. Have you ever met anyone who didn't grow to love green chiles?"

"Well, no. I guess not."

"See there, proves my point."

Norman looked hesitant and said, "Uh, I hate to be this way, but maybe you should make mine just a plain cheeseburger."

I asked Norman if he had ever eaten green chiles.

"We don't eat much Mexican food in Iowa. But my mom once made a Frito chili pie from a recipe that she got out of *Good Housekeeping....*"

"Frito chili pie! Boy, that's some recipe dreamed up in a stainless steel Yankee test kitchen. Besides, that's chili with an I. Not that it's all bad. God knows I've eaten enough of that stuff in my life, being a native Texan. But if you ever went to Santa Fe or Albuquerque and tasted the chile with an E, then you would know the New Mexicans have at least one thing on the Texans."

Buck said since he was from Texas but grew up not very far from New Mexico he would certainly have a green chile cheeseburger. Jordan said he grew up in Texas but about four hundred miles from New Mexico.

"But I'm a Texan, and I'll eat anything," he said.

"Okay, I'll have one, too," Norman said. "It's gotta be better than that Frito chili pie my mom made. The dog wouldn't even eat that."

I laughed and said, "Probably because of the chili. Some of that canned stuff is really awful. Only way you can eat it is drunk. Come to think of it, the only way you can eat a lot of the homemade chili is drunk, too. I guess that's because a lot of the chili is made by drunks. It's a wonder some of them don't die of food poisoning, but then alcohol kills a lot of germs."

I paused, remembered another funny story I once heard, and said, "That reminds me of the story about how chili was invented. There was this Montana rancher, you see, who came up with this concoction to treat his cattle for hoof and mouth disease. It worked so well that he sent it to his friend who owned a spread down in Texas. After a couple of weeks, he called his Texas friend and asked him what he thought about his remedy. 'Oh, it was delicious,' said the Texas rancher."

When Ray started to chuckle, I looked over at him and asked, "You haven't heard that one, Ray?"

"No, Flash. That's a good one. You know all the good Texas jokes."

"That's because I grew up there," I said. "I know all the Aggie jokes and all the Texas jokes. I never really was an Aggie, meaning I never went there, or any other college for that matter, but I did grow up close by after my papa opened the little grocery store in Bryan, so I kind of adopted them as my team. Norman, do you know what an Aggie is?"

"Sure do. Texas A&M Aggies."

"Well then, did you ever hear the one about the Aggie who couldn't spell, and spent the night in a warehouse?"

Norman, Buck, and Jordan smiled along with Ray, but Angelina ducked her head. I was a little bit embarrassed by my momentary thoughtlessness.

"Sorry, I guess I didn't need to tell that joke."

After a short silence, Arlene said. "What can we bring you gentlemen and the lady to drink? And what can we get you, Flash?"

I told her it was never too late for a beer, and Jordan said he would like one too.

"Please, may I have a Coca Cola," Angelina said.

"You betcha. But Jordan, I probably should ask for your I.D."

"I changed my mind. I guess I'll have a Coke too," Jordan said.

Norman and Buck also asked for Cokes, and Ray turned to fill the drink orders as Arlene went toward the kitchen.

"I've got the green chile cheeseburgers frying. They should be about ready," she said.

I said I was going to go the men's room and was glad this one was indoors.

As I closed the men's room door, Buck said, "Can you believe we're with Flash Golden? I watched him at the Saturday afternoon shoot-em-ups, and here we are with Flash Golden."

"Yeah," Norman said. "But I'll bet when you were watching those movies you never thought you would meet Flash Golden pissing in an alley outside a Tijuana cantina."

"You're right about that, buddy. But he was true to the script. He rescued the girl," Jordan said.

Buck said, "Yeah, imagine getting rescued in real life by a cowboy star you used to watch in the movies when you were in grade school."

Arlene re-entered from the kitchen bringing the cheeseburgers and overheard Buck. "Rescued? What were you young people doing that required rescue?"

"Uh, he rescued us from being late getting back to Camp Pendleton by giving us a ride," Jordan said.

"When he found out you were Marines, there was no doubt he was going to help you. He certainly has a soft spot – I believe you guys call it esprit de corps – for Marines, not to mention Texans," Arlene said as she turned to go back into the kitchen.

I returned to the table and asked, "So, how old are you boys anyway?"

Norman said, "I'm eighteen. I was born on June 6, 1944."

"D Day, the day of the Normandy invasion," I said. "So your parents, Mr. and Mrs. Victor, named you Norman."

"Yes, I'm lucky our last name wasn't Beach. They probably would have named me Omaha."

"I'm two years older, going on twenty-one," Buck said. "Jordan, who should have known better than to ask for that beer, is nineteen. So we all have to do our drinking in Tijuana and the Camp Horno Enlisted

Men's Club, where the used car dealers buy the pitchers and nobody can keep up with who's drinking out of them."

I asked them how they came to join the Corps. Buck explained that after his first year at Texas Tech he had so-so grades and an old Ford that needed a new clutch. He sold the car for fifty dollars and joined the Marine Corps, figuring he would serve a few years, maybe seeing some of the world and saving enough money with the help of the G.I. bill to go back to college.

"What did your mama think about that?" I asked.

"She's dead. So's my daddy. My mother died of cancer two summers ago right after I graduated from high school, and my daddy was killed in a car wreck two years earlier. So I'm an orphan. Don't have any brothers or sisters. Don't even have a girlfriend. Since I had no chances of getting married to avoid being drafted, I decided to join the military and thought, what the hell—I'll join the bad-asses and signed up for the Marines. I guess that's kind of funny because I've never been a bad-ass."

"Me neither," Norman said. "I was a simple farm kid. Got double-promoted in the first grade. That's why I could get out of high school at seventeen. But at least half of the guys in our boot platoon were just like me, and the rest of them really were bad-asses. Or at least pseudo bad-asses."

"Funny you should say that," Jordan said. "Here's why I joined the Marines, actually the Marine Reserves. I went to one semester of college, made decent enough grades, but wasn't sure what I wanted to do next. Over the holidays, I was at one of the local hamburger drive-in hangouts after a movie, seeing if there were any girls who might want to go for a drive, and this big guy comes up to me.

"He tells me he played football against me in high school. He said I tackled him and he thought it was dirty tackle. Then he flipped a bugger at me and asked me if I thought he should kick my ass to just to get even.

"Well, this guy was about three inches taller and twenty pounds heavier than me, so I said, no, I didn't think he should kick my ass, and I didn't want to fight him.

"He snarled and crushed my Coke cup and walked away while all of his friends were giving me intense smirks.

"I didn't sleep that much that night. I thought about guys like you, Flash, and what would have happened in one of your movies if the bully bad guy came up and essentially challenged you to a duel. I know what would have happened. The bully bad guy would have been beaten or blown away, and the good guy would have won.

"But it didn't happen that way because I wasn't sure I could beat that guy's ass. And like Buck, I didn't have a serious girlfriend and knew I would probably be drafted in a couple of years, so I thought I can join the

Marines Reserves, learn how to whip ass, and go back to college in a year."

I formed an understanding smile and said, "Jordan, that's certainly not an unusual story. I figure a lot of young men have joined the Marines for the same reason. Probably not a particularly mature or even sane one, but still a rationale that has kept the Corps in business nearly two hundred years."

The three boys told me they were radio operators in the First Marine Division's Seventh Communications Battalion at Pendleton's Camp Horno, just seven miles down the road from Camp San Onofre, where Marines go through a month of infantry training after they graduate from boot camp in San Diego.

I took a drink of my beer and said, "Yes, I know the geography. Every male in the room right now is a Marine. I served in World War II, and Ray served in Korea. I went through boot camp in 1942; Ray went through in 1952; and now you boys come along in 1962. Three decades of Marines. Ray and I had to fight wars. Maybe you boys will be able to avoid that. Anyway, I hope so, now that the Commies have the same capability as we do to blow the whole world to smithereens."

Jordan, Buck, and Norman agreed that finishing their lives as smithereens was not a scenario they had envisioned when they were growing up with the dreams and hopes that young boys got from watching Western and war movies.

"But you boys will protect us, I know. You've been through the course of how to be the world's best warriors. If you didn't know how to shoot when you went to boot camp, I'll bet you do now," I said.

"Norman did," Buck said. "He qualified expert on the rifle range. Me and Jordan, we just barely qualified as marksmen."

"What's this," I said. "Texans who aren't sure-shots? Texans who grew up on Western movies even?"

"Yeah. I guess we're not holding up the image. To tell the truth, I'm not much good at riding horses either. But I love barbeque," Buck said.

"Me too. And I played football," Jordan said.

"Those are the real marks of a Texan," said an amused Ray.

"Yes indeed," I said. "Say Ray, I guess Arlene has told you about the triple-threat asshole. Actually Arlene doesn't say asshole. She uses a more genteel term, a triple-threat in arrogance. But arrogance and asshole both start with the same letter and mean the same thing. Whether asshole or arrogant, Arlene says the ultimate A-whatever is someone who is a Texan, Marine, and Aggie, all three."

"Yeah Flash, Arlene has told me that a few times," Ray said.

I looked at Buck and Jordan and said, "So I guess you two, Ray, and I are only one qualification away from being ultimate assholes. But Ray is from El Paso, so I'm not sure he's a real Texan. You know, most Texans think El Paso ought to be part of New Mexico."

"It should be. It's even in the mountain time zone," Ray said.

Buck said mountains were not a sight that many Texans see out of their front window, adding that people on the South Plains of Texas, where he grew up, think it strange to see a hill.

"Ain't that the truth," I said. "Those Texas South Plains are as flat as Kansas. You could shoot one of those Marine rifles and the bullet could fly until it ran out of energy unless it hit a windmill or cotton gin."

Arlene returned from the kitchen, pulled a chair to the table and said, "So you are from outside of Lubbock, Buck. Oh my god, we have four Texans here. Four Texans and four Marines!"

"Five, counting Ray," I corrected. "But yeah, I already told them about your triple-threat qualifications. Heck, some people claim there's a fourth qualification -- Texan, Marine, Aggie, and Jew. I qualify for that one too. Well, halfway. My daddy was Jewish. But he wasn't really a practicing Jew. It's hard to find a synagogue or rabbi in the middle of Texas. So he married a Baptist. That's where I get my drinking genes. I'm sure you've been told that when you go fishing with Baptists, you always want to take two of that denomination. Do you know why?"

Buck and Jordan shrugged and shook their heads.

"Ray, tell them why," Flash asked.

"Because if you only take one, he'll drink all your beer. Yes, I've heard that one," Ray said.

"Of course, no one believes I'm half Jew because they never heard of a Jew from Texas. If they had, I never would have become a cowboy movie actor. But then if I hadn't been a Jew, I might never have gotten past the gates at the studios. Sometimes it helped to be named Golden when one of the most influential men in Hollywood had a similar name.But you'll have to forgive Arlene for all those comments about Texans, boys. She's from New Mexico."

Arlene shook her head and said, "I'm not sure it's safe to have this many Texans in the same room at the same time, especially talking about shooting rifles, which I believe I overheard a few minutes ago. You know it's a wonder that with so many Texans ending up in the Marine Corps and getting to play with guns, there aren't some who get out and do more damage, like shooting someone important or killing a bunch of innocent people who are just walking along minding their own business."

I told her that now she was being silly.

"Oh, I'm not saying a few crazy Texans wouldn't do something like that, but not a Texan who's been in the Marines," I said.

"The Corps teaches you values. Next thing you'll be saying is we need to watch out not only for Texans and Marines but also for Eagle Scouts."

"You never can tell," Arlene said. "But let's talk about something else. So, Buck, if you're from around Lubbock, did you know Buddy Holly?"

"No. I grew up in a small town not far from Lubbock, and we went into Lubbock to shop and see movies, but I never met Buddy Holly. He was a few years older than me. I started at Texas Tech about a year and a half after his plane crashed. I did fill up his daddy's car a few times at the gas station where I worked part-time when I was going to Tech."

"But Norman has better Buddy Holly stories. He's from Clear Lake, Iowa," Buck said."

"Yep, I saw Buddy Holly's last concert at the Surf Ballroom in Clear Lake, and the airplane went down in a corn field near my parents' farm. It was so tragic," Norman said.

"Yes, it was," Arlene said. "He was such a talented boy. I grew up in Clovis, New Mexico, and Buddy recorded his songs at a studio there. I wonder if twenty years from now whether anyone will remember Buddy."

"Oh, yes ma'am. If I'm still around, at least one person will," Norman said.

"Me too," Jordan said. "And those songs he wrote -- I'll bet people will keep them alive by recording them."

Arlene said, "Yes, but I doubt that anyone can make them hits like Buddy did. I certainly don't think anyone should even try to do *That'll Be the Day.*"

Norman said, "I knew all the people around Clear Lake who investigated the plane crash, but I never met a famous person, not even once, until tonight. Mr. Golden, I guess you know lots of famous people."

I told Norman I was going to bonk him on the head the next time he called me Mister.

"My name is Flash, or John or John Clarence or J.C. if you don't like my nickname, but don't call me Mister. And I'm not famous, at least not anymore. But, yes, I guess I have met my share of famous people. One of them is your fellow Iowa native, John Wayne -- a real man who can put away a gallon of whiskey and you won't even know it. Bill Holden is another fine man who can hold his liquor. We'd go out, and the bartenders would say, 'Look out, here comes Holden and Golden. Holden is golden because he's a star, and Golden may be holdin' because he's a Texas cowboy.'

"And Bob Mitchum is another star and good man I've tipped a few with. And there are some others, like Bill Holden's good friend, Ronnie Reagan. He and his wife, Nancy, are nice people, but Ronnie probably won't ever reach the fame of the Duke or Bill or Mitch. He may be known only as the actor who had a chimpanzee for a co-star, but he's still a good guy. Smart feller, too.

"But all of them have done better than me. Yes, life takes funny turns. I decided to stay in California after I mustered out of the Marines at the end of the war, worked as an extra in a couple of shoot-em-ups, moved up to bit parts, and when those Hollywood Jews, Baptists, atheists, or whatever they were figured out I could play the guitar and hold a note, I got a few starring parts.

"But soon kids like you were sitting in a front of a television set rather than munching your popcorn at the Saturday afternoon matinees. Now I'm living in a trailer and writing a few songs. Of course, that wasn't every singing cowboy star's fate. Roy Rogers is living a nice life with a loving wife and lots of kids on a big ranch in the middle of the California desert. Gene Autry bought a major league baseball team and just about everything else in Southern California, and Rex Allen is being paid good money by Walt Disney to narrate movies about varmints.

"And yes, I've known some really good and beautiful women, too, like Arlene who used to be in the movies, and...."

The cafe door opened, and I did a double-take when I recognized the beautiful blonde woman who had entered, slightly wobbly on her feet. She stopped and looked at the table where we were sitting.

"I'll be damned! What's beautiful lady like you doing in a place like this?" I exclaimed as I stood up and moved toward her.

The blonde woman slowly and somewhat woozily raised her eyes and recognized me.

"John? John Golden, is that you?"

"You bet your sweet, uh and beautiful, ass it is, darling. What are you doing here? Are you lost?"

"Yes," she said with a giggle. "I guess I am. I came down to have dinner with my ex-husband's son. We stayed friends after his dad and I split up. I guess I got a little confused trying to find my way back to Los Angeles. I saw this place and thought maybe someone could give me directions."

"You're on the right road. But you've only gotten as far as San Clemente, and at this time of night, I suggest you find some place to stay and go home in the daylight. No offense, beautiful lady, but I think you may have had too many champagne cocktails at dinner."

"Oh, and I suppose you're totally sober," the beautiful blonde woman said.

"Hell, I haven't been totally sober since I mustered out of the Corps. You know that. That's why I can give such good advice about these matters."

The beautiful blonde woman reached and touched my cheek and said, "I might take your advice if I could find a good place to stay. Do you live anywhere around here?"

I was not comfortable with how the conversation was going, so I pointed toward Arlene and said, "I should introduce two of the most beautiful women in California. Arlene, did you ever meet...."

Arlene spoke quickly before I could finish the sentence. "Yes, more than ten years ago, so I doubt that she will remember me. We were both movie extras."

The beautiful blonde woman looked at the beautiful brunette woman and said, "I'm sorry. You're right. I don't remember. But it's great to meet someone else from those years. Which movie was it?"

"We didn't meet on a movie set. It was at a party."

"Uh-oh. Then I'm not going to ask anything more about that," the blonde said. "I went to too many parties back in those days. As a matter of fact, I think I met Flash at a party.

"Yes, you did. Hell of a party," I said.

The blonde woman moved closer, smiled, and said, "I seem to recall it was quite a nice evening even after the party ended."

At this point I was clearly discomforted as I said, "Um, yes, uh. I have the same recollection. How could any red-blooded American male forget that night?"

"I wasn't with just any red-blooded American, Flash. I was with you – the handsomest, nicest cowboy in Hollywood." Then the blonde turned to Arlene and said, "Do you remember the year we met?"

"It was the late '40s, before either you or I met Flash, and before he got serious competition from that young fellow in

Rawhide for title of handsomest cowboy. But he's still the nicest."

I continued to be uncomfortable and said, "Oh, hush, both of you." Then I looked over at Buck, Jordan, and Norman, who were sitting pop-eyed with their mouths open.

"Boys, I must admit I can't remember a night like this, one where two beautiful women say the nicest things about a rapidly aging has-been like me."

The beautiful blonde woman moved over to the beautiful brunette woman and asked her softly but directly, "Arlene, I'm afraid I still don't remember. Were we attracted to the same men back when we met at that party?"

"I don't remember that much about the party," Arlene said. "But I'm sure all the men were chasing around to get your attention and not paying that much attention to the rest of us girls."

The blonde's expression turned really sad, almost tearful, as she said, "Yes, but now look at us. You have the great guy, and I keep getting involved with men who don't take me to happiness, even if they are famous and powerful."

Then she put her right hand up to the bridge of her nose and wiped the forming tears from her eyes and said, "Flash and Arlene, it was good to see you again. I think I'll be going now."

She turned and walked toward the door. I followed her and said, "Wait, you don't need to leave."

The beautiful blonde woman turned, smiled but with sadness still in her eyes, and said, "Yes, I do need to leave. Goodbye. You really are a nice guy. I have met some nice guys along with all the heels, and you are one of the nicest."

She kissed me on the mouth and said, "Goodbye, John Golden. Arlene's a lucky woman."

The beautiful blonde woman walked out the door of the Baja Angeles. I walked back to the table, shaking my head as I sat down.

"I don't think I've ever seen that woman when she was truly happy. She's really sad. So pretty, but since I've known her, she has been trying to find happiness. They say money can't bring happiness. Beauty sure can't either," I said.

Angelina asked, "What does bring happiness, Senor Golden?"

I looked up from my beer, motioned to Ray, and said, "Hell, if I know. Another beer maybe. Bartender?"

As I drank that beer, I thought about the woman who had walked out the door. I know some men have written about their experiences with her, some probably true, some probably not. But I'm not going to be one of those men. This book is not about her. It's not even about me. This book is about the young -- later to be older -- people I'm introducing you to. If you want to know about me, or that pretty young blonde lady, go rent an old movie, make some popcorn or pizza and have a good time remembering.

I had almost finished my beer when Arlene said, "She said I was a lucky woman to have a man like you. But I wonder if she would think I was such a lucky woman if she knew the whole story behind our relationship."

"Probably not," I said. "I'm pretty sure she wouldn't have the strength you have shown since Floyd was hurt."

The three young Marines and Angelina exchanged glances, and then Jordan, who turned out to be least timid for the next forty years, said, "Excuse me, but who's Floyd?"

"He's my husband," Arlene said.

Chapter 3
Camp Pendleton to Hollywood

Arlene realized her answer required a greater explanation, which she quickly gave before Buck, Norman, and Jordan started making plans to go back to Camp Horno.

All three no doubt had seen Floyd Bearclaw in many of the movies that consumed their Saturday afternoons, but they did not know it. Floyd was a full-blood Cherokee from Oklahoma and got some speaking parts as an Indian, but since he also had been a rodeo rider and an excellent athlete, he made most of his money as a stuntman who took the falls off cliffs, buildings, and horses that producers and sometimes the actors themselves did not want the stars of the movies to take. Floyd took one too many falls -- the last one off a horse that left him in a coma from which doctors said he would never emerge.

Floyd and I were friends who had worked on several movies together, but I did not meet Arlene until I visited her unconscious husband in the hospital. I consoled her, but our relationship was nothing more than caring friendship. Both of us were married --

Arlene to Floyd Bearclaw and I to movie starlet Debra Debaux.

Our relationship did not change until after I divorced Debra when I learned about Debra's relationship with Sam Eschidt. Sam had begun to make a name for himself by producing and directing movies in Europe -- movies that the censors would not allow to be shown in the American movie theaters. Eschidt, being a good businessman, spent time refining and softening his formula, hoping that the loosening morality would allow him to become a successful U.S. producer. In the meantime, he continued to make a good living making movies that could run in European theaters and American smut markets.

The divorce came about after I came home early from a fishing trip. I didn't make a scene. I just turned and left the house, leaving Debra and Sam in our bed, naked, moist, and wide-eyed.

Looking back, I realize why I was so amicable about the breakup probably was because I had met Arlene. With the American divorce rate today at somewhere near fifty percent, I figure a large number of Americans don't put a lot of thought into getting married. They must think romance is a thing of fate or destiny or meant to be from the time they start dating. And many of them haven't figured it out by the second marriage. Or even the third. Well, you know, I lived in Hollywood. No, come to think of it, I just lived in America.

Anyway, I guess I was a pleased after the divorce that I could spend more time with Arlene. She had a vegetative husband, but we both were still young and with active sex drives. Dear reader, you know where this is going. Yes, we succumbed to nature and started taking care of each other's needs both emotionally and physically, but Arlene, being the good Catholic she was raised to be, told me she could never divorce her husband and probably asked forgiveness in her confessions after she put me in a good mood.

I also knew that a woman who tried to follow her religious faith would not approve of how Angelina had supported herself in recent months. That is why I thought better of suggesting that Arlene take in the young woman as a houseguest on the first meeting.

After I took the last bite of my green chile cheeseburger, I suggested that the three Marines and Angelina ride with me a little farther up the road where they could find lodging near my trailer, which was in a commercial park in the hills with a view of the pier in San Clemente, the seaside town far enough from Los Angeles and close enough to a military base to still have rents in the early '60s that enabled people with moderate incomes to afford to live there.

I stopped at the first all-night supermarket we passed, gave Norman a ten-dollar bill, and instructed him to take Angelina into the store to buy a toothbrush and whatever other toiletries she might need. Then we drove to a motel where Buck,

Norman, and Jordan had spent several weekend liberty nights. It was a little seedy but inexpensive enough for Marine enlisted men.

I paid for two rooms and gave the three young men clear instructions that they should stay in one room and the young woman should stay in the other one.

"I want you boys to get a good night's rest because I'm going to be back before checkout time in the morning, and we can decide what we are going to do with Senorita Perdidos."

There was a single thought all three young Marines had about what they would like to do with the beautiful young woman, but they followed my instructions that night. They were tired, probably a little hung-over, and it had been less than eight hours since three of Angelina's colleagues had taken care of their other reason for not wanting to sleep alone.

When I woke up, as sober as I was most mornings, I wondered what I was thinking when I broke the law and stuck that girl in my car and smuggled her across the border. But when I thought about the consequences she faced, I wasn't ashamed. Maybe it was truly a heroic act, I rationalized. Never mind, what was done was done, and now I had to figure out how to make the most of it.

I knocked on the boys' door a few minutes after nine o'clock on that Southern California Sunday summer morning. Buck woke up first, pulled on his jeans, and stumbled to the door.

"Good morning, Sunshine," I said. "I hope you had a good night's sleep and have a clear head because we have to figure out what we do with this beautiful illegal citizen we perhaps not so wisely smuggled into the country last night. I'll admit if I had been completely sober I might not have been so gallant, but still I guess it was the right thing to do, and now we have to keep doing the right thing. It's important to always do the right thing."

Buck did nothing other than shrug as Norman and Jordan sat upright and started making movements aimed at getting dressed.

"I guess we can't send her back," Buck said. "So what would the law do with us if we tried to do whatever we have to do to make her a legal resident?"

"That's kind of a moot -- or maybe the better word is silly -- question, since there are procedures for legally entering the country, and crossing the border disguised as a drunk Marine is not one of those procedures," Jordan said.

I complimented Jordan for his groggy astuteness and said, "For the time being, we are going to have to deal with being lawbreakers, but Angelina is probably just one of several thousand illegal Mexicans within a hundred-mile radius of here, so I'm not losing a lot of sleep worrying about going to jail. That is, as long as we four people stick to a single story about how we picked up the girl.

"And that story needs to be that we found her on the American side of the border. It's not unusual for Mexican girls to spend their time in San Diego bars and be picked up by sailors and Marines, and from this moment on, that's what happened. You three Marines invited Angelina to have a drink, and I struck up a conversation with y'all."

"Yes sir," Jordan said as he looked at his two buddies.

"Good. Now we have to explain the plan to Angelina, but before we do that, we still need to decide what to do with her. I think I got a plan for that, too," I said.

I told them about my relationship with my ex-wife Debra, who continued to go by her stage name since she had become one of her new husband's key performers in his genre of movies.

"Now Debra and Sam have a big fancy house up in North Hollywood, a house that requires quite a few servants to keep up. I've been up there a couple of times, and I doubt that many of those maids and gardeners are American citizens," I explained.

"So you think Angelina could work for them?" Norman asked.

"Yes, but I need to figure out how to bring up the subject. As you might expect, Debra and Sam and I aren't exactly the closest of friends, but we do have a civil relationship since Debra's daughter, Tammy, took a liking to me, and Debra has asked me to come by a couple of times hoping I could talk some sense into the child, who picked up some less than desirable habits while growing up with the likes of Debra and me and now Sam. Her own daddy, Tony Dolcito, was a good jazz saxophonist, but he was a bad gambler and apparently took his own life after the bookies decided they were going to break his hands and a few other parts of his body if he didn't pay up.

"But that's another story. Let's get back to our plan for making an honest woman out of sweet Angelina. We have a little problem in timing. Debra and Sam are off on some cruise, so it will be a couple more weeks before I can present Angelina as a prospective employee. I suppose I could ask Arlene to take her in, but Arlene doesn't exactly approve of lawbreaking of any kind, and wisely so, since it would go harder on her as a business owner who's employing an illegal alien.

"I guess the other option would be for me to keep her at my place, but that's not exactly smart since neither Arlene nor the rest of the world would think it proper for me having a beautiful housekeeper young enough to be my daughter."

"So what do we do for the next couple of weeks," Buck asked.

"What can we do? I'll have to rent her a place to stay. I think I can get Arlene to do me a favor and arrange that. Arlene can go with her, and the landlord will likely think they're related. How's this place? Does it have monthly rates?"

The motel did have good rates for long-term residents, and I got Arlene to cooperate in helping Angelina get settled into her room. I also made Buck, Norman, and Jordan promise they would check on Angelina regularly. The first weekend Buck and Jordan had duty, so Norman took the assignment of looking after Angelina.

They walked along the San Clemente main street that follows the Pacific and had dinner on the pier. Then they went back to Angelina's room. Buck and Jordan could tell when Norman returned on Sunday night that their friend had enjoyed his assignment.

The next weekend Norman had duty, so Buck and Jordan looked after Angelina.

Buck and Jordan took the bus into San Clemente and picked up Angelina. They took the bus to Arlene's Baja California and ate green chile cheeseburgers.

On the weekend I was going to visit Debra and propose she hire Angelina, I wanted all of those boys to go with me. I planned to tell Debra that I wanted to introduce Tammy to some nice young men and not the druggy beatniks she seemed to hang around with.

I didn't ask Angelina to accompany us because I wanted to use the two young Marines as a pretense for the visit. I figured I would find an occasion to privately ask Debra about Angelina, telling her that she was a relative of Arlene or Ray who needed a job.

Norman declined to make the trip because he said he thought someone needed to look after Angelina, but Buck and Jordan agreed to accompany Flash because hanging out in Hollywood with people who make movies, even weird and sleazy ones, sounded cool to them.

Both of the boys were interested in meeting movie stars, but Jordan perhaps was the most interested. He was not only a Texas boy nurtured on Western movies. He also was an aspiring guitar player and songwriter, and he realized anyone who had succeeded in the entertainment business was someone he should meet.

My two young friends and I arrived at the Eschidt mansion in the early afternoon on Saturday. I could tell that Buck and Jordan both were impressed by Debra and Tammy. Debra was a beautiful blonde with the proverbial hour-glass figure. While not a classic beauty like her mother, Tammy still was an attractive young woman, certainly to a couple of horny young Marines. Tammy's father had been of Mediterranean extraction, and she inherited his big brown eyes and olive complexion. She also was about two inches shorter and maybe a few pounds heavier than her mother. The physical features both mother and daughter had in common were their ample bosoms.

Tammy was a gracious hostess to the less than dashing young men I had brought to her doorstep. After we spent about thirty minutes on the introduction and niceties, Tammy asked Buck and Jordan if they wanted to go for a tour of the Hollywood hills in her convertible.

As they walked out the door, I reminded the two young Marines that they had agreed to meet me at the corner of Hollywood and Vine at six o'clock. I told Tammy to make sure they got there. She promised they would keep their appointment and escorted Buck and Jordan outside as Debra and I were left alone to talk about what I wanted to discuss.

"So have you ever been to Hollywood before?" Tammy asked Buck and Jordan as they walked toward her car.

"Not this part. Not the nice homes part," Buck said.

"Yeah," Jordan said. "We've just seen the tourist stuff like Hollywood and Vine and the Chinese Theatre."

"So do you have girlfriends out here?" Tammy asked as she steered her car into the Hollywood hills.

"No," Jordan said. "California girls don't seem to be very interested in Marines, and it's pretty easy for them to figure out who the Marines are since we are the only ones who don't have any hair."

Tammy drove a couple of miles into the hills and pulled into a secluded groove of eucalyptus trees with a peek-a-boo view of the Pacific and parked the car. Since it was a pleasant day, Jordan wondered why Tammy put the top up. His puzzlement went away when Tammy took a small bag out of the glove compartment and rolled its contents into a cigarette.

She handed Buck the joint and said, "Want a toke?"

"Uh, no thanks." Never having smoked marijuana, Buck's discomfort was evident.

"So you don't smoke pot. How do you feel about LSD?"

"Uh, I don't really know much about them. We hardly have any Mormons back in Texas. But why do you bring them up. Do they smoke marijuana?"

Tammy and Jordan both laughed.

"Not LDS -- Latter Day Saints," Tammy said. LSD -- lysergic acid diethylamide, the new drug that the cool and hip people are using. And, unlike pot, it's legal, at least for now."

"Uh, no. I don't know about it."

Tammy took another long deep toke and said, "So they don't do drugs in Texas?"

"Yeah, I guess some people do, but I didn't, uh don't," Buck said.

"Why, Mommy and Daddy might not approve?"

"No, Mommy and Daddy are dead."

"Oh, I'm sorry. So, you're a full orphan, not just half orphan like me."

"Yeah."

"Do you miss your parents?"

"Of course."

Tammy looked a little disgusted and said, "You don't have to say it like that. Not everybody misses their parents. Especially if they never were around in the first place, like my dad. He was always off playing in some boozy jazz place. And my mom is mostly off, boozy."

Jordan didn't know what to say, so he said nothing.

"Sure you don't want a toke?" Tammy asked.

"No, thanks."

"How about you, Jordan?"

"No, I guess not. It's like Flash's joke about taking two Baptists on a fishing trip, because if you take one he'll drink all your beer. Well, smoking pot can get you court-martialed, and the two of us better not do it in front of another Marine."

Tammy inhaled again as they continued to sit silently. She said, "I wish Flash Golden was my dad. I liked it when he was married to my mother."

Buck said, "Flash is really a good guy, one of my childhood heroes. Jordan's too."

"So you like boozers rather than druggies," Tammy said.

"No, it's not that. He played a good guy in the movies, and he's a good guy in real life."

Buck had to stop himself from telling her how I had pulled four young people out of the sin pit in Tijuana and was still being nice to them even though I had nothing to gain and probably something to lose by doing that.

"You're right," Tammy said. "He is a good guy. And you two are good guys, too. I like good guys."

Like I said before, that's why I stayed in touch with Debra and Tammy after the divorce. I never had a child, but Tammy liked me and sometimes made me feel like a father, and I liked that.

Tammy got Buck and Jordan back to Hollywood and Vine on time. I was waiting for them. On the drive back to San Clemente, I told Jordan and Buck that Debra had agreed to take Angelina as a member of her household staff, but not until early November because she and Sam Eschidt were going to Europe after they sent Tammy off to college.

I was pleased to learn that Debra had finally talked her daughter, who had graduated high school two years before, into making an effort at getting a degree. Debra told me that she thought telling her daughter that she could attend college more that a thousand miles from home may have been the greatest selling point.

"Debra says she doesn't think it's a good idea to have a new girl around the house until she gets back, and she's probably right, so Angelina will just have to stay in San Clemente until then. Arlene has gotten to know and like her, and Arlene said Angelina can stay with her for the next couple of months," I explained.

A few days later, as Norman, Buck, and Jordan walked toward the enlisted men's club to drink the car dealers' beer, Norman said he was pleased that Angelina would not be moving up the road from San Clemente for a while.

Jordan said, "Norm, I suspect you may be becoming too fond of that beautiful little Mexican whore."

Jordan barely dodged the right cross aimed at his jaw and looked at Norman in surprise. Almost in unison, both said, "I'm sorry."

Jordan was sorry that he had called Angelina a whore, and Norman was sorry that he had swung at Jordan.

"I'm sorry," Norman repeated. Then he stumbled over his next words. "I, I, I -- it's just that, I think Angelina is really great. Okay, okay, she's beautiful, and we've gone to bed and she's good in bed, but she's a good person too. Jordan, she's had a hard life. Growing up in Mexico ain't easy, damn it."

Yes, Jordan thought, I know she's a good woman -- a good-looking, good-loving woman, but what else could a young man want? Maybe in truth, Jordan was jealous.

"Norman, I'm sorry, too. I deserved you trying to punch me. I won't say anything against Angelina again."

Jordan offered his hand. Norman managed a small grin as he accepted Jordan's apology.

"I haven't tried to hit anybody since the seventh grade, and here I am trying to hit a good friend," Norman said.

"And I don't make a habit of insulting a good friend's girl either," Jordan said.

The three Marines continued on to the EM club and got really drunk, consuming a couple of pitchers. As they stumbled back toward their barracks, Norman unzipped his fly and splattered the corner of building with a spray of urine that bounced back on all of them.

"Jesus, Norman, I don't need a piss shower," Buck said.

"Aw, buddy, you're a Marine. You've been pissed on plenty of times, so one more shouldn't make any difference. You know, piss ought to be a symbol of the Marines. The D.I.'s pissed on us because they wanted to make us pissed off, so pissed off that we'll jump out of dinky landing boat into who knows how deep water and charge toward some stinking beach while machine gun bullets are peppering the water all around us. Pretty stupid, isn't it?"

"Yeah, I guess it is," Buck said as he unzipped and relieved himself on the ice plants between the sidewalk and the building on the other side of the sidewalk. "But I guess it works because they've gotten a lot of dumb sons of bitches like us to do it for almost two hundred years."

"That's right. Why do you think we do it?" Norman asked.

"I don't know. Why did we join the fucking Marine Corps?" Buck asked.

"To prove we're men," Jordan said.

"I think you're probably right. I guess that means we got a whole service made up of guys trying to prove they're men," Buck said.

"When do we quit trying to prove that we're men?" Norman asked.

"I don't know," Buck said. "Maybe never."

In late September, Jordan was released from active duty to go back to his reserve unit just in time for the world to sweat out the Cuban Missile Crisis. Like most crises, this one came upon normal common people with complete surprise.

Yes, the nation's leaders knew something was going on in Cuba, but they were not sure about what was happening. President Kennedy was told what was happening on Tuesday morning, October 16, when one of his aides brought him the information that satellite photographs had confirmed the Soviets were setting up missiles in Cuba.

The president, his cabinet members, key aides, and top generals spent the rest of the week deciding what they should do about the nation's biggest rival for world dominance setting up nuclear missiles less than an hundred miles off the American coast.

I spent the same week fishing, actually mostly drinking beer, at a nondescript lake in Northern California, a place that had no telephones, no televisions sets, and no radios. I knew the world had taken a turn for the worse when I turned on my car radio as I drove toward the Los Angeles area. The newscaster speculated that the Marines were deploying from Camp Pendleton.

When I got to the Baja Angeles, Arlene was there with Angelina. Arlene asked Angelina to go into the kitchen while she told me what was going on.

"She'll be okay with me until she moves to the Eschidt's place in a couple of weeks," Arlene said. "You know it was foolish on your part, but I'm glad you rescued her from her former place of employment."

"So she told you the details of that evening," I said.

"Yes, and Angelina deserves a better life than she has. She's a beautiful girl forced into sexual slavery by a pitiful economic system and a centuries-old tradition that you macho men embrace and continue to encourage by going south of the border on weekends and taking your pleasure for a few pesos. But that's no matter. Men will be men."

I grimaced and said, "Maybe it'd be more accurate if you said, 'Boys will be boys.' I was just taking a piss in the wrong alley when I got into that mess. But on another more urgent matter at the moment, have either of you talked to Norman or Buck?"

"Yes, we finally got Buck on the phone, and they don't know or can't say what's happening," Arlene said as she poured me a big straight bourbon. "I figure you might need this tonight."

"Hell, the whole world might need this tonight," I said. "They're probably tipping their glasses everywhere, hoping we don't spend the next few days under a big mushroom cloud."

"Do you really think we'll go to war with the Soviet Union over Cuba?" Arlene asked.

"Your guess is as good as mine, but I sure as hell hope not. There ain't no way anyone can win that war. But what can we do about it? Nothing, I guess. Just wait and see what happens."

Angelina came to the kitchen entrance, and Arlene motioned for her to come to the table. As she approached, Arlene got up and put her arms around the young woman.

"We'll all be praying for Norman and Buck and the rest of the Marines," Arlene said.

"We had better pray for everyone. Not just the Marines. If we go to nuclear war, it won't matter whether you're wearing a uniform, a dress, or jeans and cowboy boots," I said.

Angelina started to cry. Arlene led her back toward the kitchen. In a few minutes, Arlene returned alone.

"As I suspected, Angelina tells me she and Norman have become lovers," Arlene said. "Angelina said since neither of them could legally drink, they went out to the hamburger places, walked along the pier, and fell in love. You know what falling in love means, don't you, cowboy?"

I smiled back and said, "Yes, ma'am, I think I do."

Norman shipped out to Guantanamo three days later. Buck never understood why the Corps had picked Norman for the assignment while Buck had been left at Pendleton. But Buck already had begun to develop his philosophy of not trying to understand what cannot be understood. The bottom line was he did not go and Norman did.

Two weeks later Arlene and I drove Angelina to Los Angeles to begin her employment with Debra Debaux Eschidt. The Cuban crisis appeared to be easing, but no one was yet uncrossing fingers. It was Friday night when we drove back to Orange County and into Pendleton to pick up Buck, now without either of his two best buddies.

As we sat at a table at Baja Angeles, Arlene brought Buck a glass and said, "Here, have a glass of my special iced tea."

Buck looked at it and said, "First iced tea I've ever seen that had foam on top of it."

"Yes, and that why Flash is going to drink his beer out of bottle. If anyone who looks like a liquor control agent comes into this bar, that glass belongs to Flash."

I asked Buck if he had heard from Norman.

"Not yet."

"Angelina told us that she and Norman were in love and that he said he wanted to marry her," Arlene said.

"Yes, ma'am, he told me that too."

"Do you think that marriage would work?" Arlene asked.

"Who knows?" Buck said. "Angelina is a nice person and a beautiful girl. Isn't that what we're all looking for? Your friend who came into this place the night we met -- what red-blooded male wouldn't want a woman that beautiful in his bed for a lifetime? Yet, see how she ended up -- dead, alone on a Saturday night. So, what can I say? I guess we're all looking for someone to love, and it's even better if that someone is beautiful like Angelina."

Arlene shook her head and said, "Sometimes beauty is a curse as in the case of our -- I guess I should say, Flash's -- friend. Even though she had a lot of men who said they loved her, I'm not sure any of them knew how to really love her. Or show her how to deal with real love. I hope Norman is prepared to show Angelina that he really loves her because I figure she's never had anyone who really loved her."

Buck looked into his glass, sighed, looked at the ceiling fan whirling above, and said, "What is love? My mama and daddy lived together for over twenty years. I guess they loved each other. My daddy went off to work, and when he came home from the road, they didn't talk about love. They just ate dinner, and while I did my homework they listened to the radio or in their later years watched television, and then they went to bed.

"Then Daddy got to drinking too much, and he died in the car wreck when he was only forty-three. Cancer took Momma two years later. Life's too short for some people. Let's hope we're not some of those people. I didn't figure when I signed up with the Marines last year that I would be sitting here worrying about whether they really have worked something out with the Russians or whether I'll have to go fight them somewhere."

I snorted and said, "What did you think, that they were just kidding about all that macho gung ho stuff?"

"No, but I thought two wars in two decades....I guess I don't know what I thought. We're here now, waiting to find out if Norman and I will get to celebrate any more birthdays – two goats ready to be sacrificed into the big war machine. I guess it's possible that Buddy Holly will have outlived me. And the beautiful lady in the bar that night had more than a dozen years on us. As I said, life's too short sometimes," Buck said.

"Yes, it is, sometimes," I said. "And you may not believe it while we wait around to find out if Misters Kennedy, Khrushchev, and Castro really have come to some kind of accommodation, but there are people who decide everyday that they've had all the fun in this life they can stand. And some of those people have some damn good reasons for not wanting to carry on – like losing all those who mean anything to you, or suffering the agonizing pain of cancer. "

"Like my mother," Buck said. "She suffered a lot, but she was brave until the end. I hope when my time comes if I have to face the pain she faced I can be as much a man about it as she was."

Buck paused, realizing his gender muff, and said. "I mean, well, you know what I mean."

"Yeah, we know what you mean," I said. "Cancer is an awful thing. Personally I'd rather have a quick heart attack and be done with it."

"But Mr. Golden, you seem to be holding up well."

"Yeah, I guess thirty-eight is not that old, but there are times I feel like I've been rode hard and put away wet. But I've learned not to worry about getting old. I think that's what makes you old – worrying about getting old. But then I -- like most people -- would prefer not to beat aging the way Buck's parents did. When were they born, Buck?"

"They were the same age, born in 1915 -- war babies. People were dying all over the world while they were learning to walk just like Norman and me thirty years later."

I took a sip of my beer and said, "Do you know how that First World War started? It started with an assassination in Sarajevo. How many people today know where Sarajevo is? It's about as obscure as San Clemente – and they're both probably two places that the world will never hear of again. But not as obscure as Crawford, Texas, where I was born and lived before my papa bought that grocery store in Bryan. Crawford is the type of town that will dry up and blow away someday. For sure no one will ever hear of it again in a few years.

"But that's immaterial. I guess what I'm saying is, some people have something to live for; others don't."

"So how come people are so afraid of dying if they don't have anything to justify their existence?" Buck asked.

"I've asked myself that plenty of times, and I don't have a real good answer. I guess we keep going because we think we're smarter than most of the other dipshits we meet. And it bothers us that a lot of those same dipshits have more to show for their lives than we do. Money, families, grandchildren. So we just keep going, hoping we'll finally get what's coming to us. And we finally do, except it's not usually what we expected. Yep, for a lot of us, life sucks and then you die."

"But it's not that way for everybody," Buck said. "Some people are optimists and go their merry way, talking about positive thinking, half-full rather than half-empty glasses, and faith in God. I guess they're lucky because they don't seem to worry. God will take care of them. It's all in his master plan, they believe."

I nodded and said, "Yeah, I've met those people -- somebody everybody loves but after a while can't stand to be around because they're always babbling those nonsense clichés that everybody says but nobody really believes. Hell, they remind me of a big dog that licks you to death.

"And like a dog, they don't seem to have a clue. I guess they may be lucky that way. But they do seem to get all the luck. Maybe they're onto something we just can't understand. Or maybe they just have never had to feel and understand the pain that others feel. But I guess we can't dwell on the pain. I guess we've got to go on, or we might as well quit living."

Buck and I lifted our glasses and sat silent a few seconds before I continued with my philosophical pondering.

"Yes, living life is kind of like fighting a war. You have to believe in something. If you're fighting an enemy that is dedicated to his cause, you can shoot 'em, bayonet 'em, burn 'em, bomb 'em, and they'll just keep on fighting. War's not something to take lightly.

"This country fought for four long years back in the '40s, killed millions of people to end all wars. I crawled over a few beaches and dodged bullets in the South Pacific and killed a few people. Then less than six years later, we were back in another bloody war, and Ray was in the goddamned Korean snow and ice trying not to get his ass either shot or frozen off.

"Now it's your turn. I guess we didn't kill enough people in those wars. We didn't know we needed to kill the Russians, Chinese, North Koreans, and Cubans then. And if we get past this crisis, maybe the Americans and Russians will someday be friends again, and we'll have some other enemies we can't imagine now – maybe one of those godforsaken countries in the middle of the Asian desert that I can't even spell.

"Oh well," I continued, "the bottom line is we'll never know what's really going to happen tonight or tomorrow. That's why we should live for now."

"But if you want to think about tomorrow," Buck said, "before Norman got on the ship, he asked Angelina to marry him."

Arlene smiled and I said, "That's a happy, almost Cinderella, story."

Some stories end with people living happily ever after, but this one didn't work out that way.

After the crisis seemed to be resolved and the world breathed more easily, Buck learned about the helicopter crash. All on board died. Buck knew the Marines had no record that would cause them to inform Angelina of Norman's death, so he called her.

"I just wanted to call and see how you're doing, and tell you I'm sorry for your loss, and, Angelina, I hope you're okay."

"I'm okay," she said.

"Can I come visit you the next time I'm in L.A.," Buck asked.

"Sure. That would be nice."

In the spring of 1963, Buck was transferred to Okinawa. Before he shipped out, Buck said goodbye to Arlene and me and took a bus to Los Angeles to say goodbye to Angelina. He figured it was the least he could do for his late buddy.

An older maid answered the door at the Eschidt mansion and apparently remembered Buck from the time when I brought him to the house with Jordan.

"I'm sorry senor, but Senora Eschidt is not here, and her daughter is away at college," she said.

Buck explained that he had not come to visit either Debra or Tammy but Angelina, who came when called by the maid and took Buck to her room in the servant's house on the grounds. They sat down on her bed because she had only a small chair. They made small talk for a while and then got around to speaking of Norman.

"You know Norman never would have really married me," she said.

"How do you know that? He loved you when you were together in San Clemente?"

"Si. He loved me in this world we lived in for a few beautiful months, this world of California, but I doubt that he could have kept that love alive in Iowa -- in a world of blue-eyed people, a world where people don't have to beg or steal or sell their bodies to survive."

Looking Buck straight in the eye she said, "Norman wouldn't take me back to Iowa as his wife, just as you wouldn't take me to Texas as your wife."

"But you and I weren't lovers," Buck said.

"No, we weren't lovers, and I'm not sure Norman and I were lovers. What are lovers, Buck? People who press their naked flesh together and share their bodies and release their emotions of pleasure and go their own ways in the morning. Is that what love is, Buck? If it is, then yes, Norman and I were lovers. But is love sharing the joys and sorrows of living together for the rest of your life in times of happiness and sadness, being proud of one another, proud to take them anywhere, proud to show them to your friends and loved ones."

Tears began to well in her eyes.

"So how are you doing? Are you going to be okay?" Buck asked.

"I can stay here. Senora Eschidt and the other women like me. They say they are happy I am here."

Buck asked her if she wanted to go to lunch. They took a bus out of the expensive Hollywood neighborhood to a Mexican food place Buck could afford. They didn't talk about Norman.

Angelina and Buck went back to the Eschidt mansion. She led Buck to a bar in an expansive room used for entertaining guests and asked if him if would like a drink. He told her he would take some whiskey. Angelina found a bottle of Canadian Club, a bottle of vodka, and a bottle of Kahlua. Then they went back to her room in the servants' house where they sat on her bed as Buck drank Canadian Club and Coke and Angelina drank the Kahlua-vodka mix called a black Russian.

She reached and held Buck's hand. "I'll be okay, Buck. Senora Eschidt pays me money and lets me live here."

"I hope things work out for you, Angelina," Buck said.

"And you too, Buck."

She leaned over and kissed him. Buck thought she meant it as the kind of kiss a sister would give a big brother, but Angelina could not give a kiss that felt sisterly. And Buck could not accept a kiss from a beautiful woman and not feel something more intense than sibling affection. As she drew her lips away, he kissed her again. This time it was not a brother-sister kiss. As they pressed against each other, their emotions ignited. In less than two minutes, Angelina was helping Buck undress her. When he removed his jeans and took the condom out of his wallet, Angelina smiled and said, "You Marines are always prepared."

"Yeah," Buck said. "I guess that's because a lot of us were Boy Scouts, too."

As they lay on the bed afterward, Buck understood why Norman was so enamored with Angelina. She was a pleasing lover and a beautiful woman -- high cheekbones, big brown eyes, a straight nose, full lips, large breasts, small waist, and shapely legs that if she lay by a giant wall map of the world would extend from the Panama Canal to Cape Horn. Maybe the only physical attribute for which some men would give her lower marks would be her butt. She almost had none. But Buck never was an ass man, and he forgot all about Norman Victor that afternoon.

Angelina also knew how to excite a man. She did not make love quietly. Buck knew that whores made noise when they were plying their trade to further excite their clients into coming and going quickly, but usually their sounds were so faked that only the biggest egotists or the most naïve believed they were true expressions of their feelings. Angelina's moans and low squeals seemed real.

In the next four decades, sometimes at night when he was alone and couldn't sleep,

Buck would remember the beautiful young Mexican woman and her sounds of pleasure.

Chapter 4
Dallas 1963

Buck wrote Jordan a letter telling him about Norman and still another one saying he had seen Angelina and that she was holding up well, but Jordan soon lost touch with everyone in Southern California after he got back to Texas. He thought about Buck often for a few months and told himself that he should try to get in touch with him and see how he was doing. He also told people about meeting Flash Golden, but as time went by, Jordan had other things to think and talk about.

He moved out of the '50s model two-bedroom house where he grew up in Arlington, got an apartment in North Dallas, and enrolled in North Texas State University. The North Dallas location made it possible for him to commute to college and work nights in a snack food production plant near Dallas Love Field Airport. He worked Sundays through Thursdays and sometimes on Fridays if production requirements called for overtime. This shift allowed him to commute thirty miles north to Denton and take day classes. By the next fall, Jordan had earned twelve more semester hours, taking six at a time. In September he enrolled in a couple of classes that met on Tuesdays and Thursdays, which left him free to take care of personal errands on Mondays, Wednesday, and Fridays when he got up after working 4 p.m. to midnight. It was on one of those errands that he again met Tammy Dolcito.

Jordan had met a young woman at the plant who stood out from the rest -- pretty face, nice figure, just about his age. After a few weeks he got the nerve to ask her if she wanted to go to a movie. After a second date, he learned that her birthday was coming up, and he decided to impress her with a gift from Neiman Marcus. He was at the perfume counter waiting for one of the well dressed and coiffured sales clerks to wait on him when he looked over and saw Tammy at the next counter completing her purchase.

His immediate reaction was disbelief that she was really Tammy. He was staring at her when she looked over, stared back, and said, "Jordan? You're Jordan, Flash's friend."

"And you're Tammy, Flash's former stepdaughter. What are you doing in Dallas?"

"I go to school here. I'm an SMU coed," she said, making a cheerleader-like gesture.

"Wow, when you said you were going to enroll in college back east, I thought they really meant back east. But then I guess Dallas is about fourteen hundred miles east of L.A."

"I don't know the mileage, but it's a long way from L.A, and I guess I'm getting a little homesick. But what are you doing here? In Dallas? And standing at the Neiman Marcus perfume counter?"

"I'm doing the same thing you are doing, going to school. Except that I can't afford a frou-frou private school like Southern Methodist University. I commute up Interstate 35 to North Texas State."

"Hey, Pat Boone is a NTSU alumnus. If it's good enough for Mister Goody White Buck Shoes, it must be okay," she said.

"Yes, it has a great music program, but I can't afford to major in a no-money degree like music although that's what I wish I could do, so I'm working toward a another degree that has some element of creativity but offers slightly better prospects of making a living. I'm majoring in journalism. I figure you don't need a degree to sing and play the guitar, and I need something that will get me a paying job in case nobody likes my music."

By this time, the perfume clerks had given up on Jordan and were waiting on other people, and he realized that he probably should forego telling Tammy he was trying to buy a gift to impress another girl. He made up a story about buying some perfume for a buddy to give to his girlfriend but said he was too confused by all the brands, so he would tell him he would have to find time to buy his own perfume.

"What kind do you like?" he asked.

"I like this kind. What do you think about it? She opened the bottle in her sack and dabbed a bit on her neck and then leaned over into Jordan's face.

"Nice," Jordan said. "I'll remember that."

Jordan remembered that sexy smell of perfume every night for the next week. He got Tammy's dorm phone number that early October day and called her three days later to ask if she wanted to go out on Friday. When he picked Tammy up in his '55 Chevy, he gave her a bottle of the perfume that he had purchased after they had said their polite goodbyes at Neiman Marcus.

"Wow. This is too much," she said. "Why are you giving me this?"

Jordan had not rehearsed an answer to a question that he should have known she would ask. He could think of only one thing to say.

"Because I appreciated how nice you were to me and Buck, two poor Texas Marines, the first time we met."

"That's nice," Tammy said. She hesitated and then said, "And, oh yeah, I don't smoke pot anymore. At least not in Texas. They'll put you in prison for life for doing that. Did you know that?"

"Yes, I know the state can sentence people up to life imprisonment for drug possession. They're tough on crime in this state. They not only can execute murderers but also rapists and armed robbers."

"So how come they have so many murders, rapes, and armed robberies in Texas?" she asked.

"Beats me. Maybe there are just a lot of mean people down here," Jordan said.

"If there are, they disguise it by acting friendly. Everyone is friendly, almost too friendly."

"Well, you know what they say about Southern hospitality, but I've always thought it was overrated," Jordan said.

"It can wear on you after a while, everyone calling you honey, sweetheart, and darling. But still it's nice to be treated with courtesy, even if a lot of these girls from the little towns in East and West Texas treat me sometimes like I'm a funny-talking slut. I do find it a little amusing when they call me a Yankee though. I mean I'm a California girl, for chrissake. Whoops, I shouldn't say that. People down here don't like it if you use Jesus's name in vain. And after all, I do go to Southern Methodist University," Tammy said, placing special emphasis on Methodist.

"Yeah, they at least pretend to be religious down here. And some of them actually are," Jordan said.

"Just like the rest of the world," Tammy said.

"I wouldn't know much about the rest of the world. I've only been in Texas and California," Jordan said. "And there's just not much religion displayed in the barracks of Camp Pendleton or the bars of San Diego and Tijuana. Although the D.I.'s did say Jesus Christ and God a lot, adding some adjectives and adverbs that would make preachers cringe. But that's enough talk about religion and the world, what do you want to do tonight?"

"What do you mean what do I want to do tonight?" she said. "It's Texas-OU weekend, and I want to go downtown Dallas and have a good time with all the thousands of other college students. It's the closest thing to Mardi Gras that Texas has. What did you think we were going to do? Go to a movie? We can do that any Friday night."

"Okay, California girl," Jordan said. "Let's party."

And party they did. Tammy already had a fifth of Cutty Sark and two plastic glasses in her purse. Jordan had never drunk Scotch before, but after a couple of ounces it tasted just fine. They skipped and stumbled down Commerce Street with all the other revelers, some of whom were actual students at the Universities of Texas and Oklahoma. Others, like Tammy and Jordan, were students at other colleges, and still others had never been on a college campus. But they all had one thing in common; they were young, horny, and looking for a good time.

Jordan got Tammy back to her dorm barely before curfew, so he only had time to tell her emphatically that he wanted to see her again. But a Marine Reserves weekend drill and overtime at the food plant kept Jordan from seeing Tammy for two weeks.

Their next date was the University of Texas-SMU game in the Cotton Bowl on November 2. Tammy was not really a football fan, but she was trying hard to get into the role of coed, so she wore a sexy short blue skirt and an even sexier red sweater. They sat on the hard bleachers and watched the first half of a game, which turned out as everyone expected. Texas slaughtered SMU, and Jordan and Tammy left at halftime. After dinner at a Mexican restaurant Jordan asked Tammy if she wanted to come back to his apartment.

She cocked her head, gave Jordan a sneering smile and said, "Maybe next time. I'm trying to learn to be a proper Southern young lady, and I don't think the debutante code calls for a girl to go to a guy's apartment on the second date."

"How about counting the time we met in California and say it's the third date?"

"Look, Jordan, I like you. You're a nice guy, but as I said, I've changed in the past few months, and you need to give me some time. I'm trying to grow up and be something other than a soft porn star's daughter."

"Okay," Jordan said. "I like you, too, and I don't want to do anything that would make you decide I'm a louse and not want to see me again."

Jordan took Tammy back to the dorm. They kissed and touched for a while in his car before he walked her to the dorm door.

"Do you like Elvis movies?" Jordan asked Tammy when he called her on the next Wednesday.

"Sometimes if I'm in that mood," she said.

"What kind of mood is that?"

"Oh, you know. A light mood, a party mood, don't want to think about anything serious, just watch a good-looking redneck making out with a bunch of pretty girls. Why do you ask, good-looking redneck? Do you want to take me to an Elvis movie?"

"*It Happened at the World's Fair* is playing at the drive-in across the Trinity River in South Oak Cliff. Have you ever been to a drive-in movie?"

"Sure," Tammy said, "but I can't remember any movies I saw. I always considered drive-in movies a place to smoke some pot and do some other things that might be more to your liking. But what the heck, a drive-in movie is a good place to watch an Elvis movie, so let's go."

"I'll pick you up at 6:30 on Friday," Jordan said.

Jordan was five minutes early, but Tammy was ready and as they drove across the Trinity River Tammy asked Jordan what other movies he had seen recently.

"Oh, let's see -- *Hud, Love With the Proper Stranger, The Great Escape* -- I'm a big Steve McQueen fan -- *The Birds, The Pink Panther,* and oh yeah, *The Manchurian Candidate,*" Jordan said.

"Which one did you like best?"

"I liked all of them. As I said I'm a big fan of Steve McQueen, also Paul Newman and Hitchcock. *The Pink Panther* was really funny."

Tammy said, "Of those movies, I think I liked *The Manchurian Candidate* best."

"It was interesting," Jordan said, "but pretty far-fetched."

"What do you mean? You don't believe there are powerful people in this country who would use conspiracy and violence to keep or increase their power?"

"Not really. In today's world it would be totally insane and very difficult to assassinate a prominent politician. And the Lawrence Harvey character -- there's no one who's that nuts. And the Angela Lansbury character -- the conniving woman using her husband and son as the front men for her own purposes. Come on -- women aren't that way. Women aren't evil. They are the mothers who keep us on the right path, the force that nurtures what is good in this world."

Tammy reached over and patted Jordan's thigh, probably a dangerous act when riding with a horny young man driving in Dallas Saturday night traffic. She said, "You really are a nice guy, Jordan, but I didn't realize you Texas boys were so naive."

"Naive? I'm not naive. I choose to think I'm just romantic," Jordan said, suddenly

more interested in her hand on his thigh than any discussions of either intellectual or psychological nature.

She took her hand off Jordan's thigh and said, "Romantic, huh. How do you define romantic?"

"Oh, I guess maybe a mix of chivalry and, uh, I can't think of another word -- horny."

"So are you horny now?" she said.

"I'm a healthy almost-twenty-one-year-old male. What do you think?"

Tammy put her hand back on his thigh and said, "So are you proposing that we do something about that?"

Jordan turned his head for a second away from the road and said, "What am I supposed to say now? If I say yes, are you going to be offended?"

"No. I guess I should be offended if you said no."

"Then the answer is yes."

She took her hand off Jordan's thigh again, leaned back against the passenger door, gave a sneering smile again and said, "After all, we are going to a drive-in, and this is our fifth date."

Jordan found a spot at the drive-in where no other cars were near and set up the speaker. Before Elvis had met the girl in the movie Jordan already had kissed Tammy and was beginning the clumsy groping that young men are prone to do. This time Tammy did a little groping of her own. Jordan was erect and almost holding his breath when Tammy unzipped his blue jeans, dropped low into the front seat, and kissed his erect and ready penis. Jordan had heard about blow jobs but never dreamed he would have the good fortune to experience one he had not given a woman money for. He came by the third sweep of her lips.

Tammy took a tissue from her purse and wiped her mouth. "Feel better now, Mr. Romantic?"

"Of course, but I guess I wasn't expecting this," Jordan said. "I thought we would do the, uh you know, the reciprocal thing. Now I guess we'll just have to watch the movie for a while."

"No," she said. "You can return the favor, and there's no risk of pregnancy. Have you ever heard of sixty-nine? We'll just do it in sequence rather than parallel."

Tammy leaned back against the passenger door, lifted her skirt, removed her panties, and said, "Come here, cowboy. I'll teach you a roping trick that will help you catch a lot of heifers."

Jordan was really looking forward to his sixth date with Tammy because even though she taught him a skill that night that would prove useful in his relationships with women in ensuing years, he still wanted to consummate their relationship in the traditional manner. But their sixth date was not really a date. It was an appointment to go downtown Dallas and get a glimpse of the president of the United States, who was coming to Texas the next week and scheduled to ride in a motorcade down the streets where they partied a few weeks before.

Friday, November 22, 1963, began with some rain but turned into a nice

autumn day in Dallas, a good day for an open-car parade -- temperatures in the sixties or low seventies with a bit of breeze. Jordan picked up Tammy about 11 a.m. and drove downtown. There had been much news coverage and controversy a month earlier when protesters had jeered and spat at former Democratic presidential candidate and now United Nations Ambassador Adlai Stephenson after he spoke in Dallas. The city's political leaders, both Democrats and Republicans, were embarrassed by the incident and called for all citizens to be on their best behavior when the president visited, but pre-presidential visit news coverage included speculation about whether the right-wing faction in Dallas would treat Kennedy with the respect normally accorded a president of the United States. Before he picked up Tammy, Jordan bought a *Dallas Morning News* and opened it to a full-page advertisement critical of the president. While he drove on Central Expressway to downtown, Jordan mentioned the ad. Both he and Tammy said they hoped that Texas hospitality would prevail. So far it had, according to the coverage on the radio. Air Force One had flown the short distance from Fort Worth and landed at Love Field, and President Kennedy and his entourage were on their way to downtown Dallas before a cheering and welcoming crowd.

"I can't believe people would treat a man like Adlai Stephenson with disrespect. It was really a redneck and bush league thing to do, but then I'm beginning to believe this is a redneck and bush league place," Tammy said.

"Oh really? What happened to make you feel that way?" Jordan said. "I hope present company is excepted."

"Yes. I've told you, you are a nice guy. But I'm meeting quite a few people who aren't. People are so racist here. That's why they don't like Stephenson or Kennedy or the other people who are trying to get this country on the right track. I mean there are almost no black people at SMU, and the things that some people say, calling them niggers and jigaboos and other awful things. And it's supposed to be a church school for chrissake."

"There are a lot of black people at North Texas State. The reason there probably aren't that many black people at SMU is probably because they can't afford it. I know I can't. And, Tammy, you have to understand the culture. I mean, I was in the first grade before I learned that nigger wasn't the proper name for black people. I had always heard them called that. Either niggers or colored people. Niggers by white people and colored people by black people. Hell, I'm not even sure the nig--, uh colored people, had ever heard the word negro."

"You almost said nigger, didn't you?"

Jordan kept his eyes straight ahead as they turned off the freeway into downtown and said, "Yes, I guess I did. I'm still trying to learn how to act in this last half of the century."

She looked at Jordan with an expression that was a mix of sympathy and disgust and said, "Well, keep trying. Oh, hell, maybe I'm just getting a little homesick. I know there are mean people in California and everyplace else in the world. My mother is married to one of them. And maybe I just miss a more cosmopolitan place like L.A. and Hollywood."

"Dallasites think they are cosmopolitan. It's Fort Worth that's the cow town," Jordan said.

"Ha! You can only legally buy a drink in one precinct in Dallas Country. That's cosmopolitan? I'm sorry Jordan, but I don't think anyone's ever going to consider Texas anything but a miserable place in the summer with a bunch of oil wells and cows. It's for sure they're not going to move here in droves, and they're never going to make a TV show about rich and hip people who live in Dallas."

"Probably not," Jordan said

He found a parking place on the west end of downtown, near the county courthouse complex and the *Morning News* building. There was a small park across from the *Morning News* offices named for the newspaper's founder. Jordan suggested to Tammy that they view the Kennedy motorcade from there. They arrived there a little after noon and pushed into the crowd beginning to line up along Elm Street, which fed into Main and Commerce onto Stemmons Expressway, the freeway that the motorcade was scheduled to take to the Dallas Trade Mart, where about two thousand people were waiting to have lunch with President Kennedy, Vice President Johnson, Texas Governor Connelly, Senator Yarborough, and just about anyone who had any level of importance at all in Dallas County.

In a few minutes, the crowd started to stir and crane their necks toward Houston Street. Soon Jordan and Tammy saw Dallas police on motorcycles make the turn from Elm onto Houston followed by more motorcycles, two cars, and then a black open convertible Lincoln limousine occupied by Governor Connelly and President Kennedy with their wives beside them, all of whom were smiling and making the perfunctory waves to the crowd.

Then they heard the first shot. No one realized what was happening, and within a second came the following shots and the president's exploding head and the blood and the panic and all the scenes to be relived in news films and print accounts for the next four decades.

Like the other people in the stunned and panicked crowd, Tammy and Jordan went to the ground instinctively to avoid any bullets that may be whizzing through Dealey Plaza. When the firing stopped and the motorcade sped to the entrance of Stemmons Expressway toward Parkland Hospital, Jordan and Tammy got to their feet. Some people, like Jordan, stood in stunned silence. Others, like Tammy, were crying hysterically.

"I want to go home," she sobbed. "I can't believe they could do this. I want to go home. Please take me out of here."

Jordan and Tammy made their way back to Jordan's car and through the chaotic traffic back to the SMU campus. It was almost 2 p.m., and Jordan was scheduled to be at work in a couple of hours.

"Are you okay?" he asked.

"Am I okay!" Tammy said. "We just saw the president of the United States murdered, and you are asking me if I'm okay!"

"Well, are you going to be okay? I mean I don't want to leave you, but I have to go to work. Are you going to be okay?"

"Go to work? Go to work! They just shot the president, and all you can think about is going to work!"

"I don't think they are going to cancel life because President Kennedy is dead. You heard the radio. We have a new president -- Lyndon Johnson, a Texan. The world will go on. The nation will survive."

"A Texan! The new president is a Texan, and the Texans killed Kennedy!"

"The Texans didn't kill Kennedy. We don't know who killed Kennedy."

She looked at Jordan with wide and sad eyes and said again, "I want to go home." Then she got out of the car.

Jordan called after her, "Tammy, I'll call you later."

But Jordan didn't know if she had heard him. She was crying and running for the door of her dorm.

Jordan called her dorm number at his dinner break, but there was no answer. On Saturday, he learned that Tammy had indeed gone home. She was at her mother's house in Beverly Hills on Sunday morning when Jack Ruby shot Lee Harvey Oswald in the basement of the Dallas police station.

Sam Eschidt and Debra Debaux, like most people with their affluence and celebrity, had unlisted phone numbers, none of which Jordan had gotten from Tammy during their two months of re-acquaintance. Tammy had Jordan's phone number, and he waited for her to call. But as the year ended, and a British band whose members later counted Buddy Holly among their inspiration for their band's name as well as their music made a sensational arrival in America and the University of Texas won its first national football championship, Jordan gave up hope that Tammy would call him.

Chapter 5
Starting Over in Santa Fe

More than twenty years after that bloody day in Dallas, I was sitting at a table in Santa Fe's Bull Ring bar when another feller got off his stool and came over to me.

"Flash! Flash Golden! Is that you?"

I looked at him, thinking I would play nice with an occasional middle-aged fan telling me how much he had enjoyed watching my movies as a child.

"I'm Jordan Roblech, a Marine buddy of Buck Leherifen and Norman Victor. We met in 1962 when I went with Buck to visit your ex-wife in Beverly Hills. Remember me?"

"Jordan Roblech. No shit! Sure, I remember. Of course, you have changed a bit in the past couple of decades."

"Yeah. I guess I've traded some of my hair for a few extra pounds and wrinkles. But you haven't changed all that much," Jordan said.

I smiled and said, "You've probably also gained a little more ability to bullshit, but I guess that comes with age, too. So what have you been doing in the past couple of decades?"

"I went back to Texas and got my college degree, got a job, got married, got divorced. I quit my job in Houston and moved to Denver where I went to work for a small oil company. Life was good for several years. Made a little money, drank good booze, ate too much, traveled to some interesting places, met some pretty women. Then the oil boom started to bust, and the company I worked for was one of the first to explode."

"Oil companies, huh. Did you go back to school after the Marines and become a geologist or petroleum engineer?" I asked.

"No. I majored in journalism because it was easy enough to work nights and still pass the courses without much studying. I worked as a reporter at one of the suburban dailies in the Dallas-Fort Worth area and then for one of the Houston dailies, but after my divorce I decided I needed a change.

"By that time I was a little jaded about newspapers so I decided I could make more money flacking for the people I had been interviewing. To make this long story short, let's just say I quit being a whore for the media to become a whore for the corporate and government establishment. Since my last beat was writing about oil and gas, I got hired as a PR guy for a small oil company in Denver, small enough that the geologists, engineers, and accountants who ran the company thought I could do double duty as both PR guy and lobbyist. And then, as I said, the oil boom went bust.

"Even though Watergate had happened and the first print journalists probably in history were starting to get rich, I figured it was too late for me to go back, aw, this story is probably too long and boring to try to explain here. Let me just say, I'm here in this bar and damn glad to meet you again."

"So what are you doing here?" I asked. "I don't think there are many oil companies in Santa Fe or many other kinds of companies for that matter. The only people in this town with money are Texans and the movie stars who have moved here and made the taxes so high that real people can't afford their houses anymore."

"I used to come down here to do some lobbying for the Denver oil company when the state legislature was in session, but mainly I just bought drinks for a few legislators, their staffers, and other hangers-on. But I got to liking the place, so I hooked up with a job with one the Los Alamos National Lab subcontractors, but that ended a couple of months ago, and I got a temporary job with the Lobos Locos," Jordan said.

"What are the Lobos Locos?"

"They're four Albuquerque boys, your typical scummy quartet of singers, guitar players, and a drummer who think playing music for a few bucks is better than working for a living. But they made their own tape of songs, and a couple of the bars up here like them, so they actually get paid for their gigs. Right now I'm just filling in for the lead guitar player, who got served with an arrest warrant for not getting his dog neutered and got mouthy with the officer. Now they need a new band member because it's going to take a while for the picker's bones to mend while he settles his legal troubles."

"So where are you playing?"

"The band's got a month-long gig at that big country-western honky-tonk out on Cerrillos Road. Come out and catch our act some night. I'm sure the guy who owns the joint would like to have some of your money," Jordan said.

I told him that I knew that pirate and I might just do that.

On Friday, the Lobos Locos were taking their first break when Jordan came over to me while I was talking with the club owner. At the next break, I came over to him and told him he was a pretty good musician.

"I got this house out on the Espanola highway with two empty bedrooms, so how about following me out to my place after the show and having a few more drinks so we can catch up on the last twenty years."

Jordan took me up on my invitation, and by the time the sun rose over the Sangre de Cristo Mountains overlooking Santa Fe he had heard the sad story about how I had changed my residence from San Clemente to Santa Fe.

Death finally released Floyd Bearclaw from his cruel unknowing fate after more than a dozen years in a coma. Arlene and I married after a respectable period of mourning. We expanded the Baja Angeles into one of the classier Mexican restaurants in Southern California. But in the mid-seventies, we became disenchanted with the increasing traffic, smog, and the various other conditions that Southern California residents complain about, so we sold our share of the restaurant to Ray Garcia and moved to Santa Fe with the intention of opening a new restaurant, this one to be called the Baja Colorado.

While we were looking for the right location, Arlene was diagnosed with ovarian cancer. She died quickly, and I lost interest in the restaurant business as well as most other things in life. Being able to write about my pain in songs and play my guitar while taking care of Arlene's middle-aged neutered tomcat was helping me to slowly recover from the loss of Arlene.

"Yeah, the guitar has gotten me through some tough times too," Jordan said.

I could tell he wasn't much happier than me, and after another beer, I said,"Why don't you save some money and move in with me? I don't need the rent since I do pretty well with song royalty checks."

Jordan finished his drink, thought about my offer for about thirty seconds, and said, "Okay. If you really mean it."

"I've never learned how to say things I don't mean," I said.

Jordan packed up his few belongings, put them into his '78 model MGB that started most of the time and moved into my place.

In subsequent evenings I told Jordan that Arlene was not the only woman who had been part of my life who was now dead. Debra Debaux had overdosed on some bad heroin several years before. After her death, I lost touch with her daughter and with Angelina.

During the time we stayed in touch I learned that Angelina had not only been a good employee but also had become one of Debra's confidants.

"I even heard Debra used her to get her drugs, but I don't know that for sure. Considering the odds against them, I doubt that either Tammy or Angelina have come to any good," I said.

Over the years since we met in Arlene's cantina Jordan and I had resisted any temptations to use any drugs other than the legal one that probably kills more people than all the illegal ones -- alcohol.

As Jordan progressed in his drinking career from beer to the harder stuff he learned to like Scotch whisky, first introduced to him by Tammy on their night of revelry in October 1963. I told Jordan it was because he was a writer. "All you writers like Scotch. I don't know why, but you do. Cowboys like me like American whiskey -- Kentucky bourbon or Tennessee mash."

"Damn, I must just be unpatriotic," Jordan said, "because I also like Canadian and Irish whiskey better than bourbon. Well, diversity is good, and you're still my friend even if you don't know good whiskey. Besides, as a good friend of mine always said, it'll all make you drunk."

I told him I was concerned about his health. "That Scotch whisky will kill you. It's got too much smoke in it. I guess you might be okay since you gave up smoking, but for a man like me it would be a quick death. That's what killed Bogey -- Scotch and cigarettes. Who knows? If he had drunk bourbon, he might be alive today."

"Did you know Humphrey Bogart?" Jordan asked.

"Met him once. He played a lot of tough, hard luck guys, but you know he really was a child of privilege from back east. I doubt that we would have been good buddies because he was probably too proper to put up with a Texas cowboy like me."

"Funny you say that, Flash. You were the most proper person I could imagine in the movies. I mean I learned more about what's right and what's wrong in your movies than I ever did in Sunday school."

I poured myself another glass of bourbon and said, "I said proper, not right. There's a big difference between right and proper, just as there's a big difference between law and justice. And knowing what is right and what is justice is a lot harder to determine. Don't ever forget that."

Jordan and I spent time over the next few weeks reminiscing about the '40s and '50s, when Jordan was growing up in a blue-collar suburb between Dallas and Fort Worth and I was fighting Japanese and then making a little money as, in more ways than one, an up-and-coming cowboy star. We also talked about the early '60s and sometimes about Norman Victor and Buck Leherifen.

"You know I probably should have tried to contact Norman's parents and tell them what a nice guy he was and how sorry I was about his death. But I didn't really know how to. I never even knew his parents' names. But I probably should have tried to get in touch. I probably made a wrong call," Jordan said late one night.

"Maybe that was the wrong call or maybe not, but it was more than twenty years ago, and if we second-guessed our life decisions, we would be here talking until way past the sun-up," I said. "I realized after Arlene died, you can't second-guess the calls or bets you make in life. It's true you have to play the hand you're dealt. Hell, I guess there is a reason I like poker so much. It's a game, but it's also a good exercise in living."

Jordan said, "I also wonder about Buck Leherifen. I also probably should have stayed in touch with him. I wonder if he had to go to Vietnam. If he did, I guess he survived because his name wasn't on the list when I visited the wall last year. I wonder where he is and what he's doing now."

Chapter 6
Lubbock 1960

What Buck Leherifen was doing at the moment Jordan mentioned his name was lying in his bed on Washington's Olympic Peninsula thinking about the girls and women besides his mother who had played a role in his life. When Buck couldn't sleep and engaged in this exercise, he always thought about Angelina. But there also were others. Beth Chertha, Candy Call, and Lisa McSwee were three of them. On this night he was thinking about Beth, Candy, and Lisa.

Buck remembered the first time he saw Beth Chertha. She was sitting in a new Pontiac, asking in her smooth and sweet voice, "Fill it, please."

From the day he had started to work at the Lubbock gas station two weeks earlier, Buck had disliked cleaning windshields, had avoided checking tires, and had detested checking under hoods, but now he was delighted to clean Beth's windshield, check her tires, and check under her hood. He hoped Clay Cotton, the station owner's nephew and night manager, would not notice the beautiful customer and come and clean her windshield before he filled the tank.

But Clay had just removed a radiator cap too quickly and was busy refilling the boiling radiator and assuring a worried woman traveler that her car not afire.

As Buck wiped extra long and extra diligently on the already clean windshield, he could not help looking at the girl. She had just finished a game of tennis and was wearing shorts and a blouse. Her racquet was in the other front seat, but the entire tennis court, including the net, could have been in the other seat and Buck would not have noticed.

She was just perfect, just perfect all over. Just the right face, just the right figure, just the right size, just the right complexion. Just beautiful.

He wanted to check the oil and water and battery and fan belt and tires. He hoped the tires were low. And the spare, too.

"No," she said. "It's a new car, and everything should be okay."

"The back tires look a little low," he lied.

"Oh, really. Then maybe you should check them."

The tires were two pounds over the recommended pressure. He was sure because he read the gauge three times.

The girl gave him a credit card. He was hoping she would give him a credit card. Not only would he have to process the ticket and get the tray and pencil and bring it to her car and reach over and hand it to her and stand beside her while she signed the ticket, he would also learn her name.

George Chertha? No, he reasoned, her name couldn't be George Chertha. George Chertha must be her father, the father of the world's most beautiful daughter.

Or was she George Chertha's wife? In his eighteen years, Buck had not yet conditioned himself to take special notice of a woman's third finger on her left hand. And with a girl like her, who notices hands?

Clay finished refilling the woman's radiator, gave her some green stamps and a road map, and came over to Buck, who was still by the pumps looking down the street.

"What did you think of that?" Clay asked.

The girl had not gone unnoticed by Clay, and Buck knew what Clay was thinking.

"Nice. What's her name, Clay?"

"Beth. Beth Chertha. And she's rich too. Her old man owns Chertha's Pontiac dealership and half of the cotton gins on the road to Amarillo.

"Does she come into the station often?" Buck asked.

"About twice a week. Mr. Chertha and his wife also are regular customers. Don't ever piss them off. Our boss, Uncle Dub, wouldn't be very pleased with you."

Piss him off? What idiot would anger people with a daughter as beautiful as Beth Chertha? Buck thought.

"Don't worry about that. Twice a week, huh," Buck said.

"Yeah, but if I were you, I wouldn't plan on getting anything going with that chick. She has a big boyfriend who's a starter on the Texas Tech freshman football team," Clay warned.

"Oh, I don't have any hopes. I just think she's cute."

"Cute!" exclaimed Clay. "Son, you just met one of the finest hides around. Every man in town would like a piece of that, and all you can say is, I think she's cute."

Clay walked away to wait on a car that had driven up to the pumps on the other side of the station, and Buck went back to fixing the flat tire. He thought about Beth as he wrestled with the tire, trying to remove it from its rim.

What Buck had told Clay was not true. He did have hopes. He would like to date Beth. But date her, not fuck her. Not get a piece like Clay had said. Clay was too single-minded, he thought. All he thinks about is screwing. Sometime Buck wondered if Clay had a mother.

If he did, she never taught her son any respect for women. Buck respected women. He respected them so much that he was still a virgin.

Guys like Clay must lie about women, he thought. Oh, he guessed Clay didn't lie very much. He had been in the Navy. Buck figured Clay had a lot of women from Tijuana to Tahiti. But he had to pay them. How could a man have relations with a whore, knowing that probably thirty minutes before she was lying with a pimpled-faced sailor and thirty minutes before lying with a Mexican pimp and thirty minutes before lying with a weird old white man, all the time sweating and crying out fake moans and receiving their passions as she was now receiving his.

Guys like Clay he could understand. He just categorized them as low class. But what about Dolph? Buck went to high school with Dolph, who dated Sheila -- a nice girl. Then one day, Dolph told him that he had sex with Sheila. Buck didn't believe him. Dolph and Sheila were going to get married in June. Dolph could have waited.

But maybe Buck just did not understand. After all he hadn't dated much. Oh, he liked girls. He liked to hold them and kiss them, and at times he wanted to sleep with a girl. Usually at these times he would masturbate. He fought it. Every time he fought it. But the biological urge within him usually won.

Lying peacefully relaxed after relieving himself, he always felt a sense of guilt and wondered why he had such a compelling urge to commit this perversion. He would then promise himself that would be the last time, and that promise would get him through the rest of the week without feeling guilty.

Candy Call came into the station and said hello. Candy was a young divorcee who managed a cafe. She was dating Clay.

"You ready for college?" Candy asked Buck.

"Since it starts next Monday, I guess I had better be."

"I'll bet you're real smart. Probably spend all your time studying and in the library and don't bother with distractions such as girls."

Buck could tell that Candy was teasing him.

"I don't have a lot of time for girls, Candy."

"If you find some time, let me know," she said, looking at him, smiling and waiting for an answer.

There was no answer. Buck just jerked harder on the tire tool and grunted a pleased sound as the rubber came loose from the wheel.

Clay came out of the office, and Candy walked toward him. They stood in the station driveway talking and laughing. Then Candy drove away.

Buck was patching the tire when Clay came over and said, "Candy's horny. I guess I'll have to take her out and make her feel better tonight."

"Does she make you feel good?" Buck asked.

"A piece of ass always feels good, Buck. You ought to try it sometime."

"How do you know I haven't?"

"Oh, I can tell a cherry. You are a cherry, aren't you, son?"

"Don't call me son."

"Why?"

"Because I'm not your son. My father is dead."

"Okay," Clay said, sounding less cocky. "I won't call you son anymore. I'll call you kid because any cherry is a kid. I don't care if he's forty years old. But then there ain't no such animal as a forty-year-old virgin--man, woman, or hippopotamus."

"What about a priest?"

Clay smiled, "You don't believe that myth, do you?"

Buck picked up the tire and carried it back to the mounting stand. He was worried about saying anymore. Clay would continue to ridicule his virginity, but he wanted to continue the conversation. Not about priests or religion because wasn't too sure about any of that himself. But about Candy and women and sex.

"Clay, what do like most about Candy?"

"What I like most about Candy is that she gives me pleasure just about anytime I need it."

Two cars pulled into the station, and Clay and Buck ended their conversation.

Beth Chertha came into the station later that week, but Buck was washing a car. Clay waited on her while Buck watched from the wash rack, hating the car he was washing and the man who had brought it to be cleaned.

Buck registered for his freshman semester on Friday. The next Friday he went to his first college class. The first student to walk into the class after him was Beth

Chertha. Almost late, she sat at the only empty desk remaining, beside Buck.

"Hi," she said. "You work at the service station near Monterrey Center, don't you?"

"Yes."

Buck wanted to say more. He searched for words that would make him witty, suave, lovable--words that would make him a Paul Newman, Elvis Presley, John F. Kennedy, words that would impress, intrigue, enrapture. But all Buck could say was, "Yes. Yes, I do."

"I thought I recognized you. I'm Beth Chertha."

"Hi, Beth. I'm Buck Leherifen."

"Your name is really Buck?"

"Actually it's Buchanan Leherifen, but they call me Buck for short."

"Yes, I think I like Buck better. Nice to meet you."

The teacher walked into the room and introduced himself and the English literature course, but Buck did not pay any attention to what he said. He was too busy reveling in Beth Chertha remembering him and speaking to him.

After class Buck followed Beth from the room. It had begun to rain, a weather condition not common in Lubbock, Texas. Beth opened her umbrella and looked at Buck.

"You didn't bring a raincoat or umbrella?" she said.

"No." He did not tell her that he did not own a raincoat or umbrella.

"You'll get wet."

"I won't melt."

"Which way are you going?" she asked.

"To the science building."

"Oh good. I'm going that way. Walk under my umbrella."

"Okay."

Okay? It's more than the okay, he thought. It's great. It's the event of the year! Thank you, rain. Thank you. Thank you! Thank you!

They began to walk toward the science building.

"Move closer," she said. "You're still getting wet."

It's the event of the decade, he thought.

They talked. Beth learned that Buck was a freshman from a nearby small town and that both of his parents were dead and he was trying to work his way through college.

Beth also was a freshman, and Buck learned the biographical facts that Clay already had told him. Then they came to the science building. It was across the campus, but Buck wished it was across town.

"Well," Beth said. "Here you are."

"Here I am. Thanks, Beth."

"You're welcome." She smiled and said, "See you Wednesday."

Buck stood in the entrance and watched her walk down the sidewalk. Yes, here I am, he thought. But where do I go from here. The rain began to blow in his face, and he walked up the stairs to his biology class.

On Tuesday the battery in Buck's car failed, and he was walking to work at the station when Beth pulled up in her Pontiac.

"Hey, want a ride?"

"Where are you going," Beth asked as he sat down beside her.

"To work."

"What time do you have to be there?"

"Not until five. I just left early because my car won't start, and I didn't know how long it would take me to walk."

"Good," said Beth. "We have time to run to the post office. I have to get some stamps. Then we can drop you off at Dub's station."

"Great," he said, wishing he did not have to be at work until six.

"Where do you live here in Lubbock?"

"I have a room at a lady's house. Her name is Grigsby."

"Oh, dear old Mrs. Grigsby. She's rented rooms to a lot of boys going to Tech. I guess she started renting rooms after her husband died. That was ten years ago. I remember because Mr. Grigsby was on the city council, and my daddy took his place, and I was eight. Nineteen fifty. Ten years ago. Do you remember ten years ago, Buck?"

"Yes, I was in the third grade, and I caught the measles the day after summer vacation began. I caught them from Lisa McSwee, the little girl who lived across the street. I was really mad at Lisa for giving me the measles. I just couldn't understand why I had to catch them after school had let out, and Lisa had got to miss a couple of weeks of school."

"How long did you stay mad at Lisa?"

"Not very long. She was the only other kid on the block. I didn't have anyone else to play with. A child can get awfully lonely by himself."

"You don't have any brothers or sisters?" she asked.

"No."

"Hey, we have something in common. I'm an only child, too. I wanted a little brother so bad. I used to beg my parents to get me one, but, well...."

They both laughed.

Beth was at the post office in about two minutes. Then they drove to the service station.

"Bye, Buck. See you tomorrow."

"You bet. Thanks for the ride."

Clay came over to Buck as he was wringing out his chamois.

"Hey, Bucky boy, you're doing okay, kid."

Buck tried to act nonchalant. "Oh, my dang car battery's dead, and she passed me walking to work and gave me a lift. And by the way, can you give me a ride home tonight?"

Clay said he could do that and went to wait on a car.

Later Clay said, "Buck, you had better watch out for Hunter Bultin."

"Who's he?"

"He's Beth's boyfriend. And not only is bigger than you, I suspect he's a whole lot meaner too."

"He doesn't have to worry about me. Do you think I could beat out a football player? Heck, I don't even have a car that I can keep running."

Clay turned toward the office, and Buck said, "Clay, how is it between Beth and this guy? I mean are they in love?"

"Love," he scoffed. "Hell, I don't know what you mean by that, kid. I imagine Hunter probably loves the good loving he gets. Of course, a young stud like him is probably getting it from a lot of girls. Beth's just probably the best-looking piece he gets."

"Clay, you don't know that."

Clay realized that Buck was becoming angry with him and said, "No, Buck. I guess I'm just hopelessly shallow and immoral. I just assume that's why guys go with girls."

"Don't you think there are other reasons?"

"Nope." Then Clay turned and walked into the office.

Buck saw Beth the next morning and every morning that the English lit class convened, and each day they would get to know each other a little bit more. He saw her when she came into the station too.

Beth learned that Buck was much more sensitive than his name implied, a young man who had little luck and no money but who wanted to make something of his life. He was different from most boys, not only more sensitive but kinder. Then she learned he was an art major. Maybe that's why he's different; he's an artist, she thought.

"Gee, I wonder if he's a homosexual. No, he doesn't act queer at all," she said out loud to herself.

Buck learned that Beth was more beautiful than she was brainy but that she had compassion for the people she knew. He often thought of asking her for a date but could never bring himself to do it.

They had known each other for six weeks. The teacher had scheduled his first exam for the next Monday. It was Friday, and they were again walking to the science building.

"Buck, do you think you are doing okay in this class."

"Yes, I think so."

"There are some things I'm having problems with, and I'm worried. What are you doing this afternoon? Do you think you could help me study?"

Buck had planned to do his laundry, but he figured he could wear dirty underwear and sox for at least a day. "Sure what time and where?"

"How about I pick you up about one o'clock and we go to my house?"

The Cherthas had a big house with a big landscaped yard and a swimming pool in the back. Buck met Beth's mother, an attractive women in her early forties who was late for her bridge club meeting, and then Beth and Buck went into what Beth called the recreation room.

They sat on a bench with cushions and reviewed the lit course, with Buck first telling Beth what he thought were the important points of the literature they had read and then Beth asking him questions.

After about an hour, Beth asked, "How about a Coke?"

She went into the kitchen and got two bottles of soda.

"All we have are soft drinks because my parents are good Baptists," she said.

Buck said, "A Coke will be just fine."

"Do you drink beer?" she asked.

"No. I'm not twenty-one yet, and besides I can't afford it, especially from bootleggers."

"I don't drink beer either," Beth said. "As I said, we're good Baptists. But some of my friends drink, mostly at parties," she said.

"I don't get invited to many parties, Beth."

"You'll have to come to my next party," she said.

"I have to work every night."

"You can come after work. Don't you want to come to my party?"

"Yes, but well, I'm pretty busy, Beth. I don't have much time for parties. Besides I don't know. I wouldn't fit in. I mean, you'll probably have football players and fraternity guys, and their pretty dates, and here I would be. I don't even know a girl to bring."

"Don't talk like that. You're very nice, and I like you. You'll fit in as well as the football players and fraternity guys. I'll see about getting you a date." Then she paused and said, "But maybe I won't have another party." Her voice trailed off, and she suddenly seemed unhappy.

Beth was holding Buck's hand. He said, "Beth, I...."

"Yes, Buck."

"Beth, I like you."

"I like you, too, Buck."

"What would you do, I mean, what would you say if, if I asked you for a date?"

There, he said it!

Beth did not say anything for a few seconds. It seemed longer to Buck.

"Buck, I guess I'd like to, but Hunter and I are going together and...."

"Are you going steady with him?"

She looked at Buck and nodded yes. "He's supposed to give me an engagement ring for Christmas."

"I see," Buck said.

"Buck, you're nice, and I do like you."

She sat still holding his hand. Buck wanted to kiss her, but he didn't. They sat there, looking at each other.

Beth went over to the stereo and put a couple of records on the turntable.

"I know I said my family are good Baptists, but some things that the minister says are evil are, I'm sorry, just ridiculous, so let's dance," she said, reaching again for his hand.

"I don't dance very well," Buck said.

"Come on," she said.

Buck held Beth in his arms, moving slowly to the soft, smooth lyrics of a Johnny Mathis song. She put her head on his shoulder. Then he saw a tear in her eye.

"What's the matter?" Buck asked. He had never made a girl cry before. "Is it something I've done?"

"No," she said. "Nothing except being the sweetest boy I've ever met."

Then she wiped the tear away and said, "I'm sorry, Buck. I guess I'm just being a girl."

She looked at her watch. "It's four o'clock. What time do you have to be at work?"

"Five. I guess I had better get back to my room and get over there."

As Buck was getting out of her car in front of Mrs. Grigsby's house, Beth said, "Buck, I wish I could have a date with you, but it's too late. I should have met you a few months earlier."

"Beth, do you love Hunter Bultin?"

"Yes." As though speaking only to herself, she added, "I had better."

She turned and smiled. "Maybe everything will be all right by Monday. I hope so. Goodbye, Buck."

The next day was a beautiful October Saturday. A Wednesday rain caused Dub's station to have many cars to wash, more than Buck and the rest of the Saturday crew could handle. It was Clay's day off. Clay did not have a phone, so at two o'clock Dub sent Buck in the station's pickup truck to see if Clay could work the rest of the day.

Clay was in his small apartment, drinking a beer and watching a football game on television.

"Hey, Buck. Come on in."

The apartment looked shoddy on the outside. It looked worse on the inside.

"Sit down, kid. Don't tell me, Uncle Dub, the old son of a bitch, wants me to work my only day off."

"We are pretty busy, Clay."

Clay lay back on the couch and put a cigarette in his mouth. "Hand me my lighter. It's on the end of the table."

Buck picked up the lighter and noticed the inscription: "Love always, Jackie."

Clay reached across the table and snatched the lighter from Buck's hand. He lit the cigarette, then looked at the lighter, then looked at Buck and said, "I guess you want to know who's Jackie."

"Yeah, I guess I do."

"Jackie, my boy, is the woman to whom I owe my worldly wisdom that you so often distain. This here lighter, kid, is a souvenir of my past, a reminder that I once was a young naive kid like you. Maybe not as naive as you, but naive. Naive enough to believe that a woman who said she loved me and who I had promised to marry could stay true for one lousy year while I was away at sea.

"Then I grew up, Buck. I grew up one day on the deck of a carrier off the coast of Japan when I read her letter -- a Dear John letter that began, "Dear Clay."

"I regret to write that I'm afraid I won't be able to marry you. You see, Clay honey, I went out and got myself knocked up. Sorry, baby, but you were there in the middle of the ocean and he was here in the middle of my pussy. Love and goodbye, Jackie."

"Maybe those weren't her exact words, but that's what she meant."

Clay turned up his beer and drank the last two swallows.

"Let's go, Buck. Uncle Dub is probably getting impatient."

Since the middle of September, Buck had looked forward to Monday mornings. The Monday after the revealing conversation with Clay, Buck went to his lit class, not thinking about the test but about Beth and hoping she would be as happy as she had been when he first met her. After the Friday afternoon conversation with Beth, Buck realized that she had seemed worried about something for the past couple of weeks. For a while, she would be happy when she was talking with him, then the worry would slip into her voice. It was as though she had forgotten whatever was troubling her, then suddenly something would remind her.

The final bell rang, and Beth was not in the seat beside Buck. The instructor passed out the test and still Beth had not come into the room. Buck finished the test about fifteen minutes before the end of the period, and still Beth had not shown.

Something must be wrong, he thought. She wouldn't cut a class when a major test was scheduled. He decided he would call her. The nearest pay phones were in the student union building. On his way down the hall to the phones, he decided to duck into the men's room.

Two other students were standing by the mirrors. Buck recognized them as linemen on the Tech freshmen football team. As one of them rubbed his hands across his flattop, he asked the other, "How do you think marriage is going to affect Hunter's playing this week?"

"I don't know," replied the other lineman. "He played pretty good the last game considering what he had to worry about."

"You mean marrying Beth?"

"I mean being afraid he would have to marry Beth."

"Huh?"

"Oh hell, you know why they're getting married, don't you?"

"You mean?"

"Yeah, I mean Hunter knocked up Beth Chertha. She found out for sure on Friday, and now they've gone up to Oklahoma to get married."

"I'll be damned. I'm afraid knowing that you're going to have a kid in about seven months could make you screw up a few plays."

Suddenly Buck didn't need to go the bathroom or to make any phone calls. He just went to his next class and then back to his room at Mrs. Grigsby's. He lay on his bed and thought about what Beth's parting words last Friday: "Maybe everything will be all right Monday. I hope so."

But it wasn't. At least not as far as Buck was concerned.

He wondered how many times Beth had let Hunter make love to her. One weak moment or every date? He tried to imagine Beth being seduced. Did she move or cry out? Did it hurt her? Did she enjoy it? He could only picture her as she had been with him, clothed and combed and smiling, not panting and sweating and clawing.

But then he didn't know.

What was it like? What was it like to have a woman under you, a partner in your lust? Was it like in the sexy novels? Does she wrap her legs around your back and draw them to your shoulders in the highest moment of ecstasy? Is there conversation? Dirty words? Tender words? How does it feel? How does she feel?

But then he didn't know.

Was he the only one who didn't know? The only kid left on the block? Has everyone else -- man, woman, or hippopotamus -- lost their virginity? Dolph and Sheila, Hunter and Beth, Clay and Candy, Jackie and the man in the middle of her pussy while Clay was in the middle of the ocean. And probably even little Lisa McSwee and some boy in Dallas, where she now lived. Buck was sorry that she had moved away in the sixth grade. Maybe they could have done it.

Was he the only clean corner on a dirty hand towel? The last virgin?

St. Paul wrote to the Corinthians: "Flee fornication." Corinth must have been a kindergarten, he thought as he reached for the tattered *Playboy* under his pillow and unzipped his blue jeans. Then he slept.

Buck went to work later in the day. When he finished his shift, he realized that he had not eaten lunch or dinner, so he went to Candy's cafe. Candy was there and he said hello to her.

"Hi, Buck. How's school?"

"It's okay. I haven't seen you in a while around the station."

"That S.O.B. you work with and I had a strong disagreement, so I'm thinking about taking my trade elsewhere."

Clay had told Buck about the disagreement. Clay said Candy called him an asshole and he called her a bitch.

She bent over to clean a table. Her sweater was V-necked with a deep V. Candy knew he was watching her as she wiped the crumbs off the table and replaced the napkins.

"You know you are really a nice guy, Buck," she said. "And a really nice looking guy."

"It seems that people keep telling me I'm a nice guy, but it's nice to hear someone say I'm nice looking too."

Candy moved over to him. "Yeah, well, you are." She moved really close to him, so close that her legs touched his legs.

"What are you doing later tonight, probably studying, huh?"

"No, I just had a test today, and really don't have that much to do."

"Want to come over to my apartment for a drink?"

Buck looked at the young woman, pretty and only a couple of years older than he. His heart began beating faster, and his throat quivered.

"Yeah, I'd like that," he said.

On his little bed on the Olympic Peninsula, a pleasant cool night like most of the nights on the Olympic Peninsula, Buck thought about that night in Lubbock with Candy, and he reached his hand down to his briefs and did what he had done for forty years to relieve those depressive passions of loneliness. But now he felt no guilt.

Chapter 7
Renewed Friendships in Albuquerque

Jordan's new source of income ended when the recalcitrant guitar picker mended, paid his fines, and suggested strongly to the singer and leader of the band that despite being a better guitarist Jordan did not know all the dirty secrets of the individual band members' pasts, which apparently included episodes ranging from racism to rape, and it would behoove his musical colleagues to reinstate the original band member. It was evidently a convincing argument.

Jordan got a friendly handshake, well-wishes, and an invitation to join the band again if any of its members quit or were unable to perform. The goodbye was okay with Jordan. He had enjoyed being a performing musician, but he had tired of being the old guy who didn't really fit in, the band member who was older than the mothers of two of the other members.

So Jordan began looking for another job, wasting phone calls and stamps only to be told sorry, there just weren't any openings available for a person of his qualifications. He told me he had already had figured out that one of these major qualifications was being over forty, and thereby not as attractive to corporate loyalists as a bright twenty-something who would work for less and probably take more crap from the expensive-suit-wearing, ass-kissing managers who had figured out the Machiavellian techniques that allowed them to keep their wives on the tennis courts and kids in private schools.

But still he went through the drill of calling and writing and following up on every lead for a job, receiving no offers.

A couple of weeks after his last gig with the Lobos Locos, Jordan was drinking his first cup of coffee after a particularly busy night of touring the bars and bistros along the Santa Fe Plaza and Canyon Road.

I walked into the kitchen and asked, "What are you looking so down about?"

"Flash, I don't know what to do with the rest of my life, whatever is left of it. I'm too old to start a new corporate career and get anywhere with it. And apparently I've lost my charm as a smoozer of politicians. So do I spend the rest of my life trying to write a hit song or go back to chasing cop cars and writing ten-inch stories for some newspaper? Or do I take up another career playing in bands organized by young men who think manhood is measured by how many women they can screw and sponge off and have no concept of honor, duty, and those obsolete values that I learned so many Saturday afternoons ago watching you and your fellow shoot-em-up heroes make everything right?"

Jordan took a sip of his coffee and continued, "Flash, I know this is going to sound a little crazy, but I've been thinking about something that would be challenging, worthwhile to mankind, and personally rewarding on a monetary basis."

"What's that?" I asked.

"Bounty hunting," Jordan said.

I gave him a bemused look and said, "Shit, I thought for a minute you were serious."

"No, I am serious. Listen to this," Jordan said. Then he read me aloud an article in the *Albuquerque Journal* about Ricardo Cajon. Known in the Mexican underworld as Big Dick Cajones, Cajon was the Mexican drug kingpin celebrity of the early '80s. He had thrived with impunity by paying off or killing the appropriate authorities until he got emboldened and ordered the killing of an undercover American drug enforcement agent. The murder might have received minimal news coverage if Cajon had not been so angered at the agent that he also gave his goons permission or perhaps even instructions to handle the execution as they did against Mexicans who crossed Cajon. After torturing the agent, they dismembered him and shipped certain body parts back to his bosses in Washington D.C. The brutal package so enraged the Reagan administration that it put a million-dollar price on Cajon's head.

"I figure it's kind of like being a journalist, except instead of going after a story, you go after a killer or a dope dealer or whoever the scumbag is who merits the bounty. And it ain't play-acting in a Saturday shoot-em-up. We'll really be catching the bad guys," Jordan said as he passed the newspaper to me.

"Just like Jim Garner in the *Rockford Files*," I said, unable to hide my skepticism. Then I told him a story about a man I once worked with.

"He was scraping by with bit parts in the movies and decided he would become a private dick. I guess he had been reading too many Raymond Carver and Dashiell Hammett novels between takes. Anyway, he got his license as a private investigator and spent his days spying on people who were having sex with people who weren't their spouses.

"But then he got it on with a woman who had hired him to spy on her husband who was fucking his secretary, and the husband found out about my former colleague fucking his wife while dishing the dirt about the husband fucking his secretary. The husband didn't take all this well and damn near beat my ex-colleague to death. Left him with a limp and a back pain that made it hard to sit a long time in cars doing all that spying that private eyes have to do and even harder to outrun men who wanted to beat the shit out of him, so he had to go back to his hometown in Oklahoma and sell washing machines and TV sets at the local Sears Roebuck store. The point is, the only person

I ever knew who took up non-government detective work didn't fare well."

"But I didn't suggest that we become peeping toms on cheating spouses," Jordan said. "I'm thinking about finding out just where Ricardo Cajon is, gathering enough information to give to the feds so they can catch him and reward us for the information."

"How could a couple of guys like us could track down a Mexican drug lord when the entire might of the United States government can't stop him?" I asked.

"That's just why I think we may have a chance. He's wary of the United States government. He won't be looking out for a couple of goofy gringos like us," Jordan said.

I took a big gulp of coffee and said, "Yeah, I guess that's so, but I think you might have better luck pursuing that dream of writing a hit song. It worked out okay for me. Hell, I may be a millionaire. I guess I could ask my accountant."

"Yes, Flash, I understand that you don't need the money, but I do."

I nodded and said, "But I admit your scenario sounds kind of exciting to an old guy like me, who's wiling away his life waiting for the big departure and hoping his true love was right about meeting again in heaven. But I guess I'm sober enough or maybe old enough to doubt we can become Travis McGee and his buddy making a living by solving crimes."

Both of us took several swigs from our coffee cups before I continued with my logic.

"And what are the technicalities of this bounty," I asked. "Is it payable dead or alive, upon conviction or what? Do you have to bring him in yourself, or just help the feds do it? And if you kidnapped him and brought him from Mexico, wouldn't you be violating Mexican law, and if you had to kill him, wouldn't you be subject to prosecution?"

"Good questions," Jordan said. "I guess it would be a good idea to check into those details. But I think we just have to be instrumental in getting him apprehended. Hell, I'm not delusional enough to believe I could haul him all the way from Mexico.

"So you aren't thinking about becoming Josh Randall," I said. "Remember that TV show that made Steve McQueen a star and probably is responsible for all these young boys walking around named Josh. The bounty hunter that McQueen played, Josh Randall, had to haul his prey back if he didn't have a reason to shoot 'em first."

Jordan said, "I watched that show a few times, and I seem to remember that he came up with that reason a lot of times. But I'm not planning on shooting anybody. I just want to use some of my investigative skills and find out what I can about this Cajon character. I don't suppose you know anybody who works for the federal government who might give us some more information about him?"

"I don't even know anybody who works for the post office," I said.

Jordan said, "I used to know a lawyer who worked for the Justice Department during the Carter administration. I don't know if Cajon was on the federal bad guy list back then, but I'm going to call him and see if he knows anything."

I shook my head and said, "Boy, you must have really tied one on last night. I'm not sure you've completely slept it off. My advice is to wait at least another day to make sure you're completely sober."

Jordan sort of took my advice. He waited two days, thought about his scheme, realized it probably made no sense, had a few more drinks, and decided even if he did not get enough information to get a million-dollar reward, he might get enough to write a freelance article about Cajon that he could sell for a few dollars. So he placed his call to Mark Paul James at his downtown Denver law office

When Jordan asked about Ricardo Cajon, Mark said, "Why are you asking about him?"

"Along with writing songs, I'm trying to be a freelance journalist, and I thought a story about a Mexican drug lord might sell."

"Maybe you should become a snakehandler instead. It would be safer,"

Mark said. "Cajon's a really bad character -- not worth the risk.

"Since you are both a musician and a journalist, why not do personality pieces on people like Willie Nelson and Jimmy Buffett. They're nice guys and won't kill you for what you write. They're both living up here in Colorado by the way. Colorado's a cool place for celebrities now, you know."

"So is Santa Fe," Jordan said. "The rich Texans colonized this place years ago, and maybe that's why the Manhattan and Left Coast crowd stayed away. As Coloradoans know, Texans aren't necessarily who you want for neighbors. But now it's the '80s, Mark. The vice president of the United States is a rich transplanted Texan; two of Charlie's Angeles are native Texans, and good ole Willie is almost as hot as Frank Sinatra was a few years ago. So people are moving here from everywhere because they're no longer put off by Texans. But me, I'm down here because I got a friend who charges me cheaper rent than I would have to pay in Colorado."

"If you get back up here, famous or not, let's get together for a drink," counselor James said.

"I'll take you up on that offer. I'll even buy if you'll tell me what you know about Ricardo Cajon, other than he's a mean motherfucker?"

"I guess the most interesting thing I remember is that he got his start supplying drugs to some people involved in showbiz out in California."

"Do you hear any of the names of the people he got drugs for?"

"I seem to recall that the Drug Enforcement Agency guys suspected he might have been the supplier for that soft porn actress who overdosed in the late '70s. What was her name -- Debra? Yeah, that's it -- Debra Debaux."

This information stunned and silenced Jordan long enough for Mark to ask him if he was still on the line.

"Yeah, I'm still here," Jordan said. "That's a bit of a coincidental shocker for me since I once met Debra Debaux."

"Really. What were doing -- working as a bit part stud?"

"It's kind of a long and convoluted story," Jordan said. "Debra had a family -- a daughter and a husband. Do you know anything about them? Were they involved in drugs?"

"Her husband was, the DEA boys said. He's probably the guy who got Debra hooked on heroin. He had a large mix of politically incorrect chemicals in his blood when he rolled his Mercedes off into the Pacific a few months after Debra overdosed. All I remember about her daughter was that she had a ditzy name, which I can't recall."

"Tammy. Tammy Dolcito," Jordan said.

"Did you know her too?"

"Yes, I knew her," Jordan said. "Do you know if Tammy was involved with Cajon, or what happened to her?"

"No, but I guess I could make a couple of phone calls and find out."

"I really would appreciate that, Mark. And if I ever get back to Denver, I buy you that drink."

"I'll be looking forward to it. But if you're really serious about trying to find Big Dick Cajon, you may be needing a blood transfusion more than a shot of Scotch. Take care, Jordan."

Jordan gave Mark the phone number at Flash's house, and Mark called back the next day.

"I don't know if you believe in serendipity or fate of whatever you want to call it, but if you want to contact Tammy Dolcito, it shouldn't be that difficult. I talked to a friend of mine with the DEA. He said as far as he knew, she wasn't involved with her mother's and stepfather's drug-taking, but she skipped town after her mother's death.

"Since she had a degree in drama from some state college in California and had spent time doing local TV commercials and had picked up a few bit parts in network sitcoms, she managed to get a job teaching acting at the University of New Mexico."

"Really," Jordan said.

"Yeah, and here is another piece of information. Tammy moved to Albuquerque with another woman who worked for her mother and may have known Cajon. Her name's Angelica or Angelina or something like that, and it's rumored that she and Tammy are lovers."

"So, what do you think about that, Flash?"

I told him I was glad they were both alive and apparently doing well.

"Me, too," Jordan said.

I asked him if he wanted to continue his bounty hunting game or forget -- to quote a recent New Mexico governor, "you ever opened this box of Pandoras." I've loved that line ever since I read Bruce King's quote. As I indicated in the beginning pages of this tale, I'll steal a good line every chance I get, especially when it's uttered by a good-natured politician who puts it [illegible] out there for posterity.

"I got this gut feeling that we should reconnect with Tammy and Angelina," Jordan said.

I asked him how he thought we should do that.

"Well, there's the telephone," he said.

Jordan was not sure why he thought it was a good idea to make contact with the two women, but I suspect he had something to do with recurring memories of those two months in the fall of 1963. He also remembered the beautiful nineteen-year-old Angelina and wondered what she looked like more than twenty years later.

"Damn, surely they haven't given up men altogether," Jordan thought.

We did nothing about contacting Tammy and Angelina for a couple of days. The next time I brought up the subject.

"I've been thinking more about it, and I've decided we should call them," I said.

"Okay, but what are we going to say? Hi. How ya'll? Sorry we haven't called in a couple of decades, but we thought we'd get in touch since we heard you were a couple of lesbians who might still know a Mexican drug lord."

"No," I said. "Look, what's wrong with calling two people you were friends with when you learn they're in the neighborhood?"

"Nothing, I guess. But I still don't know how to start the conversation. I think you should make the phone call. After all you're the one who's Tammy's ex-stepfather."

"Yeah, I guess you're right. All right, I'll do it, but not right now."

After waiting two more days, I placed the call. Tammy answered the phone. I made up a story about some old friend in Hollywood saying he had heard that she was in Albuquerque, and since I was in Santa Fe it would be a shame not to get in touch. I didn't mention Angelina, but Tammy did.

Tammy was cordial and seemed truly pleased to hear from me. She gave me a brief summary of her past two decades and told me about how she and Angelina had fled California. She even hinted of the Cajon angle when she said, "Angelina and I needed to get out of there, but that's another story."

"Let's get together for lunch or dinner sometime," I said.

"Yeah. That would be great," she said.

"And by the way," I said. "It's funny that you have Angelina as a roommate since I also have a mutual friend as my roommate."

I told her about Jordan. After the phone call, Jordan asked about Tammy's reaction at the mention of his name.

"It may have taken her a little while to remember you because she hesitated before she said anything," I said.

I followed through with a second phone call and made a date for Jordan and me to meet Tammy and Angelina at one of Albuquerque's many Mexican restaurants. I figured that lunch would be easier for everyone since if the reunion turned out to be a bad idea all of us could politely exit after an hour and go back to our business.

On the day of the lunch, Jordan overslept and skipped breakfast because he and I were determined to arrive early enough to wander through the restaurant looking for two women we were not sure we would recognize. But we recognized them immediately when they walked through the door. Tammy had shorter hair and a few more pounds than when Jordan last saw her in Dallas, but she still was an attractive woman. Angelina, with shoulder length hair, remained slender and voluptuous with her impressive bust. The only sign of early middle-age in both women were a few soft wrinkles on their faces.

After we all hugged and gave cheek kisses, Tammy said, "You're both are looking good."

"Not nearly as good looking as you two," I said.

We decided that the occasion called for a pitcher of margaritas even if it was the middle of the day. We licked the salt from the rims of the glasses and recounted how we had spent the past two decades. Both women retained the key qualities they had as the young women we knew in the early 1960s -- Angelina's calm reticence and Tammy's slightly sarcastic candor.

Tammy took the role of questioner and spokesperson. "So did you graduate from North Texas, Jordan?"

Jordan said he had indeed gotten his journalism degree, and he gave an abbreviated version of how he had become my long-term houseguest. Then Jordan asked how Tammy and Angelina had become residents of New Mexico.

"We had a rough time in our last years in California, both being abused by my hideous stepfather," Tammy said. "After my mother died, we knew we had to get away from him, so I traded in my convertible for a pickup and we loaded a few belongings we wanted to keep and headed east. We were going to Santa Fe, but about thirty miles west of Albuquerque, Angelina developed appendicitis. She had emergency surgery at the University of New Mexico Hospital.

"While she was recovering, I got bored with whiling away my days in a Central Avenue motel, so I walked around the UNM campus and bumped into a fellow I knew when he was a Hollywood screenwriter. It turned out that he's now a drama prof at UNM. Angelina's incision healed, and I got a job as an instructor in UNM's drama department."

Raising his glass, Jordan said, "Here's to all of us."

We toasted and made small talk about the advantages and disadvantages of living in our two disparate cities. Tammy agreed that Santa Fe was a more hip place but said it was tough to make a living there unless one wanted to wait on tables.

Jordan agreed, saying he could not freeload off me much longer and needed to start earning some money again.

"So, have you thought about looking for a job in Albuquerque?" Angelina asked.

"Yeah, I thought about that, but I guess I don't feel like starting over in newspapers, and there aren't many big corporations in Albuquerque, and small companies don't usually need PR guys or lobbyists, so I doubt that there are many opportunities for me here," Jordan said.

Then he hesitated and said, "And I guess not drawing a regular paycheck, besides making me poor, has spoiled me a little, not having to put up with the bullshit and assholes who inhabit the corporate world. I know that makes me sound a bit lazy, but really you would have to work in the corporate world to understand."

"Oh, and I guess the rest of us don't have to put up with bullshit and dealing with assholes," Tammy said in her best sarcastic style.

Jordan shrugged and said, "As I said, I knew saying that would make me sound lazy, or maybe simply like a jerk."

"No, you're not a jerk," said Angelina. "You're a very nice man."

"But maybe a little lazy," I said. Then I added, "Just kidding. Hey, everybody's gotta do what they gotta do."

We all laughed. The liquor on Jordan's empty stomach spurred his journalistic instincts, and he asked the question aimed at getting a confirmation or denial of Mark James' rumor.

"So how come two beautiful women like you haven't married some rich, handsome hunks who will take you out of this mediocre city of dusty strip malls and drive-by shootings and build you a hacienda in tony Taos or supercilious Santa Fe?"

Tammy didn't blink and or hesitate with her answer. She looked briefly at Angelina, took her hand, smiled at us and said, "Because Angelina and I are partners."

Angelina looked a little uncomfortable, and after a few seconds of silence, Tammy said, "Now that you two fine examples of native Texas masculinity know that you're with couple of lesbians, do you still want to have lunch?"

Jordan gave me a sideways glance and then in perhaps not the most steady voice said, "Um, lesbian, straight, or whatever, you're still a couple of foxy ladies who honor us with your presence."

When I didn't say anything, Tammy looked at me and said, "That's nice. Thank you, Jordan. And what about you, cowboy stud, albeit a little older? Do you still want to associate with your former stepdaughter?"

I gulped my last ounce of margarita, shrugged, and said, "Hey, as I said a minute ago, you gotta do what you gotta do. Why wouldn't I still want to be with a girl who I've cared about since she sometimes had bigger pimples than nipples?"

As Tammy laughed and Angelina smiled, I continued with my speech. "Look, I never have cared about what people do with other people in bedrooms, bordellos, or back seats, but most of the time I would prefer that they not tell me about those experiences.

"Still I've noticed over the years that women get a lot more emotional about other women than men get about other men. If a woman likes another woman, she doesn't say, I like you. She says, I love you. And, by the same token, if two women don't like each other, they really don't like each other and can get real catty.

"And women who like, or maybe I should say love, each other will tell just about any secret, while a man keeps his secrets much closer and when he does claim to confess something, a wise person, be it man or woman, should take what he says with a big chunk of salt.

"Aw, I guess I'm not really making my point, so I probably should shut up and just say I've wondered for a long time if maybe there's at least a little bit of lesbianism in every woman."

Angelina smiled and raised her eyebrows, and said, "I think that is true. You are a wise and observant man, amigo. Or perhaps I should say, mi salvador."

"Yes," said Tammy. "Angelina and I said several times back when we were going through the hell of putting up with my mother's slimy husband, we wished you were there to protect us, to rescue us."

"I wish I had been there, too. Sounds like you really went through some rough times. But I doubt that you want to go into the details, and I doubt that I want to hear them."

"Si," said Angelina as tears began to form in her eyes.

Tammy detected Angelina's sadness and said, "Maybe we should change the subject. Let's just say, we're glad to be back in the same town -- or at least the same state -- with you guys. Now let's enjoy our lunch. I'm hungry from some shrimp enchiladas."

All of us worked hard at making the remainder of the reunion a fun time. Jordan and I made jokes about how despite living in the American Southwest most of our lives and having friends and lovers who were Hispanic, we still butchered Spanish when we tried to speak it, and after two margaritas Angelina began to kid us and say if she could learn to speak English, we should be able to learn to speak Spanish.

"If it wasn't for those damned double R's," I said, "I might be able to do it. But when I try to pronounce something that has consecutive R's, I just end up biting my tongue or cheek, sounding like a bad ventriloquist, and splattering spit all over some rich dude or pretty girl I'm trying to impress.

"I figured out the double L's a long time ago when I lived near La Jolla. Actually, that ritzy town was good for two Spanish lessons. It helped me figure out that double L's actually are Y's and J's actually are H's."

"Yeah, same here," Jordan said. "The first time I asked a buddy in the Marines if he wanted to take bus to that beach south of Oceanside and pronounced it La Jolly or something like that, he laughed his ass off and said a Texan should know how to pronounce J's and double L's in Spanish. I set him straight when I told him that the city in the Panhandle north of Lubbock is not Amariyo and Sam Houston did not lead his band of Texans to victory at the battle of San Hacinto."

"The truth is, Texans don't just sound funny when they try to speak Spanish," Tammy said. "They also talk funny in English. For example, they don't go dancing in Dallas, they go dayncing in Dayless. They don't iron their clothes; they arn them. And we all know the reason the state is not in the economic dark ages like it probably should be is because a lot of Texans got rich in the all bidness."

Jordan smiled and said, "I see you still have the same fondness for my native state you had when we last parted."

"What do you expect me to think about state that might put Angelina and me in jail if we lived there? Besides if you like the place, why aren't you still there?"

"Touché," Jordan said.

"Aw, Tammy, darlin', don't pick on Jordan because of his roots. After all, as you're implying, he's figured out that the really smart people are from Texas," I said.

"What kind of bullshit is that?" Tammy said. "Are you trying to tell me that Texans are smarter than people from the rest of the country?"

"No. I didn't say that. I said the really smart people are from Texas, meaning they don't live there no more."

Tammy laughed and said, "Hey, I guess I was getting a little too uptight. It's just that I don't have fond memories of my time in Texas when I was an SMU coed."

"Gee, I'm hurt," Jordan said.

"I didn't mean it was all bad."

Feeling his margaritas and beer, Jordan said, "Well, I hope it wasn't me who turned you against men."

I looked at Jordan and said, "If you keep making impolitic remarks like that you're sure liable to turn a lot of women against at least one man."

"Yeah, I guess it was stupid thing to say, certainly in front of all of you."

"No," Tammy said. "It wasn't stupid. You know I like people who speak their mind. And, no, it certainly wasn't you who turned me against men. And it wasn't you or your buddy Norman who turned Angelina against men. It was Sam Eschidt and some of his low-life associates who turned us both against men."

Angelina was looking embarrassed again, so Tammy took her hand and said, "Sorry, hon, I guess Jordan and I both talk too much."

We finished our lunch, trying hard to keep the conversation confined to congenial small talk. Cats proved to be subjects that made that effort successful. Being a dog man, Jordan was relegated to the position of polite listener, a role that he welcomed after his earlier awkward questions and comments.

As we took our leave in the restaurant parking lot, Tammy said, "It was really good to see both of you."

Angelina quickly echoed with a smiling, "Si, yes, yes. It is so good to know that you are here and in good health."

"Ladies, I think Jordan will agree that this lunch has been the highlight of our year," I said.

Jordan agreed and said, "Not to get too serious again, but I was thinking about your earlier comments about me looking for a job in Albuquerque, and I think I will. I think after we get back to Santa Fe, I'll get in my MGB and come back down here, get me a room in one of these old Route 66 Central Avenue tourist courts and start pounding the pavement, seeing if anyone wants a middle-aged hack writer, PR guy, or so-called government relations specialist."

"No," Angelina said. "You will not have to stay in a motel. You can stay with us. We have a nice house over by Old Town and the zoo with two bathrooms and a nice couch that makes into a bed and becomes a third bedroom."

"No. I couldn't impose on you."

"Yes, you could," Tammy said. "It's unanimous. Angelina and I both want you to be our houseguest. We will enjoy your company, and it will blow the mind of the nosey old lady next door who is telling everyone in the neighborhood we're a couple of lesbians."

Jordan laughed and said, "Okay. Maybe I can change her mind. Who knows, maybe I can even change your minds."

Tammy jerked her head back, gave Jordan a smirk that turned into a smile, and said, "Jeez, you really did have too much to drink."

It may have been providential that we drove from Santa Fe in my pickup truck and not Jordan's little sports car since only Jordan supplemented his share of the margarita pitcher with a beer. Sometimes he drank too much, and sometimes I did. And quite often, we both did, but not when we had to drive long distances. The people who don't figure out that axiom soon end up dead or in jail. And dear reader, I never went to jail. And neither did Jordan.

Aw, I need to get off this hypocritical high horse. Probably because I never ended up in the jailhouse or anyone who ever drove with me never ended up there was because I was always the best designated drunk driver. So, don't any of you young people who might be reading this book start thinking it's smart to drink and drive. Of course, if you're old enough to read this stuff I've been telling you, you've probably already done that. Oh shit, I'm going off on a tangent again. Let's get back to the story.

"So, after you get over your luncheon buzz, are you still going to take the girls up on their hospitality offer and look for a job in Albuquerque?" I asked as we drove north toward Santa Fe.

Jordan said, "Yes, I think I will. I want to find out more about what happened with Sam Eschidt and if Cajon and his gang figured in the situation, and I think they will tell me, maybe not together, but I think each will talk to me alone."

"Yeah, you're probably right. Enjoy your stay in Albuquerque. And, who knows? Maybe you will find a job, but if you don't, you know you're still welcome at my place."

"I know, but I need to get on with my life, such as it is."

Jordan wondered if I was as comfortable with Tammy's and Angelina's alternate lifestyle as I had indicated with my clichéd comment about doing what ya gotta do.

"Flash, what do you really think about Tammy and Angelina being a couple of lesbians?"

As my truck ascended the long hill that rises to the high plateau where Santa Fe is located, I took my eyes off Interstate 25, looked at Jordan with a smile, and said, "Oh, I guess the dirty old man in me thinks it's a waste of two good-looking women."

I turned my eyes away from Jordan and the scrubby junipers that dotted the hills to the east, and neither of us said anything until we passed the state prison and neared the Santa Fe race track.

Then I said, "Jordan, as a person who really, really likes to have sex with women and would rather lick the floor of a garage than another man's dick, I admit I have never understood this homosexual thing. But in Hollywood in the business I was in, I met a lot of people who were homosexual, gay, queer, lesbian, dykes, or whatever you want to call them.

"And you know what, after I got over my Central Texas raising, I figured out that they were just like the rest of us human beings. Some of them were real assholes, but others were nice people -- as I said, just like the rest of us.

"And one of them did me a big favor and saved my career. I guess it shouldn't have taken that act of kindness to make me realize that I shouldn't judge people by their sexual proclivity, just as I had learned also not to judge people by the color of their skin or their political persuasion or their religion, but still it did, and that's all I can say."

As we rode another mile toward the Cerrillos Road exit, Jordan turned to me and looked west toward the Jemez Mountains.

"Angelina is right. You are a wise and observant man, amigo," Jordan said."

That night I lay in bed and thought about Tammy's mother. I had loved her once, and I was sad about how she had died. I also thought of another woman I had known who also died young. Soon I realized that my memories would not let me sleep, so I got up, picked up my guitar, and started to quietly compose a song.

He stopped in mid-barroom sentence with a look of surprise,
An expression that turned from loser to winner of first prize.
"Excuse me, friend," he said. "I see someone I used to know."

Then he walked over to a woman as pretty as Marilyn Monroe.
She took off her sunglasses and got up a little unsteady on her feet.
But the aging cowboy was clearly someone she was happy to greet.
She was older and still beautiful, but more than a little sad,
With the look of someone whose dreams had all gone bad.
After they hugged and sat down to talk awhile,
The beautiful sad woman soon cracked a smile
As they talked of times past, some good, others a little shady,
Shared by a daring young cowboy and his oh-so-pretty lady,
The now older man wished he could mend the broken soul
Of this woman possessing warmth in a world turned cold.
They talked, but the woman still was sad,
Longing for the real love she never had.
So the cowboy drank up and said goodbye to his friend,
Wondering and fearing how her life story would end.

I titled the song *Lost Love*, but I never wrote a chorus for it, and I never played it for anyone else.

Jordan wondered if Tammy and Angelina would really feel as hospitable after the effect of the margaritas wore off. If they regretted making the offer, they never gave any hint, and after a few days of living with two women who made him feel like he was someone who really mattered in their lives and maybe even in the world, Jordan was sitting on their daytime couch and his nighttime bed, drinking a beer while they sipped glasses of wine.

Jordan finished his beer and switched to the wine, which prompted Tammy and Angelina to open another bottle. Soon they had delayed their dinner plans, if they ever had any, and were talking about the circumstances and events that had brought them to this evening.

Jordan asked Angelina if she had any problems as an illegal alien in the years since he had helped smuggle her across the border. Had she been threatened with deportation?

Angelina said, "I'm now a legal alien and will get my citizenship because of the new law that President Reagan got through last year."

"But in the '60s and '70s, me having a no-principled stepfather who knew a lot of people with the same morals as his helped keep her in the United States," Tammy said. "However, true to his nature, Sam demanded repayment in ways that a hot-blooded male like you might imagine. But then, as Flash said, you probably don't want to hear the details."

"That's what Flash said. Not me. But maybe Angelina would rather not talk about it."

"No. I don't mind talking about it, Jordan," Angelina said. "You know what I did when you met me. Why should I try to deny that I repaid one man with sexual favors for a debt that was much more valuable than the money I took from the men in Tijuana. If sex had been all he wanted, it would not have been a problem, but when he commanded that I provide the same services for his drug dealer as well as help him bring heroin and cocaine across from Mexico, Tammy told her mother, who told Senor Eschidt that was not right."

"So Debra stopped his plans to make you a criminal?" Jordan asked.

"Yes, but it angered Sam. He hit my mother and told her to mind her own business and then he came to my apartment in Santa Monica and beat me up," Tammy said.

She paused and said. "No, he didn't just beat me up. I guess that got him aroused, so he raped me. He had slapped me a few times, but that was the first time he did that. He told me since my mother had become such a druggie that she wouldn't do it anymore, he would get his satisfaction from me."

Jordan didn't say anything, just sadly shook his head as Tammy continued.

"Then my mother turned up dead, and I knew that Angelina and I needed to get out of L.A."

"And like Flash earlier, Tammy became my rescuer -- mi salvador segunda," Angelina said.

"So Tammy knows about how you came to this country?" Jordan said.

Tammy almost scoffed. "Sure, you know that women don't keep any secrets, especially not from other women they love. Flash had it right."

It was Jordan's turn to smile. "So did you two tell each other everything?"

"If you are asking if I gave you a few lessons in Dallas on how to please women, yeah," Tammy said.

Even though Jordan had been penning words to songs and poems ever since he was a teenager, he never learned the term for a mixture of amusement and perplexity, but that's what he displayed at this point in the conversation.

"Oh well," he said. "I guess it's good that we three roommates have no secrets."

"Oh, I don't believe that. Angelina and I still have a few, and I'll bet you have a full closet. For instance, you're divorced. We haven't heard anything about that part of your life."

Jordan twisted his nose, curled up his mouth, and said, "That's right; you haven't. As you said, Flash was right."

"Oh, so you're going to withhold your secrets," Tammy said.

"Some of them, but let's talk about something else," Jordan said. "Let's talk about Ricardo Cajon and his gang of drug-running cutthroats, rapists, and just about every other sin human beings ever thought of. Do you know that our government has put a million-dollar price on his head?"

"Oh yeah," said Tammy. "Of course, we know that, and I guess you are going to be the next person to ask us if we know where Cajon is and want to help you collect that reward."

"So, other people already have approached you."

"Si," said Angelina. "The FBI, Los Angeles and San Diego police, the federal narcotics agents. That is another reason we left California. I am afraid it is only a matter of time before Cajon and his people decide that we know things we don't know and try to kill us."

"Angelina worries more than I do," Tammy said. "But then I guess she's had more experience in dealing with these beasts. I hope her concerns are unfounded because the truth is neither she nor I have any idea about where Cajon is. We assume he's been ensconced safely somewhere in Mexico since the cops and feds raided his place in San Diego after he had the narc agent butchered.

"But, come on, Jordan, please tell me that you are not seriously thinking about trying to capture Cajon?"

"Oh, I don't know. Flash and I talked about it when I could not have passed a road sobriety test, I guess out of boredom or perhaps because of my dead-end life. But it would be exciting to catch a bad guy, and I could use the money."

"Oh yeah, and how long do you think you would live to spend it?"

Angelina nodded in agreement with Tammy's last question, which Jordan thought about for a few seconds.

"Yes, I thought about that, too. But then I decided Ricardo Cajon and his gang in Tijuana aren't Soviet leaders in the Kremlin. They're a bunch of poor Mexicans led by a guy who if he had grown up in the ghettos of L.A. or New York would have probably ended up grubbing around in some dirty prison or lying dead with a couple of .22-caliber pistol bullets in his head on a dog-shit stained street, but who discovered that even average Americans have more money than they deserve and not enough principles to spend it on anything but pleasure.

"I mean he's just a cheap hood leading even cheaper hoods, and when he's out of the way, the next cheap hood who takes his place won't be spending his time and ill-gotten gains looking for who turned in Cajon and allowed him to get to that position.

"No, catching Cajon is not the hazard. Going after Cajon and him catching us before the feds catch him is the hazard. Maybe going after a Mexican drug lord is not a more reasonable plan for paying my bills on time than writing a hit song, marrying a rich woman, or winning a state lottery, but right now, those last three alternatives seem to be as impossible as the first."

Jordan shut up, and Tammy and Angelina looked at him with the pitiful expressions that women give frustrated males from the time that they see their little brothers strike out in the ninth inning of a little league game to when they have to help their fathers into wheelchairs. And at that moment Jordan felt just like both of those generations of males. So he did what a lot of males who grew up in the '40s and '50s and came of age in the '60s do in such a circumstance, he poured himself another drink.

Chapter 8
In Love in Houston

Later, when Tammy and Angelina had gone to their room, Jordan lay on the couch bed and thought about one of the secrets he had kept from Tammy and Angelina. He thought about his years with Susan.

Susan was the type of girl a man falls in love with before he realizes it. Maybe she wasn't showgirl beautiful, but she was definitely college cheerleader pretty.

But Susan was also married, and that's probably why Jordan didn't think she was showgirl beautiful the first time he met her while making his rounds on his courthouse beat with the Houston newspaper. She was a secretary for a couple of assistant district attorneys. One day he bought a sandwich in the courthouse cafeteria.

"Mind if I join you," Susan said. "The cafeteria is really crowded today."

"Please do," Jordan said.

They made small talk, and Jordan learned that Susan was married to a petroleum engineer working for one of the many Houston oil companies. Susan learned that while Jordan made his living writing newspaper articles about various crooks undergoing scrutiny by the Texas justice system, his real love was playing the guitar and writing songs.

"I thought about majoring in music in college, but I got married after my sophomore year and went to secretarial school instead so I could help put my husband through his last couple of years of college," Susan said.

"It's not too late for you to go back to school and get that music degree," Jordan said.

"You don't think so?"

"Of course not," Jordan said. "You're still young. Let your husband return the favor and put you through school."

"Oh, I don't know. We both like the money that two salaries bring in."

The next time Jordan saw Susan alone in the cafeteria, she seemed happy when he asked if he could sit at her table. Soon they were having lunch together often, and Jordan found himself thinking that Susan had beautiful eyes, a cute mouth, and a cute nose. She had nice hair, he thought, and a nice figure, even if her breasts were not as large as some of the girls Jordan had dated. And she had great legs. One noon hour, Jordan realized that Susan was just about the most beautiful woman he had ever met, and he wondered why he could not see it before.

From then on, he would glance at Susan's left hand and wish the little golden band was not on her third finger. He wished it were on someone else's finger -- someone like the girl he dated last Saturday, the girl he would date next Saturday, anyone but Susan.

Jordan told himself that it was just infatuation. Puppy love, he thought; you'll wake up. And maybe he would have, if it had not been a two-way dream.

It was Susan who suggested that they eat somewhere besides the building cafeteria for a change.

"Hey," she said. "It's spring, and it's not raining, so let's buy a couple of sandwiches and go to a park and eat."

They sat on a bench under a magnolia tree.

"Spring is pretty here," Susan said.

"Isn't it pretty everywhere?" Jordan asked.

"Yes, I guess so," she said with a faraway look came into her eyes. "But it just seems prettier this year?"

"Prettier than any of the years before?" Jordan asked.

"No," she replied. "There were pretty springs when I was a little girl. Before I got....before I grew up."

They sat silently. Susan looked sad, so Jordan reached for her hand. She held his hand tightly and smiled.

"Let's go sit in the swings," Susan said, jumping up and tugging Jordan's arm. They went over to the playground and sat in the swings with their legs extended so they would not touch the ground.

"I love to swing," she said. "My daddy built me a swing the backyard when I was a little girl, and I would sit and swing for hours. Oh, I wish I were a little girl again."

"Why?"

"Oh, she said thoughtfully, "I guess because everything was happy then."

"And everything's not happy now?"

"Now," she said. "Right now, everything is happy, but it won't stay happy."

Susan began to cry, and Jordan felt helpless, as all men do when a woman cries.

"Susan, what's the matter?"

She wiped the tears from her eyes and said, "Nothing. I guess I'm just in a bad mood."

"Please, if something is wrong, tell me."

"Nothing's wrong. All women get like this way sometime. I'm sorry."

"Don't be sorry," I said. "Be happy."

"Okay," she said. "I'm always happy when I'm with you."

"So am I with you."

She took his hand and said, "I'm glad, Jordan."

Jordan and Susan continued to have lunch at least a couple of times a week. They talked some about their work and more about their lives. At first, Susan told Jordan about her husband, Mason, about how they had started dating when both were seniors in their East Texas high school. But then Susan did not talk about Mason anymore, and Jordan was glad. They talked about Jordan and Susan, about Jordan's musical and songwriting aspirations and how they both wanted to travel.

One day they were eating again in the park, and an airplane roared above them.

"Oh," Susan said. "Wouldn't it be great if we were on that plane going to Europe or Hawaii or Japan!"

"Or Walla Walla, Washington," Jordan cracked.

Susan looked as though Jordan had just kicked over her sand castle.

"Just like a man. Walla Walla, Washington? How unromantic."

Jordan carried it farther. "Oh, I always thought the name, Walla Walla, had a lot of romance and intrigue about it."

"Intrigue, maybe," she conceded. "What's romantic about Walla Walla?"

"Well, you know, romance sometimes leads to wallowing and wallowing."

Susan laughed.

"You nut. Is this what a writer does on a date when a girl talks about romance? Make bad puns."

"No," Jordan said. "I can get romantic."

"You can?" She said it softly, sexily.

It was 12:46 p.m., and the world stopped spinning. Only in that park. The world still moved in New York, in Moscow, in Paris, and the street beyond the park. But in that park, the breeze stopped blowing in the young oak leaves above; the birds stopped singing; the basketball game between city surveyors on their lunch break stopped at the other end of the park. There, for that minute, on that bench, for Jordan, the world stopped while he tried to think of something to say next.

He knew what he wanted to say, but he did not say anything. Jordan sat there, and Susan sat there, and minutes later, it was 12:47 p.m., and the world slowly, sluggishly, like a choked automobile, began to move again.

Jordan sat in his apartment that evening, drinking a beer, thinking about Susan, and wondering why he had not told her he loved her. She knew he loved her, and now he knew that she loved him.

"I love Susan!"

He yelled it. No one heard except maybe the couple in the apartment next door, but he felt better after releasing it. He wanted to tell the world, to paint it on water towers, to run full-page ads in newspapers.

But he was afraid to tell her, to tell a married woman that he loved her and wanted to marry her.

Jordan could not muster the courage to tell her, so Susan told him.

"I love you, Jordan," she said the next time they had lunch.

"I love you, too, Susan."

Susan said that was why she was quitting her job, because she loved Jordan. And she couldn't love him because she was married, and she could not keep seeing him everyday.

"Do you love your husband, Susan?"

"Yes, sometimes, I think I do, but not in the way I love you." she said and paused. "But I married him, I promised to love him forever, and he's nice guy."

"Do you think it's fair to him? To live with him if you can't love him like you love me."

She began to cry. "It's not fair to shatter his world after letting him build on it all these years."

Jordan held her and waited until she quit crying

"Mason is a great guy," she said. "He's good looking. He's intelligent. He's ambitious. She started to cry again. "I guess that's what makes it so miserable. He's just too damn nice to hurt like this."

"Why don't you love him more?"

She was still crying. "He just doesn't make me feel like a woman."

Jordan kissed her. "I've wanted to do that for a long time."

"I've wanted you to do that for a long time."

Jordan kissed her again, longer this time. Their lips parted. Her breath was heavy on his face and his on hers.

"Oh, I want you," she said.

"No more than I want you, Darling."

She broke away from Jordan and said, "That's why I can't ever see you again. I married him. I promised to be true to him."

"Susan, divorce him. You're not being fair to any of us -- you, him, or me -- by living with him. Give him a chance, Susan. A chance to find someone who he can make feel like a woman. A chance to have someone love him as you love me. Sure, leaving will hurt him, but not as much as living with him the rest of your life. If you can't love him by now, you can't love him. That's all I can say. You know I love you and that I want to marry you. I want you to be my wife, to have my kids. But there's nothing I can do. I wish there was. I wish I could snap my fingers, and it would be before you married Mason. But I can't. It's up to you. It's a big decision, and a difficult one, I know. But please think about it. Think about what I have said. Promise?"

"Okay, I promise. But I am quitting my job."

"No, you don't have to do that. If you decide to stay with him, don't call me. If I don't hear by the end of the week, I will ask the paper to give me a new beat, and we won't talk to each other again. But if you decide to leave him and marry me -- and, God, I've never wanted anything so much in my life -- call me as soon as you can."

"Okay, Jordan."

For the rest of that day and the next, every time the phone rang, Jordan became nervous and then hated the voice on the other end of the line because it was not Susan's voice.

Susan called on Friday.

"I love you, Jordan, and I want to marry you."

Jordan had never been happier in his life than when he heard those words. Susan told him that Mason was playing golf on Saturday and that she would take her car and come to his apartment.

"I decided you're right," Susan told Jordan on Saturday. "It isn't fair to him either. For the past few days, I could only think of you and hate him for being my husband."

"Have you told him?" Jordan asked.

"No."

“When are you going to tell him?”

She sighed.

"When I get enough nerve, I guess."

"Does he love you?"

"I guess so."

"He doesn't tell you?"

"He hasn't lately."

Jordan hesitated, then said, "Maybe I shouldn't ask this, but do you make love?"

Susan looked at Jordan a little hard and said, "Well, we are married."

"Okay. I said I probably shouldn't ask."

"Look, we make love maybe once a week, and it's quick, but what am I supposed to say: I don't want you to make love to me even though you are my husband?"

"Okay, I understand," Jordan said.

Her hard look had softened.

"Jordan," she said.

"Yes?"

"I do want you to make love to me."

Jordan took her hand and led her to his bed. He began to unbutton her blouse and then unzipped her shorts. She reached for the button and zipper on his jeans. Soon they were naked, and Jordan was putting on a condom. He wanted this first time to be special, so he called upon the lessons he first learned from Tammy Dolcito. As his tongue explored the luscious area between Susan's legs, she began to utter smooth moans that grew louder and then culminated in an excited, "Oh come inside me now."

Jordan was ready to accommodate her, and he had barely entered her before he came.

Back at her car, Susan said she would try to ask Mason for a divorce that weekend. "But I'm not going to tell him about you," she said.

"What if he asks?"

"I'll deny it."

"Are you afraid of what he will do?"

"Not really. I'm not afraid he will hurt me or you or himself. But it's going to hurt him you know, and I just don't want to hurt him anymore than I have to."

Susan called Jordan Sunday night. She had told Mason the night before. She began to cry as she recounted the conversation.

"He could not understand. He kept asking why, and I could not explain. I just said I didn't love him anymore."

"Did he ask if there was another man?"

"No. I don't think it ever occurred to him that I could want another man. Last night he said that he wouldn't give me a divorce and left the house and said he would stay at a motel. This morning he came home and said that if I really wanted a divorce, he would not stop me. He moved out this afternoon."

Two days later Susan went to a lawyer. Until the divorce was final, she and Jordan were cautious in their meetings. They had no more lunches together, choosing instead to meet in the Galleria shopping mall, where they would leave Susan's car and drive to Jordan's apartment.

They were married in a civil ceremony two months after her divorce. No family members were at the wedding. Susan's East Texas parents' attitude went from disappointment about her divorcing a well-mannered engineer with a promising career to distress when she informed them she was marrying a man who made half of what her husband made and would rather be a musician than work in a corporate office. Jordan's parents, being upright and temperate Protestants who had been concerned for several years about their son's lack of reverence for God and proper behavior, also were not happy that he was marrying a woman recently divorced.

Their first year of marriage was blissful, with Jordan and Susan enjoying all the sex they could fit into their schedules. But the foundation of the relationship began to show cracks in the second year.

Susan did not understand how Jordan could like the music of Bob Dylan, a singer whom she only remembered from having a single called *Like a Rolling Stone.* Susan assumed it was a hit because it was so long that the disc jockeys could go to the bathroom and get back to their turntables before it ended.

But Susan did enjoy their weekend sojourns to Austin. She liked the musicians there, even the pretty girl singers who played for tips on the streets. And she liked the passionate endings of the day she and Jordan experienced after dinner and drinks at the Sholtz Beer Garden, the County Line, Threadgills, and other places whose names Jordan had forgotten and which were probably no longer in existence.

She, however, did not give Jordan any encouragement when, before those minutes of passion, he would tell her that his dream was to write songs and maybe live like those people whose music they had enjoyed earlier.

She also was somewhat aghast when he told her he really didn't care about finding a church to attend because he felt in the eighteen years he had to live with his parents he figured he had attended all the church he needed for the rest of his life.

He tried to explain the genius of Dylan and the incongruity of a God who sees and knows everything every human being who has ever lived has done and is doing, but Susan didn't really want to hear about it. She would rather talk about how they could come up with enough money to get out of their apartment in the hippie Montrose district and move to a nice new suburban house.

But Jordan remained in love with Susan, and sometimes they would go to the park and sit on the bench under the magnolia tree and kiss.

In their second winter together, they took a brief vacation to San Diego and Coronado, where Jordan told Susan about how he and other members of his Dallas Marine Reserve unit had spent their two weeks active duty in 1964 in amphibious training at the Coronado Naval Base, about wading ashore from landing boats and climbing up and down the slippery nets attached to the troop ship, and laughing about the Marine who got seasick and started to throw up on the deck of the ship and the Navy petty officer who told him to throw up in his helmet, which he left on the deck, and the Marine who forgot his helmet when the next drill came and ran onto the deck and was given the soiled helmet to wear. Jordan thought the story was funny as they walked by the shops near the Hotel Del Coronado. Susan wasn't really listening. She was more interested in the expensive sandals in a store window.

She wore the sandals in the Houston spring. She also was wearing them in the summer, when she told Jordan that their marriage had been a mistake. She didn't tell him about the defense attorney she had met, just as she did not tell her first husband about Jordan Roblech.

But it really didn't matter because Jordan agreed with her. The marriage had been a mistake. They just weren't suited for each other.

So they got a divorce, and Jordan quit his job and moved to Denver. And both sets of parents were happier.

Chapter 9
Up the Pacific Coast

Fifteen hundred miles to the northwest, Buck Leherifen also was finding it difficult to sleep. But he wasn't thinking about the women he had known. He was thinking about some of the men he had known -- Norman Victor and Buck's fellow platoon members in Vietnam, more than a dozen of whom were shipped back from Vietnam in flag-draped coffins. And although he tried to avoid it, he also thought about the night he received the wound that left him with the slight limp in his leg, now healed but still aching in his damp cabin on Washington's Olympic Peninsula as he tossed in his bed.

Buck kicked off the blanket that covered him and went to the bathroom. After swallowing two ibuprofen tablets, he lay back down and tried to think more pleasant thoughts. But there was no solace in thinking about his parents, both of whom died young and sad. He had few friends to remember. He wondered what happened to Beth Chertha. Was she still married to Hunter Bultin? Her child would be grown now. And what became of Jordan Roblech? Did he go back to Texas and become a songwriter like he said he wanted to be? Probably not, Buck thought. At least, not a famous songwriter. That's okay, Buck thought, I guess most of us don't realize our dreams. Certainly Buck was not a famous artist although he continued to paint and sold some of his artwork at the gallery on the ferry dock in Port Angeles. He had even won a couple of prizes in art shows on the Olympic Peninsula and one in Seattle.

A couple of prizes and an occasional sale of a painting, however, did not pay many bills. To get by and be able to continue to paint, Buck gave kayak lessons and clerked in a hardware store. Funny, he thought, how a boy from the dry West Texas plains could now be making part of his living on the chilly waters of the Elwha River and the Strait of Juan de Fuca.

Buck had no intention of settling on the Olympic Peninsula when he got out of the naval hospital with an early discharge because of the wound he received on that bloody day north of Da Nang. He just wanted to see more of the West Coast before he headed back to Texas Tech to resume pursuing a degree in advertising art. With the money he had saved while in the Marines he bought a 1962 Volkswagen van.

It was summer 1966 when Buck drove across the bay into San Francisco. He had never imagined a city so interesting and so beautiful. Buck stayed there a week, riding the cable cars, wandering through China Town and around Union Square, having a drink at the Top of the Mark and an Italian dinner in North Beach, taking the tour ferry under the Golden Gate Bridge to the Marin County village of Sausalito, and doing many of the other activities that millions of tourists have enjoyed for decades.

Buck might have stayed a few more days in San Francisco if it had not been for an incident in a bar.

Buck was the only person sitting at the bar when a quartet of Hell's Angels came through the door. They sat on stools at the other end of the bar, and Buck ordered his second beer.

"Sir, kin Ah git another Lucky Lager," Buck said.

The Hell's Angel closest to Buck looked at him and said, "Where the hell you from, boy?"

"Texas," Buck said.

"Texas," the biker said with unhidden distain. "All Texans are assholes."

Buck knew he was outnumbered and still not in any shape to take on a guy about thirty pounds heavier and a couple of inches taller, so he just said, "Some of them certainly are."

The bartender, clearly uneasy about this conversation, said, "Do you still want that beer?"

Buck took the question as a signal that he probably should move elsewhere, so he took two dollar bills from his jeans pocket, left them on the bar, and simply said, "No."

As Buck walked toward the door, the Hells Angel noticed the limp and said, "Hey, Tex, where'd you get that gimpy leg?"

Buck stopped and hesitated before he said, "I ran into some fellers in Vietnam who apparently didn't like Texans either."

Then he continued toward the door, but not before a young woman sitting with a couple of bearded men at a table, screeched, "What did he say? Is he some murdering soldier? What is this baby-killer doing in our neighborhood?"

Buck walked out the door as the Hell's Angel said, "Shut up, you hippie slut-bitch." Buck was halfway down the block before he could not hear the woman screaming as her companions tried to get her to shut up as they, too, made a quick exit. Buck was pleased that the trio of hippies turned up the street while he walked down the street. He was also pleased that the four Hell's Angels stayed inside the bar.

"Perhaps it's time to move farther north," he thought.

Buck drove across the Golden Gate Bridge through Petaluma and on to Santa Rosa. It was late afternoon when he decided he had driven enough for that day. After checking into a cheap motel, he went to a nearby tavern, where he hoped he would not meet more Hell's Angels or shrill women who thought Vietnam veterans were evil.

The only woman in the place was the bartender, and the only other customers were two middle-aged men and a young man about Buck's age. The two older men were sitting at a table talking and laughing, not paying attention to anyone else. The younger man was sitting at the bar with a full backpack beside him. He looked at Buck when Buck ordered his beer, perhaps also wondering where his accent originated, but the other young man said nothing. Buck looked over at him and nodded a hello.

Buck's gesture apparently was taken as a signal to speak. The man with the backpack asked, "Are you from around here?"

"Nope," Buck said, "just passing through on my way up the Pacific Coast."

"Me, too. Where are you coming from?"

"I was discharged out of the Marines from the Oakland Naval Hospital. I thought I would check out the rest of the Pacific Coast, or at least what I can afford to see before I run out of money."

"Small world! I just got out of the Navy a few months ago after deciding going around the world underwater in a submarine wasn't the way I wanted to spend the next decade. I worked in Oakland for a while, but I guess I got a little homesick, so I decided to go back to my home state of Washington. Unfortunately the old clunker car I bought when I got out of the Navy blew a rod this morning, and it sure as hell ain't worth fixing, so I guess I'm going to have to take a bus."

He paused, then said, "I don't suppose you would be interested in a traveling partner for a way if he paid for the gas, would you?"

Buck took a sip of his beer, shrugged, and said, "Maybe. But do you think we could work out an itinerary suitable for both of us? What's you're time-table?"

"Oh, I'm pretty flexible, but as a guy who grew up in the Pacific Northwest, I would recommend you get your traveling done before the snow starts."

"That still gives us a couple of months, I think," Buck said. "Where are you going?"

"Oh, I'm not totally sure where I want to finally land, but I need to get back and see my grandmother who raised me. She lives at the top of the Olympic Peninsula in an old house on a bluff overlooking the Strait of Juan de Fuca out onto Victoria, Canada. Port Angeles is a nice place. It's kind of gray and rainy in the winter but nice in the summer."

"I've always wanted to see the Olympic Peninsula, but I figured I would run out of money before I could get there, so maybe this will work out for both of us. My name's Buck Leherifen, by the way," Buck said as he got up from his stool and extended his hand.

"Good to meet you, Buck. I'm Jim. Jim Outseagle."

"Where are you staying tonight, Jim?"

"Since my money is running a little low, I'll probably sleep in my old car until I figure what I need to do with it."

"I got another idea. My motel room floor is probably more comfortable than your car, so drink up. Let's plan our trip."

The two young veterans drained their beers, put some change on the bar, and walked out together. They didn't hear the two older men laugh when one of them snorted and said, "Probably another couple of San Francisco fags."

The next morning after Buck and Jim found a mechanic who was willing to tow Jim's worn-out car in exchange for the title, the two young veterans threw their bags and boxes into Buck's VW bus and took the highway westward toward Bodega Bay, where they planned to take the winding Highway 1 north along the Pacific Coast. As they neared Sebastopol, Jim told Buck they were about to go through the town where Charles Schultz lived.

"Charles Shultz, the guy who draws Peanuts? He lives here?"

"Yeah," Jim said. "He's one of my heroes."

"You, too," Buck said. "Are you a comic strip fan?"

"Damn right. I was reading Mutt and Jeff before I ever knew Dick and Jane had a dog named Spot."

"Oh, man. I knew I liked you for some reason."

Buck and Jim did not really know what they were going to do when they drove into Sebastopol. They did not even know if they could find Charles Shultz's house. They were just two young men who had no specific plans for their visit to Sebastopol and the hundreds of miles north to the Olympic Peninsula or specific plans for the rest of their lives. So they did what many people do when they don't know what they should do or where they should go next. They went to a bar.

After the bartender had served their draft beers, Buck said, "Do you think he knows where Charles Shultz lives?"

"Maybe the first thing to ask him is if he knows who Charles Shultz is. Not everyone reads the comics, you know."

"Come on, everyone knows who Charlie Brown and Snoopy are."

"Maybe so, but I doubt that everyone knows the little baldheaded kid and his gang are the creations of a fellow named Charles Schultz."

"I guess you're right," Buck said. "But Sebastopol isn't that big a place. Surely just about everybody here knows who Charles Schultz is. I mean, how many celebrities can live in Sebastopol?"

"Do you think Charles Schultz qualifies as a celebrity?"

"Oh, he's not Roy Rogers or Gene Autry, but I would call Charles Schultz a celebrity."

"Roy Rogers! Heck, a cartoonist isn't in the celebrity class of any movie cowboy. Not even someone like, say, Flash Golden."

Buck's eyes widened as he grinned and said, "Flash Golden! Are you a fan of Flash Golden? I know Flash Golden!"

"You're kidding me. How do you know Flash Golden?"

As they finished their first beers, Charles Schultz was forgotten while Buck gave a summary of how he had spent time with me. He left out many of the details, basically saying that I lived in San Clemente and Buck and two of his Marine buddies got to know me and we ate green chile cheeseburgers and had some beers. He did not say anything about Angelina, Tammy, or the trip to Beverly Hills, believing that information was for people he had known for longer than a day.

"So, okay. You know Flash Golden," Jim said. "Do you think there's any chance we might get to meet another hero, Charles Schultz?

"I doubt it, but let's ask the bartender if he knows him and maybe where he hangs out."

When the bartender asked the two strangers in his bar if they wanted another round, Jim said, "One more, I guess, and could you tell us something?"

"What's that?"

"Charles Schultz, the guy who draws the Peanuts cartoon lives in Sebastopol, right?"

"That's right? Not exactly in Sebastopol, but a little ways out of town."

"So do you know him by any chance?"

"No. I hear he's not much of a boozer, and besides, this bar ain't exactly the type of place that rich and famous guys flock to."

Jim smiled and said, "So you don't think we're rich and famous."

Sensing that Jim's comment had put the bartender slightly in a defensive mode, Buck quickly said, "Don't mind him. He's just trying to be witty. But we were wondering if you might know how to get to Mr. Schultz' place?"

Now it was the bartender's turn to wisecrack. "Why, are you two rich and famous guys planning on paying him a visit?"

"No, I guess not," Buck said. "But, you see, we're big fans, and we thought it would be nice to at least see where he lives."

The bartender said the cartoonist lived on a small ranch outside of town, and he gave general directions. After they finished their second beers, Buck and Jim left what was for them a generous tip and decided to explore the outskirts of the town.

As they walked toward the door, the bartender picked up the money, smiled, and said, "Oh guys, if you spend the night in Sebastopol, you might want to have breakfast at the restaurant down the street. I hear that Schultz has coffee and even lunch there sometimes."

As they walked toward the car, Jim suggested that maybe they could have another beer at the restaurant's bar.

"Hell," said Buck, "with this method of research, if we ever do find Charles Schultz, we may be too drunk to recognize him."

"I probably wouldn't recognize him sober, and besides it's more fun than riding around in the country, trying to guess which house he lives in," Jim said.

As Buck and Jim walked into the bar, they passed a slender bespectacled man going out the door with another man and two women. The four people walked out into the street as Buck and Jim turned toward the restaurant foyer.

Buck said, "Jim, I think that was Charles Schultz!"

Buck and Jim turned and walked back toward the street just in time to see the four people get into a car. The man who looked like Schultz got into the driver's seat. The car pulled out and passed them.

"Let's go back inside and ask if that was Charles Schultz," Jim said.

"No," said Buck. "Let's go back to that other bar and tell the bartender we saw Charles Schultz. I'll tell you why over another beer, which I'll even buy."

"I guess having someone else buy me a beer beats -- as you said -- wandering around looking for the house of some guy we never met," Jim said.

The bartender looked up with slight bemusement when Buck and Jim walked back through the door. "That didn't take long. Did you learn anymore about Charles Schultz?"

"As a matter of fact," Buck said. "We went over to the restaurant, and he was leaving as we walked through the door."

"So did you say hello, introduce yourself?"

"No," Buck said. "We didn't realize who he was until he was almost in his car. But we saw him, so I guess that's good enough for a couple of poor slobs like us."

"So the trip was a success," the bartender said. "Do you want some more beers?"

"Yeah, we'll take another round," Buck said. "I promised Jim I would buy in celebration of seeing our favorite cartoonist in person."

This time Buck suggested that they sit at a table in the corner rather than at the bar. While the bartender pulled their drafts from the tap, Jim said in almost a whisper, "So you're sure that was Charles Schultz? Why didn't you want to go inside and confirm it?"

"Because I want to believe he was Charles Schultz, and if nobody tells me otherwise, that man will be Charles Schultz for the rest of my life. But if we went back inside and the waitress told us that man is a tourist from Nebraska or a local optometrist, then we would have to keep looking for Charles Schultz, and what do you think the chances are that we would find him?"

"Probably pretty slim."

"Yeah, so let's just believe he was really Charles Schultz, and we can get on our way north toward Oregon."

Jim shrugged, tilted his head, and said, "I guess that's one way to look at it."

"Let me tell you a personal story to illustrate the folly of knowing too much about your dreams," Buck said.

"My real first name's not Buck. It's Buchanan. My mama named me that because she believed she was a direct descendent of James Buchanan, the fifteenth president of the United States. You know -- the guy who was there just before Lincoln. Anyway, my mama never was much of a history student, or any other kind of student for that matter. She dropped out of high school to marry my daddy. But her mama's last name was Buchanan and her relatives told her she was related to James Buchanan, so she assumed that meant she was a great or great-great granddaughter, and she told me I was descended from a president of the United States.

"My daddy also didn't read any history. He said it didn't matter what happened in the past; what counts is what happens now and in the future. So he didn't care anything about who my mama's alleged ancestors were, and when she said she wanted to name me Buchanan Leherifen, he said that's fine because he could call me Buck and he thought Buck was a good name for a boy.

"When I was about eight or nine, my mama told me why she named me

Buchanan. She said she named me in honor of her mother's family and that I was the great-great-great grandson or something like that of a president.

"Of course I was impressed to know that I came from the closest thing to American royalty, even if it lasts only four or eight years, and I puffed up and bragged about my lineage to some of my third-grade friends about being a descendent of President James Buchanan.

"You know in every class you always have the smart kid who knows more about things than a kid should be expected to know, and as luck would have it, I bragged about being descended from James Buchanan in front of that particular kid. He laughed and asked me how I could be descended from the only American president who never married.

"I know today kids know it's possible for a man to have children even if he never married, but back in 1950, in rural Texas at least, third-graders considered that an impossibility, so I was flustered and found an encyclopedia that sure nuff confirmed my smart aleck classmate was correct. I then confronted my mother with this puzzling set of facts, and I guess I never saw her more disappointed in her life. As time has gone by, I realize how important the myth was to my mother and how the truth had cut a hole in her heart. Here she was a poor girl living in a podunk West Texas town with no hope of glamour and fortune, but holding on to her dream that some smartass kid destroyed.

"I've wished many times that I had just quietly taken silent pride in my alleged ancestor and not said anything to my classmates, and then when I learned the truth, never told my mother."

There was sympathy in Jim's eyes as Buck finished his story and said, "So you see, Jim, it's better to just believe your dreams than talk too much and ask questions that will destroy them."

Buck and Jim began their journey along the snake-configured coastal highway at Bodega Bay. The town was small without many stores or other businesses, but the view from the cliffs overlooking the Pacific was impressive. Buck told Jim that it and the neighboring town to the east, Bodega, was where Alfred Hitchcock's horror movie *The Birds* was filmed.

"I never saw the movie," Jim said. "When did it come out?"

"I think it was 1963. Yeah, that's when, because I saw it after I transferred from Camp Pendleton and before they sent me on my fun trip to 'Nam, so it must have been '63."

"That's probably why I didn't see it. I spent most of 1963 under the world's oceans."

"It was a pretty scary movie," Buck said. "Maybe not as scary as eerie. I mean, how scary can a bunch of birds be?"

Jim laughed and said, "Yeah, I guess the only thing that's ever frightened me about birds is their crapping on me. Those damned seagulls are pretty bad about that."

"Oh, so were you ever crapped on by a bird?" Buck asked.

"No, I managed to dodge them. I haven't been so lucky with people though. I've been crapped on by people several times, starting with my mother, who was too busy looking in the bars for my father's replacement to spend much time with me. That's why I'm close to my grandmother. She pretty well raised me."

"But you still have her. I mean, she's still alive, right?"

"Oh yeah, she's going strong, works as a practical nurse at the hospital in Port Angeles."

Buck asked, "What happened to your parents?"

"My father, a member of one of the native American tribes on the Olympic Peninsula, died on a fishing boat off the Alaskan coast a couple of months before I was born. My pretty blonde mother moved in with my grandmother with my sister and me and then got killed one night when she and some Coast Guardsman stationed on Ediz Hook ran off the road after boozing and boogying in Bremerton. So my grandmother raised both of her grandkids."

"But you still have your grandmother and a sister," Buck said. "I don't have anybody. I can't really say I've been crapped on by anyone, unless you want to count the U.S. government, which sent me on the other side of the world to almost get killed by people I never met."

"Hell, we all get crapped on by the U.S. government. It never stops. First, they draft you or get you to join up under the threat of a draft. Then if you're lucky enough to survive that, they tax you for the rest of your life, unless you're some rich guy who knows how to shelter your income."

"Shelter your income? What's that mean?"

"See, you're so poor, you don't even know the meaning of the phrase. It means you put your big bucks in some investment that the government doesn't tax or you hide it in some company offshore. But the catch is you have to have enough money that you don't need to spend it all on food and rent and maybe a couple of beers or a movie ticket."

"I certainly can't argue that I'm not a poor boy -- just a West Texas orphan kid. But maybe I won't be a poor boy forever. This is America, you know."

"Yep, and maybe we'll both get rich and then we can live like the rich guys, traveling around the country first class on an airplane rather than an old Volkswagen bus. We can be drinking European beers and twelve-year-old Scotch served to us by a pretty stewardess and not caring a bit about those poor slobs who don't have any income to shelter."

"Maybe so," said Buck. "But for now we got this old Volkswagen bus, and I say we head it north up the coast and see the country while we can still associate with the little people."

"Yeah, they will probably be intimidated by us after we get rich," Jim said with a sarcastic laugh. "We'd probably have to spend our time having coffee and beers with folks like Charles Schultz."

The ride was slow as the highway constantly curved to fit the contour of the coast. Buck and Jim went through approximately a dozen coastal villages before they decided to call it a day and find a motel in Mendocino, which is less than two hundred miles north of San Francisco but seemed much farther because of the winding road.

Checking their wallets, both men decided it would be prudent to buy a six-pack at a small grocery store near the motel than spend two or three times as much for the same number of beers at a bar.

As he settled onto one of the twin beds and opened his first bottle, Buck said, "Whew. It was an awesome view but, dang, it was tiring trying not to run off the road into the ocean. Sure seems like we went farther than about a hundred or so miles today."

"Yeah. I once heard a fellow compare looking at a map and calculating the time it takes to go between Point A and Point B on roads out west to choosing what you're going to wear on a winter day by just looking at the temperature," Jim said. He could tell by Buck's vague facial expression that Buck did not understand his point, so Jim elaborated on his analogy.

"I mean the humidity and the wind can make the weather seem a lot colder, just as mountain ranges and coastal curves can make the trip a lot longer. I guess the bottom line is, like your imagined ancestor, things aren't always what they seem when you look more closely at the details."

Jim then moved the discussion into another subject when he said, "By the way, I guess I don't follow your philosophy that it's better to believe a false dream than find out the unpleasant truth."

"That's okay," Buck said. "But I know some people can't deal with unpleasant truths. For instance, dying. We all die, but no one wants to think about that. You and I obviously have had to at an early age because of our parents. But a lot of people, maybe most, don't have to deal with consequential deaths that early."

Jim laughed. "So what's an inconsequential death?"

Buck smiled. "I guess it's the death of someone you don't care about."

"That being the case," Jim said, "I would submit that just about all deaths are inconsequential to most people."

"Bingo," Buck said.

"So, see that's one of those false dreams that people say that believe -- that everyone in their roles as God's children are our brothers and sisters, and we love them all. But then I don't really believe in God, so I don't have to buy into that hypocritical piousness," Jim said.

"You don't believe in God?"

"No. Do you?"

"I suppose so. At least I prayed to him when I was walking around in Vietnam, wondering if some Cong or punji stick was waiting for me a few feet ahead."

"That's different," Jim said.

"What do you mean?"

"When people pray because they are scared, that doesn't really mean they believe in God. It just means they are desperate and figure it can't hurt to clutch at straws. It's kind of like the people who go to faith healers or take the quack cancer medicines."

Buck looked at his beer and didn't say anything. Then he took a sip, looked up, and said, "Yeah, you're probably right. I'm not sure I believe in God, either. Maybe he's just another one of those dreams that it would hurt to give up. Maybe God is like my mythical great-great-whatever presidential grandfather. But, you know what, when my mama believed that James Buchanan was our ancestor, it was like he really was.

"She believed in God, too. When she was in pain with the cancer, telling me she was going to a better place and that she knew God would look after me, she felt better. And

I did, too. So maybe that's a good example of a dream that's better to believe even if it ain't real."

This time it was Jim who did not say anything and looked down at his beer. Then he looked up with a slight smile but sad eyes and said, "I can understand that. And actually I shouldn't speak disparagingly of faith healers. I guess that's what you could call the Native American medicine men. I'm half Native American, you know."

Buck gave Jim a shy grin and said, "Don't take offense, but when we met I wondered what the heck you were. I thought maybe you were part Asian."

"Where the hell do you think the Native Americans came from?"

"Yeah, that's right. I knew that. Actually I'm quite a Western history buff. I guess it's hard to grow up in West Texas in the era of the cowboy movies and not be one."

Jim started to say something else but paused to take a large gulp of his beer. Then he said with eyes that seemed even sadder than before, "But back to this religion and God stuff, It's just, it's just that...if there is a God, I guess he doesn't have much love for a couple of poor orphan schmuck veterans like you and me."

"Have you ever read the *Book of Job* in the *Bible*?" Buck asked.

"No. I don't read the *Bible*. I prefer to get my truth from science books," Jim said in a tone that was slow and deliberant enough for

Buck to think maybe he should change the subject.

"So you read science books?"

"Yeah, the other half of me is Scandinavian, so maybe that cancels out the Native American mysticism. And I want to be an engineer. That's why I spent six years in the Navy. So I could earn enough money to go to college."

"What kind of engineer?"

"Oh, I'm not really sure." Jim said. "Maybe electrical, maybe chemical, or maybe nuclear. That seems to be a coming field. So what do you plan to do with the rest of your life, Buck?"

"I would like to be an artist -- a painter, an illustrator, and maybe even a cartoonist like Charles Schulz."

"So you like to draw? I like to draw, too. I thought about becoming an architect, but then I found out you have to go to school for an extra year and then you don't make as much money as engineers. I don't like to draw so much that I want to live poor for the rest of my life," Jim said.

Buck smiled and said, "I'm not that fond of being poor forever either, but I can't do math well enough to be an engineer. I never impressed any of my science teachers either, except when I would draw pictures of a brain or a skeleton or an atom or something like that for a science fair project."

Jim raised his beer bottle and said, "Well, here's to our ambitions. May they be realized. Maybe, twenty or thirty years from now, we can be looking out at the Pacific from our private mansions rather than a motel room."

"Or at least from a really fancy hotel room," Buck said.

The next day Buck and Jim began their journey with intentions of crossing into Oregon before sundown. They realized they did not have enough money to tarry at every town along the way. At Rockport, Highway 1 turned northeast back into U.S. 101, an inland road until it meets the coast again at Eureka, where they followed the coast the last hundred or so miles to Oregon. They did spend some time in Crescent City, looking at the remaining scars created by one of the more uncommon disasters to strike an American city.

"This is the city that was hit by the giant tidal wave created by the big Alaska earthquake in 1964," Jim explained to Buck as they passed a road mileage sign featuring Crescent City. "They call it a tsunami, which I think is Japanese for harbor wave. It's pretty scary for those of us who live on the Pacific coast. The earthquakes are bad enough, but every now and then an earthquake causes a tidal wave, so it's a double whammy. I guess I worry a little about it for my grandmother's sake. But Port Angeles is not on the direct coast. It's on the Strait of Juan de Fuca, and she lives on a big high bluff, so I just hope she's safe. Now south of there, much of the coast of Washington is just flat, and I guess there's a real danger for those people if a tsunami were to hit them."

"Really? The coast is flat in Washington? I figured it probably looked like the rest of the Pacific Coast," Buck said.

"No. The coast from about Ocean Shores in Washington to Seaside in Oregon is not all that spectacular if you like rocks and bluffs and all those scenes we've been looking at for the past several days," Jim said.

"Sounds like the Gulf Coast in Texas," Buck said. "My mama and daddy took me down there on a little vacation when I was ten years old. It was the only time I saw the ocean before I joined the Marines.

"Texans who live on the coast don't have to worry about earthquakes or tidal waves, but they do have hurricanes. They had a really bad one in 1961 after I joined the Marines."

Buck was getting weary of the slow pace of driving along the coast. He had looked at his map and saw that just north of Crescent City, he could take Highway 199 inland. He asked Jim about the Oregon coast.

"What does it look like?"

"Until Seaside, pretty much like what we've been seeing for the last five hundred or so miles," Jim said.

Buck asked, "Do you want to cut inland and make a little better time?"

"Yeah, that's fine with me. There's some pretty country inland in Oregon," Jim said.

Buck and Jim entered Oregon through the Siskiyou Mountains and spent that night in Medford. After the next night in Portland, they followed the highway along the Columbia River to its mouth in Astoria.

"So this is the end of the Lewis and Clark Trail of Discovery," Buck said. "I've always been fascinated by the Lewis and Clark expedition. One night in the enlisted men's club at Camp Pendleton, a friend of mine in the Marine Corps -- another Texan named Jordan Roblech -- and I had a few beers and started talking about following the same route of their expedition all the way from St. Louis to here. Jordan wants to be a writer, specifically a songwriter, and he's also interested in history. Me, I would just like to see the country and maybe paint some pictures."

"If you really want to see some picturesque country, let's get moving on toward the Olympic Peninsula. There may be some places on the planet that are just as beautiful, but I'd be willing to bet there aren't any that are more beautiful," Jim said.

After two more days, including an overnight stay in Seattle, Buck and Jim crossed the Tacoma Narrows Bridge, drove along the Bremerton Navy yards, and Buck got his first view of the Olympic Mountains from the Hood Canal Bridge. An hour later they were in Port Angeles. It was August 1.

Jim's grandmother was at work, but the key he had kept since he joined the Navy six years earlier still worked. Jim opened two of the beers he had bought at the nearest grocery store and put the remaining four in his grandmother's refrigerator. He handed one to Buck and turned on the bulky black-and-white television set in his grandmother's living room.

As Buck came into the room from the bathroom, Jim said, "Your home state is in the news again. Somebody is shooting people from the big tower on the University of Texas campus. What's with you Texans and snipers anyway?"

The next evening as they drank more beers in the summer sunset on the side deck of the house, Buck pondered the question and recalled the ironic barroom conversation in the fall of 1962 and how Flash had pooh-poohed Arlene's comment about Texans, Marines, and Boy Scouts shooting people. And he wondered what Flash and Arlene thought about those two violent days in the fall of '63 and the summer of '66 that will forever remain in the memories of all Texans old enough to remember them.

But with each new day he spent on the Olympic Peninsula, Buck found himself thinking less and less about Texas and Texans. Jim had told him the truth. He had found a place as beautiful as any on the planet, and before the year 1966 ended he decided he had found a new home, a decision he had not doubted through the next two decades.

Chapter 10
Adventure in the Animas Valley

The morning after Jordan Roblech and his hostesses had stayed up late discussing their memories -- both good and bad -- of the past two decades, Jordan asked, "If I did want to make the acquaintance of Ricardo Cajon, did either of you ever meet anyone who actually knew him? Other than Sam Eschidt, of course."

"Harold Ash probably did," Tammy said. "He was a drinking and doping buddy of Sam's, so they probably both did business with Cajon."

"Harold Ash? It seems like I've heard that name before," Jordan said.

"He made a nice living playing bit-parts in movies and then went into television and made a small fortune as a clueless but funny sidekick in television sit-coms. But even though he never got the girl in the shows, he was quite a cocksman in real life. I think he scored with just about every starlet he met. The ladies like a guy with a sense of humor, you know."

"So I've heard, but I must have the wrong set of jokes because it never seemed to do me any good."

"They also like it if you're good-looking, hung like a race horse, and rich, too," Tammy said. "But since you aren't exactly ugly and, as I recall, all of your parts work quite well, I figure that gives you at least a sixty-forty chance. I'll bet you broke a few hearts over the years."

"Yeah," Jordan said with a smirk. "My parents when I didn't major in something that paid big money, my ex-in-laws when I married their daughter, my high school football coach when I missed the tackle that cost us the game, maybe a couple of bosses. But enough of that. Let's get back to Harold."

"Actually, his real name is Horace," Tammy said. "But he changed it to Harold when the guys in the first movie he made started calling him Horse's Ass. Then they started calling him Harry Ass, but he figured he didn't want to go through the trouble of changing his name again and he really didn't mind being a harry ass."

"Yeah, I think I remember him, now," Jordan said. "He was pretty funny. So do you know how I can get in touch with Harold, or Harry, or whatever Mr. Ash wants to be called?

"It so happens I do. Angelina and I ran into him one afternoon in Santa Fe at the Pink Adobe. He had come down to shop some of the galleries for artwork to put in his place outside of Durango. He moved there a few years ago. He's always been a big skier, and he likes Telluride."

Ash had given Tammy his private phone number, which Tammy had saved although she really didn't understand why. Tammy wrote the number on a slip of paper and gave it to Jordan as she wished Angelina and Jordan a good morning and left for the UNM campus. Jordan put the slip of paper in his shirt pocket.

Angelina looked at him across the table as she put a dollop of Kahlua in her coffee.

"Want some?" she asked, holding up the Kahlua.

"Yeah," Jordan said. Then he smiled and said, "Oh, you mean the Kahlua."

Angelina looked surprised for no more than two seconds and returned Jordan's smile.

"Such a raunchy muchacho you are this morning, senor."

Jordan wondered for another two seconds if he had committed a major faux pas with his attempt at risqué humor. Angelina eased his concern when she unbuttoned her robe, revealing the same beautiful breasts that had enticed Norman Victor and then Buck Leherifen.

Jordan pushed back his chair, put his hands on the table and just breathed and mouthed a sound that came out as something between "wow" and "whew."

"I guess you may think I am not a good person, Jordan," Angelina said. "I love Tammy. I will always love Tammy. She is the best amiga I ever had. I would do anything for her."

Then she smiled and said, "And I guess I have done just about anything with her. But, Jordan, I cannot help being who I am. I have come to realize that I need a man, at least sometimes."

More often than sometimes, Jordan needed a woman. Angelina led him to the bedroom and undressed him. She took a condom from the chest by the bed, an act that made Jordan wonder if the moment before had not been altogether spontaneous. No matter, he thought as he lay back and enjoyed Angelina's lips on his lips and grew cross-eyed as she moved lower. Then he was thrusting, thrusting, as the beautiful woman moaned under him. He, too, would never forget those wonderful sounds of pleasure.

It was not difficult for Jordan to get an appointment with Ash, especially after he mentioned Tammy. It also turned out that Ash and I had met when Ash played a bartender in one of my movies. That was good because Jordan wanted me to go with him when he talked with Ash.

We took my truck to Durango and followed Ash's directions into a long gravel driveway outside of the city. A foppish man in his early sixties greeted us at the door.

Jordan explained that he was a freelance journalist working on a piece about drug lords. He did not qualify his mission by saying the article was only a fall-back option if he could not get enough information to collect the reward. Jordan told me he knew that sort of deception was frowned upon by practicing journalists who believe it makes people distrust their profession and less likely to cooperate in providing information for fear they are really talking to a bill collector, private eye, and duly constituted undercover law officer. But Jordan also figured that a sensible person would rather talk to those categories of people than a reporter and therefore considered the journalists' concerns unfounded. And what the hell, he said, news reporting is just another way to make a living, not a priesthood, and besides he had sold his journalistic soul a decade ago when he became a flack and then a lobbyist.

So Jordan proceeded with his questions, and Ash frowned when Jordan mentioned Ricardo Cajon.

"Why would you ask me about Cajon?"

Jordan said, "I've heard that Sam Eschidt and Debra Debaux may have had dealings with Cajon, and since you were good friends with them, I just wondered if you had any knowledge of that."

"No," Ash said. "And I would like to give you perhaps lifesaving advice of which you may already be aware. Asking too many questions about Ricardo Cajon can get you in a shallow desert grave. That's what happened to a lot of people who know too much about Ricardo Cajon. I think you should think hard about that, Mr. Roblech.

There are plenty of other, safer people to write about."

In a fake jocular manner, Ash said, "You might even reconsider your efforts and focus instead on a veteran TV sitcom player who hasn't been offered a part in more than a year and could use a little publicity."

"Maybe that's a later story," Jordan said.

"Keep me in mind if you decide to write it, but I'm afraid I can't help you with any information about Ricardo Cajon or any other drug dealers."

"Thank you," Jordan said. "Now can I ask you one other perhaps slightly indelicate question, and that is, did you ever suspect that perhaps that your good friends, Sam Eschidt and Debra Debaux, met their deaths by means other than accidental?"

Ash looked hard and directly at Jordan for several seconds and said, "It appears that you are not going to take my good advice. I'm sorry, gentlemen, I have no further information. Have a safe trip back to Santa Fe."

Jordan thanked Ash for his time, and he and I got into my truck and began our trip back to Santa Fe. As we drove down the winding road from Durango to Farmington, I asked Jordan if he thought Ash was lying.

"Oh yeah," Jordan said. "For sure, he knows more than he was telling us."

"How do you know?"

"Oh, it's nothing I can pinpoint. I guess it's just an intuitive sense that you develop after you've interviewed scores of people for news stories and then dealt with politicians and their henchmen. Perhaps it's one of the few valuable life skills I've developed. Or, on second thought, perhaps it's a detriment. I guess if I believed all the bullshit people told me I might be richer, or at least have a few more friends."

"Yeah, you may be right," I said as we crossed the Colorado border into New Mexico.

Ricardo Cajon had been in the business of corruption long enough to ensure that Anselmo and Jesus made their way across the border without any problems. The two men, like Jordan and me, were almost twenty years apart in age. They had established a base in one of the fine hotels near the plaza in Santa Fe and leased a nondescript but plush American car in which they could travel to Albuquerque and wherever else they needed to go to complete their mission.

Jordan was surprised but pleased to receive Harold Ash's phone call and invitation to meet with two acquaintances he said may have information about Ricardo Cajon. As we drove to our meeting at the Pink Adobe, I said, "There's something puzzling about this. Why would Mr. Prissy Horse's Ass suddenly decide he wanted to help you when he was so cold during our visit?"

Jordan, who was driving this time because I had begun my day with two Irish coffees and a bloody mary before Ash called, nodded his head and said, "As private eyes and bounty hunters soon learn, you have to be willing to follow all leads. We'll just have to see what these two Mexicanos have to say."

What Anselmo and Jesus had to say was that they were affluent Mexicans who hated Ricardo Cajon and his kind and wondered if they could help Jordan and Flash in what they hoped was an investigative piece of journalism "that would get rid of those drug-dealing vermin like Ricardo Cajon."

Anselmo, the older man, continued, "Please understand that we do not want to be part of your article. You must respect our confidences."

Jordan took a large gulp of his beer and said, "No problem. I'll protect you as well as Woodward and Bernstein protected old Deep Throat." Seeing the puzzlement on the two men's' faces, he explained, "I mean, senors, I will honor your request for anonymity, but I at this point I do not know what you want to confide."

"What we want to confide, Senor Roblech, is that, while we have no immediate information, we do have contacts who may help you find Ricardo Cajon, but we do not want to waste our time with people who are not serious. What we need to know, Senor Roblech, is why are you looking for Ricardo Cajon?"

I interrupted the conversation with coughing laughter because my capability for discretion had not recovered from the earlier drinks and had become even more hampered by the fresh beer in front of me.

I asked, "Sorry, boys, but is this what they call a cat-and-mouse game?"

Jordan looked at me with a perplexed smile and said, "I think so."

Harold Ash looked at his Mexican friends, apparently concerned that Anselmo was beginning to show anger and Jesus was simply looking bewildered.

"Please, gentlemen," Ash said. "I think you have mutual interests, and Mr. Golden is correct. Mr. Roblech, if you would not mind simply explaining as you did to me why you are interested in finding Ricardo Cajon, I think Anselmo would be able to continue his discussion."

"Okay, I'm a journalist working on a story about drug lords, and from what I've heard about Cajon, I figure he should be included," I said. "So what can you tell me about Cajon?"

"That he is an hombre muy mal," Anselmo said.

"I've already heard that from several people. Do you have any additional information, like where he is?"

Anselmo shook his head and said, "Surely you aren't so foolish to want to interview him personally. I think maybe you aren't a journalist. I think maybe you think you could use the million dollars the United

States government has put on Ricardo Cajon's head."

I took the cigarette from my mouth and said, "Aw, come on, does that middle-aged gringo look like a bounty hunter?"

"Yo no sabe. What do bounty hunters look like?" Anselmo replied.

As I shrugged, Jordan said, "What if we were bounty hunters? Would you be concerned that we might be in competition with you?"

"We do not seek money," Anselmo said. "We seek revenge, but we were hoping that maybe you had some information about Cajon."

"We are sorry to disappoint you. Now would you be willing to tell us about the people who may have some information that can help us?"

"Yo arrenpentido, but not tonight. We need to talk with them first and see if they want to meet with you."

"Fair enough," Jordan said as he took a pen from his pocket and wrote down my phone number. "Call us when you know when they want to meet."

Anselmo stood up, took a fifty-dollar bill out of his pocket, put it on the table, and said, "I think that will take care of the drinks and the tip. Adios, senors. We will call you after we talk with our contacts."

As the two Mexicans walked toward the door, Ash said, "I had better be going too." Then he hurried out the door after his friends.

Jordan called Tammy to tell her he was coming down to Albuquerque to pick up the few belongings that he had left at their place. "I've imposed upon your hospitality long enough," he said. "I'm moving back to find my fortune in Santa Fe and perhaps beyond."

Of course, he did not mention that he felt guilty that he had made love to Angelina. He wondered what would be the proper word for what he had done. Can a heterosexual man cuckold a lesbian? But Jordan remembered his times with Tammy, and he figured it would not be pleasant for either Angelina or him if Tammy discovered that Angelina had been -- Jordan again searched for the correct word -- unfaithful.

The day Jordan picked to drive to Albuquerque was the day Tammy and Angelina planned to have dinner with Kendrick and Barbara Dahl. Kendrick was the drama professor who had used his connections to get Tammy her position at the University of New Mexico. Jordan had met the couple while he was staying with Tammy and Angelina, and Tammy said Jordan would be welcome to join them for dinner.

They ate dinner and drank beers and margaritas at a small chic restaurant near the UNM campus. Then they drove back to Kendrick's and Barbara's place a few blocks away in a neighborhood called Nob Hill, not nearly as exquisite or lovely as the more famous San Francisco neighborhood with the same name. They had an after-dinner drink, and Kendrick and Barbara decided to follow Tammy and Angelina home to pick up a book Tammy had promised to loan to Barbara. Barbara needed the book quickly because it was going to be the topic of discussion at her next book group meeting.

Kendrick and Barbara had a Labrador retriever, which -- true to the nature of the breed -- won the heart of Jordan after a few drinks, and he suggested they bring the Lab along to Tammy's place. Kendrick, Barbara, and the dog were in their car. Jordan was driving Tammy's car with Angelina in the back seat.

The dog spotted the two intruders as they ran out of Tammy's and Angelina's back door. Jordan was turning the corner when they ran down the sidewalk toward a nearby park. He thought he recognized them and wondered what those guys would be doing in this neighborhood. Jordan did not have time to reflect or wonder anymore before he parked on the street across from Tammy's and Angelina's house.

The Lab and Kendrick were coming back from the end of the block. Barbara was outside. All went inside together to see if the two men who ran from the house had taken anything. Nothing seemed to be missing.

"Shouldn't you call the police?" Barbara asked.

Tammy looked at her with a slightly bemused smile and said, "Barbara, you've lived in Albuquerque longer than I have. You know how many burglaries we have in this city, burglaries where the burglars actually take something. These guys didn't even break a window or bust a door frame. They just messed up our back door lock. You know the cops wouldn't do anything but walk around the house and shrug, so why waste our time?"

"Yeah, you're probably right," Barbara said.

Jordan was relieved that Tammy didn't want to call police although he felt guilty that the two women were probably in an unaware danger. He wanted to collect his thoughts and to not have to worry about explaining to law enforcement people that he might have been the reason Anselmo and Jesus were snooping inside the house.

"Since nothing is missing," Angelina said. "I wonder what those men were doing in our house. Usually even if a burglary is interrupted, the thieves take something."

Although Jordan thought he knew the answer to Angelina's question, he did not feel comfortable telling Tammy and Angelina in the presence of Kendrick and Barbara. After the Dahls and their lovable pet left, Jordan, Tammy, and Angelina each poured a favorite trauma-reducing, relaxing nightcap.

Jordan finished his drink in less than five minutes and said, "Ladies, we have a problem. I recognized those two men who ran away from your house. Their names are Anselmo and Jesus. They said their last names are Carrasco and Perez, but I doubt they gave their real last names when Harold Ash introduced them to Flash and me, so they could ask us why we were asking questions about Ricardo Cajon. I think they probably are allied with Cajon, and I'm afraid Flash and I have put your lives in danger. I'm sorry."

Angelina looked more agitated than Tammy, but it was Tammy who spoke after a half-minute of silence. "What do we do, now?"

"I think you probably should take a little vacation. You're not teaching this summer, right? I can stay here at your house. Maybe Flash will come down too. We can get Flash's shotgun and pistol and see if those guys come back," Jordan said.

Tammy's scoffed, and Angelina's look of agitation evolved into a mix of anger and frustration. No one said anything. Jordan wished he still had a drink to sip.

It was Tammy who finally spoke after lighting a cigarette.

"Look, a big clue to whatever is going on here lies with Harold Ash. He's the one who introduced you to these two characters. He obviously knows who they really are. We just need to talk to him and see if we can decipher the truth."

"I haven't had much luck getting the truth out of Mr. Harry Ass," Jordan said.

"Maybe I can," Tammy said. "He called the other day to get my address, said he wanted to send me a photo of my mother...." Tammy's voice trailed off as Jordan gave an enlightened nod. Then she shrieked, "That how they got our address! That son of a bitch called to get our address so they could find us."

Angelina finally spoke, "And if they would break into the house, they did not come here to talk to us. They came here to kill us."

Jordan said, "I'm afraid you may be right."

Tammy said, "I repeat: so what do we do now?"

"And I repeat: I think you should take a little vacation," Jordan said.

"What good would that do?" Tammy said. "They can just wait us out until we return. We either have to run away again, as we did from California, or we can make an effort to get out of this mess once and for all."

"I guess you just finally made a good case for us to get rid of this hombre muy mal Big Dick Cajon, but our immediate problem is Anselmo and Jesus. I agree that Ash may be the key to all of our problems. We need to connect with him, but in the meantime, you need to get out of this place. There's no guarantee that those two sons of bitches won't come back tonight, so start packing. You two ladies are going to be the guests of Mr. Flash Sinclair until we figure out what we need to do. At least he has a shotgun and a pistol, and tomorrow perhaps we can come up with a plan to get out of this mess."

The plan, after we spent the next morning in my dining room drinking coffee without Irish whiskey and tomato juice without vodka, was to not wait around for the next shoe to drop but to take the crisis north to Durango and involve Harold Ash, whom Tammy remembered as an unprincipled coward, a man who was friendly to whoever could help him but who was nowhere to be found when there was no gain but some risk for him. Jordan told Tammy that Harold Ash would have had a successful career as a corporate vice president.

"Hello, Harold," Tammy said when Ash answered his phone. "You don't have to mail that photo if you haven't already because Angelina and I have decided to take a few days vacation in the lovely Animas River Valley, so if you don't mind we'll just drop by and buy you that drink and dinner you promised me."

As Tammy had expected, Ash did not know how to react to the unexpected phone call, and his brain stumbled over his tongue as he gave a conditional acceptance to her invitation.

"I think I may be able to meet with you," he said. "But I have some other things going on, and I need to rearrange my schedule a bit. Can I call you back?"

Later that day Ash called and said he could meet with Tammy and Angelina in a couple of days.

I suggested that the four of us rent a big cabin on a small lake outside of Durango, explaining that it's on a gravel road not on most maps and we could operate out of there. I also suggested that since none of us owned a vehicle that would comfortably accommodate all of us we should rent a van for the trip.

Tammy called Ash to tell him that she and Angelina were driving to Colorado and would call after they got there. Late that same afternoon, we checked into a two-floor, three-bedroom cabin overlooking the lake. On the ride from Santa Fe, we discussed ploys for getting the truth out of Harold Ash and quickly reached a consensus that Jordan and I needed to remain in the background. We continued the discussion after unloading the van.

"I think we all agree that Ash will be uneasy if you show up with Jordan and me," I said. "But we need to make sure you two are safe. That's where the van also comes in handy. Jordan and I don't yet have enough arthritic joints to prevent us from crouching down in the back without anyone knowing we are in the vehicle."

Jordan said, "Since we know his two south-of-the-border buddies don't worry about committing felonies, like breaking and entering and who knows what else, I think any meetings you have with Harold Ash, especially if he wants to bring Anselmo and Jesus along, should be in a very public place. If he tries to get you to come out to his place, make up some excuse. Tell him you don't have time. Maybe you could say you want to have breakfast before you catch the narrow gauge train to Silverton."

"Hey, that's a good idea," Tammy said. "Actually I always wanted to ride that train. I hear in the summer it's the biggest tourist attraction in the town -- spectacular scenery along the Animas River Canyon. So maybe we don't even have to make up a story for Harold. Pardon me, boys, but do want to ride the Durango choo-choo?"

Jordan had ridden the narrow-gauge tourist train from Durango to Silverton once when he explored Colorado while he lived in Denver. He told Tammy it was fun one way but tiring and even a little boring on the ride back.

"People who have more than two or three in their party often divide up. Some of them take the train up to Silverton, the rest ride in a car. Then they switch, and the ones driving up ride the train and the morning rail riders bring the car back.

"Since I've already ridden the train, I could be the driver and you two ladies -- and Flash if he wants -- could ride the train," Jordan said.

"Let the girls have a little time to themselves," I said. "I've already done the train too, so I'll be your shotgun rider in the van."

"By the way, Flash, I noticed that you pronounced Jesus as Heysus. With an H. Wow, I guess you're finally mastering the Spanish language," Tammy said. I smiled as Angelina and Jordan laughed.

Tammy placed a phone call to Harold Ash. She suggested that she and Angelina meet him for breakfast at the Streeter Hotel coffee shop prior to the two women's morning train tour.

Ash said that would work for him if he could bring two friends along.

Jordan and I watched from the van as Harold Ash walked into the hotel with Anselmo and Jesus. As we sat in the van, Jordan wished we had not stayed up so late planning and drinking. In Jordan's case it had been more drinking than planning. The only way he stayed awake was getting out of the van and walking around when I lit a cigarette.

About an hour after Tammy and Angelina went into the hotel, all five of the breakfast companions walked out together. It was nearing time for departure of the train, but Jordan and I expected Tammy and Angelina to return to the van to report at least briefly about the breakfast meeting.

As the two women walked toward the depot with Anselmo and Jesus and Ash turned the other way and walked toward his Mercedes, Jordan said, "What the hell? Are they going to ride the train, too?"

"Maybe so," I said. "I think this calls for a quick change of plans. One of us needs to be on that train if those two goons get on it with Tammy and Angelina. Since I still occasionally have some old fans who waylay me on vacation venues, you run over and get a train ticket. I'll be waiting for the train at the Needleton Creek stop. Check in with me then."

As Jordan opened the van's passenger door I said, "Here, take my hat. You may need it."

Jordan looked at me puzzled but did not have time to ask why I thought he might need the hat, so he just took it and ran toward the station. As he went through the door, Anselmo and Jesus were completing their ticket purchases. Jordan stayed behind vending machines and corners so they would not see him. After they had moved toward the train, Jordan bought a ticket and boarded. Anselmo and Jesus were walking ahead at the other end of the car. Then Jordan realized why I had given him the hat. By moving it from one side to the other, he could hide his face.

So now Jordan was wondering what he was going to do. Why did Anselmo and Jesus get on the train? Were they truly just being tourists? No, he thought. They broke into Tammy's and Angelina's house. They are clearly up to no good, he thought. Why didn't

Flash give me his pistol along with the hat? But what the hell could he do if he had a gun?

Jordan took comfort in that last question. He realized that if he could not shoot somebody on a crowded tourist train -- though he did not want to shoot anybody even if he were where he could -- then Anselmo and Jesus could not shoot anybody either.

So Jordan thought he would just keep my hat positioned well on his head and he would attempt to be a guardian angel watching over Tammy and Angelina and keeping them from harm.

Jesus, how ironic, Jordan thought. Here are some Mexican gangsters trying to do harm to two nice women, and one of them is named Jesus. Jordan wondered again if the two Mexicans had given their real names. He still doubted it.

Jordan saw Tammy, Angelina, and the two Mexican men as he entered the rail car and settled into the last seat in the car. He pulled the hat lower over his face. Maybe he pulled it too low, or maybe he simply was exhausted from the night before, but for whatever reason, Jordan was soon asleep.

Not much of a bodyguard, Jordan thought when he was gently shaken awake by Tammy. Jordan looked at her and at my hat, which had fallen off his face onto the seat. Then he looked at his watch. He really must have been tired because he had been asleep for almost two hours.

"Where's Angelina?" Jordan asked.

"That what I was trying to determine when I got up from my seat and walked down the aisle only to look down at this man snoring in his seat while the beautiful country rolled by. What are you doing here? I thought you were riding with Flash."

Jordan didn't pay any attention to her question. He was too concerned about getting an answer to the one he had asked.

"Is Angelina with those two Mexicans?" Jordan's apprehension was obvious in the tone of his voice.

"She went toward the back of the train, outside the railcar with Jesus, when he asked to talk with her privately. Anselmo looked agitated but stayed and made some small talk with me for a few minutes, then said he had to go to the men's room. When he didn't return in about fifteen minutes, I decided I probably should see what was going on. I got up to look for them, and that's when I saw you snoozing."

Jordan stumble-jumped out of his seat and started toward the railcar door, remembered he had forgotten my hat, went back and got it, and took Tammy's upper arm and said, "We got to find them."

They did not have to go far, meeting Angelina as she came the other way outside the next car. She looked at them with a stunned stare.

Tammy asked her if she was okay.

"Si, yes, yes, I'm fine," she said. "Maybe a little bit nauseous from looking into the cliffs along the river. I'll be okay. I just need to sit down."

"Let's go back inside," Tammy said.

When they had returned to where Tammy and Angelina had been sitting with Jesus and Anselmo, Tammy asked Angelina what happened with Jesus and Anselmo.

"Please, just let me rest for un momento," Angelina said.

"Okay," Tammy said as she motioned for Jordan to follow her.

They went to the smoking car, where Tammy fumbled for a cigarette and said, "Something happened. Oh, I wish we could get off this train."

"We can get off when we come to the rest stop where they drop the backpackers off. I think that should be pretty soon. Flash said he would be waiting for us there. We'll get off and get the hell back to Durango," Jordan said.

"Yes, that's what we should do," Tammy said.

I was waiting when they got off the train. Jordan, breathing easier because he did not see the two Mexicans, hurried the two women toward the van. Angelina sat silent in the back with Tammy as Jordan told me to waste no time getting back to Durango down the winding highway that shared the river canyon with the railroad. He quickly recounted the events on the train as well as he knew them.

"What are we going to do now?" Tammy asked.

"Hold on, girl," I said. "It's my turn to ask a few more questions. For starters, what did you learn at breakfast?"

"Nothing that we didn't already know," Tammy said. "That Harold Ash is still the same prissy asshole he always was and is obviously tied with Anselmo and Jesus, but we got no truth out of any of them about what that connection is. They spent most of the time trying to grill us about what we are doing in New Mexico and, oh, by the way, they asked about you two and how we had come to be connected again."

Jordan turned from the front seat, looked at Tammy sitting behind me and said, "So you didn't ask Anselmo and Jesus what they were doing in your house?"

She glared at Jordan and said, "What do you think, Jordan? Here we were, two unarmed women having breakfast with three sleazy men, at least two of whom are probably assassins, and you want us to say, 'Oh, by the way, why did you break into our house the other night?"

Jordan said, "I was just asking. I understand."

"Okay," Tammy said. "You two big heroes who thought it was such a good idea to go after a Mexican drug lord, I ask my question again, what do we do now?"

Jordan had decided to keep his mouth shut for a few minutes, and I resisted the impulse to explain that the bounty hunting idea was solely Jordan's, figuring we had more important issues to discuss at the moment.

"We go back to our place by the lake and get our wits together. You girls didn't tell those guys where we are staying, did you?" I asked.

Tammy shot me a look as mean as the one she had given Jordan.

"Jeez," she said. "Can you two ask more condescending questions? I repeat, we were having breakfast with a known sleazebag and two probable assassins. Now, Flash, what do you think? Do you think I said, here guys, here's our address and a map to our place, so you can come out and finish the job you flubbed up a week ago."

That girl should have been a lawyer, I thought. She was really good at putting men on the defense.

"Okay. I was just asking," I said.

Back at the cabin we tried to make sense of our predicament. There was only one answer, or maybe if there were more than one, we could find only one. Someone would have to tell Harold Ash that we knew he was allied with a couple of drug operatives who had broken into Tammy's and Angelina's house and likely want to kill them and then demand that Ash tell us what he knew.

Without an explanation, Angelina simply but firmly said she was not going to confront Harold Ash, and Tammy agreed that she did not want to see Harold Ash and certainly not his two Mexican friends again.

"Then maybe Jordan and I will go out there and confront him. Ask him what the hell is going on. But just to give us a little more of a sanity check, let's hang out here one more day and think about it," I said.

So we sat outside and drank bourbon, beer, and margaritas and ate pizza and chips and salsa.

The next day Jordan and I planned to drive out to Ash's mountain retreat after we had breakfast in Durango and Tammy and Angelina slept late. The banner headline on the newspaper Jordan bought outside the restaurant changed our plans. It read:

TV Actor Found Slain
In Home Outside City

The article told of a FedEx employee seeing Ash's body through a window in his living room. He had been shot.

We drove back to the lake cabin with the newspaper.

"So, do we go the police and tell them what we know?" Jordan asked after Tammy and Angelina read the article.

"No," Tammy almost screamed. "What good would that do, other than get us more involved in this than we already are."

I said, "She's probably right. I don't think there is anything to tie us to these characters, and when you think about it, what could we offer? Jordan, we already got these two girls in way too much trouble. I say, let's all go back to Santa Fe, and then maybe take a little vacation and wait and see how all this plays out."

"No," Jordan said. "I think we should stay in the cabin for a couple more days. Jesus and Anselmo are still on the loose, and we know they know where Tammy and Angelina live. They probably know where your house is too, Flash. So let's give them a few days to either high-tail it back to Mexico, get caught by the authorities -- be they Coloradoan, New Mexican, or federal -- or perhaps try to make some mischief with us in Santa Fe and Albuquerque.

"No," Tammy said, "We are going to have to face this issue, and two or three more days won't make any difference. Look guys, I really think we'll be okay. Angelina and I want to go back to Albuquerque and get the rest of our life organized."

Jordan and I wondered what Tammy meant by her last sentence, and we tried to convince her that while waiting two or three days to return to Albuquerque might not make any difference, neither would it cause any harm. But there were no words of reason we could find to make the two women change their minds, so we packed and headed south toward New Mexico.

As the van moved along the highway by the Rio Grande, Jordan suffered through another siege of conscience and civic duty and said, "I'm wondering if we are doing the right thing about not going to the authorities and tell them about Anselmo and Jesus. I mean I've always been a law-abiding citizen, and we have some information that might help catch Ash's killers. And what if the law finds out we associated with those characters?"

"I hear what you're saying, boy," I said. "But I think we also have to think about the welfare and feelings of the two ladies in the back seat. If they don't want to get involved, it's their call.

"But I figure telling some yahoo cowboy lawmen we've met a couple of Mexican drug dealers through our connection with the murder victim will just make our lives much more complicated.

"And how do we explain that we met Ash in the first place? If we involve Tammy and Angelina, we'll really screw up their lives. Angelina might not be able to complete her citizenship process."

Jordan sat silent, looking out at the rocks along Abiquiu. Then he said, "Yeah, I guess you're right. As you once told me, there's a big difference between right and proper and legal and just. I guess getting us all in trouble might be proper and legal, but it wouldn't be right and just."

Everyone sat silent as I drove toward Espanola. When the road turned south toward Santa Fe, Jordan spoke again.

"Well, right or proper, legal or just, I hope if we don't go around asking anymore questions about Ricardo Cajon, he'll forget about us. I've lost my interest in bounty hunting or even writing about drug dealers. I think I'll just concentrate on looking for a regular job."

"I'm glad you've regained your sanity," I said. "But I still recommend that we all take a little vacation, if for no other reason, just to refresh ourselves. But of course, you are all grownups, and that's just a suggestion. I'm thinking about going back to Texas and see how things have changed in the past half-century. What do the rest of you think?"

"I wouldn't mind a little relaxation time," Jordan said.

Tammy said, "Don't take offense, guys, but Angelina and I have had about all the fun with you two that we can take for awhile, so, yes, we may take some time off, but right now, we just need to get back to Albuquerque."

"Now, I don't mean to frighten you," I said. "But I would be remiss not to at least mention the possibility that Cajon might still be concerned about your whereabouts."

"Of course, we've thought about that," Tammy said. "But guys, trust me! I think we'll be okay."

"Si," said Angelina, who had sat silent throughout the trip.

Again we wondered why the two women did not appear to be scared of the prospect of returning to the house that Anselmo and Jesus had burglarized.

When Jordan pleaded with Tammy and Angelina to accompany them back to Albuquerque, Tammy said, " Jordan, we wouldn't be in this mess if you had not involved us. We can take care of ourselves. We'll be in touch."

Tammy and Angelina did not call. Jordan called them several times but got no answer. After five days, he got the message that the number was no longer in service. He drove to Albuquerque. The house was locked, and no furniture was inside. He drove back to Santa Fe.

A few days later Tammy's letter came in the mail. It had a Tucson postmark.

"Dear Jordan and Flash,

"Since you're both nice guys, we thought we owed you this letter so you won't worry about us and to tell you not to worry about Jesus or Ricardo Cajon. Trust me on that one. It's okay.
"Angelina and I decided we need to disappear, and so that's what we are going to do. I repeat -- don't worry. We're fine, and you'll be fine. We just need to start a new life where no one has ever heard of us or Ricardo Cajon, Sam Eschidt, Debra Debaux, Harold Ash, and, yes, Flash Golden and Jordan Roblech.

"So don't worry, and have a good life! That's what we are going to try to do.

"Love,
"Tammy and Angelina."

Jordan and I found it to be a puzzling letter, talked about it, and came to the conclusion there was nothing we could do -- neither about the flight of Tammy and Angelina nor the foolish failed bounty hunting adventure. Later Jordan found a brief story in the *Albuquerque Journal* about how two hikers had found the body of a man in the canyon below the Durango & Silverton Railroad. He was middle-aged, most likely Hispanic, and his injuries appeared to be caused by a fall.

Chapter 11
Back and Forth Across the West

So Tammy Dolcito went out of Jordan's life for the second time.

For a couple of weeks after Tammy's letter arrived in the mail, Jordan and I warily kept our eyes out for unwanted visitors, but the only person who showed up at my place was the mailman. Breathing easier, I again invited Jordan to accompany me on a trip to Texas, and Jordan still thought it sounded like a good idea.

We drove to Clovis and visited Arlene's grave. Then we drove into Texas, past Lubbock and east toward Fort Worth.

"Hey, this is the home town of Buck Leherifen," Jordan said as we approached a city limits sign a half-hour out of Lubbock.

I brightened at the mention of Buck's name and said, "Buck. Yeah, he was good boy. Arlene and I lost track of him after he got transferred to Okinawa."

"He's someone we both liked," Jordan said. "Maybe I can do a little research sometime and see if I can find him. For sure, it will be safer than trying to track down Ricardo Cajon."

We spent the night in Mineral Wells, about an hour's drive west of Fort Worth. As we pulled out of the motel parking lot the next morning, Jordan said, "Look up at the sky, Flash. Back in the '60s, there were a lot of helicopters up there. The young Army men in them were learning how to be pilots at Fort Wolters. It seems in my memory that one of those copters crashed about every week. Maybe not, but quite a few young men died in training here, getting ready to go to Vietnam. They didn't get the honor of having their names put on that big black wall. Still, they're just as dead."

"Yeah, my buddies who died in the South Pacific or Ray's buddies who died in Korea don't have their names on any big black walls either. Just on their tombstones," I said.

"So let's go visit another set of tombstones," Jordan said as we drove east on Interstate 20.

By mid-morning, we were at the cemetery west of the Six Flags Amusement Park and the baseball stadium where the Texas Rangers play baseball, standing over the graves of Jordan's parents. They had been dead for less than a decade. First his mother died of cancer. Jordan told me that after his mother died, his father did not have much to live for. Jordan [illegible] came from Denver [illegible] to see his father and told him he ought to get a medical checkup. Maybe if he had followed Jordan's advice, the doctors would have discovered the blockage that caused his father's fatal heart attack.

"Yeah, I guess that's what happens when you get older," I said. "You get up in the morning, read the obit page, feel slightly relieved you're not there, think about all the friends and relatives who once were breathing and having as good a time as you were, and when you're lonely and hurting from whatever ailment is bothering you at the moment, wonder if you or them are better off, and then you go visit their graves every now and then and remember again and wait for whatever is going to happen."

We drove through Arlington and Grand Prairie and turned south on our way to a small cemetery outside of Bryan. After the same ritual over my parents' graves, I told Jordan I was ready to head northwest back to some mountains and cooler weather.

Somewhere in the Trans-Pecos area -- the part of Texas that looks like what people think Texas looks like but really should be in New Mexico -- Jordan said, "I probably should go back to Texas every now and then in the summer, so I can remind myself how goddamned hot it is. When I was in that cemetery where your parents are buried, I damned near passed out."

"I know what you're saying," I said. "I've been telling people for more than forty years, I like Texas, I just don't like where they built it."

Two weeks after we returned to Santa Fe still with no disturbances to my property, Jordan said, "New Mexico is a nice place, a good refuge for Texans, but here's one native Texan who's going to move on west."

I asked him if he was tired of my company.

Jordan said, "You know I've been fishing for jobs for a while, sending out letters, making some phone calls. I think I might have gotten a bite from Sandia National Laboratories' California location in Livermore, writing some technical stuff. They seem to think my oil and gas writing background makes me qualified."

I pumped his hand in celebration and said, "As I've always said, you got to do what you got to do, so go do what you got to do, but if you ever need a place to stay, you know you're welcome."

Jordan put his arms around me and said, "Thank you, partner. You've become almost like a father to me. Well, maybe an older brother. I don't think I would have ever gotten into as much trouble or had as much fun with my father as I've had with you."

I have to admit that my eyes watered up a bit when I hugged him back and said, "And you've been like a son to me, a son I never had."

Jordan grabbed both of my biceps and stepped back and said, "I never had a son either, and I guess at this point in my life, I'm never going to have one, so we got that in common too.

"Come to think of it, we have another thing in common. We don't have any brothers or sisters either. I guess the two of us were just destined to meet. Two lonely guys with no one to care about us."

"Yeah, I guess so," I said. "I had a few buddies once, people like Ray the bartender, but he had his own life to live, and I haven't heard from him in years. And I've had a lot of acquaintances. You know about them -- all those famous movie stars, most now dead, except for one -- that nice feller, Ronnie Reagan. I remember all the times I told folks he was a nice guy but probably would be remembered for playing second-fiddle to a chimpanzee and selling General Electric products on television. Shows you what I know and why I would have never made any money playing the stock market."

I blinked, wiped my eyes the way men do when they are trying to hide their vulnerability, and said, "What about you, Jordan? Do you have any real friends, more than acquaintances?"

"No, I guess not. Like you, I've known some people who I thought were worth caring about and staying in touch with, but for whatever reason, I didn't. People like Buck Leherifen and maybe less than a dozen people I've worked with in Houston and Denver."

"Buck. Yeah, Buck. When we rolled through his hometown, you said we should try to find Buck. Are you going to do that? I sure would like to see him again," Flash said.

That conversation occurred toward the end of the 1980s, before the Internet had become a tool that allowed people to click on the various national phone directories and find old friends, lovers, relatives, or whomever, so Jordan said, "It may take a little time, but I'll see what I can do."

Jordan remembered how relieved he had been to learn that Buck's name was not on that long black wall in Washington D.C. He told me about walking along the wall on a beautiful spring day in 1984. He was in D.C. for a job interview with a defense contractor based in the Virginia suburbs. He visited the wall after the interview, which he knew had not gone well. Jordan was disheartened because he really wanted the job. He thought the Washington area would be a fun place to live for at least a little while.

Jordan remembered some lyrics he wrote on the airplane back from D.C. to Denver, and he dug it out of the box where he kept the various lyrics he had written. He read them to me and suggested maybe we could come up with a tune.

He wasn't quite the handsome cowboy he used to be,
But he was still a hero to me.
A man of honor and member of the generation
That fought and gave their youth to save this nation.
He bought me a beer in that California bar
And gave me advice I've carried near and far.
He said, "Son, life ain't fair and life ain't kind,

But it's all we get, so don't go through it blind
To the good times that will count so dear
When you chalk up the end of another year."
He took a swig and wiped his chin
And gave this advice with a little grin.
"As you pick up that rifle and hide your fears
Remember your loved ones will cry real tears
If you die trying to prove you're a hero.
The sum of their hopes will add up to zero.
Because life ain't fair and life ain't kind,
But it's all we get, so don't go through it blind
To the good times that will count so dear
When you chalk up the end of another year."
As I listened to him on that hot August night,
I didn't realize how much we would have to fight
When our government sent us to a place called Vietnam,
Telling us those Commies can't stand up to Uncle Sam.
But they did, and we lost friends and more faith
And I remembered the words of that old cowboy sage.
Life ain't fair and life ain't kind.
But it's all we get, so don't go through it blind
To the good times that count so dear
When you chalk up the end of another year.
The years went by and they built a wall of black stone
Honoring fifty-eight thousand who have never known
The joys and sorrows of living as the century ended

Or that we forgave and forgot as the nation mended.
And I didn't hold back the emotions as I thought
Of lost friends and all life's battles I had fought.
Yes, life ain't fair and life ain't kind,
But it's all we get, and I'm not blind
To life's basic truth that when all is said and done,
I'd rather have my back against the wall than my name on one.

Jordan and I picked up our guitars, and in less than an hour we had a tune.

"Too bad no one cares about Vietnam anymore," I said. "Back in the late '60s or early '70s, we might have sold this to some protest singer. Let's hope we never have another era when Americans understand what the song is trying to tell them."

Jordan nodded his head and started packing for his interview trip to Livermore.

Jordan got the job and moved to the rolling hills southeast across San Francisco Bay. He called and told me life was good out there. The job was not difficult, even interesting every now and then. His paycheck was generous, and most of his co-workers were pleasant. There was always an asshole anywhere, Jordan said, but on the whole the scientists and engineers who lived the sheltered life offered by a national laboratory were intelligent and congenial Americans. Taking home a hefty paycheck, spending work hours doing interesting research, writing messages to buddies on the latest model computer, or traveling around the country and the world collecting airplane mileage to be used during generous vacation time would make just about anyone congenial. Jordan said he knew some people might find it ironic that such nice people are working at places with a principal reason for existence being the creation of horrendous weapons that may someday wipe out the human race, but, what the hell, what would life be without irony, he said.

Jordan's work kept him busy enough that he soon forgot about his promise to try to locate Buck Leherifen. But Jordan did stay in touch with me and came back to visit a couple of times a year when he needed his green chile fix. Jordan told his California colleagues that anyone who lives in New Mexico and doesn't get addicted to chiles probably is some sort of robot. I've known that ever since I tasted one of Arlene's burgers.

I also came to California to visit Jordan. We promised each other to get together once a season. Since Livermore gets the inland California heat in the summer, we decided that Santa Fe, at seven thousand feet, was better in the summer. Since the April and May winds can really be beastly in New Mexico, we opted to meet in California in the spring. Fall is nice in both places, but since Jordan came to New Mexico in the summer, I usually went to California in the fall. Then Jordan would come to New Mexico in the winter because he had learned to ski when he lived in Denver.

We had a good time, and almost a decade drifted by before we realized it. Jordan dated his share of the lovely ladies who populate Northern California and had what is politely described as affairs with some of them. I also met a few women who apparently enjoyed my personality, sense of humor, or whatever other attributes they were seeking in a man.

When Jordan and I got together, we would discuss our romantic situations without getting too graphic. Primarily we would just ask each other if we had met anyone we might marry and then spend the rest of the conversation explaining how this or that woman was really an intelligent, caring, and attractive person but we were not quite ready to make the commitment.

Maybe I had a more understandable reason. I always seemed to close my conversation with an explanation that in effect said: "She's nice, but she's not Arlene, and it just wouldn't be fair to her to be lying there in bed or sitting and looking across the table at breakfast and wishing she was Arlene."

Jordan's explanations were more varied but had the same theme: "Our relationship was going well until I did something that made her realize that I wasn't the man she wanted to spend the rest of her life with."

In 1994 I finally asked Jordan how his search for Buck was going.

"Oh, just about like my search for Big Dick Cajon went. Actually, Flash, I got busy with the move and then enjoying my time in California, and, like most selfish human beings, forgot all about trying to find Buck."

"I wish we could find him," I said. "I would like to see that boy again. I don't really know why, other than I just liked him just as I like you. You're both good boys from Texas, and you're as close as anything I ever came to having sons."

"Flash, I think we can find Buck now. This modern computer world -- which I'm not all that comfortable with, except as a writer it's nice to be able to correct my typos without a pencil -- anyway we now have the Internet, and the computer entrepreneurs have created all sorts of so-called websites that provide information through the use of these newfangled so-called search engines. At least one of those websites functions as a kind of national phone directory. Now if you have a computer and an Internet connection, we might be able to look up Buck."

I looked at him like he had just asked if I enjoyed going to the dentist.

"I never even learned how to use a typewriter, so do you think I would embrace some technology that seems to be a painful way to spend your time on this earth?"

"Yeah, I figured you would say something like that. When I get back to Livermore, I'll try to look up Buck, and if I can find him, we'll both come down to visit or maybe get together in the Bay Area as soon as we can arrange it."

Jordan found Buck without much trouble. There are not that many Leherifens in this world, not in the United States at least, so when Jordan punched in Buck's last name, there he was on the short list. He was not listed as Buck but as B.J. for Buchanan James Leherifen. As Jordan punched in the Port Angeles phone number, he was hoping Buck would remember him, and Jordan was getting ready to explain to any woman or teenager who answered that he was an old friend of their husband, boyfriend, or father.

The conversation was easy since Buck answered and, yes, he did remember Jordan, although Jordan could tell by the tone of his voice that Buck was a bit puzzled about why he called. So Jordan quickly told him.

Jordan said Buck remembered me even better than he remembered Jordan, who invited him down to visit in the fall when I was planning to come to California. Jordan told Buck that I had offered to pay for the flight.

"That's mighty generous, and I wish I could say you don't have to bother, but I'm afraid that's the only way I could fly down there," Buck said. "You see -- and I hope you have made more of a fortune in the last thirty years -- but I'm just a starving artist who lives in a little hut by a river that flows out of the mountains, and I make a meager living by giving kayak lessons in the summer and working in a hardware store in the winter. About all the travel I can afford is a trip every now and then to British Columbia or Seattle and an occasional summer trip to Montana or the Minnesota boundary waters."

Buck said he would plan on making the trip, and in the meantime the two former Marine buddies caught up by telephone on what had happened in their lives since they said goodbye in early 1963. Both learned that neither had spent the last three decades living a life that Donald Trump, Donald Rumsfeld, or maybe even Donald Duck would envy. Hell, Buck thought, even Donald Duck had three nephews. All Buck had was a goofy Labrador retriever, and the only other creatures sharing Jordan's property were a family of squirrels living in the tree that hovered ominously over his townhouse.

All three of us felt better when we got together at Jordan's place. Here we were -- Jordan and Buck in their early fifties and me just turned seventy -- drinking, laughing, and for a little while at least glad to be alive. Jordan and I were really happy to have Buck back in our world, and we told him he had to be part of our seasonal get-togethers for the rest of our lives.

It was at that first gathering in Livermore when Buck told the story about how he traveled up the coast after getting out of the

Marines, met Jim Outseagle, and ended up on the Olympic Peninsula. After he told the story about maybe seeing Charles Schultz, we drove up to Santa Rosa and went to Snoopy's Gallery & Gift Shop. Of course, Charles Schultz was not there, but a man wearing a baggy pair of shorts and sneakers with black sox recognized me from my movie days, handed Jordan a Japanese camera, and asked me if I wouldn't mind posing with him and his wife.

"Hell, this is better than meeting Charles Schultz any day," the tourist said.

I could not believe anybody still remembered me and that any celebrity I ever had could ever compare to that of the creator of Charlie Brown, Linus, Lucy, and Snoopy. But I told the aging fan I was flattered and it would be an honor to have my picture taken with him and his wife. Jordan snapped the photograph. The man and his wife got in their RV with big smiles on their faces, and us three Texan former Marines drove back to Livermore.

Buck told enough enchanting stories about the Pacific Northwest that Jordan and I decided our next gathering would be at Buck's place in the early summer of 1995. Buck explained that the Olympic Peninsula is especially nice in the summer. It does not rain as much then. The daytime temperatures are usually in the sixties, and the scenery, he said, is awesome in the true sense of the word.

Buck didn't exaggerate. The scenery was so awesome that Jordan, after his first visit, thought he might be willing to forsake the San Francisco Bay Area for the Olympic Peninsula if there were a way he could make a living there. He revealed that inclination to Buck and me the next time we met, this time again in Livermore.

"Better stay where you are," Buck said. "It's a pretty place, but there aren't many good jobs up here."

I understood what Buck was saying and said, "Yes, like my old daddy said, you can't eat pretty. But then I guess my old daddy wasn't right about everything because I've eaten quite a few pretties."

I could tell that Buck and Jordan were somewhat surprised when they heard those words coming from me because for all the years I had been discreet about my sexual experiences. So I said, "Sorry, boys, I guess I shouldn't have said that. Guess I'm just in a raunchy mood. Maybe it's these trips I've been making to see you in California. This state does that to me. I miss it. Knew a lot of pretty women out here, and I get those old-time feelings every time I visit, even if I'm too old to do anything with them.

"Maybe that's why I'm willing to get on that goddamned airplane. I believe, those feelings keep a feller alive. Maybe there are a lot of guys out there who don't care about sex, but I never was one of them. And I suspect you two aren't either."

It was a comment that led to a more candid, although not especially sober, discussion. All three of us were raised to be gentlemen, at least when it comes to treating women with respect, even if we were paying to fuck them or trying our hardest to get it for free. And we had a common trait that forbade us from bragging and talking about our sexual experiences.

Jordan and Buck knew these were not especially Texas traits, certainly not refraining from bragging. Jordan wished he had a dollar for all the places he had been in his careers as a reporter and lobbyist or even science writer traveling around the country when somebody told everyone in the room that he or she was from Texas and then proceeded to tell how he or she liked everybody within earshot and said if they ever found themselves in that great state he or she would be happy to accommodate them at his or her great hacienda because he or she had a made a fortune in oil, computers, cotton-farming, heart surgery, entertainment, multi-level marketing, tort law, politics, war -- be it starting them, fighting them, or profiting from them -- you name it, - the Texans have done it.

The truth is, Texans are no better or no worse about talking about their sex lives than other folks. I figure that trait has something to do with one's raising, or maybe just genetics. I told my two surrogate sons that I wondered why some men have to talk about their sexual experiences, and often lie about them, while others make you wonder if they have ever even put a finger in a woman's pussy. Buck said he quit thinking about the question when he realized he could not find the answer.

"Yeah, but I wish I had known about blow jobs when I was in high school," Jordan said.

I chuckled and said, "Boy, don't we all."

Buck took a swig of his drink and agreed.

I could tell that Jordan and Buck were surprised at my comments. But I was not speaking those words because I was a horny septuagenarian. I was speaking them because I probably was drunker than they had ever seen me. For all of my adult life, I had drunk way more than the doctors recommend, but I had been doing that for a half-century and during those fifty years a lot of those doctors had died and I was still alive.

That's when I told Jordan and Buck I was not destined to be in that breathing condition for much longer. I said I already had figured out the diagnosis before I went to my doctor about the cough that would not go away.

"Yeah, it's the big C," I said. "Same thing that took Arlene, both of your mamas, my buddy John Wayne, Bogart, McQueen, and several million other good folks."

"What's the prognosis?" Jordan asked.

"Not good. At best a year, likely less."

Jordan and Buck sat silent.

"But you know, boys, we got to have something to take us out," I said. "This old earth just doesn't have room for all of us, least not any decent room. I guess we could still put a bunch of people up near the Artic Circle, in the Amazon jungle, or maybe even around Las Vegas, Nevada, but who the hell would want to live their whole year in one of those places.

"So I'm not looking at this with any regret. Hell, with all those heart bypasses and blood pressure pills, if we didn't have the great equalizer of cancer, then we'd all live way past the age we had anything to live for anyway. I just wish it was a fair disease and pick someone like me who's managed to live past seventy despite all my evil habits and not good people like Arlene and your mamas when they still had something more to live for.

"So, as I said, I'm not looking at this with regret. Sadness, dread, maybe even a little fear, a wish I could stay longer, but no regret. So, fill up your glasses, boys, the drinks are on me. And try to get as much pussy as you can before you leave this earth."

The reunion ended too soon for all of us, but Jordan and Buck had to go back to work. Jordan urged me to stay in California with him, but I told him I needed to go back to Santa Fe, where my doctor was.

"Then I'll be coming back to Santa Fe about once a month," Jordan said. Buck just stood in silence with a sad look, and said, "I wish I could, too, but...."

"I know, Buck. Don't fret about it," I said. Then I handed each man a fat envelope. "Maybe this will help you get back here every now and then."

In unison they opened their envelopes that each contained fifty one-hundred dollar bills.

Jordan and Buck both realized the proper and common reaction to such generosity from a dying man would be to say something like, "You don't have to do this." But with their mentor standing before them, they had outgrown propriety and replaced it with honesty.

Buck spoke first. "Thank you," he said through his tears.

Jordan simply shook his head and said, "Yeah, thank you." Then he added, "As I said, I'll see you in a month."

"Me too," Buck said.

I should remind you, dear reader, at this point that I've already said this book is not about me. It's about those two boys, Jordan and Buck. But I have to talk about me a little bit so that this story makes sense

After I got the fatal diagnosis, I didn't sleep much at night unless I took the pills the doctor gave me. But some nights I did not want to sleep. I just wanted to remember. I figured I would soon sleep forever with no memories, so I savored my memories in my bed or favorite chair.

The bed held special memories. I had driven to the San Diego furniture store to haul it to Arlene's house in San Clemente. She had made me a special dinner to repay the favor, a big steak, smothered in onions and chiles, and Arlene's special rice and beans. Dessert was fried apple ice cream. Arlene made coffee and put an array of whiskeys and liquors on the table.

We had equally consumed the large bottle of Napa Valley red wine, and now we were on Arlene's sofa. I was drinking my version of Irish coffee -- three eighths coffee, one eighth milk, and one half Irish whiskey. Arlene was sipping coffee with Kahlua. She turned and gave me a brief kiss.

"Thank you for hauling the bed. Thank you for being a good friend. A friend to both me and Floyd."

"You're welcome. I just wish the circumstances were different."

"But they aren't, and they never will be, not as far as Floyd is concerned. I realize that now," Arlene said.

I looked at the beautiful woman beside me and said, "Yeah, I'm afraid you're correct. I know how hard that it is."

"Do you?"

"No, I guess I can't really know," I said.

Arlene said, "Don't be sorry. I should not have said that. You are such a good man." Then she paused and said, "I need a good man."

I did not know what to say next, so I just took a drink of my Irish coffee.

"Flash," Arlene said.

"Yes?"

"I think I love you, Flash."

"Arlene, I know I love you."

She put her arms around me with tears in her eyes and we kissed hard and long. When our lips parted, Arlene said, "I've made the bed. Let's put it to good use."

As I lay alone in the same bed, almost forty years later, I remembered that first time. I never imagined she would be a screamer. But she was, and she made me feel I was a better lover than I had even been with all the other women. I enjoyed the times with her better than with Debra, better than with the beautiful blonde actress, and better than with all the others.I remembered the last time Arlene and I had been in bed. Arlene's cancer had made it too difficult for us to make love. I just held her and said, "I can't tell you how much I love you."

Arlene pressed her frail body against me and said, "I'm sorry I have to leave you. I'll look forward to when we are together again."

So as I pulled the trigger, I hoped that that Arlene's faith was well founded and the reunion would be sweet.

So now you know I'm dead. And I'm not John Clarence "Flash" Golden anymore. I'm nobody, just like everybody else who's dead. Just like all those dead Texas entrepreneurs. Just like all those dead politicians. Just like all those boys killed in the score or so of declared or undeclared wars Americans have fought since the Europeans -- those descendants of the killers of that poor unfortunate white ape -- arrived on this beautiful continent.

And dear reader, let's get the questions out of the way.

So if I'm dead, you ask, what's it like up there?

I'm going to handle your questions like the prissy politicians or petulant policemen on the televised so-called news conferences you see on those cable so-called news channels. I'm going to tell you a little bit but not nearly what you want to know.

The first answer you want of course is whose version of eternity is correct -- Christians, Jews, Muslims, Hindus, Buddhists, Wiccans....?

I'm not going to comment on that. I'll bet you've heard that before. I'm not going to comment because no matter what I said, you wouldn't believe me. You, like the people who watch those cable news conferences, still would believe what you want to believe and figure the rest of it is bullshit.

But I will tell you this: I ain't burning in eternal fire, and I haven't had sex with forty virgins. Come to think of it, I'm not sure I've even met any virgins since I got into this state. And, oh by the way, I haven't seen any old guys with flowing beards playing harps while lounging on clouds or any old guys wearing fancy robes and high hats or any of those fellers I heard screaming about salvation on television while telling me I needed to send them some money.

Thank you for coming. This news conference is over, because, as I've said, this story is not about me. It's about Buck and Jordan.

My lawyer called Jordan first. I had slipped a note under the lawyer's office door on Sunday night, telling him to call the police and come to my house on Monday. They found my body in the garage. The pistol, the one I had worn in all of my movies, was nearby. I left notes to both Jordan and Buck, telling them I had seen the toll that waiting takes on those who care about the dying person and that I already had come to terms with my imminent departure.

"And besides," I wrote, *"ever since I stood in line so many times in the Marine Corps, I never had liked to wait."*

I closed the notes with this message: *"It was among my lucky moments when I met you two more than thirty years ago, and I thank whatever God or Gods there may be that we got reunited again. I consider you the sons I never had, and I'm leaving you my inheritance, which, thanks to a couple of silly songs, is more than I ever thought I would have when I was a boy back in Brazos County. I had hoped to leave it to Arlene, but you know how that turned out.*

"Maybe I'll see you somewhere else in eternity. Or maybe these few years were all we had. No matter. There's not anything we can do about it anyways. So have a drink on me and enjoy the rest of your lives."

I also included in my last messages to Jordan, Buck, and the lawyer my desire to be buried next to Arlene in Clovis. I asked that Jordan and Buck accompany my coffin and oversee the burial in a cemetery that is only a few miles west of my native state.

My body was flown in the coffin to Lubbock and trucked to a funeral home in Clovis to await the arrival of Buck and Jordan. They flew to Albuquerque, rented a car that took them through the low pass that separates the Sandia and Manzano Mountains on the eastern edge of Albuquerque, and headed east on Interstate 40. At Santa Rosa they turned south of U.S. 94 and then east toward Clovis at Fort Sumner, the town known by every Western history buff as the place where Sheriff Pat

Garrett shot William Bonney in the summer of 1881.

"We've got to stop and see Billy the Kid's grave," Jordan said.

"I've already seen it," Buck said. "Remember, I grew up not all that far from here. But if you haven't seen it, by all means, we can't go through Fort Sumner without visiting the Kid's grave."

The grave is on a road a few miles outside of the town, and, like all graves, it is not a place where one wants to tarry. It is in a small fenced plot with a few other graves of people never known and long forgotten next to the museum and gift shop with overpriced coffee cups and t-shirts. Visitors read the inscription that says it holds the body of the infamous young outlaw and a couple of his outlaw buddies and then get in their cars and drive on to the Grand Canyon, Carlsbad Caverns, or wherever they really were going when they found themselves in Fort Sumner.

Buck and Jordan got back in their rental car and talked about Billy the Kid and many of the other Western legends as Jordan drove toward Clovis.

"You know we probably are the last generation to give a shit about Billy the Kid, Wild Bill Hickok, Wyatt Earp, Buffalo Bill Cody, Kit Carson, and all those other great icons who rode horses with six-guns on their belts and Winchesters in their saddles," Jordan said.

"Every Saturday afternoon along with the rest of the boys in the neighborhood, I would get a dime and maybe an extra nickel for popcorn and go to the movie theater and sit and watch the movie until, as we kids described it, the screen went blank. That was our under-ten-year-old terminology for sitting through all three or four showings of the featured movie and the accompanying serials and cartoons."

"Me too," Buck said. "Saturday afternoon shoot-em-ups were as certain as the sunrise. But when I got older I also went to the nighttime Western movies. And both the Saturday afternoon and weekend night good guys always did what was right in the end and always defeated the bad guys."

"The bad guys were always the same," Jordan said. "Roy Bancroft and Myron Healy must have made nice livings playing Saturday afternoon Western villains. I don't remember the names of all of their henchmen, but I remember their faces. There was the tall one with the soft voice and the stocky one with the broken nose who looked funny when he shot his pistol because he held it with his left hand."

"Yeah, I remember that guy, too, maybe because I'm also left-handed," Buck said. "Left-handed people look funny using almost any instrument, be it a pistol, golf club, or a pair of scissors. But I don't remember his name either.

"I guess Randolph Scott or Rod Cameron were the most frequent nighttime Western heroes, along with the great John Wayne and real-life war heroes Audie Murphy and

Jimmy Stewart. They and all the Saturday afternoon heroes, Roy, Gene, Rex, Tim Holt, the Durango Kid, and all the rest were really good guys."

"Yeah," Jordan said, "And when you're eight or nine years old, you still believe in good guys. Guys like the one who's going to be in that that new grave in Clovis."

I appreciated the comment.

A few hours later, as the funeral attendants lowered my body to rest forever beside my beloved Arlene, Jordan wiped his eyes and said, "Rest in peace, good guy." Then he and maybe his only living friend walked toward the rental car.

"So what do we do now?" Jordan said as they pulled back onto the highway.

"Do you have a few days to spare?" Buck asked.

"Considering the royalties that Flash bequeathed to us, I may have the rest of my life to spare," Jordan said.

"That's what I was thinking, too. I expect I'll quit working at the hardware store, cut back on my kayak lessons, and paint more when I get back to Port Angeles. I figure I can spend the rest of my life painting, especially since I never needed much to live on. But I asked the question since I'm this close, and since the theme of this trip seems to be visiting graves, I would like to drive over to my parents' graves," Buck said.

"Okay, I'm up to a trip into Texas. I went through your hometown with Flash a few years ago."

In less than a half-hour, they had crossed into Texas and were heading southeast toward Lubbock on U.S. 84. As they passed through Littlefield, Buck asked, "Do you know whose hometown this is?"

"Sure. Waylon Jennings. Now are you going to ask me whose seat he gave up on that plane?"

"Okay. I should have known you'd know all that, seeing how you're the musician."

Jordan scoffed, "Yeah, fine musician I am."

They spent the night in a Lubbock motel, and by mid-morning the next day they were in Buck's hometown. After driving past the small stores and vacant buildings just off the highway, Buck turned back to the cemetery on the outskirts of the town. He found the graves of his parents, stood over them for a few minutes, commented that he was pleased that the cemetery was well tended, then walked around, finding the graves of other people he had known in his teen years.

"I guess I should be a bit more emotional," he said, "but it's like a different world. The town pretty much looks the same with its streets and early twentieth century buildings. The road between here and Lubbock looks pretty much the same with the flat cotton fields and occasional oak trees. The sky pretty much looks the same, going on forever and speckled with white clouds.

"But it's not the same. The only tangible part of my world of forty years ago, the part that's not whirling around in some ethereal place, lies in four coffins in two flatland cemeteries that I may never visit again. I guess Thomas Wolfe was right. You know what I mean?"

"Yes," Jordan said with a slow sadness. "Yes, I do."

As they walked through the brown grass of the cemetery, Jordan said, "There's certainly not much scenic about these South Plains, just brown grass, dust, and miles and miles of cotton fields."

"Yeah, I guess so," Buck said. "But a few miles from here, there's actually some scenery."

"You got to be kidding," Jordan said.

"No. It actually is kind of pretty when you go off the Caprock and look out over the mesas. That's the scenery that, along with the Big Bend country, the rest of the country might believe is really Texas. They've damned up one of the Brazos River tributaries for water and made a pretty little lake, where some people have homes and weekend cabins.

"I'll show you the lake, and then we can double back and I'll show you the falls on the river. They aren't Niagara or even Washington's Snoqualmie, but not bad for Texas." Buck said.

A few hours later, when they stood outside the car looking at the falls near a sign warning tourists to watch out for snakes, Jordan said, "You're right Buck. Not bad for Texas. Now let's head back west."

Chapter 12
Century's End at Land's End

So Buck and Jordan went back to their homes of the last few years of the twentieth century, and after Jordan got a couple of royalty checks from my inheritance, he quit his job too. He liked the Bay Area, but he had made no real friends, particularly no real women friends.

Buck already had turned in his notice at the hardware store, but he never gave a thought about leaving his beloved Olympic Peninsula even if it meant risking his life every time he drove his old pickup onto the winding two-lane, frequently wet and slick U.S. 101. After Jordan listed his townhouse with a realtor, Buck called him and told him to come up for a long visit.

"Maybe you'll realize there is not a place nicer in the whole world and decide to live here," Buck said.

"It's one of the places I'm considering," Jordan said. "But I suspect I'm more of a city boy than you. Maybe I'll get me a place in Seattle. Then we can get together anytime we want after a short drive and a ferry ride."

"Yeah, that would work," Buck said. "So what would you do in Seattle?"

"I want to indulge my fantasy of earning a few song royalties on my own, and I hear Seattle has a good music scene. Ray Charles got his start there."

"I thought he was from Georgia?"

"He was born and raised in Georgia, but when he grew up he moved to Seattle and met Quincy Jones and moved on to fame from Seattle."

"So come on up. I don't think Quincy still lives here, but they do have some good music up here, especially if you like folk music. Maybe it's because we're close to Canada. Lot of good folk musicians come from there. They've put together a music festival up here in Port Angeles on Memorial Day weekend. It's called the Juan de Fuca Arts Festival. And I got a friend in Richland who tells me they're working on organizing one on the eastern side of the state on the banks of the Columbia River."

"I know about Richland," Jordan said. "It got its start as the company town for the Hanford Nuclear Reservation, where they processed plutonium for nuclear weapons for forty years, supposedly the most contaminated place on Earth, but I guess that's all relative. I figure the Mississippi River around New Orleans or some other river estuaries on the East Coast could kill you as easily as radiation if you spent time in their polluted waters."

"Actually, the Columbia is really a clean river, probably one of the cleanest big rivers in the country, because it doesn't have a bunch of big cities to dump sewage into it. And the radioactive contamination on the Hanford site is mostly stewing in more than a hundred huge old underground tanks, so you're okay as long as those tanks don't all break apart and start leaking a bunch of the radioactive mess. At least that's what my friend tells me. But I still worry a little because more than sixty of those tanks already have leaked," Buck said.

"I also have a friend -- well, maybe acquaintance would be more accurate, anyway a PR associate who works at Hanford -- who says there's no evidence that any are leaking now," Jordan said.

"I'll leave it to you to decide if you want to believe a guy who makes his living trying to polish the actions of a federal government contractor. All I can tell you is that Hanford scares the hell out of the frou-frou people over here on the west side of the state and all those aging hippies in Portland."

"Yeah, my friend told me that, too," Jordan said. "As far as making your living working for a federal government contractor, remember that I comfortably did that for the past decade or so. And I was working for a company that's still making deadly weapons, not cleaning up after them."

"Yes, I know that. I wasn't making any judgments. I was just telling you what the people on the west side of Washington and Oregon think."

"So what do you think?" Jordan said.

Buck was silent for a few seconds. Then he said, "What do I think? I really can't tell you what I think over the phone. Some things are too hard to explain in a brief conversation. I'll tell you what; I'll send you an e-mail."

The message came three days later.

"Jordan,

"You asked what I think about the nuclear society. It's something I have thought about over the years. Here's what I think:

"There's a contingent of people who think milking a cow is animal abuse, not to mention knocking one in the head with a hammer and turning it into steaks. But we don't seem all that upset about killing human beings.

"I read somewhere that Americans had spent almost seventy trillion of their tax dollars on nuclear weapons. That's trillion with a T, not billion with a B, not a measly million with an M, and certain not hundreds with an H -- the only multiple zero dollar figure that I ever figured I would count.

"So what did we get for our money? We ended World War II, but we did that with two bombs that killed more than a hundred thousand people immediately and probably twice that many from the residual effects of the injuries and radiation rained on Hiroshima and Nagasaki.

"We haven't used those weapons since then, but we've spent those trillions of dollars making sure we got thousands of them, I think somewhere in the range of 30,000 to

40,000. And each one of those weapons, about four times more powerful than those puny firecrackers we dropped on the Japanese, could wipe out more than a million people.

"And because we got those weapons, the rest of the nations that want to play in this frivolous game of military insanity decided they needed these weapons too. So now about ten nations have a combined total of thousands of nuclear weapons that could put this old earth back in the same condition it was when the cockroaches were the highest form of life.

"But those weapons have been a deterrent to World War III, people say. Maybe so; maybe not. Maybe the United States and the Soviet Union would have gone to war if the two K's -- Kennedy and Khrushchev -- had not possessed the diplomatic wisdom to work out a way to save their collective political faces and the rest of the world's asses. Remember the whole crisis was caused because the Soviets were trying to set up nuclear missiles in Cuba. If we had no nuclear missiles, then what would have been the crisis?

"What would have happened if Harry Truman had told the soldiers and scientists to go home and throw out the witches brew magic formula they had spent three years developing? The bombs had done their job; we don't need them anymore. Would the world have been at peace? Would the Russians or English or French or Chinese have not

pursued their development of these horrible weapons? Probably not, but who knows. Was it worth sixty or so trillion dollars to bring the world to this state of edgy peace? Probably not, but who knows.

"So what do I think, Jordan? I think I would have liked to live back when a dorky-looking William Bonney could gain fame by shooting people with six-guns and shotguns in range wars and jail breaks. Today he wouldn't even make the front page unless he kidnapped a pretty white girl while doing all his killing.

"So when are you moving to the Pacific Northwest? We can always move a few miles north across the Strait of Juan de Fuca to Canada, where they devastate their government budgets on healthcare rather than war planes and bombs.

"Your friend, Buck."

Jim Outseagle was Buck's friend who lived in Richland. Jim never found the money or perhaps the time to finish his college education, but his experience on nuclear submarines had allowed him to get a job with the Hanford contractor responsible for managing the waste tanks.

Jim had a house in Port Angeles, which he acquired when he paid his sister for her half of the inheritance from their grandmother. Shortly after his daughter and only child had gone away to the University of

Washington, Jim learned that his wife had been screwing his boss. Jim quit his job, took his pension money, filed for divorce, and moved to his grandmother's old house. He was glad to be away from Hanford and its memories and closer to his daughter.

In December 1999 Buck and Jim were at a restaurant on First Street in Port Angeles when two Customs inspectors chased and tackled a Mideastern man who ran away from them after they asked him to get out of the car he was driving off the Victoria ferry.

"It turned out the rented car had explosives in it," Buck told Jordan when he called him. "The authorities are speculating that he planned to blow something up and spoil the millennium celebration for a lot of people."

Jordan and Buck celebrated the millennium in Seattle, slept off their New Year's Eve revelry at Jordan's condo in the Lower Queen Anne section of the city near the Space Needle. Around noon they walked a few blocks to their favorite sports bar, Floyds, where they had a couple of bloody marys and some appetizers. Then they walked back to Jordan's place and watched football bowl games for what was left of the day and into the night. The next day Jordan drove Buck to his house on the peninsula. As they crossed the Hood Canal Bridge, Jordan said, "Well, it's a new century. Wonder what it will hold?"

"Oh, I imagine some joy, some sorrow, a little fun, and a lot of pain -- just like the previous ones," Buck said.

"I guess you're right," Jordan said. "But I wonder what the big news will be. Like will we get into any more wars? Or will the big earthquake finally hit? Or will a hurricane blow away Miami or drown New Orleans? Or will another nut blow up a building? And where will the next serial killer put everybody in his town on edge?"

"I expect the answer to all those questions probably is yes, except maybe the first one. I figure this country learned its lesson about wars -- big ones anyway -- in Vietnam. Now we only get in ones we can win real quick and not get bogged down. Surely we won't have a congress and president stupid enough to get us into another quagmire war.

"And maybe the earthquakes and hurricanes that destroy major American cities will hold off for another century, but I think we've been living on borrowed time, so I figure we'll have at least one event that will have all the journalists and politicians crying crocodile tears and looking for somebody to blame and hoping this horrible turn of fortune furthers their careers."

"And the recent arrest in my little hometown proves that we still got the nuts who want to blow up buildings, and serial killers. Maybe if our leaders have learned their lesson about wars, we could paraphrase that Biblical passage to read,

'There will always be serial killers or rumors of serial killers,' in America at least."

Buck and Jordan sat silent for a few minutes as the car moved past the trees on Highway 104. As they neared the junction of 104 and 101, Jordan said, "Why do you think America has so many wacko killers?"

"I don't know," Buck said. "Maybe it's because we got so many white people."

"Say what?"

"Think about it," Buck said. "How many serial killers have been black guys or Asians or even Hispanics? Yeah, they got that guy in Atlanta, but he's still claiming his innocence. But it seems the majority of serial killers are white guys who look like every other white guy and most of the time, except when they are strangling, raping, or stabbing their victims, apparently act like every other white guy.

"White guys are mean motherfuckers. Maybe not literally. No, maybe literally. Oedipus was a white guy, wasn't he? But I guess he wasn't really mean, just a motherfucker. Anyway, what nations have killed more people than any others in the history of the world? What nations dropped the bombs that killed all those women and children in Dresden and Hiroshima and Nagasaki? What nations have almost wiped out entire races, be they European Jews, or the people who inhabited this continent before the white guys showed up? What nation had a king who cut off several of his wives' heads and lived a long life honored by his people? What nation had legal slavery longer than most of the rest of the world, and then had a war in which thousands of white guys killed each other when their leaders could not be rational about dealing with an economic and social problem that surely could have been solved some other way? I mean, what do Stalin, Hitler, and Saddam Hussein have in common? All white guys."

Clean-shaven Jordan looked over at his passenger with a full beard as they approached the junction to U.S. 101 and Discovery Bay, smiled, and said, "Yeah, and they all had hair under their noses. Seriously what about the African dictator Edi Amin, that fat Chinese guy, Mao the Dung or whatever his name was, and those Japanese warlords of the '30s and '40s who tortured everybody they took prisoner in their effort to conquer all of Asia?"

Jordan continued with his counter-argument. "I suspect the white guys come off as the baddest badasses because they've gotten more efficient at killing people. Given the opportunity, the blacks, browns, and those with the different eye angles can be just as deadly and vicious as us honkies. I tend to subscribe to Mark Twain's theory that our problem is that we're all members of the damned human race."

"Still I believe in evolution, and I say the living apes give evidence of how proficient white guys are at killing," Buck said.

"Oh, how's that?" Jordan asked.

"You see, Africa has chimpanzees and the gorillas, and Asia has orangutans, but Europe has no white apes. I figure that's because the white humans killed them all."

"Maybe so," Jordan said. "But I suspect you are giving the white guys too much credit in the killing area. Heck, I wouldn't be surprised -- if we don't do something about letting every crazy person have guns -- in the coming years to see some non-Caucasian try to outdo Charles Whitman and those other whacko white shooters."

Buck shrugged and said, "Well, I hope not, but you may be right. Maybe we'll be lucky and not live long enough to see that."

Early in February of that first year of the new century, Jordan could sense that Buck was in a gloomy mood. Jordan asked his friend," What's the matter?"

"Oh, I guess I'm just sad about Charles Schultz dying. You know I might have had the opportunity to meet him once if only I had not been timid or afraid to burst another of the many balloons in my life. Just think, I might have been able to claim both Flash Golden and Charles Schulz as friends."

"Well, one out of two ain't bad," Jordan said. "And, who knows? Maybe you'll meet some more famous people. To paraphrase a line in our mutual favorite movie, 'Sooner or later, everybody comes to the Olympic Peninsula.' If they live long enough most famous people will explore the beautiful Pacific Northwest and will cross the Strait of Juan de Fuca to equally beautiful British Columbia."

But it was Jordan in the summer of that year whose courage faded when he had the opportunity to say hello to someone who came to the Olympic Peninsula. He and Buck were on the ferry returning to Port Angeles after having a few beers in Victoria and spending a long weekend wandering around Vancouver Island.

As they drank coffee in the ferry commissary, Jordan recognized the voice in the booth behind him that still sounded familiar after thirty years. When the man sitting across from the woman called her Susan and asked when the flight from Sea-Tac arrived in Houston, Jordan motioned to Buck, who followed him to the other end of the ferry.

"Why not say hello to her?" Buck said. "It's been thirty years for chrissake."

"What good would it do?" Jordan said. "I don't know, but I guess I've decided that lost and failed loves should stay in the past unless there is some hope for reviving those loves. And there's no hope for that, not that I would want to, even though she still appeared to be a lovely woman. I mean as I glanced back she had a few wrinkles, but I guess, who doesn't when you reach your sixth decade of living. I guess I wouldn't mind saying hello to her, but....

"But what?"

"Look, I don't mean to be mean. I just mean....Oh, hell, I don't know what I mean. I just don't want to talk to Susan, who I haven't seen since the '70s. Maybe I'm afraid she won't speak to me. Or maybe I'm afraid of what she might say to me. Maybe I'm afraid she will say something like, 'God, Jordan, you've gotten old and ugly.' And maybe I'm afraid she might be right."

The next encounter with a friend from decades past came a year later on the first Sunday in September. Many of the people who catch the Port Angeles-Victoria ferry kill some time wandering through a building of shops and restaurants called the Landing. The most prominent of the shops in that year was an art gallery that was a cooperative effort by a collection of amateur and professional artists who lived on the Olympic Peninsula. The artists took turns minding the gallery. Buck was a member of the art guild, and it was his day on duty when the two women walked through the door to view the artwork.

Buck and Beth did not recognize each other, but they recognized their common accent, and Beth recognized Buck's name immediately, before he remembered that Beth Chertha had become Beth Bultin.

Beth's middle-aged daughter was somewhat surprised at the vigorous hug her mother gave this man in the little shop two thousand miles away from Texas. Buck and Beth quickly exchanged abbreviated biographies. Beth was a recent widow. Her late husband, Hunter, had taken over her father's car business, and they had a good life in Lubbock until he dropped dead from a heart attack in the dealership showroom.

As Beth and her daughter, Barbara, headed toward the ferry, Buck asked them if they were returning from Victoria through Port Angeles.

"Yes," Beth said.

"When?" Buck asked.

"Two days from now on the midday ferry," Beth said.

"Do you have time for a late lunch?" Buck asked.

Beth looked at Barbara and took her daughter's puzzled shrug as meaning "up to you Mom."

"Maybe," Beth replied.

"Are you taking your car across?" Buck asked.

"No, we parked it at the lot at the end of the street," Barbara said.

"Good. Since you're walking off the ferry, I'll be waiting and see if you have time for lunch. If you don't, that's okay. At least I'll see you again. I'll be waiting on Tuesday. That's the eleventh, right?"

Americans will forever remember what happened on that Tuesday morning and how they watched their television sets in horror and wondered how nineteen crazed young men armed with nothing but boxcutters could kill more than three thousand people in three airliners, Lower Manhattan's Twin Towers, and the Pentagon.

But Buck was not watching television. Buck seldom watched television, and on this day he was waiting for the Coho Ferry to arrive from Victoria. He heard the few other people on the pier talking about the terrorists and the chaos, but he could not leave to watch television because he did not want to miss greeting Beth and her daughter. He already had made reservations for lunch at the hotel seafood restaurant overlooking the little downtown beach and the pier tower.

The trio ate their lunch in an angry daze, the same emotional state in which most Americans found themselves on that late summer day. Then Beth and Barbara learned that all U.S. flights were grounded indefinitely.

"What do we do now?" Barbara asked. "Do we rent a car and drive back to Lubbock?"

"No," said her mother. "I'm sure they will resume flights as soon as they figure out what's happening. We'll just have to rent a hotel room in Seattle and bide our time."

It was the first time that Buck wished he had a big house rather than his two-bunk, one-bathroom cabin, so he could offer the two women a free room. Instead, he said, "Why not just stay here at this downtown hotel for at least a day? I could be your personal guide to Olympic National Park's

Hurricane Ridge or maybe we could drive over to Sol Duc.? I would offer my place for you to stay, but it's so small."

The two women looked at each other. Then Barbara asked, "What do you think, Mom? We don't know anyone in Seattle, and besides we've already seen the Space Needle and the waterfront, so I guess we'd just be bored."

Beth looked pleased at her daughter's positive attitude toward Buck's suggestion. She looked down at her glass of iced tea and said, "Okay. Let's see if we can get a room here."

There were rooms available, and Buck wondered where he should take Beth and Barbara to dinner. For more than two decades Buck had told visitors that for a poor port town, Port Angeles has a surprising number of really good restaurants encompassing most of the international cuisines as well as good solid American food. Jordan, a more experienced traveler than Buck, had agreed with him that the Port Angeles restaurants compared with those in Seattle and other large cities.

Buck left the two women to get settled in their rooms and drove west back to his cabin. He wanted to collect his thoughts, put on more cheap aftershave lotion, and recheck his appearance. He wondered why he was so excited about meeting Beth Chertha Bultin forty years after they were emerging adults in another era. Maybe it was because in the ensuing years he had never met a woman he thought he wanted to marry.

He had met women. He had dated women. He had taken women to his bed. He remembered Candy, the young divorcee who freed him from virginity. He remembered the brothels of Tijuana and the pretty young women in Okinawa. He remembered the single women tourists who had been his kayak clients. He remembered the women he met in the Victoria and Vancouver pubs and the two schoolteachers from Colorado who were having drinks at the First Street bar the night before they would embark on a four-day hiking trek into the park. How could he forget that night -- his first and only ménage a trois.

He also remembered how some of those women had looked with a mixture of pity and horror at his scarred leg. He also remembered how the woman in Vancouver in 1970 had arisen from the hotel room bed and dressed when he told her how he had gotten the scars.

"I'm sorry," she said, "but I don't sleep with war criminals."

As she walked out the door, Buck wondered if she had ever spent time in San Francisco.

Now as Beth and her daughter unpacked in their hotel room, he asked himself, "Why do I find this widowed grandmother more attractive than just about every other woman I have known since I met her in the fall of 1960?"

Then as he remembered the other woman who had remained in his memory as long as Beth. He remembered Angelina. She was even more beautiful than Beth. But Angelina was a beautiful Mexican whore, and Beth was a pretty privileged daughter of a Texas businessman. And now Beth was a wealthy widow, and Buck, while delivered from his lifetime of poverty by my inheritance, was in some ways still the insecure West Texas kid who had never been on an airplane until one took him to the Marine Corps Recruit Depot in San Diego.

He made dinner reservations at his favorite restaurant on First Street. A few minutes past six o'clock, he arrived at the hotel and used the house phone to call Beth in her room. She was in the lobby in less than five minutes, but Barbara was not with her.

"Barbara is tired from all the traveling," Beth explained. "And she's worried about her daughter, who is understandably upset about today's events, as of course we all are. She wants to call her and comfort her and tell her everything will be okay. And I guess she wants to watch television. But I told her that I thought I would feel better if I could get this awful event off my mind for a while, so I'm looking forward to our dinner."

Buck made the perfunctory comments about being sorry that Barbara couldn't join them, but he was politely lying. He was happy that he would be alone with Beth. After all he had waited forty years for this evening even if it had come to pass on such a tragic day. When the waitress came, Buck asked Beth what kind of wine she liked.

"Oh, I don't drink wine," she said. "I'm a Southern Baptist, you know."

Buck smiled, remembered my joke, and said, "So, do you want a beer? I guess you've heard that you always need to go fishing with two Baptists because if you take just one, he'll drink all your beer."

Beth didn't laugh. Buck was not sure she even smiled. He was sorry he tried to be funny.

Then Beth said, "But that's okay. You go ahead and order whatever wine you like. I'm a Southern Baptist, but I'm also a modern woman. My husband and I entertained many times, and we served liquor. Hunter, unfortunately, did drink liquor, not much wine but bourbon and beer. Maybe that's one of the reasons he died in his early sixties." Then Buck was sure she did smile when she finished her little speech by saying, "So you go ahead and order whatever drink you like."

After what Buck took as a mild temperance lecture, he knew he needed a drink so he ordered a bottle of Washington wine. The waitress brought two glasses. Beth did not protest but simply raised her hand after the waitress had poured about an ounce. "That's enough," she said.

Buck let the waitress fill his glass and drank it quicker than he should have because he already had drunk two beers before he picked up Beth. He drank the beers because Buck never got over being a shy boy, and he found that a couple of ounces of alcohol reduced his timidity and made him an acceptable social person, and he wanted to be social with Beth Chertha Bultin.

"So, Buck, you never married?" Beth said. He had heard the question many times before, and he never knew how to answer other than to say, "No."

Most of the time he was content with that simple answer because he was talking with someone whose opinion of him did not matter. This evening was different, and after the two beers and glass of wine, Buck felt compelled to say in a voice loud enough to garner glances from the people at a nearby table, "But I'm not gay."

Buck could see that Beth was embarrassed, and he was even more embarrassed by his elaboration on a simple answer to a simply question.

"I'm sorry, Buck. I certainly did not mean to imply that just because you have not married that you are..." Beth paused and then finished her sentence, "...homosexual."

Buck finished his second glass of wine and said, "Gay."

"Pardon me?" Beth said.

"Gay," Buck said. "The politically correct word is gay. I know it's screwed up the meaning of a long established adjective in the English language, but homosexual men seem to want to be called gay. I guess homosexual is still okay to say in polite company, certainly better than fruit, fag, or queer, just as Negro is better than nigger or jigaboo. But if you want to be PC, the word is gay."

Beth looked down at her salad, this time apparently feeling that she had been the subject of a lecture, and said, "I'm sorry, I guess I was trying to be politically correct, and I thought homosexual would be the best word because, well, in Texas, there are people who still use those words you just mentioned. But, Buck, I'm not one of those people."

Then Beth smiled and said, "I know this sounds almost bigoted, certainly a cliché, but, Buck, some of my friends -- maybe not my best friends -- are gay and lesbian. Still I must admit that I am not comfortable with saying I think it's proper and normal because it's not normal and the Bible says it's a sin. Still I don't hate my friends who are homosexual. Or gay or lesbian, if that is what they want to be called.

"I know you people up here don't agree with our politics down in Texas. That's clear by your votes for Bill Clinton and Al Gore. But still I'm not going to apologize for believing in proper behavior."

Now Buck was not only embarrassed; he was ashamed -- ashamed that he had made the comment that had led to ruining what he had hoped would be a wonderful evening. He also was a little ashamed that he could not stand up for his libertarian belief that human beings have the right to do whatever they want in their lives without judgment or condemnation as long as they don't hurt other people. But Buck knew that he was the host for the evening and Beth was a nice lady, and he should follow a basic longstanding principle of decency and subjugate argument for politeness. He had learned that from his mother.

"I'm sorry, Beth," Buck said. "Let's talk about something else. Let's just stay off the subject of morals, religion, politics, or the merits or evils of alcohol and talk about whatever you want to talk about. Tell me about your grandchildren, and I'll tell you about my Labrador retriever."

Then Buck paused and said, "Damn, I didn't mean to equate your grandchildren with my dog."

Beth laughed, took his hand, and said, "No, that's all right. I have a dog I love like a grandchild, too. Sometimes maybe more because dogs often are a lot easier to deal with than teenagers."

They completed the dinner without anymore awkward moments. The topic of the conversation naturally came around to the horrific acts of the hijackers.

"The world is really getting scary. Almost makes you want to go back in the woods and hide," Beth said.

Buck smiled and said, "Yeah. I guess I got a head start on that. I guess I've been hiding in the woods every since I got back from Vietnam."

When he walked Beth back to the hotel, Buck asked her what time she and her daughter wanted to meet for the trip up the Olympic Mountains.

"I'll have to call you, Buck. Barbara has started to miss her family, and she's concerned about getting home to her kids, so we may need to drive back to Seattle so we can get home as soon as they start flying planes again."

Buck was not surprised when Beth called shortly after eight o'clock the next morning and said she and Barbara had decided to drive back to Seattle that morning.

"Thank you for the evening and your hospitality. You're a nice man," she said.

Buck hung up the phone and thought about her comment, 'You're a nice man.' He had heard it before. He had been a nice boy, now a nice man. Now he realized that Jordan perhaps knew what he was doing when he hurried out of the booth to the other end of the ferry the year before. I guess lost loves and lost dreams are forever lost, he thought.

But he thought maybe not when he received the letter from Beth two weeks later thanking him for the nice evening and offering to return his hospitality.

"If you ever decide to quit hiding in the woods, I hope you will consider visiting your native state. Although we are a long way from an ocean and the South Plains are nothing like the Olympic Mountains, the people are nice, like you. I hope you will keep in touch."

In between their separate encounters with women in their past, Buck and Jordan expanded their friendship with Jim Outseagle, whom Buck met when he was getting a bicycle tire fixed in a shop on Port Angeles' Front Street. They spent time reminiscing in various restaurants, pubs, and sports bars in Port Angeles, Victoria, and Seattle.

Buck and Jordan drank beers while Jim had coffee, tea, or club soda. He explained to his two friends that one of the reasons his wife gave for leaving him was he was getting drunk too often. He believed the main reason she left was because she would rather have the other, richer man as a husband, but he thought about her comments about his drinking and decided she probably was right, that he was drinking too much. Jim had read about how Native Americans seemed to be more affected by alcohol than Caucasians and thought perhaps his genealogy was coming into play, so he decided to quit boozing, something he did without obvious pain, and something that Buck and Jordan doubted they could do.

After a few rounds of the regionally produced brews, Buck and Jordan often would begin the political discussions. Buck, who never had company-paid insurance or filled out a timecard, probably could best be described as a libertarian. Jim, being a union man, voted for Democrats, although he was finding it more difficult to get excited about all of their Hollywood fans and gun-control advocates. Jordan, who had worked for oil companies and then government contractors and had voted for several Republicans in his lifetime, considered himself a middle-of-the-roader. In the twentieth century his votes had been for Johnson, Humphrey, McGovern, Ford, Reagan, Reagan, Bush, Clinton, and Clinton.

Even though that record might not appear to be a middle-of-the-roader but rather a guy who went from a Democrat to Republican to Democrat again, Jordan never considered himself either a Democrat or a Republican. He voted for Johnson because LBJ's campaign people convinced Jordan and the majority of voters that Goldwater would rush to get the country into some nuclear war. He voted for Humphrey because, even though he was Johnson's vice president, Jordan thought he would work harder than Nixon to get the nation out the bloody mess in Vietnam. He voted for McGovern because Nixon proved Jordan's fears about him four years before were well founded. He voted for Ford probably because he had recently gone to work for the oil company and was trying to fit in with his co-workers, and besides Jerry Ford had done a good job of getting the country back on track after the Watergate scandal. He voted for Ronald Reagan because -- well, because he was Ronald Reagan. How could a fellow who was a kid in the 1950s not vote for a guy who starred in all those Western movies and hosted TV's *Death Valley Days*? He voted for the first George Bush, who had been Jordan's congressman when he moved to Houston and seemed like a nice guy. He voted for Clinton twice because he also seemed like a nice guy who was smarter than the two nice guys he was running against. Now, Jordan thought, the Oval Office anteroom escapades had proved that Jordan had been mistaken about Clinton being that smart. He didn't believe George H.W. Bush or Bob Dole would ever have done something as dumb as what got Bill Clinton into trouble. Actually the only vote Jordan cast before 2000 he probably didn't regret was the one he cast for Jerry Ford.

Buck had not voted for a Democratic or Republican presidential candidate since he voted for Barry Goldwater, the closest thing to a libertarian that the Republicans ever produced with the exception of an obscure congressman named Ron Paul from a district on the coast of Texas. Buck also voted for former Colorado Governor Dick Lamm one year, but most of the time he figured the choices were akin to choosing between being shot or hanged and went fishing on the second Tuesday in November. Jim also skipped most of the elections, but he voted for Bill Clinton both times because he figured he might get some programs like healthcare for all Americans through the Congress. He, like Jordan, was disappointed.

But still they would argue politics after a few beers. The next morning Jordan and Buck would agree that it probably wasn't their convictions that sparked the spirited discussions -- the cliché that Jordan and Buck would use. It was more likely the alcohol that ignited the fire in their aging male egos.

But sooner or later, everybody -- be they ex-wives, lost loves, or first ladies -- comes to the Olympic Peninsula. The first lady came in the summer of 2003.Buck, Jordan, and Jim were going to dinner when they saw her and her contingent going into the Italian restaurant across First Street.

"She's obviously a lot smarter than he is," Jordan said.

Jim asked, "What makes you think that?"

Jordan said, "My reasoning isn't political. It's this: while he's packing for his summer vacation in Texas, his wife is spending a week with friends on the Olympic Peninsula in the other Washington, the one that's about thirty degrees cooler. I've spent some time in our nation's capital, and it often is as hot and miserable as Texas."

"Remember what Flash used to say," Buck said. "He liked Texas. He just didn't like where they built it. But I guess millions of people aren't as troubled by hundred-degree weather and ocean beaches lacking mountains in the background as we are. Otherwise Texas would not be the nation's second most populous state."

"I still say most Texans, given a choice, would not vacation in Texas in August," Jordan said.

"Maybe the fact that he spends his summer vacation in Texas is a clue to why so many of us who lack riches or power tend to vote Democratic," Jim said. "You have to wonder about the leadership of people who have the resources and opportunity to enjoy the summer rather than working on roads, mowing yards, or standing over fast-food grills and yet still choose to spend their time risking melanoma or heat stroke."

"Maybe his wife will go back to the ranch and say, 'You've got to get over this weird affectation for making journalists and your cabinet members suffer in the Texas heat. Come with me next summer to someplace where Anglos like us are supposed to spend our time," Buck said. "Of course, she won't say that, but the country and the world would be better off if she did."

"What do you mean by that?" Jordan asked.

"I mean if he hadn't bought that goddamned ranch and if he had stayed in Houston, Dallas, or Austin, where rich city boys like him belong, maybe he wouldn't have wanted to start playing cowboys and Iraqis," Buck said.

"So you don't believe we should have gone into Iraq?" Jim asked.

"No, at least not this time," Buck said. "We should have kept all of our guns in Afghanistan, where the villains really are. I'm afraid Iraq is going to turn into a quagmire, just like the place where I got this ugly leg. You know why?"

"No. Why?"

"Because, just like in Vietnam. We can't tell the good guys from the bad guys."

"I got another problem with going into Iraq this time," Jordan said.

"What's that?" Jim asked.

"Let me explain my reasoning in a parable. I don't know about you Jim, but Buck and I, being Texas kids, grew up on western movies. There were two kinds of western movies -- the Saturday afternoon shoot-em-up and the weeknight western. They differed mainly in their heroes. Saturday afternoon movie heroes had moral fibers beyond reproach. They didn't smoke, drink, kiss girls, or fight dirty by doing anything other than pounding the bad guy into submission with their fists or shooting him in a fair gun duel. And if the situation had to come to gunplay, the western hero never drew his gun first.

"The heroes of the weeknight westerns, often the same men who were in the post-World War II battle movies, could do things that were forbidden in the Saturday afternoon movies. Sometimes they smoked. Often they would walk into a saloon and tell the barkeep to give them a glass of whiskey. And by the end of the movie they kissed some girl. Hell, some of them kicked the bad guy in a fight or even hit him over the head with a chair. But, like their Saturday afternoon counterparts, none of them ever drew his gun and shot first.

"I never thought about it then, but it has since occurred to me in the ensuing years of grueling adulthood that most of the Saturday afternoon heroes had no visible means of support. They just rode from town to town with their sidekick and saved the citizens from villains who usually were trying to cheat good people out of their ranches or secretly running a stagecoach-robbing business or quite often pursuing both endeavors at the same time.

"Perhaps these Saturday afternoon good guys were like the current foreman on this big ranch called the United States of America -- born into wealth and privilege, never having to worry about whether they could afford that fine stallion and fancy saddle. Maybe never having to worry about money for his education or feeding his family is why he was willing to spend billions of dollars to invade a country that has no nuclear weapons and made no noises about attacking our country while saying we can use diplomacy to deal with a country that has nuclear weapons and has threatened to hurl them at the American West Coast, where they could land smack dab in the middle of Front Street here or maybe on my condo at the bottom of Seattle's Queen Anne Hill.

"Now I know this won't be the first time that we've devastated the national treasury on a war, but I think it's the first time in our lifetimes that we drew our guns and began shooting while the other guy was standing there claiming to the rest of the people in the world saloon that he didn't want to fight and wasn't wearing any guns.

"And most of the other guys in the saloon -- the Frenchies, the Germans, the Canadians -- were saying, 'Hold on, let him explain, give him a little more time. He's not threatening you. We don't see any guns. Yes, he is a low-life sidewinder, but you just cain't go shootin' everybody you think is a no-good varmint.'

"The foreman and his ranchhands are mostly of the age that surely watched Saturday afternoon movies. But if they did, I guess they missed the lessons about not shooting first."

When Jordan finished his parable, Buck said, "Yeah, and I guess they didn't read *The Ox-Bow Incident* either."

Jim took a sip of his club soda and said, "Let me tell you one other thing wrong with how we're going about straightening out everybody else when we got plenty of problems of our own in this country. I can explain the cause for this international mess in a single word -- religion."

"Oh shit," Jordan said with a big grin. "We've already got off on a tangent talking politics. Now you want to talk religion?"

"I can't really separate it from politics," Jim said. "To continue in your parable mode, I figure the ranch foreman figured he was right because of that ancient but enduring canard of having God on his side.

"It doesn't matter that all the members of that outlaw gang called Al Qaeda also are claiming they have God on their side, except they call him Allah. Still, our American ranch foreman knows he's right, and it's okay to shoot whomever we decide are bad guys because we're riding with Jesus and our leader says he's getting his guidance from the big guy himself.

"And I know there are people who are asking what about all those other guys who claim they're riding with Jesus? People like that old guy over in Rome and a whole bunch of other preachers, even if they don't have their own universities and television shows. And that former president who goes around the country building houses for poor people and around the world trying to help people get along. They say they talk to Jesus and God everyday, too, and they don't think he wants us to be shooting anyone.

"But they're just misguided old guys or pansies or appeasers, people who didn't understand that Americans, least not Texans, take no shit from anyone, say the hands who ride with the foreman," Jim said.

Buck said, "That's enough of this serious talk for tonight, you goddamned atheist. Let's drink up and talk about some things fine or fun, things like fishing, football, or even fucking. Something that counts in this world."

Buck, the kayak guide, knew the most about fishing. Jordan, who had been a second-string defensive back in high school and once met Tom Landry as a young reporter, knew the most about football. Buck and Jordan figured that Jim knew the most about fucking because he had slept next to a woman every night for twenty years before she left him for the contractor executive whose penis may have been smaller but whose monthly paycheck was three times bigger than Jim's.

Jim was better looking than Buck and Jordan. At least that's what Buck and Jordan thought. Buck had never been able to accept the fact that some women found his scarred leg anything but repulsive. Jordan wished he still had the hair he put under his football helmet. Both Buck and Jordan wished they had Jim's smooth blended complexion rather than the wrinkled, ruddy faces they inherited from their ancestors -- the ancestors who, according to Buck, killed all the white apes in Europe.

Jim wished he had not been cuckolded. He knew Buck had not been cuckolded since he had never been married. He didn't know whether Jordan had been cuckolded by some admirer of Susan. Jordan had been cuckolded, but he never knew it, just as

Mason never knew that he had been cuckolded by Jordan. Or maybe he did. Jordan sometimes wondered about how Mason really felt about losing his wife to another man.

Jordan and Buck did not have to wonder how Jim felt about losing his wife to his boss. At first he was bitter. He was mostly bitter because the breakup came at a crucial time in his daughter's life. Shanna Outseagle had not expected to spend her first college year wondering about her parents' acrimonious divorce. But she was able to persevere in her classes and spend an occasional weekend with her father on the Olympic Peninsula.

After Jim had pondered his breakup for several months, he concluded that it was destined to be. He realized he and his wife had little in common, and he wondered how they had stayed together as long as they had. Jim, because of his near-poverty childhood, was frugal. Brenda had no concept of saving money. Jim wanted more children, but after a difficult pregnancy with Shanna, Brenda said one was enough. Brenda enjoyed the social opportunities afforded to her by the church she had attended since she was child. Jim, the atheist, went inside churches only for weddings and funerals. Brenda, for most of their marriage, had an occasional glass of wine while Jim guzzled several beers and whiskeys.

Yes, Jim thought, she and the asshole executive are a better match, but still the fact that his wife had left him for another man, a man he considered less of a man than he, gnawed at him, and the raw wound to his ego would sometime be obvious to Jordan and Buck by his comments.

"Remember, money makes the man," he would say.

Sometimes Jim would lament not completing college. "I figure with an engineering degree and a few years of apprenticeship in corporate sycophancy, I could have been as good a brown-noser and ass-kisser as the rest of them," he would say.

"I got a college degree, and you probably made as much money at Hanford with your Navy nuke experience as I ever did with my journalism degree," Jordan said.

"What can I say? I guess you didn't master the skills of sycophancy either," Jim said.

"It's for sure, I never did," Buck said. "You both made a lot more money than I have."

"Yeah, but you got to be your own boss," Jim said. "You didn't have to take a bunch of shit from prissy executives or crude supervisors, some of whom were dumber than dirt."

"No," Buck said. "But you can't eat pride."

"Who says you can't? I've had to swallow mine many times," Jim said.

In 2003 Jim suffered a hurt a thousand times greater than any pain caused by wounded pride. His daughter was murdered. She was in Seattle's downtown Pioneer Square district on a Saturday night with a boyfriend when what started out as a simple mugging turned bloody. The young mugger had a pistol and, intentionally or unintentionally -- no one will ever know but the shooter -- the pistol was fired into Shanna's chest. The killer ran into the night, and the coroner's office called Jim about an hour before the sun rose over the Strait of Juan de Fuca.

Jim claimed his daughter's body, and Buck and Jordan drove him across the Cascade Mountains to the funeral. Shanna was buried in a cemetery overlooking the Yakima River. Jim hugged his ex-wife as both sobbed. The new husband stood by as helpless as Buck and Jordan. Jim wiped his eyes and got into Jordan's car, and the three friends headed back west to spend the night at Jordan's condo. The three-hour ride was mostly silent and sad, as sad as the one Jordan and Buck had taken from Albuquerque to Clovis almost ten years earlier.

Jordan and Buck figured that Jim needed to do something that might take his mind off his bitterness and grief. They suggested a weeklong exploration of the beaches of Vancouver Island. During the first night at a small town watering hole and eatery, Jordan and Buck ordered beers.

"Make it three," Jim said.

Jordan and Buck were not concerned that their friend, going through an experience that most people would agree is one of the worst that can happen, was not worrying about riding on the sobriety wagon. Nor did they begrudge him when he ordered a second and third beer and then a shot of Canadian whiskey.

After he ordered a second whiskey, Jim looked into his glass and said, "I damn near lost it when that preacher started talking about God helping us get through this. I mean, how can anyone believe if there was a God, he would play with us miserable human beings like this?"

Neither Jordan nor Buck spoke. Both figured it would be good for Jim to express what he was feeling.

"I guess the most puzzling things about people's insane religious beliefs are how they could believe in a single all-mighty being who knows every little thought and act of billions of human beings and why would this supreme being care? Why, as Rick asked Ilsa, would anyone care about the problems of two little people in this crazy world?

"I know the answers to these questions are relatively simple to the believers. They are quick to tell me that this almighty God cares about us, God loves us. That rationale leads to my next questions. If God loves us, he has a funny way of showing it. If God is all powerful, if God is able to control all forces in the universe, why does he 'sendeth rain on the just and the unjust'? Why would God let my precious daughter, who had a lot to give this world, be killed by some low-life punk? Does God have ideas about justice different from most of the human beings who walk this earth? I believe most of us, if we had the power to prevent bad things from happening to good people, would do that. We wouldn't reward the greedy while punishing the benevolent. We wouldn't empower the evil while crippling the ethical.

"But, we human beings aren't God."

Jordan and Buck tried to think of something to say. Jordan thought about quoting, "This, too, will pass." Buck knew that Jim was speaking the truth and thought only of quoting John Kennedy's advice that "Life is not fair." But both sat silent, and Jim began to speak again.

"I guess it would be comforting if I believed in a heaven. It would be nice to believe that Shanna is in heaven. But I just can't make myself believe it. I mean, I wonder if people who believe there's a heaven ever really thought about eternity. Oh yes, they know it never ends, but did they ever think about when it started?

"Maybe my skepticism rests not so much with the creators and prophets as with the disciples. I mean, why can't they all get along? After all, the origins of Judaism, Christianity, and Islam have common roots back to Adam and Abraham. And they can't even agree among themselves on what is really the truth and proper ways to practice their religions. Let's see, there are the Orthodox Jews, the Reformed Jews, the Shiite Muslims, the Sunni Muslims, the Eastern Orthodox Christians, the Catholics, and more Protestant denominations than a rock star has girlfriends. And a great deal of those different religious groups, all professing a belief in the same God, Allah, or supreme being without a name seem to think anyone who doesn't toe the same line they do on the finer points of piety is going to burn in hell. Now I doubt that Adolph Hitler, Joe Stalin, or Saddam Hussein ever dreamed up a torture equal to having someone burn in eternal fire. I ask, does that sound like a merciful God to you?

"And if all the Christians and Muslims take their respective prophets at their words about damnation of nonbelievers, isn't it more than a bit absurd that hundreds of Christian soldiers are dying and thousands more are being maimed in a war to free Muslims to practice for a few transient years a lifestyle that will send them to that eternal torture?

"It just doesn't make any sense," Jim said as a wave of sad anger forced tears down his cheeks. Jordan paid the check, and they walked back to their rooms at the hotel and slept fitfully.

Neither alcohol nor exercise helped Jim's mood. Halfway through the week, he said he wanted to go back to Port Angeles. "I'm sorry, guys," Jim explained. "But I think I need to be alone for while. I'm just not in the mood to pretend I'm enjoying a vacation."

Jordan and Buck understood. They drove back to Victoria and caught the last ferry of the day across the strait.

"Are you sure you're going to be okay?" Buck asked Jim as they helped him carry his bags into his house.

Jim didn't say anything. Dumb question, Buck thought. No, he's not sure he will ever be okay again. But maybe time alone to reflect will help him. Or maybe it won't.

"We'll leave you now, but be forewarned we're going to check in with you by phone to make sure you're doing okay," Buck said.

Jim looked at his friend and gave him the closest thing to a smile he had mustered in weeks. "Thanks for caring about me," he said. "But I'm going to have to figure out how to deal with this on my own."

The next day Buck kept his word and called Jim. Jim told Buck he had decided to insulate the garage he had built behind the house after his grandmother died. "I think I just need to stay really busy, and this will help me," he said.

Buck offered to help, but Jim again declined, explaining that he still needed to be alone. Alone and busy, he said.

So Jordan went back to his condo in Seattle and Buck started painting again. He went down to Ediz Hook between the paper mill and the Coast Guard station and made sketches and took photographs of the decrepit piers, the gulls on the riprap rocks, the driftwood stumps on the black sand beach, the mountains on Vancouver Island across the water, and the mountains that rose above Port Angeles. Then he went back to his cabin and began putting acrylic paint on the cheap canvas boards he purchased at the Wal-Mart on the other end of town.

On the evening of the day he spent on the hook, Buck called Jim and asked him how the garage project was going.

"All right. May be more work than I planned though. Going a little slow."

"So do you want to take a break and come over for dinner? I'll find something to cook."

Jim thought about the invitation for a few seconds, and then said, "Maybe in a couple of days."

"Okay, so I'll expect you over on Friday night."

Jim said, "How about you come over here? You bring some beer. I probably got a pizza at the bottom the freezer if you want that."

"Tell you what, I'll bring some beer and stop and pick up a pizza."

Buck wondered if he indeed should bring some beer but realized that if Jim didn't want it, Buck needed it. When he arrived at Jim's house, Buck soon realized that Jim probably did not need any beer. On the dining table strewn with unopened mail and old newspapers was an almost empty bottle of cheap Canadian whiskey.

Still Buck needed a beer. Dealing with a friend's heartaches is not easy, Buck thought. It's not as hard as what the friend is enduring, but still it's not easy to watch a friend go through agony. And maybe a beer or two or three sometimes helps to endure that painful vigil.

Buck and Jim made their way through the twelve-pack and halfway through another bottle of Canadian whiskey that Jim pulled from the cabinet after he finished the bottle on the table.

Buck spent the night at Jim's place. He figured that he had several characteristics that made him a successful drinker. One was a strong liver. The other, like his friends Flash and Jordan, was the ability to know when not to do something foolish like insult armed men or try to drive on Highway 101 after he had consumed more than a few ounces of alcohol.

The two men's moods may have been merry when they finally went to sleep, but the serotonin levels were much lower when they stumbled awake as the sun positioned itself almost perpendicularly in the sky over the Olympic Mountains.

Buck called Jordan before he left for the ferry and told Jordan to meet Jim and him at a First Street cafe, where they could get a late breakfast.

As they ate omelets, Jim said, "I think it's time for me to go back on the wagon. I think it's time for me to see if what I find myself thinking makes sense when I'm sober."

Buck said, "You're reasonably sober now, what are you thinking?"

"I'm thinking I'm going to find the son of a bitch who took the life of my beautiful and wonderful daughter. I'm thinking I can never rest until that son of a bitch gets what's due him."

"So how do you think you are going to find him easier than the police?" Jordan asked.

"I think I have more impetus to look for him than the police do. To them, he's just one more worthless bastard who's wandering around this country killing people -- more than sixteen thousand each year. To the cops my daughter is just a statistic. To me and my ex-wife, she was a large part of our reason for living. Now just about the only reason for living I have is to bring that goddamned low-life to justice. Or maybe just kill him without bothering with a trial."

"Jim," Jordan said. "I think both Buck and I know how you feel. I'm sure it's the same way we would feel. Hell, we hate him too because of the pain he's caused a friend and his family. But let me tell you I learned from personal experience that bringing criminals to justice is better left to the authorities."

"So do you care to tell me about your experience?"

"Maybe some other time. It's kind of a complicated story."

"Okay. Maybe we can go into details later. As I said, I probably need to get a little more sober before really deciding to play avenging angel. Maybe I'll come to my senses."

"Fair enough," Jordan said. "In the meantime, just know that you have at least two friends who are here for you when you need us. But don't ask us to do any bounty hunting. As I said, I've already learned my lesson in that area."

"Will you do me one favor?" Jim asked. "Can I ride back with you to Seattle and spend a night or two at your place? I do want to talk to the police to see where they are in the investigation of my daughter's death."

"Sure," Jordan said. "Will you be ready to go in the morning? I got the cot and the futon at my place. Buck also is coming back with me. He wants to do some painting along Elliott Bay."

The next day was a typical early spring day on the Olympic Peninsula, a little rain and then a mid-day temperature near sixty degrees. The rain had stopped when the three friends came upon the two-car wreck that had blocked traffic on both lanes of U.S. 101 on the outskirts of Sequim.

Jordan and Buck saw the woman leaning hysterically against a state patrolman. Jordan recognized her immediately despite the passage of almost twenty years. She was still a beautiful woman. But he wondered if maybe his mind was playing tricks. He had reached the age when he saw many people on the streets who looked like someone he used to know. Jordan and Buck watched as EMTs led her toward the ambulance as their comrades worked to free one of the drivers from the gnarled wreckage of the two cars.

Jordan looked at Buck and said, "Do you remember Angelina Perdidos? That woman really looks like her."

Buck hesitated and said, "Of course I remember Angelina, but it's been more than forty years since I last saw her."

Jim, never having met Angelina, was concentrating on the accident. He interrupted the conversation, saying, "Looks bad. A T-bone wreck like that. Somebody must have run the light. I don't see how the driver who was broadsided could survive."

"Yeah," Jordan said, "And the other guy in the pickup is halfway through the windshield. I guess he wasn't wearing his seatbelt. Damn, it's really early in the morning for a wreck like this."

Jim said, "Jordan, I've lived more than half my life on this highway, and it's never safe -- day or night --probably not all the way from the top of the peninsula to the bottom of California."

"I guess I've spent a good part of my life on this highway, too. And it's like life anywhere. It's never safe," Buck said.

Jordan looked at his friends with perplexed resolution and said, "Look, you two, at this moment, I'm interested in neither safety statistics nor philosophy. I still think the woman they put in that ambulance may be Angelina. Let's follow it back to Port Angeles. We can wait at least one day to get to Seattle."

Jordan and Buck dropped Jim off at his house and went to the hospital. They asked about the woman involved in the wreck and were told she had been admitted for examination because of the severity of the accident.

"The gentlemen driving the cars apparently weren't that lucky. I think both of them have been declared dead," the hospital clerk said.

Jordan said, "I think the woman may be a friend of mine I knew several years ago. Was her name per chance Angelina Perdidos?

The clerk looked at her records and said, "No. Her first name is Angelina. But her last name is Renaci. Maybe she got married."

"Maybe so. What was the name of the man with her? Was his name Renaci also?

"I don't have that information. He unfortunately didn't live to be admitted," the clerk said.

Jordan asked, "Is there any way we could talk with Angelina, at the appropriate time I mean?"

"Yes. She can have visitors."

"Can we see her now?"

"I'll check with the nurses. What are your names?"

After time on the phone, the clerk came out into the hospital lobby and told Jordan and Buck that she had told the nurses to tell Angelina that former acquaintances may be inquiring about her.

"The nurse said when she mentioned your names, Ms. Renaci smiled and said to please have them come up."

As Jordan and Buck rode the elevator, Jordan thought of the other chance reunions he had -- meeting Tammy Dolcito in Neiman Marcus in Dallas and me -- formerly Flash Golden -- in the Santa Fe bar. And he thought of the one he avoided -- Susan on the ferry.

He wondered out loud to Buck what they would say to Angelina?

"What the hell happened? Where's Tammy? Who's Renaci? And how did you -- who has had such an exotic or erotic life -- land in a small town hospital after an accident leaving Costco?"

Maybe it was the pain medication or maybe it was the shock of the accident that dimmed Angelina's inhibitions. Whatever the reason, she answered all of his questions and explained the mystery that Jordan had pondered for almost twenty years.

Chapter 13
Mind Journeys to the Past

"Buck, remember how I told you when we met in 1962 I had a baby brother and I believed he had died.

"Jordan, remember the trip on the train out of Durango and the young man named Jesus who took me out of the railcar to the rear of the train. That's when he told me he was my brother. His real name was not Perez. It was Perdidos.

"And remember Anselmo, the man with my brother. As we talked, Anselmo came upon us. Jesus hurriedly motioned for me to go back into the railcar. As I closed the door I could tell that Anselmo was angry with my brother.

"I waited near the door of the car, and after, maybe five or ten minutes, Jesus came to get me. He took me back outside the car and told me how he fought with Anselmo because Anselmo wanted to kill me and Tammy -- and you and Flash.

"Jesus said he did not care about you and Flash or even Tammy. But he said, 'You are mi hermana, the only family I have. No one harms you.'

"He told me how he and Anselmo had tussled and Anselmo fell off the train into the canyon below, unnoticed because the confrontation had occurred between two closed cars.

"Jesus said he would protect me and Tammy. He promised that he would see that no one harmed us. I told him he also must promise that no one would hurt you and Flash. I told him how Flash had saved me twenty years before and how you were a good and loyal amigo. I promised him that you would not cause him any trouble. I did not know that to be true at the time, but what else could I say? Then Jesus told me to go back to Albuquerque. He said he still had my address, and he told me to wait for his letter.

"I do not know what happened with Harold Ash, but I suppose Jesus killed him. I do not know why. It could have been he and Anselmo had been sent by Cajon to kill Ash, but more likely Jesus killed him because he did not trust him. He knew that Ash was an American operative for Cajon and his main contact was Anselmo.

"The day after Tammy and I returned to Albuquerque, I got a package from Jesus. It contained thousands of dollars in cash and a letter telling me where to meet him in Tucson. Tammy was very upset about all of the things that happened, but I convinced her that we needed to get away, and she went with me to Tucson, where Jesus repeated his promise to not only protect us but also to not hurt you or Flash.

"Tammy told me that she did not bargain for a plight like this -- being stalked by Mexican drug dealers and then establishing a personal relationship with a lieutenant of the drug lord who had caused all the trouble. She said we left California to get away from these people.

"I told her, 'I know, but he's my brother. I did not know I had any family still alive. He's my little brother. I cannot abandon him.'

"Then I realized that I was being unfair to Tammy. So I told her that I would be okay, that I was a survivor and I could survive in the United States or I could survive in Mexico. 'It is not fair to involve you anymore in this because you have been so good to me,' I said. Then I told her I would like someday to find a good man to love me.

"Tammy smiled and looked at me with teary eyes and said, 'You know what, mi corazon -- sometimes I think I would too, but are there any good men out there?'

"We agreed to remain friends. I told Tammy that I would not leave her in this time of turmoil.

"Tammy said, 'Let's go to a place I think where we can hide and think. Let's go to Reno, Nevada. It's an easy city, one that we can relax in, and one that is near many pretty places.'

"Now, Buck and Jordan, you sweet men," Angelina said, "I'm grateful that you are here. I would say happy that you are here, but I cannot be happy at this time. The doctors just told me that Raul, my husband, did not survive. Raul was a good man. He was another savior. I am sorry that he is dead. I will miss him. And now I need to sleep."

While Angelina slept, Jordan and Buck asked questions of hospital officials and police officers and learned that the man who had been driving the car was Raul Renaci. The investigating officer was happy to talk with them after he learned they knew Angelina because he was trying to find out more information about both Raul and Angelina.

"His driver's license says his home address is in Reno, Nevada. He also had a passport that says he was born in Santiago, Chile," the policeman said. "The lady with him, I assume, is his wife because her driver's license says her name is Angelina Renaci. It's a Nevada license with the same address in Reno. So that's what I know. What do you know?"

"Not as much as you," Jordan said. "I knew Angelina years ago before she ever met Mr. Renaci. It was just one of those strange coincidences that Buck and I happened to come upon the wreck."

Both men were savvy enough not to mention that it was Buck who first met Angelina because neither wanted to go into details about that part of her life.

"So is she a U.S. citizen?" the policeman asked.

"Yes," Jordan said.

Jordan hoped that he was correct, that Angelina had indeed acquired her citizenship. He was growing nervous about the police learning about her past and whatever relationship she might have with her brother and his business partners. There were nights he could not sleep when he remembered the events outside of Durango and wondered what would happen if government agents ever started asking questions about his association with Jesus, Anselmo, and Harold Ash.

Jordan and I -- when I was Flash Gordon -- had never told Buck about that experience in our lives. Only seven people knew what happened on the journey from Durango to Silverton, and Jordan knew that at least three of them were now dead. He wondered about Tammy. She might be dead too. Jordan wondered not only because Tammy knew so many of the secrets in his life but also because, as he had realized when he could not sleep at night, that he had never quit caring about Tammy Dolcito.

Jordan never told Buck about Angelina's and Tammy's relationship in Albuquerque, not even when Buck commented in the hospital hall after they left Angelina's room, "Damn, it almost sounded as though Angelina and Tammy had a thing going -- with that corazon reference. That means lover in Spanish, I think. But that's the way women are, I guess. They show their affection better than us guys."

Jordan, with an inner relief, said, "Actually, it means heart, but Tammy called all of her good friends that. You understand how women are. Since we never had sisters, I guess it's good we had mothers who helped us understand that."

But as they continued to walk toward the hospital lobby, Jordan added, "Hell, the truth is, old buddy, I'll probably never understand women."

"Me neither," Buck said.

The doctors said Angelina had no injuries that required a longer stay in the hospital, just severe bruises and sprains from the impact of the collision. Jordan and Buck told her they were available to help with anything she needed.

"The first thing I must do is see that Raul's wishes are carried out. He wanted to be cremated and his ashes to be scattered in the Pacific Ocean. Raul loved the ocean. That's why we have the boat. He said he wanted his ashes scattered because he hoped some of them would someday float to the shores of his homeland."

Jordan and Buck soon learned that what Angelina called a boat was really a small yacht. It was moored in the Port Angeles harbor. Raul and Angelina also had a small boat that transported them from where the yacht was moored to the Port Angeles pier. Jordan and Buck went with Angelina in the small boat to her yacht so she could change clothes and make arrangements for Raul's cremation. They also went with Angelina when she sailed past Cape Flattery to scatter her husband's ashes in the ocean. Jim also was with them on this funeral journey. He, after all, was the seaman of the trio.

Buck and Jordan recognized the immediate attraction that Jim had for Angelina. Both understood Jim's attraction to Angelina. "It's quite normal that Jim would be attracted to Angelina," Jordan said. "She's still a beautiful woman even after entering the sixth decade of her life, just like Sophia Loren or Ann-Margret."

"I think Angelina likes Jim, too," Buck said when he and Jordan sat on the yacht's deck, drinking twelve-year-old Scotch whisky that Raul had stocked in the boat's bar. Jim and Angelina were in the steering room.

"So you think the attraction is mutual," Jordan said.

"Yeah," Buck said. "I think they got this immediate thing going. I'm happy about that. Jim needs a woman, and Angelina -- she's a woman that any man would like to have."

Buck paused and wistfully finished his thought, "She's a woman a man can't forget."

Jordan looked at his friend, smiled, and said, "Are we going to have one of those rare sessions like that time with Flash at my place in Livermore when we tell secrets that gentlemen don't tell."

Buck took a sip from his cup and said, "Naah. At least not until we have quite a bit more of this whisky."

They had more whisky, but they learned no more secrets about each other, maybe because Angelina came out from the steering room and sat with them.

"I decided not to put Raul's ashes into the ocean here," she said. "I know he wanted to be near his homeland, so I am going to sail south in a few weeks and put them into the Pacific off the coast of Chile."

Buck asked, "So, how did you meet, Raul?"

Angelina smiled and then recounted the events of the past twenty years that had resulted in her talking with her friends while looking out over the waters of the Strait of Juan de Fuca onto the mountains of Vancouver Island.

"I met Raul in Reno. He was living there because, as Tammy said, it was an easy place to live, and Raul needed an easy place to live. He and his brother, Luis, were the sons of a rich man who died shortly before Salvador Allende was elected president in 1970. Their mother had died about ten years before. When Allende became president, Raul and Luis were afraid the country would become communist, so they took their wealth and came to this country. When Pinochet came to power three years later, they thought about returning, but before they could, they realized that the country was now run by a man who cared little for freedom or human life, so they stayed in the United States.

"When I met Raul in a Reno casino, I was immediately attracted to him. I am like that. I know I like a man when I meet him. Why were we attracted to each other? Quien sabe? Maybe it was our mutual Hispanic heritage. Maybe it was because he was a nice-looking man even though he was ten years my elder. Maybe it was because I knew he had money. But probably it was a little bit of all those things. Anyway we fell in love, as much as I can fall in love.

"Tammy, mi amiga, could not handle my relationship with Raul. I sometimes think she may have had a little crush on him, too."

The last comment brought a surprised look into Jordan's eyes as Angelina continued to speak.

"One day Tammy hugged me closely, kissed, and said, 'Via con dios, mi corazon. Have a good life. I'm sorry, but I must go.' Then she left, and I never heard from her again. I do not know where she is today. I do not even know if she is alive. It makes me sad.

"Raul and I were married. I stayed in touch with mi hermano, Jesus, for a year after we met him in Tucson. He sent me some money, but I never told Raul about him. I told Jesus that I did not need any money, that I had found a good, rich man. Jesus said he was happy for me. I heard nothing more from him. I do not know if he is dead or alive, but I fear that he is morte.

"I know Ricardo Cajon is dead. I read in the newspapers that there was a big war between Cajon and another drug lord and Cajon lost that war. I read that the war not only claimed Cajon but also many of his people. I fear that Jesus Perdidos was one of the victims. If he was, I hope he is with the other Jesus now and trust that God will have mercy on muchachos like him who had no chance in life."

"Now I should get back to the steering room. Jim may need some relief from the wheel."

"Here," Buck said. "I know a little bit about boats also. I can take over."

"I'll keep you company. Maybe you can teach a landlubber like me how to steer," Jordan said.

After the boat moved through the strait and its anchor was again dropped in the harbor, Jim said, "I've invited Angelina to come stay at my place. She doesn't need to be alone on this boat in her time of sorrow, and -- no offense, Buck -- I'm the only one with decent accommodations."

Neither Buck nor Jordan pointed out that Angelina was surely affluent enough to get a nice hotel room. They figured if Angelina wanted to stay at Jim's place, the arrangement probably would be good for both Jim and his beautiful guest.

"No offense to you either, Jordan," Jim continued, "but tomorrow I'm going to drive Angelina to Seattle. She needs to see a lawyer there to start the process of settling

Raul's estate, and I still need to talk to the police."

Jordan said, "I understand. I wish I had a place to offer for both of you to stay, but you know my condo has only one bedroom and the futon and a cot are the only other accommodations I got. But one of you is welcome to stay. "

"That's okay. We have quite a bit of business to take care of, so I guess we'll both get a room at one of the hotels downtown," Jim said.

After Jordan and Buck dropped Jim and Angelina off at Jim's house, they bought a twelve-pack of beer. When they had only four bottles left, both men had switched to the fifth of Canadian whiskey that Buck had not opened until that night.

After midnight when the bottle was half empty, Jordan said, "You know, old buddy, on that boat I asked if maybe we were going to share a few secrets, and you said, not until we had more to drink. Well, we've reached that point, and I don't know why, but I have something I would like to tell you, but only if you will tell me something."

"Okay, you're just about the only living friend I got left in this world, so I guess I can share secrets with you. What is it you want to tell me and what is it you want to know?"

"I guess I will start out like a true Texan and brag a little. I once fucked Angelina, and it was one of the best fucks I ever had in my life."

"What?" Buck said. "Was she fucking you while she was making poor Norman think she and him were star-crossed lovers?"

"No! No, no, No! I never fucked her when we were in the Corps. I fucked her twenty years ago in New Mexico. I'll tell you that story later, but now it's your turn to tell me something. On the boat you said, I believe your exact words were, Angelina is a woman a man can never forget. Now my question to you, my good friend, is, what did Angelina do to make you never forget her? Or in good Texas lingo, did you fuck her, too? And if you did, you must have fucked her while she and Norman were those star-crossed lovers."

"No! No, damn it. I didn't fuck her while Norman was alive. I fucked her when I visited her to see how she was doing and to say goodbye when I transferred to Okinawa. I guess.... I guess she was just lonely and needed someone. Hell, I don't know why it happened."

Buck looked embarrassed and took a big gulp of his drink. Neither man said anything for at least a minute. Then Buck said, "But, just like you said, it was one of the best fucks in my life."

"Damn, that might have been the best I ever had."

Angelina turned on her side, smiled as she gazed at Jim through her naked, still firm breasts, and said, "Tambien."

In a king-sized bed in the downtown hotel room, they lay naked for perhaps two more minutes before Angelina said, "Do you think I am a loose woman, making love to you with my husband dead for less than a month?"

"No. If it happens, it happens, and I guess it was meant to happen. I've been attracted to you since we went out on your boat. And I haven't made love to a woman in almost two years."

"And I haven't made love to a man in more than two years."

"You and your husband didn't have sex? I'm sorry. I guess that's none of my business."

"No. I want to tell you. Raul and I used to make passionate love, but less and less as the years passed. Then he had prostate surgery for cancer."

"Yeah, I've heard that sometime can put a real crimp in a guy's love life if the surgeon cuts too many nerves."

"Is that what causes it? I wondered why I could not make him ready like I used to. Would you like to see if I can make you ready again?"

"Help yourself," Jim said as Angelina's tresses tickled his naked thighs.

While the Seattle lawyer took care of the details required for transferring Raul's estate to his widow, Jim met with Seattle homicide detectives. The lead detective invited Jim to have a chair and took a sympathetic tone as he told Jim he understood his anger and frustration.

"These cases are sometimes the most difficult to solve because they are so random. Crimes of passion, such as jealous lovers killing lovers or drunken friends killing friends -- or where money is a clear motive, such as beneficiaries of large insurance policies or inheritances -- they are usually easier to solve because we have people to question and investigate.

"But that doesn't mean we won't find the person who killed your daughter. Often we solve these cases when the killer commits or tries to commit a similar crime. Or when someone who knows something has a conscience attack and gives us a tip. Sometimes the guilty person succumbs to remorse and confesses. But unfortunately Mr. Outseagle, it is often years before that break in the case comes, and I know that's hard on you and the rest of the loved ones of the victim waiting for justice and not knowing if you will ever get it."

"Yes," Jim said. "It is very hard. I keep thinking maybe there is something I can do to help you. Maybe go door to door in the neighborhood and ask questions."

The detective shook his head and said, "I wish it was that simple. The problem in this case is there is no neighborhood. That is, not one where people live. Your daughter was killed downtown, and the killer could be from anywhere -- Capitol Hill, South Seattle, SeaTac, or even Bremerton or Tacoma. Who knows where? Pioneer Square is only a few blocks from the ferry."

"Yeah, I guess you're right. I guess there's not much anybody can do, just hope that we get a break someday," Jim said with a disgusted sniffle. "A break. That's an ironic word. When something goes right, people say, 'I got a break for once.' It seems like it ought to be the other way around because a break means something's broken."

"Good point," the detective said. "Mr. Outseagle, unfortunately, in this society today, there are a good many things in the criminal justice system that are broken."

"Yeah, well, thanks for your time, and keep me informed if you get any.... breaks," Jim said as he turned and walked out of the police station.

Meanwhile real breaks were beginning to have their effects on both Buck and Jordan. They had talked about the pains they felt in their joints, especially their legs. Buck's aching leg brought back the bitter memories of the battle in 1965 near Da Nang. Maybe it was the aching at night that brought back the nightmares.

The nightmares had been frequent through his twenties. They had faded as he moved into his thirties and quiet times in the mountains, the ocean, the forests, and putting those scenes on paper with watercolors began to replace bad memories with more pleasant ones.

Now the bad memories were returning. He did not know why. Maybe it was because he had reached another stage in his life when people his age again were dying around him. This time they were natural deaths. This time the deaths reminded him that it would soon be his time, that his generation was the one at the gate, and when he thought about death, he remembered those who died so many years ago that rainy night in Vietnam.

He remembered the lieutenant, maybe one year older or one year younger than Buck, who took Buck's radio receiver from him to tell headquarters that there were VC in the area. He remembered the grenade blast and how the lieutenant's body flew into the air and came down in more than one piece. And Buck remembered the sharp pain as the shrapnel tore into his leg and head. And he remembered the rifle fire before he passed out, and the screaming as bullets tore through young men's bodies.

He did not remember the time at the field hospital or much from the flight over the Pacific to the naval hospital in California. But he remembered the months he spent there in physical therapy recovering from his wounds, and the nightmares he had over and over, each time emblazoning them more into his memory.

Jordan's knee gave him no nightmares, but the pain more frequently reminded him of the sideline tackle he had taken when he intercepted a pass and was running for a touchdown on a Texas Friday night in November 1959. He had surgery a half decade later when a doctor finally figured out that the tear had been so clean that the cartilage would go cleanly back into place before x-rays could be taken, but the torn cartilage had taken its toll on his knee ligaments, which ached more often as the weather grew cool and damp.

His knee had been aching earlier in the day, but he no longer felt any pain as he sat on his condo balcony enjoying the end of a beautiful fall day in Seattle. Maybe it was the two ibuprofens he had taken a couple of hours earlier, or more likely it was the combination of Scotch and beers he had consumed after he gave up on trying to write a song and sat outside watching the people walk by on the sidewalk below.

Jordan had come to the realization that, like many writers and journalists, he was a consummate people-watcher. He liked to sit on his balcony and watch and listen. He noticed that many of the voices were young, using all of the words and phrases of the generation that would be his grandchildren's if he had any grandchildren.

"Hey, dude."

"Whassup?"

"Oh, we are so like not going to that place again."

Jordan tried to recall the slang of his teen and early twenties years. Was it his generation or Kerouac's that came up with "cat" -- the "dude" of the middle twentieth century? No matter, he thought. A cat has gone back to being a four-legged creature, so he wondered if a generation from now whether a dude would again be a novice cowboy or a dandy dresser.

He also had gathered from listening to the conversations below and in bars and retail stores that the current generation had deemed that the word "like" was neither a preposition nor an adjective but rather a verbal punctuation mark.

"And I was -- like, oh you're so totally full of shit."

"And she was -- like, fuck you."

Jordan could, like, not be slightly surprised at the profanity the young people used on a public street, not that he and his generation did not say the same words when they were that age. They just said them in the privacy of closed rooms and cars. He also marveled at how when two young men with two young women would all greet each other with cheek kisses.

For sure, his generation did not do that. He and his contemporary males would have reveled in getting to casually kiss the girls, except they would probably have gone for the lips. But kiss the boys, even on the cheeks? Not likely.

He had been marveling at the tattoo craze for more than a decade. He remembered how surprised he was in the late '80s summer when he saw the pretty young woman walking across the Santa Fe plaza with tattoos on her back. He remembered how he debated with himself in 1962 about getting a tattoo of the Marine emblem on his arm and decided against it because while it would tell everyone he was macho it also probably would hinder his attracting upper-class women or getting the better jobs. Now he wondered if anyone -- male, female, or transgender -- younger than forty did not have a tattoo somewhere on his or her body.

"So I guess you're just becoming old and obsolete -- an aching archaism," he muttered to himself, taking a wordsmith's arcane pleasure at his almost alliteration. Perhaps he had not yet become obsolete and archaic, but he knew there was no argument that he was growing old and aching.

Funny how the booze sometimes failed to take him from these melancholic moments, Jordan thought. He would be glad when Buck returned from his kayak guide gig off the San Juan Islands. Jordan would tell his friend about his plan to move on, maybe one final attempt at finding the right place or woman.

He took another sip and looked over at the Space Needle, clearly visible from his balcony. He always had a fondness for the Seattle landmark because it been a backdrop in *It Happened at the World's Fair,* a movie he would never forget even if he paid little attention to it on that fall night in 1963 at the drive-in movie with Tammy Dolcito.

He wished he could see Tammy again. He wished it was 1963 again. Maybe he even wished he was in Texas again.

"I'm not sure the Puget Sound area or the Olympic Peninsula is the best place for a guy in his sixties to spend his remaining winters," Jordan told Buck as they finished beers in Jordan's condo after a disappointing Seahawks' game.

Jordan expected Buck to say something like, 'Don't be a wuss; the scenery's worth the pain.' Instead his friend simply said, "Yeah, I'm beginning to understand what you mean."

With undisguised amazement, Jordan said, "What? You aren't thinking about moving, are you? You, who has been so in love with this peninsula for more than thirty years!"

"Have you ever heard of falling in love with a place that didn't fall in love with you? I think Tom T. Hall wrote a song about that once, except it was Texas that didn't fall in love with him. Tom T. Hall wrote a lot of good songs about the times and circumstances in our lives. Anyway, I've been thinking about being somewhere you love but no one loves you," Buck said.

"Remember I'm a year older than you," Buck continued. "We've talked about not having any family. Lately I've come to realize that I don't have many friends either. Really only you and Jim. The people up here are nice, but it seems they've always had all the friends they need. Or maybe they just don't need a gimpy guy with a Texas accent who didn't have anything better to do than paint pictures and take people out in a little boat that a person in his right mind would know better than to get in.

"Now, I'm not whining or bitching. What I'm saying is the fact that I've reached this stage in my life and don't have much to show for it is my own fault. I know I could have taken my G.I. bill and finished college and got a normal job and maybe got married and had kids and bought a nice house in a suburb somewhere and a fancy SUV for my wife and a nice pickup for me. But, for whatever reason, I didn't, and now if you're thinking about moving away, I might be, too. After all, my dog died last year, and I told you then that I didn't want to get another pet that might outlive me."

"So where are you thinking about moving to?" Jordan asked.

Buck said, "I don't know. No. Yes, I do know. Don't laugh or faint, but I've been thinking about Texas."

"I must admit that I'm a bit surprised," Jordan said. "You've said a few disparaging things about our native state a few times, like it's hotter than hell, doesn't have any decent rivers, etcetera. All of which are still true, by the way."

"Yeah, I know I said those things, but that's before I got to aching so, before I realized that I've lived up here all these years and never really made any friends. Before I realized that there still ain't any women in the world prettier or nicer than Texas women. Damn it, Jordan, I know I'm getting to be long in the tooth, but my cock ain't getting any shorter, and it still gets hard, just not as often. And I'd like to have a nice lady that I could spend more time with."

"Don't you think you could meet some nice ladies up here?"

"It seems that the ones I meet here are all married or vacationing and back on an airplane a few days after I meet them. Besides, as I said, I'm starting to ache a lot from the old 'Nam wound. I wonder if it would be better in a warmer, drier climate."

"Well, it's drier on the east side of this state and certainly warmer -- in the summer anyway -- and there's certainly at least one good-sized river called the Columbia."

"That may be true," Buck said. "But we're back to the subject of available women. From everything I've heard and read, there are fewer single women looking for guys like me on the east side than there are on the west side."

"How do you know there are any available women in Texas?"

"I don't really know. But what I'm saying is, I'm thinking about making a trip down there, maybe spend a few weeks and see what I think about it. I guess I'm just thinking out loud, and maybe not thinking all that clear. Maybe the arthritis has gone all the way to my brain."

"No," Jordan said. "I think you're not displaying any evidence of an unhealthy brain. If I had to diagnose your case, I would say you are suffering from nostalgia brought on by age and compounded by a little bit of both loneliness and -- this one is a little bit like having a high reading of the good cholesterol -- horniness."

Buck smiled and said, "Yeah, I guess I shouldn't be complaining about still being a little bit horny when I'm about to apply for Medicare and Social Security."

"Damn straight. But this conversation isn't just about you. Remember I started it. I was the one who said he was thinking about seeking warmer climes, and damn it, old pard, you just went and usurped my plan. I guess I wasn't thinking about Texas. I was thinking maybe about Southern California, Arizona, or New Mexico. When I think about California and New Mexico, I conjure up memories that I'm not sure I want to revisit. And Arizona is even hotter than Texas in the summer. Besides, it's like Florida -- too damn many snowbirds and white-bread retirees to suit my taste."

"Recalling our conversation on the ferry when we encountered your ex-wife, I guess I can understand why Texas isn't one of your top choices," Buck said.

"Funny you should say that," Jordan said. "I've also been thinking about that quite a bit lately, and, just as I was surprised when you said you've been thinking about moving back to Texas, I've been thinking about reconnecting with the women who have meant something in my life. Maybe I would just like to thank them for doing that -- being a person that meant something. Or treating me for at least a little while or maybe longer like I once meant something to them."

"Wow," Buck said. "You're talking about reconnecting with your ex-wife who you haven't seen in three decades, and -- judging from the ferry trip -- is still connected with another man. Okay, I don't feel so bad. I think you are the one whose arthritis has gone to his brain."

"Maybe I'm not that crazy, although I sometimes think I would like to see her just one more time to say no hard feelings."

"Really, no hard feelings? Not ever having been married, I've wondered about guys who have taken that step and find that it didn't work out since it happened to my two best friends, you and Jim. No hard feelings, huh?"

"Maybe there were a few at first. But I got over it, and I hope she did too. I'll bet she married a guy who's made more money that I ever did. Probably has that fancy SUV and maybe even a Mercedes or Lexis to boot."

Both men took drinks from their glasses, and Buck said, "Take heart though. As you said, at least you ain't fat. That guy on the ferry easily weighed over two hundred pounds, and he wasn't any taller that we are."

"So we may outlive him," Jordan said. "Who was it who said living well is the best revenge. Sometimes living longer is the best revenge, if you can live well while you're living longer.

"I mean, I saw Jack Kennedy get his brains blown out. He was president of the United States, very rich, who allegedly had fucked Marilyn Monroe while he had a smart and beautiful wife who put up with his dalliances. Still, who would you want to be -- me or some corpse in a long box that millions of tourists have walked over?"

"Is this a trick question?" Buck said.

Jordan took another drink from his glass and said, "I've asked myself that about life a lot of times. Is it a trick question? Is someone fooling with me? Just to see if I can be smart enough to figure it out."

"Shit, old buddy, now you're beginning to not make much sense, but that happens when we drink too much whiskey. So let's get off philosophy and talk about something else -- like phishing, phucking, or phootball. You know all three activities have one aspect in common," Buck said.

"What's that? I might guess that there are mostly enjoyed by men if you're talking about fishing or football, but the third -- I think some women like it just as much."

"No, here's the clue," Buck said. "You get tackled going for the touchdown and lose the game; your line breaks and the big salmon swims safely away, and you say or do something stupid or don't do anything and lose the woman who might have made your life fulfilled. See what I mean?"

"Okay, I get it. The one that got away," Jordan said.

Angelina could tell that Jim was upset when he met her back at the hotel, but she did not ask him any questions about his conversation with the police. Angelina did not like to think about policemen or the circumstances that make their profession necessary. She asked herself why she was so attracted to this man -- a man with much more emotional pain than money.

Angelina knew about emotional pain, but she had suffered so much so early that she felt she had become immune to it. Still Angelina believed that she knew how to help ease a man's emotional pain. As she reached toward the zipper of Jim's slacks, she licked her lips and said, "Checkout time is in an hour, but I'm all packed. I think that gives us enough time for me to take that worried look off your face."

On the drive back to the boat in the Port Angeles harbor, Jim noticed the tears in Angelina's eyes as the car passed the scene of the fatal collision. Angelina realized that maybe she was not immune from emotional pain.

"It's going to be tough for awhile. I know. I guess we never get over losing someone we love," Jim said.

"Yes, maybe that's why we are good for each other. We can comfort each other in our losses. But I know mine is nothing equal to yours," Angelina said.

"Everybody's loss is unique," he said. "Grief, like love, is something that should not be analyzed, certainly not compared. Hell, I remember when Buck's old Lab died. I could tell the poor guy was suffering as much as if he had lost a brother. Maybe more."

"Anyway, I've been thinking. I need to get away. Nothing I can do will bring my daughter back. I thought maybe if I could find the worthless bastard who killed her and take my personal revenge, like killing him and cutting his heart out and feeding it to a flock of crows or something really bitter like that, I would feel better.

"But now I realize I wouldn't. Nothing would change. My daughter would still be dead. Her mother's life would still be ruined. I would still hate the heartless son of a bitch who killed her. And the next day, probably several hundred more people would be senselessly murdered by other Americans all across this country.

"As I said, I think the only thing that I can do is get out of here. Maybe leave the country. I guess right now I don't feel that good about it anyway."

"Do you want to come with me?" Angelina asked.

"What? Where are you going?"

"I can't leave the boat in the harbor forever. And I need a boat captain. I can't take care of it by myself all the way to Chile," Angelina said.

" Sounds like an intriguing proposition. What else do I have to do?"

Angelina put her hand on his thigh and said, "We can certainly have a muy bueno time while we make our way south, stopping at the ports along the way. Have you ever had a blow job on the high seas, hombre?"

"No, but I'm looking forward to it."

The next morning Buck and Jordan continued their conversation over coffee and breakfast burritos that Jordan has fashioned from ingredients in his refrigerator. Jordan's gypsy ways had made him an eclectic eater. Gulf Coast gumbo, Texas barbeque, California cioppino, Dungeness crabs, oysters from Puget Sound tide-pools, salmon from the Columbia River, or Thai food from his favorite restaurant in upper Queen Anne -- Jordan liked it all. But perhaps his favorite food was Mexican, specifically New Mexican.

As Jordan took the first bite of his burrito, he said, "You know, Buck, all my life I've heard people talk about growing older and tired and trying to simplify their lives. Now I'm beginning to understand what they were talking about."

Buck, already halfway through his breakfast, said, "I've never had an issue with simplifying my life. It's probably always been too simple. A little house, one vehicle, not much money, one pet, no wife, no children. But go ahead, make your point."

"I guess I was just making early morning conversation. I was going to say after eating a lot of fancy, even exotic food over the years, I'm coming to realize that I just want to spend the rest of my life eating what I really like -- grilling barbeque outside in the summer, cooking pasta in a crock pot in the winter, and eating Mexican food all year round. And when I want a change of taste, I'll go out to some good Asian restaurant and have spring rolls, pad thai, sushi, or whatever."

"No offense, old friend, but it sounds like you've come to a conclusion that most of us figured out a long time ago," Buck said.

Jordan took a sip of his coffee, smiled, and said, "Yeah, I guess I was trying to be a sophisticate despite my accent. But lately I've come to the conclusion, as the cliché goes, I gotta be me. I even wrote a little poem about it. Here it is:

It's true as Keynes said,
In the long run
We are all dead.
Human, cat, or elephant,
Rich or famous,
Dumb or elegant,
All creatures you've known

Will be reduced
To ash or bone.
So take what you've got
And don't waste time
Being someone you're not."

When Jordan finished his recitation, Buck clapped his hands and said, "I like it."

After the two men drank their coffees in silence for a minute, it was Buck who renewed the conversation.

"I've been going though a bit of life passage too, and it has nothing to do with simplifying my taste in food, something that I never have gotten really excited about. I probably could exist on oatmeal and peanut butter sandwiches, just like I did when I was a little boy. But lately I've been needing something else."

"And what's that?" Jordan asked.

"I've been needing a good woman's hug. Everybody needs a hug sometime."

"Yeah, and a few other close encounters like kisses and blow jobs," Jordan said.

"No. That's not what I'm trying to explain. Often kisses and blow jobs are easier to get than hugs. Kisses and blow jobs are reciprocal acts. People kiss people because they want to be kissed back. And women give men blow jobs because they...." He paused because he realized that maybe blow jobs are acts that are the hugs of the last half century.

"But your mama didn't give you blow jobs. She hugged you. And when you get to be our age, we want a woman who will hold you and hug you and tell you that she loves you."

Jordan interrupted, "And, since she ain't your mama -- give you a blow job."

"Ah shit, we've spent too much time analyzing sex and love. And, as we know, there are things that just can't be analyzed," Buck said.

"Yeah, I guess you're right," Jordan said.

Jordan finished his first burrito and asked, "Were you really serious about considering moving back to Texas?"

"Yes. I've been thinking about it. That's what I was getting at a few minutes ago. What I was trying to say is, I know this area is beautiful, but I need some friends, and I think I might be able to make more back in Texas. Maybe some will give me hugs and kisses. Not to mention an occasional a blow job."

"Buck, if you leave, I won't have much reason to stay. You and Jim are really the only friends I've made up here. But I'm still leery about going back to Texas. It hasn't gotten any cooler, maybe even hotter, from what I hear. I might be more inclined to move back to Colorado. But not Denver. I hear the traffic there has gotten awful, just like California -- or Seattle, for that matter.

"Still, Texas might be worth checking out. Of course, Houston and the Dallas-Fort Worth area have as much traffic as Denver, I'm sure. But I've been hearing some good things about Austin. It has quite a music scene."

"That's what you said about Seattle," Buck said.

"Yeah, but I guess I spent too much time with you and Jim. Never did get to meet all the cool musicians who are supposed to live up here. I probably should have gotten a clue when I couldn't find but a couple of country-western stations on the radio."

"Speaking of Jim," Buck said. "He called me yesterday. He's leaving too. He's going to sail off with Angelina, be the skipper of her boat."

Both men looked at each and smiled. Jordan said, "I guess poor old Jim deserves some fun after all he's been through."

Buck's smile faded as he said, "I was thinking last night. It was almost forty years ago when Jim and I met and we made our trek up the Pacific Coast from the Bay Area. I remember telling him about you and me planning to take a similar trip along the Lewis and Clark Trail. Why didn't we ever do that?"

"Don't know. Still sounds like a good idea," Jordan said.

"Then let's do it. Yeah, it's the long way, but we follow a route that eventually would take us to Texas -- across Washington, Oregon, Idaho, Montana, the Dakotas, along the borders of Iowa, Nebraska, Kansas, Missouri, then down to Texas. How about it?"

"As I said, sounds like a good idea. Whose vehicle do you want to take? Or do you want to take both?" Jordan asked.

"I think I'll sell my old truck and buy a new one in Texas," Buck said. "So can we take your SUV?"

Jim sold his house on the bluff overlooking the strait to a retired California highway patrolman and his wife. He told Angelina that even if he decided the life of sea gypsy did not turn out to be what he had hoped for, he wanted to get away from any place with memories. He said he could not walk through the house without tearing up while remembering Shanna visiting her grandma and walking on the rocks of Ediz Hook.

Jordan thought about leasing his Seattle condo, but when the young woman who moved to Seattle to take a software engineer job with Microsoft offered him more than three hundred thousand dollars, he decided it was too good a deal to turn down. Buck's place was worth nothing near that price, and besides, he said, he wanted to keep his place, thinking it would be more practical to test his plan to abandon the Pacific Northwest before getting rid of the only real estate he had ever owned.

On the evening of the day Jim closed on the sale of his house, Angelina hosted a going-away party. She piloted the small boat alone to pick up Jordan and Buck at the Port Angeles pier and take them to her big boat moored in the harbor.

She hugged both men and said, "Before we go out to the boat, let's take a walk down Front Street. I want to discuss something with both of you."

"Uh oh, what did we do?" Jordan joked. "You sound like my mother when she had found out I had done something that I shouldn't have."

"No. It's the other way around. I have done many things that I should not have done, and Jim does not know of that part of my past. I do not want him to ever know."

Jordan said, "Angelina, all three of us have done some things together that we do not want to discuss with others. I think I can speak for both Buck and me. We'll keep your secrets if you will keep ours."

"Well said, amigo," Buck said.

Angelina, walking in the middle, took both men's hands and said, "Gracias, you two hombres have always been two of my best amigos. To you and Senor Flash and mi amiga, Tammy, I probably owe my life."

Alcohol fueled the going-away party. Angelina had told Buck and Jordan that they should not even consider leaving the boat that night. Recalling it later, Jordan told Buck he thought the night was fun and maudlin but mostly fun. Still, alcohol can bring out truth, feelings, foolishness, and memories.

Jordan and Buck recalled their childhoods in Texas. Buck and Jim recalled their sojourn up U.S. 101. Jim recalled how he had moved from the Olympic Peninsula with its rain forests and green mountains to the Mid-Columbia Valley, where the mountains have no trees and, if human beings had not learned the techniques of irrigation, the only vegetation probably would be tumbleweeds and sagebrush.

"But I could make a whole lot more money with my nuclear sub experience on the Hanford Nuclear Reservation than I ever could on the Olympic Peninsula. And, you know what? For quite a few years, I didn't miss the ocean at all. We had the Columbia if we wanted to get in a boat. But after those years in the Navy, I guess I had gotten my fill of boats.

"Now I'm going back on a boat to go damned near from one end of the world to the other, just like I did when I was in my twenties, except my shipmate is a whole lot prettier than the ones I spent those days and nights with in the '60s.

"But, still, it's interesting how I'm going back to the sea, and you two are going back to the place where you spent your childhoods. Why is it that when people get near the end of their lives, they want to do that -- return to their childhoods," Jim said.

"Because life's not a line; it's a circle," Jordan said. "I wrote this song a couple of days ago, just about the only song I've written since I left California. I didn't bring my guitar, so I guess I'll have to sing it a cappella."

I *was at the bar drinking doubles,*
Thinking about all my troubles
When an old cowboy told me it's okay
If things ain't always what they say.
Like:
Blueberries ain't blue;
They're purple.
Life's not a line;
It's a circle.
And tie don't always go to the runner.
And it may not get better come summer.
I looked at him and shook my head,
Puzzled by the rhyme he just said.
What kind of crazy has this man got?
Talking about what is and what's not,
Telling me:
Blueberries ain't blue;
They're purple.
Life's not a line;
It's a circle.
And tie don't always go to the runner.
And who knows what'll happen come summer?
I thought of friends who left when times got lean.
And bosses who treated me mean,
Telling me to strive, strive, strive
When it was all just jive, jive, jive.
So I know:
Blueberries ain't blue;

They're purple.
Life's not a line;
It's a circle.
And tie don't always go to the runner.
And I doubt it'll get better come summer.
Still this old man sitting beside me
Wasn't trying to hurt or deride me,
Just trying to pick me up when I'm down.
So I told the barkeep to give us another round.
And we sang:
Blueberries ain't blue;
They're purple.
Life's not a line;
It's a circle.
And tie don't always go to the runner.
But maybe it'll get better come summer.
So when some sorry sons of bitches
Put you in one of life's many ditches,
Crawl out and find a friendly bar,
Where you can be who you really are.
And sing:
Blueberries ain't blue;
They're purple.
Life's not a line;
It's a circle.
And tie don't always go to the runner.
But it may get better come summer.

Angelina, who had sat sipping a glass of red wine throughout her friends' conversation, said, "Si, let us hope so."

Chapter 14
Following the Lewis and Clark Trail

A week later, Jim and Angelina were sailing out of the strait into the open ocean as Jordan and Buck drove into Astoria, Oregon, near the mouth of the Columbia River.

After they visited the Fort Clatsop historical site, where the Lewis and Clark expedition spent a bitter winter two centuries before, they drove to Portland and checked into a hotel. After a few beers, Jordan told Buck the story of the week around Durango in 1987. He recounted the prior weeks that he had spent with Tammy and Angelina at their Albuquerque home and the erotic morning when he, like Buck and Norman more than twenty years earlier, was initiated into the pleasures that Angelina could provide.

But he did not tell Buck about Tammy's and Angelina's lesbian relationship. He had been confused about that relationship twenty years before, and after meeting Angelina again and learning about her relationship with her late husband and now her relationship with Jim, he followed his and his friends' axiom that love is not something to be analyzed. He wondered also about

Tammy. Had she remained a lesbian? He remembered Angelina's comment about Tammy possibly having a crush on Raul. Did she, like Angelina, find a man who could satisfy her?

Jordan thought about how Tammy had been part of his life during three crucial times. And he realized that not only had an assassin's bullet changed world history on a Dallas November Friday. It may also have changed his and Tammy's lives.

The next morning he talked about Tammy after they drove east on Interstate 84 past the spectacular scenery of the Columbia River Gorge into the barren grasslands of eastern Oregon and Washington.

"I really wish I knew what happened to Tammy," he told Buck. "I guess I never told you this, but we kind of had a thing going when she was going to SMU."

"Oh yeah?"

"Yeah, but then we witnessed the Kennedy assassination, and Tammy was so upset she left without saying goodbye, and I never heard from her again until she and Angelina showed up in Albuquerque two decades later."

After the road curved northward over the Columbia into Washington, and the two friends neared the Tri-Cities of Richland, Kennewick, and Pasco, Jordan told Buck that they soon had some choices about which routes to take along the Lewis and Clark Trail.

"You see the expedition didn't exactly follow the same route going and returning. On the way west, they went down the Snake River from its confluence with the Clearwater River where the Washington-Idaho border is today to where the Snake joins the Columbia at Pasco. On the way home, they went overland a little to the south of the Snake. I recommend we take the overland route -- Highway 12 to the Washington-Idaho border -- especially since there aren't any real highways along the Snake," Jordan explained.

"Besides, I've always wanted to go through Walla Walla," Jordan added, remembering that day more than thirty years ago in the Houston park when he and Susan talked about their travel dreams.

Jordan wished he had found the nerve to talk to Susan on the ferry. Now he would never know how her life had been after their divorce. He did not even know her last name. All he knew was that two years ago she was spending a vacation with an overweight man close to his and her age, presumably her husband.

He wondered why he wanted to know about Susan. Just curiosity, he thought. But he knew it was more than curiosity that made him want to see Tammy again.

"You know, Buck, sometimes I think the best I ever had was what I never had," Jordan said as they crossed the Columbia again in the Tri-Cities.

Buck thought of Beth Chertha Bultin and said, "Yes, I think you may be right."

As they approached the outskirts of Walla Walla, Buck said, "I guess you know this place, besides being a pleasant little college town, is also the location of Washington's main penitentiary."

"I read that in at least a couple of crime stories in the Seattle papers. But you know ever since that scary little adventure outside of Durango, I haven't been particularly interested in crime or prisons," Jordan said.

"I understand," Buck said. "That was quite an adventure, but not one that I would necessarily want to experience."

"Come to think of it, it probably sounds silly to talk about encountering a couple of poor Mexican drug dealers to a guy who damned near got killed in Vietnam," Jordan said.

"No. No, it doesn't. Getting killed is the same result, no matter how it happens, whether it's by some slant with an AK-47 in a jungle, a Mexican trying to better himself by protecting his drug trade business, or some worthless trigger-happy kid trying to get a few dollars from more fortunate kids partying in downtown Seattle. As I said, the result is the same. You're dead."

What can you say after that, Jordan thought, and the two friends drove in silence to Walla Walla, where they spent the night.

All the way from Seattle, they had played their favorite music CDs. They started out with discs they had bought at the local festivals, self-financed by talented musicians known only by a few people in their region -- the fate of most entertainers. Some of the women reminded Jordan of Emmy Lou Harris and Nanci Griffith, whose CDs he and Buck played on the second day of the journey. Perhaps because Emmy Lou and Nanci had recorded so many songs with so many of the two friends' favorite male singers, Jordan and Buck decided the third day was time for Willie Nelson, Waylon Jennings, and some of their other favorite Texas singers -- Jerry Jeff Walker, Guy Clark, Townes Van Zandt, Lyle Lovett, and Robert Earl Keen.

"Hey," Jordan said. "You would think that every guy who ever wrote a country song, at least the country songs I like, was born in Texas."

"Okay. We'll take a break and listen to Kris Kristofferson," Buck said.

"You lose, old buddy," Jordan said. "Kristofferson is also a native Texan, born in Brownsville, but he was a service brat, so he moved around as a kid. California is as much a home state for him as Texas, I figure. And Jerry Jeff is a native of New York, but he's certainly lived in Texas long enough to qualify as a genuine Texan."

"I didn't even know Kristofferson was born in Texas. I guess I'm proud to know that. A service brat, huh. I've often wondered where service brats tell people they are from. What state do they consider home? For that matter, what state do we consider home? I lived in Washington for more than thirty years. I guess that would qualify as my home state. But I never really felt at home. I just liked the mountains, the forests, and the water.

"And you, Jordan, you've lived in how many states -- a half dozen? Which state do you consider home?"

"I don't know. I think maybe I don't have a home. Home is something you have with a wife and kids. But since you asked the question, I guess that's why I'm in this car with you. I guess if you're raised a Texan, you're always a Texan, no matter how hard you try not to be."

"Yeah, I reckon you're right. Maybe that's why I'm glad to learn that Kristofferson was born a Texan. I really like his songs, especially this song."

Buck flicked to *Good Christian Soldier*, the song about a platoon of soldiers in Vietnam trying to get through their one year of war.

They drove in silence for a mile or so after the song ended. Then Buck said, "I never killed anyone, but I watched some grown men cry -- including me -- and a few of them die." Buck said.

"You never killed anyone?" Jordan asked.

"I wasn't there long enough. Got wounded on my first patrol. Sometimes I wish I had killed someone, especially the

Cong who tore up my leg, gave me these scars on my face that nobody sees because of my beard, and killed the lieutenant and some of my other buddies. And other times, I'm glad I never killed anyone. The nightmares are bad enough, just dealing with my wounds and my friend's deaths. I guess they would be worse dealing with thinking about the people I killed.

"After all, most of them were just young guys like me -- fighting for their country, as they saw it. I'm glad I don't have to think about killing them. And I'm sorry for my buddies who stayed over there to have those memories even if they came back without a limp or any scars, visible scars at least."

Jordan still did not know what to say. He was glad he never went to Vietnam and had to face the prospects of cowardice, death, or cruelty to the enemy. He had told friends in the past three decades that he was glad that Presidents Johnson and Nixon had not called up the reserve units. He had reasoned that their decision was political. The reservists were more affluent Americans -- college students, sons of people who might have influence or at least were registered to vote.

Now, he thought, in this new century the situation had not changed and yet it had. Now the reservists and National Guard members were the ones having to fight and die in a war.

"Maybe we should have the draft," he said to Buck. "If we still had the draft, I'll bet we never would have invaded Iraq, and we wouldn't be in the mess we are in."

"The draft didn't stop us from invading Vietnam and getting in that mess," Buck said.

"Yeah, but I thought we learned our lesson in Vietnam," Jordan said. "I still think we learned our lesson in Vietnam. I still think if all those upper middle class people had thought their kids could be thrown into the carnage without any say in the matter, I don't think people would have stood for this war."

"I don't know," Buck said. "I'm beginning to think men just need to go to war every so often, just because that's what human beings do. Come on, you know we didn't join the Marines because of its benefits, certainly not because it was easier, or because we could see more of the world. We joined the Marines for the same reason kids have joined the Marines for over two hundred years. We joined the Marines to prove we were men. And, Jordan, you know more than forty years later, you're proud of that fact that you were a Marine. If you're not, you're the first Marine I've ever met who wasn't."

"There's no denying that," Jordan said. "I suspect one impetus for me joining the Marines and maybe playing football was my parents' giving me a name that sounds like a girl's. I guess I wanted to show people once and for all I was a male."

"Never thought about that," Buck said with a smile. "I guess you could have told people to call you Jord, like I was called Buck. It would have been really miserable to be called Buchanan."

Both men smiled and Jordan said, "But what made us think being a Marine was special? As far as I know, we never had a president of the United States who was a Marine. You don't have to be a Marine to be a success in politics, to get rich, or to get women. Why did we think it would be important for the rest of our lives?"

"Wasn't it?" Buck asked.

"I guess it was," Jordan said. "But what about Norman? And all your buddies who died, shot all to pieces in that Asian mud? Yeah, it was certainly important in their lives. It was -- as they say -- a life-changing experience, except in their case, it was a life-ending experience."

"As you said, there's no denying that," Buck said.

Jordan remembered the song he had written almost twenty years before, the one that I had given a tune.

"Life ain't fair and life ain't kind,
But it's all we get, so don't go through it blind....
If you die trying to prove you're a hero.
The sum of their hopes will add up to zero."

Jordan and Buck went across Idaho and the Lolo Pass into Montana and decided to take the Lewis and Clark southern return route along the Yellowstone River. When they checked into a motel in Missoula, Buck looked at the road atlas they had bought for the trip and told Jordan the battleground where Sitting Bull's and Crazy Horse's Sioux and Cheyenne warriors had wiped out George Custer's Seventh Cavalry would be a short side trip south of Billings, where they spent their fourth night on the road.

"Well, it would a shame to be that close and not see that piece of western history," Jordan said.

After touring the battlefield and having a late dinner in Miles City, Montana, each man could see that the other was beginning to grow a bit weary of the road. Buck brought up the subject.

"You know the only way we really could reenact the Lewis and Clark route just north of here would be to get a boat and go down the Missouri River, and you know we're not going to do that, so how about we just do an approximation by taking Interstate 94 to Bismarck and then take whatever highway hugs closest to the river down to St. Louis?"

"I was pretty much thinking the same thing, except I was thinking maybe we could skip St. Louis and head south toward Texas at Kansas City. I mean the practical purpose of this trip is to see what type of country is along the expedition's route, and by Kansas City we will pretty well have done that," Jordan said.

"Okay with me. I guess I'm itching to get to Texas," Buck said.

"After we get to Kansas City, I will be wanting to haul ass down Interstate 35 through Kansas, Oklahoma, toward Dallas-Fort Worth because I've seen that part of the country, and it's not exactly a tourist spot," Jordan said.

"I'm really glad, though, you reminded me of our long-ago plans," he continued. "I consider the Lewis and Clark Expedition basically the conception of the Western United States, and I love the West."

"I do too," Buck said. "Maybe it was all those western movies we saw as kids. I guess we were imprinted forever by what we watched every Saturday afternoon from first grade to junior high, seeing the bad guys get what they deserve from the barrel of a six-gun and the good guys ride away to another town to solve more of the world's problems. Is it any wonder that we grew up and joined the Marines and moved where there were real mountains."

"Yeah," Jordan said, "And is it any wonder, speaking for myself, that I'm somewhat disgusted with the world we're going out in -- a world being directed by leaders I can't respect. Wishy-washy Democrats who try to ride the wind but are so clueless they can't figure out that the wind changes directions often. Or Republican snakes who could step right into roles as those banker villains who were secretly leading the stagecoach robbers while acting like they were the town's most stalwart citizens.

"I was wondering last night why I was fleeing from the land of the wishy-washiness to a place that seems to be a breeding ground for those banker, secret-stagecoach-robbing ring leaders?"

"I guess that's a good question," Buck said. "I told you I'm going back because even though they may not have as many crooks up in the Northwest, they also don't seem to have many heroes. And I'm hoping to meet a pretty school marm or widow who owns the boarding house. You know what they say about Texas women. I don't know why, but there are a bunch of pretty women down in Texas. Even the ones close to our age."

"You sure you're not just wishing that's true?"

Buck thought about the question for a half-minute and then said, "No. No, I'm not sure about anything anymore, but it seems that most of the women from Texas I met who came up to explore the Olympic Peninsula or cross over to Victoria were good-looking."

"Old buddy, in less than a week I reckon we'll start learning whether the women are as pretty as we imagine them and if our return to the past is a solution to our aging angst or just a silly dream of a couple of long-time losers."

After they crossed into North Dakota and were driving a few miles south of Theodore Roosevelt National Park in the Badlands along the Little Missouri River, Buck said he considered Teddy Roosevelt one of his hero presidents.

"Maybe it's because of what we were talking about last night. Like us, he was a kid who wanted to prove himself by being a cowboy and a soldier. Hell, I'd rather be called Buchanan or Jordan than Theodore.

"Anyway, Teddy believed in doing what he thought was right -- a rich kid who confronted the rich robber barrens and brought them to heel, a loving husband and father of six, including four sons, one who died in the First World War and the other three who were wounded and received a slew of medals. And when the Second World War happened, all three of the surviving sons were using their contacts to get back into the Army, not stay out of it. There were certainly no draft dodgers in that family. Ted the third, by that time an infantry general, was awarded the Congressional Medal of Honor for his leadership in the first wave on Utah Beach on D-Day. No sir, no chicken hawks in that family."

"Yeah," Jordan said. "I wish we had a few more politicians like Teddy and his progeny today."

The sixth night of the trip was spent on the west side of the Missouri River across from Bismarck, in Mandan, where Lewis and Clark spent the winter of 1804-1805 enjoying the hospitality of the tribe after which the town is named.

"Two hundred years ago, Lewis and Clark were here," Jordan said.

"Yeah, and a hundred years after that, Teddy Roosevelt was president," Buck said.

"And now a hundred years later, here we are. I guess you could call it a bicentennial circle," Jordan said.

The next day Buck and Jordan turned south. After crossing into South Dakota, they were playing the first of two albums made by the Highwaymen, a short-lived impromptu quartet made of singers considered by Buck and Jordan to be among the greatest who ever strolled down Nashville's Sixteenth Avenue.

"Yep, the current generation of music industry pirates are going to have a tough time finding anyone who can equal Willie, Waylon, Kris, and Johnny," Buck said.

"No argument from me about that," Jordan said as the last song on the disc began to play. Buck noted the title of the song, *The Twentieth Century Is Almost Over*, and joked: "I guess our music collection is getting as obsolete as we are."

Jordan chuckled and said, "Yeah. Remember when we were teen-agers and young Marines and George Orwell's masterpiece was a futuristic novel. And this year the babies born in 1984 can legally buy their first booze."

Both men were suddenly sadder, and neither said anything for a mile. Then Jordan said, "Maybe that's why I'm getting to be such a curmudgeon."

"I'm sorry. I guess I missed your explanation of being a curmudgeon. Besides, I'm not really sure what a curmudgeon is anyway. Remember, you're the wordsmith. I paint pictures," Buck said.

"A curmudgeon," Jordan explained, "is, by my definition, someone who doesn't like anybody or anything very much. I'm afraid I'm getting that way, and I'm wondering why. I was just offering the theory that I'm becoming a disagreeable old grouch because I'm not doing a very good job of adjusting to time passing and societies changing.

"I mean, I don't like the Republicans; I don't like the Democrats. But then maybe I've always been this way. I got disgusted with working for newspapers, so I got into the corporate world, which I didn't like any better, so I got involved with the government, which may even be worse than the other two environments. I damn sure never wanted to spend much time in a military environment, and I think most of the entertainment crowd come off as a bunch of phony loons, just like the squirrels in the academic world.

"See what I mean?"

"Yeah, I think I understand. I guess I managed to deal with those feelings by going off in the woods and voting for Libertarians whenever I bothered to vote at all," Buck said. "But then, if everybody was like us, where would this country be?"

Jordan shrugged, smirked, smiled, and said, "Back in the nineteenth century, where I probably would like to be right now."

"I guess we'll be splitting up at Dallas," Buck said three days later as they crossed the Red River out of Oklahoma into Texas. "I'll catch a flight to Lubbock."

"Are you sure you don't want to explore Austin with me first?" Jordan asked. "Somehow I never figured Lubbock for a place that anyone would want to retire to."

Buck smiled and said, "It may not be, but if either you or I had ever figured anything right, then I guess we'd be rich rather than handsome."

"Anyway, I know a lady out there who owns a car dealership. Maybe she'll give me a good deal."

Jordan dropped Buck off at Love Field, where he caught his Southwest Airlines flight. Then Jordan drove to Arlington, visited his parents' graves, and checked into a hotel on the interstate loop that surrounds where he grew up, then a town with a population of approximately forty thousand, now a city of more than three-hundred thousand. Jordan called Buck on his cell phone.

He told Buck that the traffic in the so-called Metroplex was as heavy but not as fierce as some places he had lived.

"I guess that might be because they have so many freeways. Unlike Seattle, it seems like Dallas-Fort Worth has more freeways than real streets."

"Hell," Buck said, "I think Lubbock has as many freeways as Seattle. That's one thing Texans know how to do -- build roads.

"Speaking of roads, or maybe the reason for building them, it turns out that Beth Bultin no longer owns the dealership. She sold it to her son-in-law. Anyway, I still made a deal for a car and a dinner date with Beth. Maybe it's just wishful thinking, but I got the idea that she was glad I asked her."

"Well, best of luck. Maybe romance will blossom."

"Oh, I'm not going to get my hopes up, but I'll keep you posted. Stay in touch, Jordan."

"I'll do that, and let me know when you get your hopes up. And maybe you'll be able to get something else up."

Chapter 15
An Unexpected Reunion in Austin

Jordan continued on Interstate 35 south from Dallas toward Austin. He had read in a news article that the road was favored by Mexican drug dealers because it runs all the way from Laredo to Duluth -- a main transportation artery for the entire central United States, a concrete Mississippi River.

One of the hundreds of little towns that Interstate 35 bypasses is Abbot, Texas. This hamlet of three hundred people about seventy miles south of Dallas is the hometown of a man who was already famous when Mary Kay Ash was selling cosmetics out of a small store, when George W. Bush was working influential connections to get into the Texas Air National Guard, and when Michael Dell was learning to walk.

As Jordan drove past the sign outside Abbot proudly proclaiming its favorite son, he was pleased that he had now passed through where both Willie and Waylon got their starts in life and by nightfall he would be in Willie's current hometown. He played a Willie CD, then put in a Jimmy Buffet disc.

Jimmy's not a Texan, Jordan thought, but he's given Texas and places in Texas credit for some of his success -- playing in the Texas community colleges as a fledgling minstrel and composing perhaps his breakthrough hit, *Margaritaville*, while enjoying the subject of the song in an Austin bar.

Jordan had been in Austin several times before. He had competed unsuccessfully for state honors at the University of Texas in 1959 when he won a Texas Interscholastic League regional impromptu essay writing contest. He had toured the State Capitol and drank beer at Scholtz Beer Garden on a spring weekend with Susan. It was on that trip that he had seen Kinky Friedman perform. Jordan knew that Kinky had gone from being the lead musician for the Texas Jewboys to a successful mystery novelist. But not having heard Don Imus's morning radio show since he moved to Seattle, Jordan did not know that Kinky had mounted an impressive campaign as an independent candidate for Texas governor with a slogan of "How Hard Could It Be."

Austin had changed in the thirty years since Jordan last visited. Now more than a million people lived in the city and suburbs that used to be rustic towns such as the place where outlaw Sam Bass was killed. That city, Round Rock, was now the headquarters city for Dell's computing empire. It also had traffic that equaled any city in the West.

One thing that had not changed was Austin's reputation as being the liberal bastion of the state. If he decided to settle in

Austin, Jordan figured his fellow citizens would quickly accept him when they learned his former places of residents had included Santa Fe, the Bay Area, and Seattle -- other famous frou-frou liberal havens.

After checking into a hotel, Jordan took a copy of the *Austin American-Statesman* to his room. An article in the newspaper informed him of Kinky Friedman's campaign. Jordan first thought it was just some of Friedman's ironic humor, but after reading the article he realized the University of Texas graduate, former successful musician, and successful novelist had serious political ambitions. Then he remembered his Texas history and thought maybe Kinky's ambition was not absurd. After all, no one -- not me -- formerly Flash Golden, nor anyone else -- expected their amiable, capable, but not particularly impressive actor friend of the 1950s to be elected twice as governor of California and president of the United States.

Jordan also remembered his Texas history and recalled that Pappy O'Daniel, a radio personality who also started his own band -- called Doughboys rather than Jewboys -- had been elected governor of Texas in the 1940s and defeated future President Lyndon Johnson in Johnson's first run for the U.S. Senate.

Maybe history will inevitably repeat itself, Jordan thought. After all, life's not a line; it's a circle.

He turned the page and a photograph accompanying an article caught his eye. It was a studio portrait of a member of one of the many Texas state commissions. Jordan could not recall why the man in the picture looked slightly familiar. The headline read, "Prominent Attorney, Wife Die in Plane Crash."

Darwin Argwell was the name of the lawyer piloting the private airplane that malfunctioned as he and his wife were on their way to their summer retreat in Colorado. From a dusty corner of his brain, Jordan recalled that he had met Darwin Argwell when Jordan worked the courthouse beat for the Houston newspaper. He remembered Argwell as a young attorney -- a smooth, articulate, and congenial professional, a man who Jordan thought would do well in his chosen profession. When he read that Argwell's wife was named Susan, he recognized the man in the photo as the same man he saw on a ferry in 2002. Jordan put down the newspaper, realizing that he would never again get the chance to speak with his former wife.

It was not only a day of surprising revelations. It also had been a tiring one, and Jordan needed a relaxing drink. He decided to go to the historic drinking place in Austin, the place in the city that got the first liquor license after prohibition ended -- Threadgills.

"What's this?" Jordan asked as he walked into the famous watering hole. "Why the cameras? Did someone shoot someone here?"

His greeter laughed and said, "No. They're just filming some footage for a documentary on Janis Joplin. This is one of the first places she ever sang in back in the '60s."

Jordan looked over and saw a woman directing the cameraman. Her back was to him. Then she turned around and Jordan recognized her as quickly as he had recognized Angelina on Highway 101. But this woman was not trembling in the arms of a state trooper. She was not crying. She was a woman in control of the moment.

At this point Jordan was not a man in control of the moment. He looked for a chair where he could sit and contemplate what he would say to Tammy Dolcito at this third reunion. He ordered a beer and sipped it, waiting to see if Tammy and her crew would take a break. When they did, Jordan walked over to Tammy and asked, "Remember me?"

Tammy put her cigarette in an ashtray, gave him a puzzled look, then cocked her head, squinted, and said, "Jordan? Jordan Roblech, is it you?"

"Yep. You win the prize for guessing who this old geezer..."

He was unable to finish his sentence as Tammy through her arms around him and said loudly and happily, "Jordan, what are you doing here?"

"Excuse me," Jordan said with almost a laugh. "But I think I should be asking you that question. The last time I talked to you in

Texas, you certainly didn't sound like you'd ever come back to the state."

"Yeah, well, things change. You know that. I can't explain it all to you right now since we're busy shooting, but let's get together after we finish. Uh, I guess I should ask if you are here by yourself. If you're not, whoever you're with I hope will indulge us in an hour or two of catching up on old times."

"I'm alone, and I got all night. Or the rest of my life, for that matter. So do you want to settle down at a table here, or go someplace else?"

"No. Not here. It's too busy. I'm staying at the Driskill Hotel. Let's meet at the bar there. You can find it, can't you? We should be finished here in an hour or so. Do you want to hang around?"

"No. I think I'll go back to my hotel and then meet you at the Driskill."

As Jordan walked away, Tammy called after him. "Wait, Jordan, let me get your cell phone number, so if I get delayed I can call you."

"No," Jordan said as he looked back. "I'm not going to give you any excuses for running out on me this time. If you're late, I can wait all night." Then he turned and walked to settle his tab and muttered, "After all, I've waited most of my life."

As he laid down his money, he did not see the flushed smile on Tammy's face.

Tammy was only thirty minutes past her estimate, an interval that gave Jordan time to have a Scotch on the rocks.

"I'll have another," he told the waitress when Tammy arrived.

"Me, too," Tammy said.

When the drinks arrived, Tammy reached into her purse and said, "What do we owe you for this one and whatever he had before?"

"No," Jordan said. "Let me take care of this. Besides I might want another one."

Tammy raised her flat hand in front of Jordan's face and said, "This is my treat, and I have a better place if you want another drink."

As they walked from the bar into the lobby, Tammy said, "It's been a while since I invited a fellow to come up to my hotel room at this time of night."

"Oh, so that's where the better place to drink is."

"Yes. It's cheaper anyway. I have my own bottle."

Then Tammy stopped as they neared the elevator, looked at Jordan, and said, "Remember the first time we shared my own bottle of Scotch on that Texas-OU weekend."

"I'll never forget it," Jordan said.

As Tammy pushed the elevator button, he muttered almost to himself, "Life's not a line but a circle."

Tammy turned and asked, "What did you say?"

"Oh, nothing. I was just quoting a line from a song I wrote."

As they got out of the elevator, Tammy said, "So you're still writing songs."

"Every now and then. But I'm probably just a dilettante. Maybe I've been one my whole life -- flitting from job to job, dream to dream, place to place. Hell of a legacy, I guess."

Opening the door, Tammy said, "I see you're still pretty good at trying to get a woman's sympathy by putting yourself down."

"And I see you're still pretty good at putting a guy in his place by speaking the truth."

"I'm sorry," Tammy said. "I shouldn't have said that. But, yes, I'm apparently still pretty good at alienating people when I should know better, especially guys I like."

"Hey, don't worry about it," Jordan said. "We know each other, even if we do get together only every twenty years or so."

Tammy pointed with both of her hands toward her bed and a chair and said, "Have a seat anywhere you want and we'll get this reunion started. Do you want your Scotch straight, with ice, or with water?"

"Probably should put some water in it. I'm getting too old to drink it straight. I'm liable to start acting like I was twenty years old again, and that probably ain't smart for a guy my age."

"What are you trying to do? Make me feel old? I seem to recall that I'm a few months older than you. That's why I could buy that bottle in 1963," Tammy said. "And what's wrong with acting like you're twenty years old?"

"Nothing, I guess. Come to think of it, I've probably been doing that most of my life, even when I was fifteen. But I guess what I was getting at is, I've come to realize that women, many of them anyway, seem to not care much for a forty, fifty, or sixty-year-old man who's still trying to be twenty or thirty."

Tammy handed him a drink and sat down on the bed beside him.

Jordan took a sip and said, "Twenty-five."

Tammy waited for Jordan to finish his sentence, but when he simply stared at the wall, she said, "Twenty five? Is that another song title like the circle of life or whatever?"

Jordan laughed and put his arm around Tammy. "No, I was just thinking about a friend I met when I was a lobbyist. We would be sitting in a bar in Denver, Cheyenne, or Santa Fe, buying drinks for state legislators or anyone who worked for legislators or who claimed to know legislators, especially if they were pretty women, and my friend would say, 'My body is fifty years old, but my mind is twenty-five.' I guess that's why I liked that guy so much. I was in my mid-thirties at the time, but I decided I wasn't going to let my mind grow any older than twenty-five.

"I lost touch with that guy when I lost my lobbying job, and I guess my friend is dead now. Certainly he's dead if he stayed true to his creed of being twenty-five in a sixty or seventy-year-old body."

"But at least he probably died happy," Tammy said with Jordan's arm still on her shoulder. She put her hand on Jordan's thigh and said, "Do you want to go back to 1963?"

Jordan looked at Tammy with a pained smile and said, "Don't we all? Don't all of us want to go back to when we were starting to make our way in life, knowing what we know now?"

"Not necessarily," Tammy said. "Some of us have come to understand the song that was inspired in this hotel. You know the one about not looking back because you probably would make the same mistakes again."

"Guy Clark's *Ramlin' Jack and Mahan.* How did you know that song?" Jordan asked.

"Because I've spent some time in Texas doing this documentary. I've met quite a few people, especially the blue staters who live in Austin. Actually, I've come to like Texans, because even the jerks are usually polite and mostly straightforward."

"Wow! Tammy Dolcito, an advocate of Texas! This is really too much for my mind to assimilate tonight."

"What does your mind want to assimilate?"

"Oh, I don't know, maybe just get caught up with you, find out how you've been spending the last couple of decades, and maybe giving you some news you didn't know, some of it sad, some not so sad."

"I suspect a piece of the sad news is that Flash is no long riding this planet."

"Yes. He died about ten years ago. He had cancer and chose to go out in his own way."

"Are you saying he committed suicide?"

"Yes. Used the same pistol he used in all of his movies."

"Oh, that's so sad."

"In one way it is, but in retrospect I don't fault him for not wanting to spend his last days in a morphine haze in some hospital bed."

"So what's some of the better news?"

Jordan spent more than an hour telling Tammy about reuniting with both Buck and then Angelina. Jordan was not surprised that Tammy was more interested in what Angelina was doing now than what Buck was doing. After all she had met Buck only once.

"Angelina and I were close once, as you will remember," Tammy said.

"Yes, I remember."

"That was during my lesbian stage."

Even after consuming several drinks, Jordan felt awkward about reacting to Tammy's last comment, but he knew he would have to say something.

"So, you like guys again?"

Tammy gave Jordan a wry smile and said, "I guess I've always liked some guys. Guys like you."

"Are you coming on to me?"

"Maybe, maybe not," Tammy said.

"What would you do if I said I was coming on to you?" Jordan asked.

"Oh hell," she said looking away. "What are we doing? Here we are a couple of people in their early sixties but acting like we're sixteen."

Then as she turned and looked Jordan straight in the eyes, she said, "Do you want to fuck me?"

"Tammy, I've wanted to fuck you for forty years."

She looked at Jordan for a time that seemed to him much longer to ten seconds it actually was, then pulled her sweater over her bra, and said, "As they say, better late than never."

Jordan awoke when Tammy came out of the shower. She was running a towel over her hair, which was short with bleached blonde highlights that contrasted with the gray that was dark brown when Jordan last saw her twenty years before. Like Angelina, she remained a beautiful woman. Jordan thought maybe she had lost a little weight in the past two decades. All things considered, he figured he was fortunate to have been offered such an enjoyable evening since he did not think he had aged nearly as well as Tammy.

"So," she said. "I guess we didn't stay up all night in the Driskill Hotel as the song goes, but I'll bet we had as much fun as those three cowboys had drinking and singing philosophy."

"I certainly did," Jordan said.

"Me too," Tammy said as she stepped into her jeans. "Maybe we can do it again, sometime."

"Let's not wait twenty years to get together again. I may not be able to make the appointment if we do."

"Okay. How about tonight?"

"That sounds good. I don't know if that hotel room I paid for last night is any good or not, but I probably should find some place that gives me a discount for staying a week or two. That should give me time to determine if I want to stay any longer."

"If you decide two weeks is enough time, I might have another proposition for you."

"Oh yeah, what?"

"I've got to go now, or I won't get this first project wrapped up on time. But just check out of your hotel and don't rent anything until we talk again tonight. You probably need to get dressed now and get out of here in case the maid thinks you're some hotel burglar. Meet you in the bar at six."

Tammy arrived on time. Jordan was early, so he again had a Scotch before she arrived and began telling him about the Joplin piece.

"We actually did a lot of the shooting in San Francisco and will do the editing in Vancouver...."

"Vancouver?" Jordan interrupted. "I assume that's the Vancouver in Canada, not the Vancouver in Washington state. But either one is only two or three hours away from the condo I had in Seattle."

"Yes, it's Vancouver, B.C. That's where I live now."

"We got so involved in, uh, other activities last night that I never asked you where you live now. I assumed it was somewhere in California."

"Yes, being the same somewhat self-absorbed male you've always been, like most of the other self-absorbed males I know, you never asked. But I understand, and for the record, I live in Vancouver, B.C., because it's a good place for making films, which I do mostly for public television and cable channels.

Tammy told Jordan more about her movie on Janis Joplin, a bright, talented, iconoclastic woman who never felt as though she fit in with her teen-age environment of the 1950s and was not embraced by her peers at her Port Arthur high school and then went on to further humiliation by ridicule at the University of Texas. A woman who had all the feelings and desires experienced by most human beings -- someone who found women sometimes more loving than men.

"I found her story dramatic and interesting. And I identified with her in some ways, although she had a loving family -- a father, mother, and siblings. But she and I, like you, were toddlers in the '40s, grade school kids and teens in the '50s, and came to adulthood in the early '60s. She left Texas because she didn't fit in. When I was her age and in Texas for that brief time, I didn't feel like I fit in either. I felt like an outsider at SMU."

"Do you think if you could go back forty years and know what you know now, you would still feel like an outsider at SMU?"

Tammy thought for a minute, shrugged, and said, "I'm certainly neither Harriet Meyers nor Laura Bush, bless their loyal hearts. But, hey, let's not go there. That might lead into a political discussion, and I gave up on politics years ago. Besides I might find out you've become some kind of weird ideologue instead of the clueless journalist, worn-out lobbyist, would-be songwriter, dreamer nice guy I knew and liked twenty years ago."

Jordan laughed and said, "No. You can relax. I think I'm still that same old clueless -- and now I sometimes think, worthless -- dreamer you used to know."

"You left out that adjective, nice," Tammy said. "That's a key word. You know I don't use that word casually. And stop that talk about being worthless. We're all worth something to somebody and nothing to others."

"Damn. That's a good line. You should have been a writer."

Tammy kicked him gently in the calf and said, "Oh, so you're trying to go from nice guy to asshole. What do you think I've been doing for these past years?"

"I thought you were a TV director-producer."

"I make independent documentaries, nice-guy asshole! That means I have to be a writer, director, camera operator, production manager -- you name it. I have to do just about everything because I can't afford to hire a bunch of people to help me. When I go into a new town, I find local old pros who need the money or talented kids who want the experience as a crew for a few days. Sometimes, if I sell the piece, I make a little money; other times, I have to go into my savings or inheritance."

"Oh, so your parents left you some money?"

"My mother did. My father, my real father, had no money. That's why he killed himself. My mother -- maybe she wouldn't win any prizes for mommy of the year, but she did love me in her own way. She wasn't a bad person. Otherwise Flash would never have married her. Anyway, even as she became more addicted to the drugs, she had enough sense to provide for me.

"But enough of that, too. I don't like to talk about family, probably because it brings back some memories I don't want to revisit. Let's talk about you. What are you doing nowadays? Did you get a good retirement or did you come into money some other way? Or are you just, as you said, a worthless drifter?"

Jordan felt it would be awkward to tell Tammy that her former stepfather had left him enough money to live not luxuriously but reasonably comfortable, so he just said, "Maybe a little of all those things."

"Okay, so you don't need a job?"

"Depends. Are you offering employment?"

"Yes, that's what I wanted to talk to you about. Here's the deal. In the couple of weeks we spent down here, I've become interested in doing another documentary. This one will be about the Mexican immigrants who come to the United States to make a better life or make enough money to help their families in Mexico have a better life.

"As I mentioned, I have to make do with local talent, and I was wondering if you wanted to help me with my next project. I think you probably have enough of the all-round creative talents and experience."

"Sounds interesting. What the heck; I don't have anything else better to do. It might be good for me to actually be engaged in something useful again."

"Great," Tammy said. "Now let's talk about some possible fringe benefits."

Two weeks later Tammy had wrapped up the Janis Joplin film and she and Jordan were making plans to set up operations along the Texas-Mexico border. Jordan checked in by phone with Buck and learned that he had dinner with Beth Bultin and her daughter and son-in-law.

"I think she likes me better than the rest of her family does," Buck said.

"What do you mean by that?"

"Oh, I don't know. They kept asking me questions aimed basically at what I'm doing down here and how did I get enough money to get down here. I made the mistake of telling them that I might start painting cowboy pictures and try to sell them. I get the feeling they think I'm some sort of ne'er-do-well. Maybe it's the beard and the fact that I don't own a tie."

"What counts is what Beth thinks of you," Jordan said.

"She seems to like me okay. I just had iced tea, and tried to keep the conversation on safe subjects -- the weather, her grandkids, the Texas Tech basketball teams, things like that."

"I didn't know you were a basketball fan," Jordan said.

"I'm not, but everybody out here in Lubbock seems to be, what with them naming a freeway after the national champion woman Tech coach and that colorful former Indiana legend coaching the men. So I guess I had better learn to like basketball if I'm going to fit in."

"So where are you staying?" Jordan asked.

"Oh yeah, that's some good news for sure. I figured I just couldn't go cold turkey away from the water, so I mentioned to Beth that I wouldn't mind getting a place on White River Lake, and it turns out that she knows this other widow who's trying to sell her second home out there and she's not getting any bites, so she rented it to me without a lease so long as I agreed to let her show it with me living there and to move out if she gets a buyer.

"Of course, it's an hour drive into Lubbock, but that's not as bad as the drive from Port Angeles to Seattle, so that works out well. It also gives me some impetus to just have iced tea if I ever get another dinner with Beth. So where are you staying?"

Jordan said, "If you're not sitting down, you might want to find a chair."

After Jordan finished telling Buck about reconnecting with Tammy and taking up a new trade as a film production assistant and co-writer, Buck said, "Damn, that's good news. I mean I'm glad Tammy's still alive and well, and you're not having to drink iced tea with your steak and burritos or whatever you eat down there in South Texas."

"Yeah, the only thing I'm having a problem getting used to is the smoke from Tammy's cigarettes. It's been a long time since I've lived with that smell. Reminds me of when I was a kid or a young reporter in the newsroom. But she says they keep her slim and calm."

Chapter 16
A Dream Blown Away in the Texas Wind

Buck was having his second Lubbock meal with Beth, this time lunch with her and Barbara, when Jim called to say he and Angelina were in Panama. "About halfway there," Jim said.

Buck excused himself for a few minutes, and the two friends gave quick summaries of the past weeks. Buck's interest in resuming his lunch caused him to shorten his report, which in a sentence could be summarized as, "We made it to Texas and are having good times with old friends in Lubbock and elsewhere."

"Glad to hear that. Angelina says hello. I'll keep in touch," Jim said.

"So, who was that?" Beth asked.

"A friend of mine from the peninsula. I met him years ago when I got out of the Marines. He had just gotten out of the Navy. We went up the coast together and reconnected in the last few years. It's a long story, but now he's sailing down to Chile with another friend."

After Buck paid the tab and he and his two lunch companions were walking out the restaurant, Beth said, "Barbara and her husband, Mike, are giving me a party, and I would like for you to come. Remember when we first met in 1960 and I invited you to a party and you said you didn't go to parties, or whatever you said. Well, it's more than forty years later, and I want you to come to my party."

"Just tell me where and when," Buck said.

Buck bought a tie for the party held at Barbara and Mike Stuggart's residence, a four-thousand-square-foot house near Lubbock's most prestigious country club. He had to call upon a forty-year-old memory of getting into his Marine Corps uniform to fashion a knot that looked acceptable, and he still felt awkward when he was met at the door by Barbara and Mike.

"Mom's in the media room right now, getting caught up on the game scores," Barbara said. "What would you like to drink? We have beer, wine, or soft drinks."

So the party includes alcohol, Buck thought. It was as if Barbara read his mind when she said, "Yes, we have beer and wine. Mother is the teetotaler of the family, but, in her own words, she's not a fanatic."

"Okay, I'll have a beer," Buck said.

"Come with me, and you can pick out which one?"

Buck followed Barbara, wondering what a media room was. As he reached into the iced tub near the door to the patio and pool, he overheard a man in the kitchen ask in a whisper, "Who's the hippie-looking guy?"

"Some artist guy my mother-in-law met when she and Barbara took their vacation in the Pacific Northwest. Apparently he is originally from around here, and he and Beth knew each other in college."

"Artist, huh? I guess that's why he's wearing that beard and those funky shoes."

Buck looked down at his Earth Shoes and wondered why he bothered to wear a tie.

"But never mind about him," Mike said to his conversation partner. "I got somebody important I want you to meet."

Buck walked out to the patio. The strong spring wind discouraged him from staying outside for any longer than it took for him to quickly drink his beer. He went back into the house and helped himself to another beer. He saw Mike with the man who critiqued Buck's shoes and a tall man about Buck's age. Must be the important fellow, Buck thought.

Buck moved closer to the trio, close enough to overhear Mike say, "Yeah, Dan here played football with my father-in-law, got his petroleum engineering degree, and went off to Houston and got rich. Now he's sold his interest in his oil company and decided he wanted to come back to where the air is dryer and the traffic and the people are friendlier."

The tall man laughed and said, "The people are friendly in Houston too, that is them who aren't planning on stealing your car or burglarizing your place. But Mike is right. The traffic certainly is friendlier out here on the South Plains.

"No, I guess I just got homesick after my wife died, so I sold my place in River Oaks and headed back west."

Mike took a more serious tone when he said, "Yes. Dan lost his wife about the same time Hunter died."

Beth came up behind Buck and asked, "Getting to know anyone?"

"Oh, hi. Not really," Buck said. "I guess I've been in the woods too long. Still kind of shy probably."

Beth smiled and said, "Come on. I'll introduce you to some more people."

She took Buck's hand and walked toward her son-in-law and the other two men.

"Oh, you're going to introduce me to the important guy?"

Beth stopped and said, "Excuse me?"

Buck blushed and said, "I'm sorry. Never mind. I just overheard your son-in-law telling the other guy, not the tall one but the other one, that he was going to introduce him to somebody important."

"Mike is impressed by people with money. He figures the more money they have the more cars they can buy."

"Are you?"

"Am I what?"

"Are you impressed by people with money?"

Beth expression changed from friendly accommodation to slightly pained puzzlement.

"I suppose so," she said. "Isn't everybody?"

Buck finished his second beer, put the bottle on a tray, and said, "Yes. I suppose so too. Let's meet this important guy. And the other guy, too, the one who thinks my shoes are funny."

"Did he say that?"

"Not to me. He just talks a little too loud."

"Yes, he does. Howard is a little crude, but he owns an electrical contracting company and buys all of his trucks from Mike. Dan McKenmon, however, is a really nice guy, money or no money, so let me introduce you."

Dan McKenmon was a nice guy. At least he was courteous and seemingly gracious. Howard Harkle, on the other hand, was as big a jerk up close as he was a room away.

"Artist, huh. What kind of pictures you paint? Something a feller can recognize or some of those weirdo abstract pieces? People up there in Seattle with all of them leftist voters, puny computer nerds, and grungy musicians probably like weird art, too."

"No, I think you could recognize what I paint, but, you know what they say, beauty is in the eye of the beholder. Excuse me. I'm going to get another beer."

Beth soon came over to Buck as he solitarily drank his beer, looking out toward the sun as it went below the South Plains. She was accompanied by Dan.

"Buck, don't let Howard's comments bother you. I told you he was a bit uncouth sometimes, but he doesn't really mean to be offensive."

Buck shrugged and said, "Oh, I'm not upset. I understand. A guy like me is not likely to be a good customer for electrical work, especially since the only property I own is a little cabin about two thousand miles from here. I didn't excuse myself because I was offended. I just couldn't think of anything worthwhile to say and figured another beer might help me be more sociable."

Dan then picked up the sociable mantle, saying, "So Beth tells me you went to Tech the same time we did."

"For a while. Before I ran out of money and joined the Marines."

"Marines, huh. Did you go to Vietnam?"

"Fraid so. If I had not decided I needed a little more money and extended my enlistment, I probably could have gotten out before the Gulf of Tonkin incident really heated up things. That being the case, I probably would have come back to Texas on two good legs and, who knows? I might own an electric company or car dealership."

"Yeah, it's funny how life's events shape us. Speaking of two good legs, I might have ended up in Vietnam, too, if I hadn't got my knee torn up when I got cracked from the side by an Aggie cornerback. Anyway, the doc signed a paper that made the draft board classify me 1-Y.

"But, hey, I just want you to know that all of us appreciate the sacrifices you and the other guys who went to Vietnam made, just as we appreciate the sacrifices that our young soldiers are making now in Iraq and Afghanistan to keep our country safe."

Buck wondered to himself if Dan had any children who were young adults. If he did, he wondered if any of them were in the armed forces or veterans of the armed forces. But the two and a half beers had neither taken away his judgment nor given him the courage to ask that question. Besides, he thought, I don't really want to have this discussion with some rich ex-jock who missed his chance to get killed because he got a boo-boo playing football.

"Beth," Buck said. "I really appreciate you inviting me to the party. It was nice, and I appreciate meeting all these nice people like Dan, but you know I have an hour's drive to the place on White River Lake, and I guess I'm finally showing my age, so I probably should excuse myself soon. So, in case...."

"No, Buck you can't leave yet. You have to stay for the occasion for the party."

"Oh, and what's that?"

"We have an announcement to make," Barbara said.

"So you can't give me -- as my buddy, Jordan says -- a break on the story, an advance tip. Did the car dealership win some sort of sales award? Is your granddaughter her high school's valedictorian, or did she get accepted to a high-falooting university? Did you win the Texas lottery? What's the exciting news?"

"Okay," Beth said, addressing Buck but gazing at Dan. "I'll give you an exclusive. Dan has asked me to marry him, and I've accepted."

"Yeah, Buck, I won the best Texas lottery I can imagine," Dan said.

Chapter 17
One More Sad Journey

Jordan felt he had won the lottery also. He was enjoying researching the documentary with Tammy. It's a fun collaboration, he thought. But it was an even more fun cohabitation.

Jim was enjoying being pilot and crew of Angelina's yacht. Angelina also was appreciative of her new crewman. They were especially enjoying their time in port in Panama, perhaps because it had been a long trip along the coasts of the United States, Mexico, Guatemala, Honduras, El Salvador, Nicaragua, and Costa Rica. Jim said he was tired and needed a break.

There's that word again -- break, he thought. But he needed a rest, and a break would be good.

Angelina was weary of the boat and the sea too, so tired that she wondered why she felt compelled to carry Raul's ashes back to Chile. If it had been her choice, Angelina would have buried Raul in California. She did not favor cremation. But Raul did not expect to arise from the grave. He often told Angelina that, being agnostic, he did not know what to expect after death.

Angelina wondered why two of the three men she had loved did not believe in the power of Jesus. The beliefs of her first lover she never knew. She and Norman did not have enough time together to discuss religion, but she remembered when he left for Guantanamo, he told her to pray for him. She prayed to Jesus to keep Norman safe, and within a month he was dead.

She also prayed to the big Jesus to take care of her brother, the little Jesus. Now she figured her brother was dead too. Otherwise he would have kept in touch. She prayed to Jesus to look after Raul, and Raul died in a stupid traffic accident. Now she prayed every night to Jesus to take care of Jim and console him in his grief over the loss of his only child and keep him safe as they journeyed toward Chile.

She prayed the night before they rented the motorcycles to tour the highlands of Panama. She also said a silent prayer as they stopped at a cantina on the road back to the city and Jim had a couple of stiff drinks. She also prayed as she ran down the hill after Jim missed the curve. Now she prayed for Jim's soul, just as she prayed for the soul of her brother and her husband. And for her own.

It was the most unexpected phone call in Buck Leherifen's life. In his four decades of adulthood, Buck had not received many phone calls, and the single land line in his small kitchen outside of Port Angeles had been adequate to handle all of them. He bought the cell phone just before he and Jordan began their journey to Texas after he had canceled telephone and electric service in his cabin. The cell phone had made its shrill -- Buck thought, irritating -- sound only a few times, and most of the time the caller had been Jordan.

He expected this call to be from Jordan also, but the voice coming from the phone was that of a woman.

"I did not know anyone to call but you. You and Jordan are his only friends I know, and I thought you, rather than Jordan, might know Jim's family. Oh, I just do not know what to do. Oh, I feel so alone. Please, Buck, I hope you can help me."

By this time, Buck recognized the voice as being Angelina's. And her words and the terror and sadness in her voice told him that something bad had happened to Jim Outseagle.

Buck was on an airplane to Houston before sundown and on another plane to Panama City early the next morning. He called Jordan on his cell phone but got Jordan's not-here-leave-message answer. Buck never learned to be comfortable talking to cell phone answer recorders, and he certainly did not know how to explain this turn of events in an abbreviated ethereal digital world, so he hung up.

Buck had never anticipated traveling out of the country, so his cell phone did not work in Panama. He called Jordan and explained the sad demise of Jim Outseagle on Angelina's phone.

Like Buck, Jordan was not prepared to receive the news. And neither was Buck prepared to receive the news that Jordan was with Tammy Dolcito.

"Maybe we should just keep that between us for now," Jordan said. "I'm not sure Angelina needs to deal with trying to reunite via international telephone."

"Agreed," Buck said.

"I'll meet you in Seattle when you get back with Jim's body," Jordan said.

"First, we need to know what to do with Jim's body. Remember, he wasn't into religious services. He might just want to go into the ocean with Raul. I need to find his sister in Ohio. Can you help me do that?"

"What's her name?"

"Mariah."

"Mariah what?"

"I don't know? Wait! Yes, I remember, only because she married a guy whose surname made her name ironic. Mariah Winn. Remember the verse from the song about calling the wind Mariah. I remember Jim laughing about that."

"Okay. Here's all I can do. I can get on one of those Internet phone directory sites, where I found you, remember, and see if I can find a Mariah Winn. But here's the other thing you ought to do. Oh shit -- I guess since I'm in the United States -- I ought to do, we should call his ex-wife. I think she might be able to give us more information about his family."

"Yeah. That makes sense. I guess all of us haven't been thinking that straight. Will you do that? Angelina would appreciate it very much."

The Internet failed to deliver a phone number for a Mariah Winn. Probably has a damned cell phone like the rest of us, Jordan thought. Then he called Jim's ex-wife Brenda. He was glad she and her new husband were listed. He got a recorded greeting and left a message. Brenda called him back within a couple of hours, naturally quite shocked.

"I don't have Mariah's number, but she lived in a little town in Wisconsin the last time I heard," Brenda said. She hesitated and said, "I guess I should tell you that Jim called me before he left on his trip. He said he wanted to tell me there were no hard feelings, that he hoped I could overcome our mutual tragedy and -- I don't know if he had some kind of premonition -- he said if anything happened to him, he wanted to be buried near our daughter."

"Oh, thank you, Brenda. That's what we needed to know."

"But you still need to reach Mariah. She, after all, is the only living kin he has as far as I know."

Jordan found a man named Winn listed in the Wisconsin town and dialed the number. It was the number for Mariah and her husband. By this time, Jordan was beginning to feel like it was thirty years before and he was working the newspaper police beat, talking with grieving loved ones, except then he was not the person who had to deliver the sad news. At least, he was not supposed to be the one who delivered the bad news. He remembered the time when he talked to a survivor who had not been called by anyone else. He knew he would never forget that awkward conversation.

Mariah did not seem nearly as upset as the shocked unsuspecting survivor thirty years in the past. She told Jordan she was sorry to hear the news but, no, she would not be able to attend the funeral, and they could do anything with Jim's body that they thought appropriate. Yes, she said, it would be very appropriate to bury him near his daughter. Thank you for calling, she said, and, oh by the way, did he leave a will?

Chapter 18
Along the Rio Grande

"Who would have thought forty years ago we would be back together -- four friends, four decades later," Buck said.

"Certainly would not have thought we all would be together looking out at the Rio Grande in -- dare I say -- Texas," Jordan said as he put his arm around Tammy.

"Es voluntad del Dios," Angelina said.

Tammy smiled back at Jordan and said, "Yes, I guess that's the only answer -- the will of God. Or maybe el Diablo -- the devil."

The reunion happened after Buck and Jordan finally told Angelina about Jordan's reconnection and liaison with Tammy. They were returning to Seattle in their rental car after Jim's burial. Jordan wrapped up his account of the reunion as they topped the Yakima Ridge looking down on the Kittitas Valley.

Angelina beamed when Jordan said, "Tammy said to tell you hola and that she would like to see you again even if she now has taken up with a reprobate like me."

Angelina said she had moored the boat in Panama, that Raul's ashes were safe in a box in a Panama bank, and she had no urgent need to get back to Panama.

"I don't know what I will do. Maybe I will sell the boat and fly to Chile, but I do not need to make a decision quickly. The dead are going nowhere," she said.

"So come with me back to Texas. Tammy and I could use the help," Jordan said.

"Can I come too?" Buck asked. "I'm getting kind of lonely looking out at that little lake off the Llano Estacado. The people are nice and friendly, but the scenery just can't compete with the strait."

So here they were -- four friends, sometime lovers, now past sixty -- looking out at the Rio Grande, a small stream compared to the mighty Columbia but historically equal.They spoke briefly about Jim's funeral. It turns out that he did leave a will, which he had not updated after his divorce or the death of his daughter, so the will left all of his holdings to Brenda. None of the four knew who would eventually inherit the money Jim received from the sale of his house and his 401K investments. And none of them cared. They figured that Brenda and Mariah deserved each other and whatever legal battle that might ensue. Jim was dead and in the ground next to his daughter and now only a memory, like the other friends and relatives Buck, Jordan, Angelina, and Tammy had outlived.

"Jim would have scoffed at my statement about God's will. Jim did not believe in God.

I hope God will be merciful to him. He was a good man," Angelina said.

"Yes, if there is a God, I believe he will understand that some of us don't believe everything that we read even if it's in the *Bible,*" Jordan said.

"You mean like homosexuality is an abomination?" Tammy said. "Or that a man cannot take a divorced woman as his wife or that you can't eat pork or lobster."

"Yeah, stuff like that."

"There are some things in the *Bible* that clearly this country has discarded," Buck said. "Passages like Jesus telling the rich kid that he needed to give away all of his wealth because there ain't no way a rich man is going to heaven."

"So, mi amigos, you do not believe in God?" Angelina asked. "What is there to hope for; what is there to keep us going in this world if there is no God?"

Jordan said, "I guess that's the question mankind -- excuse me, humankind -- has been pondering for thousands of years. Just how many thousands of years, I guess, depends upon whether you believe in the *Genesis* version of the creation of the world or the geological and biological evidence that science has provided to us."

Buck took a drink of his beer and said, "What difference does it make?"

"Por favor." Angelina said. "You do not believe it makes any difference if there is a God?"

"I believe it does not make any difference to the conglomerate humankind. It only makes a difference to the individual humankind. Some people have to believe in God to get through their lives, and some people just can't buy into the totally nonscientific and apparently mythological diverse explanations for supreme beings that range from the edges of Australia to the Arctic," Buck said.

"But I repeat, what difference does it make to the individual human beings who inhabit this third planet in the solar system? The president of the United States holds hands with the leader of Saudi Arabia when he gets off the helicopter outside of Flash's hometown like they're kinfolk or gay lovers, yet their two religions say officially and literally that each is condemned to whatever versions of eternal hells that their common prophets predicted back when people believed that a flat world existed only a few hundred miles from the Red Sea.

"Okay, so Angelina, you believe in God. You want to believe probably after the hard times you have had in your life that you'll get an easier life in a world above this world.

"And Jordan, you evidently believe, like the Buddhists, that we get many chances in this same world, that life is a circle.

"And Tammy, I don't know what you believe, just as I don't know what I believe. I would like to believe in a God. I certainly would like to believe in Jesus. I believe just about everything printed in red in the *New*

Testament. That we should love everyone and forgive our enemies, that building up riches on this earth is not an admirable ambition, all of those admirable moral principles that Jesus is quoted as saying."

Tammy took a drink and said, "I'll pretend this is a panel discussion on the PBS *News Hour* and you just gave the microphone to me for my sixty seconds. And being a good PBS panelist, I will agree with most of what you said. Like you, I don't know that there are certainties in religion, but I am certain about what I believe about goodness.

"I believe that if you can't go to heaven unless you believe exactly what certain people believe about the nature of God, that if an evil person can go to heaven because he or she follows a certain creed while a kind person can go to hell because he or she doesn't follow that creed, then I don't think I want to spend any time, certainly not eternity, in a place run by that guy.

"But I do disagree with you about religion not making a difference. It does make a difference when religious beliefs cause people to start wars that cost billions of dollars and thousands of lives. It does make a difference when people discriminate in the name of religion. And, as I said, it does make a difference when someone thinks they can do anything they damn well please as long as they go to confession or profess to their savior or pray toward Mecca or get right with their particular little tin god in whatever way they want."

Jordan shook his head as he held up his hand, "Well, Buck -- if he is the moderator of this panel show -- didn't give me a chance to get in my sixty seconds, so here they are. First, I'm not a Buddhist. Buddhists are too nice. I was raised a Methodist, a reasonably tolerant mainstream Protestant denomination, at least back when I was a kid. We could dance with girls, and the preachers didn't care how we got baptized. But I also took a few science classes in high school and college, and...."

Jordan paused and said, "Aw, my sixty seconds is up. Let's just say my religion today is -- as Rick Blaine said when he was asked what was his nationality. What is my religion? I'm a drunkard.

"That means we are getting too deep for a conversation beside a very shallow river, so let's have another round and talk about some fun things."

Buck laughed and said, "Ladies, that's code for Jordan wanting to talk about football, fishing, and other activities that start with the letter F. Now, I doubt that either of you played football, but then maybe you're fans. Angelina, since you own a pretty nice boat, maybe you're into fishing."

Tammy interrupted, "Oh, so you guys never talked about fucking?"

Buck just couldn't get over being embarrassed when a woman was as straightforward as Tammy.

When Buck blushed and looked down at his newly purchased boots, Jordan said, "Yeah, but probably not as much as women do."

Angelina, even though she had perhaps had the most expertise, did not like to talk about fucking. She took a drink and said, "Hey, I do like to fish, and I am a Forty Niners fan, so we can talk about other things. Just so long as you don't talk about fighting. I had much rather -- uh I prefer to use a more gentile term -- make love than fight or argue, but I had rather talk about other things."

"So what do we talk about?" Tammy asked.

"Let's talk about that shallow river Jordan referenced," Tammy said. "It may be a shallow river compared to the other great rivers of the United States -- the Mississippi, the Columbia, the Ohio, the Potomac, the Hudson, all those rivers that helped shape our country in the first two centuries.

"But this relatively shallow river we looking at, I believe, will be the river of destiny for this country in the twenty-first century."

"Oh yeah, how's that?" Buck asked.

"Because it's the river that millions of immigrants have crossed, most of them illegally, seeking the opportunity afforded two centuries of Americans who came before them. It's a story I want to tell. That's why I stayed in Texas after we finished the video for the Joplin piece. That's what Jordan is helping me with."

"Yeah," Jordan said. "She's made a journalist -- well, kind of -- out of me again."

"Some of us did not have to cross the Rio Grande to get to America," Angelina said.

"Yes," Tammy said. "I plan to go to California and Arizona next."

"I hope you aren't going to make this story too personal," Angelina said.

"No, mi amiga. Do not worry. This is not going to be a story about you or me or a couple of clueless young Texas Marines and their and your well-meaning but equally clueless mentor and salvador -- my beloved ex-stepfather. And it's certainly not going to be a story about drug runners. I just want to do a story about good people who were not graced by God -- if there is such a creature -- to be born a few hundred miles to the north. But good people who said to hell with that, we're going to wade or swim that river or sneak across that border and get some of that good life for ourselves."

Buck said, "You may be right. But I have another theory. I think the river of destiny is not a river at all. I think it's much wider, thousands of miles wider. It's an ocean, the Pacific -- the ocean that separates this country from China and the rest of Asia. And I believe the Chinese will be the people who come to rule the world, just as they did thousands of years before the Brits and Spaniards had their countries."

"Tammy, mi amiga, I hope it is a good story you tell," Angelina said. Her three friends pretended they did not see the tears in her still beautiful brown eyes.

The next morning Buck, Jordan, and Tammy were having coffee as Angelina took a shower. Buck said, "Angelina told me last night that she wanted to get back to Panama and finish her mission. She still wants to deposit Raul's ashes into the Pacific off Chile. And I've offered to take Jim's place."

Tammy took a sip of her coffee, smiled, and started to speak, then paused.

"What were you going to say?" Buck said.

"Oh, nothing. It's too early in the morning for weak attempts at what is probably inappropriate black humor."

"So go ahead and say it," Jordan said. "I was thinking it, too. Buck, we wish you well in taking Jim's place as Angelina's companion. We just hope you have a better fate than Jim. Or Raul. Or Norman for that matter."

Buck said, "Yeah, I guess she hasn't exactly been a lucky charm for the men in her life. Then his sneer turned into a grin, and he said, "But what the hell. No one lives forever, and it will be a heck of way to go out."

"So what's the plan?" Jordan asked.

Buck said, "We'll fly up to Lubbock, settle up with the lady renting me the lake place, get whatever I need for the ocean, drive back to San Antonio, store the car someplace I guess, and figure out the best flight back to Panama City."

"I guess that will work," Tammy said. "Maybe we can finish this project down here along the border, and then we four can decide what we are going to do with the rest of our lives."

Buck and Angelina packed up and went northeast toward the Llano Estacado. Jordan and Tammy took her video cameras and prowled the counties along the Rio Grande.

In one of those counties, they met a man named Lofton Victor. He was a rancher who said he was becoming concerned about all the illegal immigrants traipsing across his property.

"It wasn't a real problem when I first moved down here from Iowa in the '70s. A few people came across. We even fed some of them. But now, it's getting ridiculous. They are fogging across. Some days I think I have more illegal immigrants on my property than I have cows. And some of them aren't nearly as nice as the people we fed in the '70s and '80s. Some of them are just criminals. Frankly, I'm getting afraid for my family. This just isn't right. If I still lived in Iowa and hundreds of people came across my property illegally, the sheriff would come out and help me."

The name Victor and the state Iowa clicked with Jordan.

"I had a friend in the Marines from Iowa whose last name was Victor," Jordan said.

"Really," Lofton said. "What was his name?"

"Norman. Norman Victor."

Lofton eyes widened as he raised his hands.

"He was my brother."

Jordan and Tammy were as stunned as Lofton, both thinking the small world cliché at the same instant.

"He died for his country in a silly helicopter crash while the world was faced with a threat from people speaking Spanish south of our border. Maybe the world hasn't changed much in the past forty years," Lofton said.

Jordan wondered why Tammy did not react to a remark in which he detected at least a little racism but instead put down her notebook and said, "Excuse me, but let's set up the camera."

Then Jordan remembered that despite what Lofton had just said, the world had changed in the past forty years. And Jordan had not been a journalist for more than twenty years while Tammy had spent the past twenty years as a journalist, or at least practicing what has evolved into what passes for journalism nowadays.

Jordan remembered the day he covered a politician, cabinet secretary, or somebody else deemed newsworthy speaking at a

Houston luncheon back in the '70s. Jordan was at the press table when the young television reporter sitting next to him scoffed and said, "Yeah, they talk about Edward R. Murrow, Walter Cronkite, and all those other dead and aging icons. They talk about journalism like it was some sort of priesthood, but let me tell you print guys the truth is that the new journalism is neither truth nor literature; it's show biz."

Jordan realized that Tammy was busy setting up her show biz interview. Get the redneck on tape denouncing the wetbacks, he thought. And Tammy had learned her trade well. Lofton Victor went unsuspecting into the interview, just as his brother had gone unsuspecting into oblivion on a helicopter over the Caribbean.

"So, Lofton, please repeat what you just said about your brother and how he had been protecting his country from the threats then and how you are protecting your country now."

Lofton had lost his word cadence when Tammy stopped the interview to set up the camera, but he soon regained it with Tammy's coaching. He talked about protecting the country from threats to its border, equating the Mexicans wading across the Rio Grande to the missiles that Castro had encouraged the Russians to set up in Cuba.

When Jordan interjected that perhaps the North Koreans and Iranians were bigger threats than poor Mexican immigrants,

Tammy gave Jordan a hard look he had never before seen on her face. Jordan wondered why he had always been intimidated by Tammy, but that thought was obliterated when he heard Lofton's next comments.

"The Mexicans come over illegally, and the men get their women pregnant, some married and some not. And more babies are born who the parents or the American taxpayer cannot afford to support. We just need to do something."

To hell with Tammy's hard stare, Jordan thought as he asked, "So what should we do? Maybe encourage more abortion?"

"Oh lord, no!" Lofton said. "Abortion is wrong. It's a sin. It's killing innocent children."

This time Tammy's look at Jordan was one of approval, and she picked up on his question: "So what should we do?"

"Well, uh, we, uh, we should do what's right and moral and obey the laws of this country -- the greatest country God ever made, a country founded on Christian principles and blessed by our Lord for two hundred years."

"So what is immoral about trying to find a better life for your family? What goes against Jesus Christ's principles about working hard -- doing, as our politicians say, necessary jobs that Americans won't do -- so you can send money back to your poor parents, wife, and children back in Mexico?"

Now the hard stare came from Lofton Victor. "What's going one here?" he said. "I thought this was going to be a straight interview, but I guess I should have known better, that I couldn't get any honest treatment from the media. So maybe I should just tell you this interview is over and ask you politely to leave my property."

"No, please," Tammy said. "My assistant did not mean to insult you. He was just asking questions that other people might ask."

Then Tammy looked at Jordan and said, "Please, Jordan. I know you are new in this television interviewing business, and I mainly hired you to work the camera and take care of production aspects, so would you kindly take the camera and let me interview Mr. Victor, so he will not misunderstand our intentions."

Tammy handed the camera to Jordan and then addressed Lofton Victor.

"I'm sorry, Mr. Victor. We are here to do a truthful story on the illegal immigration situation along the southwestern United States border, and we would like to hear what you have to say, since you are obviously, to use a cliché, on the front lines."

"Lady, I would be happy to explain the situation to you, but I'm getting just a little bit suspicious about where you're going with this story considering the questions that your, uh, assistant started asking. I'm not interested in talking with anyone that is trying to make me out to be an abortion proponent or implying that I don't care about my fellow brothers and sisters in God."

"We apologize, Mr. Victor. I'm sure Jordan did not mean to imply either of those things."

"No sir. I did not," Jordan said, feeling appropriately contrite for almost ruining Tammy's interview.

"Look. Here's the deal if I continue with this interview," Lofton Victor said. "You let me speak my piece. And then you can ask questions."

"Fair enough," Tammy said. "We are rolling, Mr. Victor. You say whatever you like."

"Okay, here's what I was trying to say. I believe in this country. It's a good country. My only brother, Mr. Roblech's former Marine buddy, died in the service of this country. He believed in doing what's right because he was taught by my parents -- good God-fearing people -- to do what's right. We didn't grow up watching MTV videos. We grew up watching Hopalong Cassidy, Roy Rogers, Gene Autry, and all those other cowboy good guys, who did what's right.

"Now disobeying the laws of this country is not right, and aiding and abetting people to break the laws of this country is not right. I don't care if it is helping them to drink alcohol or take drugs illegally or helping them come illegally into this country. Those are acts that are against the law, just like burglarizing someone's home or murdering someone is against the law.

"Please understand that I have nothing against Hispanic people. They are, for the most part, as good as white people. Or I guess I should say Anglo people. And I guess I shouldn't leave out black people or Asian people or any other people in this world. As I said, we are all God's children.

"I just think we need to enforce our laws, and people should not come into this country illegally. And I shouldn't have to worry about the safety of my family everyday because illegal people are on my land."

Tammy asked, "Have any of these people harmed you or your family?"

"They haven't done any physical harm, but maybe that's because we keep our rifles and shotguns handy. But they leave trash strewn around, and a couple of my outlying buildings have been broken into."

Lofton Victor paused and continued, "But that's not the point. Are we supposed to wait until they hurt somebody before we do something? I just believe that we live in a country of laws, and it makes no sense to me to just let people disobey the laws and then make those of us who try to do right look like the bad guys. That's all. You can ask your questions now."

"I realize you make a good case, Mr. Victor," Tammy said. "But I also think you must be aware that many people think that rounding up and sending twelve million people back to Mexico would be an impossible task, and many others think it is just as impossible to prevent those people from coming to this country to seek a better life. I guess my question to you is: what would you do to prevent illegal immigration?"

"First, you got to police the borders. Then you got to prosecute the people who give jobs to the illegal aliens. If no one hired them, they would go back to Mexico."

Tammy looked at Jordan and said, "Okay, I think we're just about done. Mr. Victor, thank you for your time and cooperation. It's a complicated issue, and I hope we can help people understand it."

"Okay, ma'am. It is a difficult issue; I'll grant you that, but as I said, I don't think it's all that complicated. Just enforce the law. Black is black; white is white; wrong is wrong, and right is right. That's what my parents taught me and my brother. Norman was a big fan of those cowboy movies, the ones where the good guys always win. I wonder what he would think about what's happening in this country today if he had lived."

"Did Norman ever write your parents about meeting Flash Golden?" Jordan asked.

"Flash Golden, the cowboy actor? Norman met him? No, I don't believe he ever told Mama and Daddy about that? If he did, they didn't tell me. How did he meet him?"

"Excuse me, Jordan," Tammy said with perhaps one of the hardest stares she had ever given. "But we need to go; we'll be late for our next interview."

Jordan understood her message. They had no more interviews scheduled that day, and he knew her stare meant she did not want Jordan to talk about his relationship with her former father-in-law.

"Oh, we just met him once in a cafe in Southern California," Jordan said. "No big deal. He was a nice guy. No big deal, though."

"You know I was in junior high when Norman joined the Marines, and I've often wondered about his time in the Corps before the copter crash. Maybe you could come back sometime and tell me more about your friendship with my brother."

"Yeah, maybe we could meet for a beer sometime," Jordan said.

"Except I don't drink," Lofton said.

Figures, Jordan thought to himself.

"I'll see if I can find time to get together again," Jordan said. "But to tell you the truth, I was not Norman's main buddy. I was in the reserves and got out of active duty before Norman shipped out to Gitmo. My buddy, Buck, who's a long ways from here was Norman's best buddy. Did Norman ever mention Buck?"

"He might have to my parents. Of course, both of them are dead now. If you want to come back sometime, give me a call. And I'm sorry about getting so testy about the questioning. It's just that a lot of people don't understand how important I feel this issue is."

"Sure. No problem. I should have let Tammy ask the questions. I'll call you if I get a moment before we leave the area."

"What's your cell phone number?" Lofton asked.

"Are you really going to call that asshole?" Tammy said as she drove off Lofton Victor's ranch.

"Asshole? You were kissing up to him pretty much when I screwed up and started asking those questions he didn't like."

"I needed that interview. It explains the mindset of that pious redneck crowd who don't want anyone but good white people in this country."

"He didn't say that," Jordan countered.

"Oh yeah. He said it. You just have to know the code. What did he say? 'I have nothing against Hispanic people. Most of them are as good as white people.' Then he realized he had shown his hand and added the rest of the people who make up more of the human race than white people.

"And, 'Black is black; white is white; wrong is wrong, and right is right.' What the hell did he mean by that?"

"I took it to mean he's an absolutist," Jordan replied. "You know, like the guy who's running the country right now. No shades of gray. No waffling on good or bad, right or wrong. I sometimes envy that type of person. Life must be simpler without moral dilemmas. The only problem is that I just never could learn to buy into moral certainty."

Tammy voice softened as she smiled and looked at Jordan, "Mister, you had better watch it with being so understanding and forgiving of rigid arrogant assholes. Otherwise people are really going to think either you've become one of their allies or, perhaps even more dangerous, a proponent of one of those mellow Eastern religions."

They rode in silence for a couple of minutes. Then Jordan said, "Maybe your former father-in-law is to blame for me getting mellow in my old age."

"How's that?"

"I remember a conversation Flash and I had late one night at his place in Santa Fe when I told him I had learned more about right and wrong watching his movies on Saturday afternoon than I ever did in church on Sunday morning. That's when Flash told me there often are big differences between right and proper and between justice and law. Knowing what is right and what is justice is a lot harder to determine, he said. I've never forgotten that lesson."

"Funny you should mention Flash," Tammy said. "That's another irony from our conversation with Mr. Lofton Victor. He too said he got his convictions from cowboy movies. I wonder how he would have reacted if you had told him the real story about his brother and Buck and Flash and Angelina. I wonder how he would have reacted if you had told him he could have had an illegal alien ex-prostitute as a sister-in-law."

"I think he probably would not have been able to handle that bit of news," Jordan said. "That's why I tried to politely dodge his invitation to talk about the last few months of 1962. I have to comment that you, too, did not take the opportunity to burst his moral bubble by telling him what you know."

"No. But I have to admit I was tempted. But I thought, what good would it do? First, it probably would have ruined a good interview with maybe my best source for that point of view. And...."

Tammy shrugged, and Jordan asked, "And, what?"

"I don't want to do anything to hurt Angelina. I'm careful about protecting her past and her identity, just as I know that you and Buck are. We've all been through a lot together, much of it we probably wish we could forget, especially the saga of Durango and Harold, Anselmo, and Jesus."

"I'm hoping we can bury those memories just as those three ghosts are buried," Jordan said.

But ghosts don't die, and some ghosts were never dead.

The dirty bedraggled unshaven man making his way along the Mexican side of the Rio Grande remembered when he was a young man. He remembered how he had impressed the man who was the feared leader by being fearless, ruthless, and savvy enough to avoid arrest. Maybe that was why he was given the assignment to accompany the leader's trusted lieutenant on that long-ago mission.

Now middle-aged and looking and feeling older, the man wondered how his life would have turned out if his father had not died of thirst and become buzzard food in the Sonoran Desert trying to find work so he could feed his family.

Maybe the man should have never gone back to Mexico after the mission across the border. Still he survived after he went back across the border. He told the leader a story about how the two gringo males had killed his partner, and how he had to kill the American connection to keep him from talking, and how the American connection had made up the story that had caused the leader to send him and his partner across the border.

But he felt that the leader never really trusted him after that episode. It was a good intuition. The young man, rapidly growing older and more savvy, allied with one of his first boss's rivals in the drug trade business, and it was the young man grown older who killed his first boss.

But no business is more dangerous than the Mexican drug trade, and the now middle-aged man was lucky that he was caught by the police and imprisoned before one of his drug trade rivals or perhaps even a fellow cartel member found some reason to kill him.

He was also lucky enough to be in the right place at the right time when other drug gangsters instigated a mass escape, and now his luck had continued until he was hiding in the scrubby bushes looking for a chance to cross into the United States.

But he was tired, and he was hungry. He told himself that after crossing the river, he would find some place to sleep and some food to eat. He knew the Texas ranches along the river should offer those opportunities. If he could find no food on the ranch, he knew he could survive with the pistol he took from one of the weaker escapees. The pistol would allow him to take what he wanted and kill anyone who threatened his effort at a new life north of the border.

"Here are my edits," Tammy said as she inserted the tape into the player.

"....I believe in this country. It's a good country....my older brother died in the service of this country....He died for his country in a helicopter crash while the world was faced with threat from people speaking Spanish south of our border. Maybe the world hasn't changed much in the past forty years.

"....we should do what's right and moral and obey the laws of this country -- the greatest country God ever made, a country founded on Christian principles and blessed by our Lord for two hundred years.

"Now disobeying the laws of this country is not right, and aiding and abetting people to break the laws of this country is not right. I don't care if it is helping them to drink alcohol or take drugs illegally or helping them come illegally into this country. Those are acts that are against the law just like burglarizing someone's home or murdering someone is against the law....I shouldn't have to worry about the safety of my family everyday because illegal people are on my land.

"....Are we supposed to wait until they hurt somebody before we do something? I just believe that we live in a country of laws, and it makes no sense to me to just let people disobey the laws and then make those of us who try to do right look like the bad guys....

"The Mexicans come over illegally, and the men get their women pregnant, some married and some not. And more babies are born who the parents or the American taxpayer cannot afford to support. We just need to do something.

"First, you got to police the borders. Then you got to prosecute the people who give jobs to the illegal aliens. If no one hired them, they would go back to Mexico.

"Please understand that I have nothing against Hispanic people. They are, for the most part, as good as white people....

"I just think we need to enforce our laws, and people should not come into this country illegally.

"It is a difficult issue....but....I don't think it's all that complicated. Just enforce the law. Black is black; white is white; wrong is wrong, and right is right...."

Tammy clicked the button and said, "I think I captured his points. What do you think?"

Jordan scrunched his shoulders, pursed his lips, and said, "Well..."

"Well, what?"

"I don't know, Tammy. Maybe I'm not cut out for this TV journalism."

"Jordan, this is not really journalism. I'm making a documentary. But I'm asking you what you think about the edits. Did I capture his points in a way the viewer can grasp in the time I have? Of course, I may still have to trim it some, depending upon what else I have."

"Well, Tammy, you have it on tape. He said it, but he didn't say it in that sequence, and he said more. I....well, I guess it's like the old saying, 'I guess you had to be there...."

"Look, Jordan. Just tell me what you think is wrong with the edit, and let's get on with our project."

"Tammy, I think the edit makes Lofton look like a bigot, well, more of a bigot than he may be."

"So what would you do?"

"For starters, I would run the tape in sequence....

Tammy interrupted. "You just don't understand. Sometimes you can't run comments from an interview in sequence. Look, if I'm going to sell this documentary, I have to keep it under an hour. I have to capture what people say without leaving in all of their asides, duhs and uhs, coughs, stammers, and other stupid speech patterns that all of us have when we are just sitting around talking and especially when we get exercised about some issue."

"Okay. You're the boss. I just work here, but I'm not sure I belong in this job."

"Do you want out? If you do, that's okay. But stay with me until I can get another camera operator. I probably can get the woman who worked with me in Austin on the Joplin piece."

"No. No, I agreed to work with you, and I'm not going to bail out now. Please, don't take any of this personally. It's not your problem. I thought it might be fun to get back into reporting. I guess it's reporting whether you call it journalism or a documentary, right? But now I'm having second thoughts.

"Let's see. I thought I might like to be a newspaperman. Then I thought I might like to be a lobbyist. Then I thought I might like to be a science writer. And I've always told people I wanted to be a songwriter, but when I got the financial independence to do that, I didn't spend hours a day with my guitar and writing pen. Then I thought I would enjoy working on this project, and here I am whining about it.

"I guess there is a disadvantage of having a mind that is perpetually twenty-five. I haven't decided what I want to be when I grow up, and now it's beginning to look like I'll die before I figure it out."

"Jordan, I don't think I can help you with that. But thanks for sticking with me."

Then Tammy smiled a sexy smile and touched Jordan's cheek. "But I hope the off-hours have been fun for you."

Fun was a rare experience for the man looking for a chance to cross the Rio Grande out of sight of the Mexican police or U.S. Border Patrol. It had not been fun growing up without parents, one more child for an aunt to provide for, a child who was not her own. But his aunt did the best she could. She wished that the young boy's sister had not disappeared after her mother and her little brother had become ill. But the teen-aged sister thought both her mother and her baby brother were dead.

"Your mother is dead, and it is only a day or maybe hours before your little brother joins her in heaven." That's what the aunt told the girl.

Fun was even rarer when the baby who was supposed to die lived and made his way through the urban Mexican world of the 1970s. By the 1980s he was an accomplished gangster -- making money any way that was most profitable, killing with impunity.

But it was not fun.

And certainly the years in the Mexican prison were not fun.

And now exploring his last hope -- to escape to the United States and disappear in the crowd of millions of illegal aliens and make a new life was not fun. But the thought of making that new life excited the man. He knew he could make it as an American. He had met Americans, and he was as smart or smarter than most of them. And he thought he was as honest and moral as many of them.

But honesty and morality were not characteristics he had been taught. Nor were they characteristics that he thought were particularly valuable in progressing through the tough world of the last few decades of this planet's millions of years of existence.

And now he was watching as three men waded across the river. He watched as they stepped onto the Texas shore and ran into the scrubby trees that lined the river. He waited to see if any men in uniforms or badges came forward to apprehend them.

None did, so the man walked from his hiding place and put his foot into the water. Maybe when he got across the river into the new land, he could find his sister again.

Jordan Roblech had reached a stage in his life when he really did not care if anyone spared his life. He had no children, no living family, no wife, and, now, no living ex-wife. Unlike me -- the former Flash Golden -- and Buck, Jordan thought, he never even had the comfort of a loving dog or cat. When he took account, he realized he had only three friends -- Buck, Tammy, and Angelina.

"Quit feeling sorry for yourself," he said to himself in the morning. "Three friends are better than none."

But before the sun set, he was feeling sorry for himself again. He wished he had someone to talk to, but he knew that Tammy would look at him with her expression that was a mix of ridicule and sympathy when he started whining, bitching, complaining, or whatever one wanted to call his manly cries of pain.

Maybe his loneliness was the condition that led him to accept Lofton Victor's invitation to come back to Victor's ranch and tell him more about his late big brother. Tammy had flown to Vancouver for some finishing touches on her Joplin piece when Lofton called.

"I'll even buy some beer and maybe have one with you," Lofton said. "The wife won't know. She's in Dallas visiting our daughter."

"I'll also drive you out to a spot where all the illegals come onto my ranch. Show you some of the garbage they leave and the buildings they break into. Just don't bring the camera this time. This will be, as those liberal news guys say, off the record."

Jordan repeated to Lofton Victor that he was just the camera operator and off-duty, so Lofton did not have to bother with the trip to the ranch outskirts.

"No, I want to show you this place. Besides it's a nice drive. You can drink your beer and enjoy the South Texas scenery while we talk about the 1960s -- a world that doesn't exist anymore."

As they headed down the dirt road toward the river, Jordan looked out the window at the desolate landscape and wondered if Lofton was really serious when he made the comment about enjoying the scenery.

He wondered if his fellow native Texans who had remained in the state really thought the landscape of Texas was something to savor. He knew that many of them -- probably more than most other Americans -- traveled to other places in the world, and wondered what these loyal citizens found so attractive about their native state. Certainly it was not the weather -- intense humidity in the eastern half, blazing heat all over, hurricanes along the Gulf, flash floods in the Hill Country, ice and snow storms in the Panhandle, tornadoes anywhere. And, after living in Colorado, New Mexico, California, and Washington, Jordan was not impressed with the scenery. He would tell people that much of the countryside that people take for granted in those states would be national parks in Texas.

But Lofton did not grow up in Texas. He grew up in Iowa. Jordan had driven through Iowa once. He was on a road trip with a woman he met in Denver. They thought they might be in love. She asked Jordan to accompany her for a visit to her parents in a suburb of Minneapolis. It turned out Jordan liked Iowa and Minnesota better than his girlfriend's parents liked him.

He overheard her mother talking to her daughter when the two women went outside for a smoke. The mother asked if she really thought she was in love with "that redneck." He knew it was time to catch a plane back to Denver when his girlfriend answered, "I thought I might be, but now I guess not. But Mom, don't call him a redneck just because he talks funny."

Jordan did not talk as funny now. He had slowly lost his accent while Lofton Victor had picked up a Texas drawl.

Jordan sipped from his can of beer and asked, "So Lofton, what drew you to Texas?"

"My wife," Lofton said as he turned onto a dirt road that led to a small building near the river. "She's from Texas. We worked together in the Twin Cities. We fell in love, and she wanted to move back home, so we did. I had majored in agriculture at Iowa State, but I didn't want to be a farmer. Thought I wanted to be a corporate executive, so I got a job with one of the big food corporations, met my future wife, who was a company home economist. But she didn't like the North, thought the weather was too cold, and the people were, too.

"I tried to tell her they weren't cold, just more reserved than Southerners. Anyway, she wanted to come back to Texas, and I wanted her to marry me, and that's how I won her heart. Told her we could move back to Texas. We got married, and I became a rancher.

"And now I love it down here. I even like the weather. And my wife was right. The people are friendlier.

"But that's enough about me. Tell me about my brother. Was he a good Marine?"

"Oh yeah. We were all good Marines. The Marines don't put up with any other kind. But as I told you, I didn't know Norman as well as our friend, Buck. They were best friends.

"We were all radio operators. You know, the same job as the heroes in Leon Uris's great World War II novel, *Battle Cry*.

"But I guess the most memorable thing about Norman's, Buck's, and my time together back in 1962 was meeting Flash Golden."

Then Jordan spent the next half-hour telling about how he and Lofton's big brother had got to be my young pals back in California. But he only talked about times that Lofton could tell his wife or anyone's mother or aunt. He did not tell about Angelina. He did not mention that Tammy was my former stepdaughter. He just said he and Norman and Buck met me at Arlene's cantina, and Arlene and I were nice to them.

"Damn, I wonder why Norman didn't write us about that. He always was a big fan of Flash Golden."

Then Lofton's good-natured musing turned into cautious alarm as he pulled the truck up to the small building.

"Uh oh. Looks like we've had some more visitors. I just wish they wouldn't tear up stuff," Lofton said as he pointed toward the broken door. Then he reached for the shotgun that was behind the seat of the pickup.

Jordan opened the passenger door, heard the pistol shot, felt the bullet graze his upper shoulder, and then heard the blast from the shotgun and saw the blood spurt from the chest of the dirty, unshaven man as Lofton fired two more shots."

"Shit! Son of a bitch! Are you hurt bad? We got to get you to a doctor," Lofton said as he fumbled for his cell phone.

"No. I think he only grazed me. One thing for sure, I'm not hurt as bad as he is," Jordan said pointing to the man whose blood was flowing into thc dirt.

"Hell no! I figure he's one of the many illegals I've been trying to tell you and your woman friend about. Maybe he's an outlaw. I never had one shoot at me before."

Jordan said. "You still never had one shoot at you. He shot at me, and I probably owe my life to your good shooting."

"No, Mr. Roblech," Lofton said. "We both owe our lives to the fact that I had this shotgun to protect us. I don't know how you feel about gun control, but remember today the next time one of your journalist or liberal friends starts talking about restricting peoples' rights under the Second Amendment."

"Yes, I will certainly remember this day," Jordan said.

"You sure you're okay?" Lofton said.

"No. I'm not sure, but I'm pretty sure I'm not going to die from the bullet wound. Might have a heart attack or stroke, though, if I don't calm down."

Chapter 19
Pacific Waves and Caprock Mesas

It was not Jordan who had the heart attack. And his heart beat even faster when he got the phone call from the Canadian hospital.

"Ms. Dolcito asked me to contact you," said the person on the other telephone. "I'm the doctor treating her after she had the heart attack, and she and I thought it would be better if I informed you. It might be a little too tough on her at this point in her treatment."

Jordan was still in shock from being shot and seeing Lofton Victor fire three shotgun blasts into the desperate man who had fired the pistol, but Jordan quickly realized he had no time to process the events of yesterday. He had been treated at the South Texas hospital for the slight wound. He had given the sheriff a statement about how the man had stepped from the out building and fired a pistol at him and how Lofton had defended himself and Jordan with the shotgun.

Now he was wondering how fast he could get a flight from San Antonio to Vancouver, British Columbia. He asked the physician on the phone if he really thought it was better that he did not talk to Tammy.

"Yes. I'm sorry, but Ms. Dolcito is at a critical point right now. I promise you I will keep you informed."

"No worry about that, Doc. I'll be up there as soon as I can be there."

"Okay. That would be good," the doctor said.

Jordan knew it was an ominous sign when the clerk at the hospital desk picked up the phone after he told her he was there to see Ms. Tammy Dolcito. His pulse began racing as it had after the ranch shooting when the clerk asked him to take a chair in the waiting room and that a doctor would be meet with him in few minutes.

"I'm sorry, Mr. Roblech. Ms. Dolcito had a second heart attack last night, and it was fatal."

Those were the only words from the doctor that Jordan remembered. The rest of his time in Vancouver was a haze. He had been almost killed by some unknown man on a South Texas ranch, and before he could recover from that event, one of the few women who had meant something to him in his life had died of a sudden heart attack. Nature has a way of protecting humans from the overload of emotions that would blow their brain circuits in those traumatic times in their lives. It puts them into a state of shock. But the shock has different effects. Some people become hysterical; some just act goofy; and others -- like Jordan -- become matter-of-fact robots who do all the things necessary to get through whatever tragedy they are facing. That was what Jordan did when his mother died. That was what he did when his father died. And that was what he did when Tammy died.

Jordan had not expected to be Tammy's unofficial next-of-kin. She had no kin. But Jordan was relieved to learn she had a lawyer and a will. It divided her estate between Planned Parenthood, the American Humane Society, and an organization that protects abused women.

Tammy also stipulated that she wanted no funeral, no burial, no cremation, no dumping into the sea. She donated her body to a medical school. She had made her death simple, much more simple than her life. Jordan contacted the lawyer who had helped Tammy write the will. After the lawyer said he would take care of the details, Jordan realized there was little else for him to do in Vancouver.

Jordan had called the cell phones of both Buck and Angelina several times. No service, the message said. He dialed the numbers again. No service. Jordan knew that Buck and Angelina were somewhere in the Pacific along the South American coast.

Rather than return immediately back to San Antonio, Jordan decided to take a few days and revisit the Olympic Peninsula before flying out of SeaTac. He was under no time pressure because he had purchased a one-way ticket, not knowing when he would return.

Jordan drove back across the border at Blaine, through Bellingham, and turned west onto Highway 20, over Deception Pass, down the length of Whidbey Island to the ferry to Port Townsend. He spent a day walking around Dungeness Spit and then driving up to Hurricane Ridge. That night in Port Angeles he bought a Seattle newspaper and settled down to read it before going out for a late dinner.

On the front page of the local section was a story about a teen-ager who had been killed when a woman using her cell phone had lost control of her SUV and hit him as he walked along the sidewalk. The accident had happened a week earlier, and the boy had died at the scene. The article that Jordan was reading was not so much about the dead teenager, whose body lay unclaimed for days because his single mother was in prison. Rather the follow-up story was about the pistol found on his body. Ballistics had shown it to be the gun used to kill Shanna Outseagle, and the youth's description -- young black male -- matched that of the shooter.

A young impoverished, illiterate adolescent with a pistol. Jordan wondered what Lofton Victor would say about this case. Probably that Shanna Outseagle and her friends should have taken along a couple of constitutionally ensured weapons on their weekend outing in downtown Seattle.

Jordan put down the newspaper, picked up his cell phone, and made a reservation to fly back to San Antonio. He realized the Pacific Northwest no longer held any good memories either.

From the San Antonio airport, Jordan drove west toward the Rio Grande. He wanted to check in with Lofton Victor and make sure Lofton was clear with the law, make sure that the authorities understood that Lofton had saved Jordan's life and had killed the unknown gunman in self-defense. He called Lofton, who suggested that they meet at the sheriff's office.

"It's all settled. It was an unfortunate happening, but we need to move on with our lives. I know God was looking after us, and we need to thank him for that," Lofton said.

"Yes," the sheriff said. "There's no doubt about what happened. You and Mr. Victor stopped a viscous criminal from going any farther and doing more damage in this country. Who knows what this animal would have done if he had gotten past the borderland into cities like San Antonio, Houston, or Dallas."

Jordan took a deep breath and said, "So you know who he was. He was a criminal from Mexico?"

"Yes," the sheriff said. "We identified him. He was a drug gangster and killer who escaped from a Mexican prison along with several others."

"Have you got time for lunch?" Lofton asked.

"Sure," Jordan said. "I guess I got the rest of my life. Thanks to you."

As they ate their barbecue sandwiches, Jordan told Lofton that Tammy had died and consequently Lofton would not be featured in a future documentary.

"I'm sorry to hear about your friend," Lofton said. "So you're not going to pick up the project?"

"No. No, I was just a friend helping her out. I don't have any interest in illegal immigration, certainly not anymore. I just want to go somewhere and try not to think about anything unpleasant for a while -- some place that's peaceful and doesn't have many distractions and allows me to be by myself for a while. I think I know a place up the road a few hundred miles, a little lake outside of Lubbock."

Lofton said, "There probably won't be many people bothering you up there. So good luck."

Jordan picked up the check, and the two men shook hands as they walked out of the cafe.

"Sorry again about Ms. Dolcito, and I hope you find some peace on the lake," Lofton said.

"Thank you," Jordan said. "By the way, I never did ask you the name of the man who tried to kill us. I guess I should at least know that."

"Oh yeah," Lofton said. "They shipped his body back across the border. The sheriff said no one claimed it, so I guess he didn't have any family. Or at least, none who wanted to admit to being his family. It's hard to imagine having kin like that.

"Anyway, his first name for this low-life scum was ironic. It was Jesus, except, as you know the Mexicans pronounce it Haysus. Yeah, his name was Jesus. Jesus Perdidos."

Ironic, Jordan thought as he drove Buck's car up the spine of Texas -- through the Hill Country, north toward Abilene, west on Interstate 20, and northwest on U.S. 84 to the farm-to-market roads leading to White River Lake. Buck had given him the key to the house overlooking the lake and said he would tell his landlady that a friend might be staying there bcforc Buck returned from his sea journey.

So much irony, he thought. Ironic that the man Lofton Victor shot could have been his brother's brother-in-law if the world had turned differently a half century ago. Should he tell Angelina about her brother's ignoble end, that her former lover's brother had killed her brother after her brother had tried to kill another of her former lovers? But, he thought, lovers was not the right term for his relationship with Angelina. Angelina and Norman had been lovers. He and Angelina in that hung-over morning in the 1980s had just been two people who needed release from horniness.

Were Buck and Angelina lovers on the boat, Jordan wondered. Or were they just two people taking care of each others' aching loneliness and desires?

Jordan dialed Buck's cell phone again. Still no service. He had decided that he would not tell Angelina about her brother -- one more secret that he would keep into eternity. Angelina believed her brother had died years before.

It would have been good if her brother had died years before, Jordan thought. It would have been good if her brother had never been born. Maybe it would have been best if none of us had been born, he thought.

"No, that's not right," he said out loud to himself. "It's been a good ride even if the horse stumbled, and I got bucked off a few times."

Jordan finally connected with Buck by cell phone a week after Jordan settled into the house by the lake. Buck and Angelina had docked in Chile. Raul's remains were splashing about in the waters off his homeland. Jordan could tell by the tenor of

Buck's voice that his friend was having a good time.

But moods changed when Jordan told Buck about Tammy. Jordan heard Angelina crying in the background when Buck turned and told her the sad news.

"I'll call you later," Jordan said.

The next day, the two friends talked again after several aborted connections.

"We like this place," Buck said. "We might stay here for a while. Let's try to stay in touch by e-mail. That's more reliable than cell phones," Buck said.

"Yeah, I guess I'm becoming addicted to this laptop, too," Jordan said. "Hell, as a would-be writer, I've even thought about starting a blog. Then I come to my senses and ask myself, who are these people who sit around and surf the Internet all day? Got to be a bunch of wackos."

"Or people who are too old or infirm to do anything else -- people who can't jog, so they blog," Buck said.

Buck sent the first e-mail.

"It was good to hear from you. Angelina and I are both really sad about Tammy. It seems that so many of our friends and loved ones have died before their time -- my parents, Norman, Arlene, Raul, Jim, and now Tammy. I guess Flash is the only one who lived his allotted seventy-odd years. But damn, I wish

he had lived longer. Anyway, he will live forever in my mind. You know, I've been thinking a lot about your song -- the one about life being a circle. I hope that's right, and I hope somewhere in this world there are some little boys and girls and adults walking around, doing good deeds, not knowing that they have lived before with the likes of us, but having the good lives they deserve. Still, if life is really just a line, I'm glad I had the chance to walk it with you, buddy."

Jordan wrote back:

"Whoa, you're being way too philosophical, buddy. You need to go back to painting. I'm having a good time sitting out watching this little lake and the nondescript but pretty mesas that surround it. I'm writing a few songs and getting better and finding the right keys and strings on the guitar. Maybe my mood has been changed by the lady I've met. She's a couple of years older than us, but she's still one foxy-looking woman. She retired out here after she and her late husband Clay sold the liquor store they owned on the strip outside of Lubbock. Her name is Candy, and I think she likes me. For some reason, I'm feeling good again, even in this god-awful Texas summer."

Overlooking the Pacific, Buck read Jordan's reply and remembered back to the fall of 1960. Angelina gave him a puzzled smile when he began singing:

"Blueberries ain't blue; they're purple.
"Life's not a line; it's a circle.
"Tie don't go to the runner,
"But it'll get better come summer."

Angelina smiled and said, "But it's winter down here."

"Oh! Oh! Eiahh!!! Ah! Ah! Oh! My God, it's so good! So good! Ah."

Jordan released his passion, took a few breaths on top of Candy, pulled out, wiped, and rolled over on his back. Candy smiled at him as they looked out the window at the dwindling little lake shimmering in the July heat.

"Damned global warming," Jordan said.

"What does that have to do with fucking?" Candy asked. "The weather hasn't seemed to slow you down any."

"No. I wasn't talking about sex. I was just looking out at the lake drying up and thinking about why the damned politicians haven't recognized how we're fucking up the whole world."

Candy did not say anything, so Jordan continued with what he later realized was a strange rant after pleasant sexual activity.

"But then the stupid Republicans couldn't and can't recognize how they've fucked up everything by this stupid war in Iraq."

Now Candy reacted.

"What? Are you a goddamned stupid liberal Democrat?"

Jordan realized they had never talked politics, and he gathered from Candy's question that she was, like most of her fellow Texas voters in the first decade of the twenty-first century, a Republican voter, if she voted.

"No. I'm not anything. But I would vote for the proverbial yellow dog before I would vote for Bush," Jordan said.

"Shit!" Candy exclaimed. "If you didn't provide such a good time in bed, I might throw you out of this house right now. Dubya is the best thing that has happened to this country in a long time."

"You got to be kidding?"

"No, I'm not kidding, and I'm serious. I ain't going to let any goddamned liberal fuck me, neither literally nor figuratively."

"I told you I'm not a liberal. I don't particularly like any of the current Democrats either."

"You better not. I guess I can put up with someone who doesn't like any politicians," Candy said.

"I didn't say I don't like any politicians. Hell, I used to make my living talking and working with politicians. I'm just disgusted with what's happened to politicians and the political system in the past couple of decades."

Neither said anything for at least a minute. Then Candy spoke.

"I'm sorry. I didn't mean to sound like such a bitch. But I just can't stand most of those Northeast and West Coast politicians preening on television. They're almost like all those nig -- I mean, black -- football players who dance around in the end zone after they catch a football. Sons of bitches! That's what they pay millions of dollars for those bastards to do -- catch the football. And I find myself screaming at those pompous Democrats on my widescreen TV. If you don't like what the current leadership is doing, then get the balls to come up with a better plan."

Jordan smiled as Candy took a breath and continued as she put her left hand between Jordan's legs.

"But then a lot of them literally don't have any balls, and I like people who have balls, so let's see if I can get a little more juice out of this set," Candy said as she bent her head over Jordan's midsection.

As she puckered her lips, she and Jordan looked up as a car pulled into the driveway.

"Shit!"

"Who's that?" Jordan asked.

"It's my son. Get dressed quick."

"Your son? I didn't know you had a son."

Get dressed, goddammit! And go quickly out the back door. I'll talk to you after he leaves."

"Oh! Oh! Eiahh!!! Ah! Ah! Oh! Dios mio, es bueno! Muy bueno! Oh Luis!!! Oh Luis!!! Si! Si! Oh, es muy bueno! Oh! Oh!! Oh!!!"

Buck had enjoyed those sounds of pleasure all the way from Panama to Chile and for a month in the apartment he and Angelina rented in the beautiful beach town.

But this time it was not Buck who was inspiring Angelina's moans and squeals. She obviously had not expected him to return so soon from Santiago, where he had gone to inquire about how to get a long-term visa.

Now he realized that he probably would not need that visa. He turned and walked out of the apartment before Angelina and the man in bed with her realized he was there.

In the small beach cantina, he drank his wine and wondered about what he had just heard. Whose name did she call out? Luis? Yes, that was it. He had met only one Luis in the month they had been in Chile. Luis Renaci, Angelina's brother-in-law.

Luis was a few years younger than his brother, near Buck and Angelina in age. And even though he was probably at least sixty, Luis was still fit and, certainly for his age, physically attractive, characteristics he shared with his sister-in-law.

He also was, like his late brother, a rich heir. He had fled Chile with the rest of his family, but he returned in the early '90s when the right-wing Pinochet was no longer president and the leftist Allende was long dead.

Angelina made contact with Luis soon after they arrived in Chile. He was on the boat with them when they placed his brother's ashes into the Pacific. He seemed like a gentleman to Buck, and perhaps that is why Buck did not question why Angelina seemed so fond of her brother-in-law.

"But I guess I'll have to find out what's going on, and I guess the only way to do that is ask Angelina," Buck told himself as he finished the wine.

"You didn't tell me you had a son."

"You didn't ask. Does it matter?"

"No. I guess I should ask about the rest of your family. Do you have any other children?"

"No. He's the only one."

Candy and Jordan were in the living room of Jordan's rented place. She had knocked on his door before eight o'clock. They were drinking coffee.

"Are those tears in your eyes?" Jordan asked.

"Yes," Candy said.

"What's the matter?"

"I didn't know whether he was alive or not." Then Candy broke into a full sob. "And it may have been better if he wasn't."

Jordan reached over and put his hand on hers.

"So do you want to tell me what's going on?"

"He's a meth addict. He's really fucked up. Just like his father, except Clay was only a drunk."

She wiped the tears from her eyes and continued.

"Only a drunk." Her tone moved from pity to derision. "A drunk that gave me a few black eyes and broke my nose once."

"Your son hasn't hit you, has he?"

"No, at least, not yet."

"Are you worried that he might hurt you?"

Candy sighed and sat silent.

"So you are worried," Jordan said.

"I'm not really worried about myself at this point. I'm worried about my son. I don't know what to do to help him, just as I couldn't help his father quit his drinking."

"So, has he committed any crimes?" Jordan asked.

"I don't know. Probably."

"Maybe going to prison would be best for him. Maybe that would straighten him out," Jordan said.

Candy gave Jordan a look of disgust and said, "Have you ever been in prison? No, of course not. But what good would it do for him to be in prison with a bunch of niggers and Mexicans. Oh shit, Mr. Liberal, I forgot to be politically correct. But I don't give a shit right now."

Jordan ignored the last part of Candy's dialogue and did not remind her that he was not really a liberal by the current definition. He realized that his tolerance of intolerance was thinning. He already knew he had never been very forgiving of criminality. Or stupidity, even though he knew he had been stupid, like everyone.

Still, he thought, it's stupid for this woman to come over and unload all of her trouble on him before he had his second cup of coffee.

Then compassion came in and pushed irritation toward the end of the bench in his brain. After all, we've been intimate and she needs help, he thought.

"So, what can I do to help you?"

The tears came back as Candy looked into her cup.

"Probably nothing. Just be here for the next few days. I may need a friend."

Luis was gone when Buck returned to the beach apartment. Angelina was in the shower. Buck was in a chair with a beer when Angelina walked into the front room.

"Oh, you have returned. What did you learn about visas?"

"We can get them easily for six months," he said.

"Bueno," she said.

"But I guess I don't need one."

"What?"

"I'll be heading back to the States."

"What are you talking about?"

"Angelina, I came back a couple of hours ago. You and he were in the bedroom. I heard you."

"Oh," she said as she slumped into the other chair in the room.

Neither said anything for more than a minute. Then Angelina said, "Buck, I'm sorry."

Buck still did not say anything.

"I'm so sorry," she repeated. "I knew that I would have to tell you, but I did not know how."

"So how long have you two been, uh, lovers?"

"It depends upon what you call lovers," Angelina said. "We first made love two years ago after Raul had his surgery. But we knew it was not right, and we vowed to not do it again.

"Buck, I did not mean for this to happen. It's just that....I suppose I am not a good woman. But I can't help it."

Again they sat in silence.

"Oh, don't beat yourself up, woman," Buck finally said. "If you love him, you love him. I don't guess there's anything either one of us can do to change that. We had a good time, and now I guess it's over."

Buck put the beer bottle on the table beside the chair, got up, and said, "I'll be packing now."

"You don't have to go," she said.

"Yes," he said. "Yes, I do."

As he walked toward the closet where he had put all of his belongings, Angelina called out, "Buck."

"Yes?"

"Remember when we met in the alley in Tijuana?"

"Of course."

"Remember when the pimp who was going to cut me said I stole the sailor's money?"

"Yes."

"I did take the sailor's money. I've always wanted money as much as I have wanted a man. See, I told you I guess I'm just no good."

"My little lost angel," Buck said. "I'll tell you one more time. Don't beat yourself up. There's nothing wrong with wanting a man with money, no more wrong than all of us men wanting a woman as beautiful as you. I hope it works out for you."

He moved again to get his belongings, then turned with a smile and said, "And I hope things really do get better come summer."

Summer was almost over when Jordan got the phone call from Buck.

"How's it going?" Buck asked.

"Not so well," Jordan said.

"Oh yeah? What's happening?"

"I guess I've been reminded that I shouldn't get too close to my neighbors. How's it going with you and Angelina?"

"It's not going at all. She found someone who's richer, more handsome, and just all around has more to offer than I have."

"Oh, so I guess we both have some news to convey. How many minutes do you have left on your cell phone?"

Jordan told his story first. It was not easy for him to recount.

Candy had left Jordan's lake house after telling him she probably would not talk to him for at least a couple of days. Jordan did not know how to react. When Candy closed the door behind her, he went to the kitchen cabinets and got his bottle of Irish whiskey. He poured an ounce into his coffee cup and thought about how he was fortunate to have no living family to complicate his life or cause him to worry.

Before noon Jordan looked out a window and saw the car pull out of Candy's garage. Both Candy and her son were in the car. Jordan went to the cabinet and prepared another Irish coffee. He was still glad he had no family. No kids or grandkids to worry about in this world careening wildly into ignominy, illegality, irresponsibility, and insanity.

Jordan finished his coffee, made a bloody mary, and got his guitar from a closet. He began strumming it and singing lyrics he had composed the day before. He put them to a blues tune:

Oh Mama, you wouldn't believe the world today.
Mama, ain't that what old folks are supposed to say?
But I miss when the funny papers and those great folk songs
Made us think we'd be the ones to right all the world's wrongs.
But, Mama, we didn't do that, according to the news I read,
And now Dylan's past sixty and Schultz is dead,
And the world's no better, just crazier instead.
So I got the Bob and Charlie blues.
Yeah, the Bob and Charlie blues.
Bob's past sixty and Charlie's dead,
And the world's no better, just crazier instead.
And I got the Bob and Charlie blues.
Oh yeah, the Bob and Charlie blues.
Oh Mama, politicians tell us we're in the land of plenty
While the corporate pirates raid the fortunes of many.
And so many people, young and old, suffer and die
Without health care as no one bothers to ask why.
Yeah, Mama, more of us are finding it hard to get ahead.
And Dylan's past sixty and Schultz is dead,
And the world's no better, just crazier instead.

So I got the Bob and Charles blues.
Yeah, the Bob and Charlie blues.
Bob's past sixty and Charlie's dead,
And the world's no better, just crazier instead.
And I got the Bob and Charles blues.
Oh yeah, the Bob and Charlie blues.
In jungles, deserts, even the streets of L.A.,
We've fought to preserve the American way.
But it seems a lot of this world don't give a damn
About the sacrifices or principles of Uncle Sam.
And it don't matter if we vote blue or vote red,
When Dylan's past sixty and Schultz is dead,
And the world's no better, just crazier instead.
So I got the Bob and Charles blues.
Yeah, the Bob and Charlie blues.
Bob's past sixty and Charlie's dead,
And the world's no better, just crazier instead.
And I got the Bob and Charles blues.
Oh yeah, the Bob and Charlie blues.
Oh Mama, we got computers twice as smart as us,
Microwaves, Botox, and GPS for our fancy trucks.
And going to the moon's no longer science fiction,
But we still can't cure hatred, poverty, or addiction.
Now we're running out of time, and, Mama, as I've said,
Dylan's past sixty and Schultz is dead
And the world's no better, just crazier instead.
So I got the Bob and Charles blues.
Yeah, the Bob and Charlie blues.

Bob's past sixty and Charlie's dead,
And the world's no better, just crazier instead.
And I got the Bob and Charlie blues.
Oh yeah, the Bob and Charlie blues.
Oh Mama, we drove our big rigs from ocean to ocean,
Never once having the slightest notion
That our grandkids and generations after that
Would be left with a messed-up world thermostat.
Oh, I'm afraid someday the last boomer will go to bed
After me and Dylan and Schultz are all dead,
Gone from a world no better, just crazier instead.
So I got the Bob and Charlie blues.
Yeah, the Bob and Charlie blues.
Bob's past sixty and Charlie's dead,
And the world's no better, just crazier instead.
And I got the Bob and Charlie blues.
Oh yeah, the Bob and Charlie blues.
Yeah Mama, this old world's gone plumb insane,
Oh, if there's any truth to this reincarnation thang,
I hope I can wait a while before coming back again.
Cause sometimes I envy the people already dead,
And gone from a world no better, just crazier instead.
Oh, it's true, I got a bad case of the blues,
Yeah, a real bad case of the Bob and Charlie blues.

The former Flash here, dear reader. I think that may be the best piece that Jordan ever wrote, probably because I've been waiting to come back again. I just hope I don't have to come back as some poor urban kid with an unmarried mother; a child of impoverished parents in Mexico, Africa, or wherever; a baby born in Jaffa or Baghdad; or a clueless kid who thinks he's special because he was born rich. Oh well, in seventy or eighty or fewer years, it won't matter anymore again. We'll all be dead and nobody again.

Candy did not return to her house within two days, three days, four days, five days, or six days.

During that week Jordan sat on the ramshackle deck of his rented house and finished off the liquor in the bottles he had bought from Candy's former establishment. He looked out at the little lake, the scrubby vegetation like that around Albuquerque, the flat mesas standing timidly against the clear sky but nothing like the majestic mountains of Colorado, Washington, or even New Mexico.

He remembered his and Buck's side trip to the Custer Battlefield along the Little Big Horn River, a landscape that was as scenically unimpressive as the Caprock. On the edge of Montana, Wyoming, and South Dakota, Jordan and Buck were in the heartland of the Sioux and Cheyenne. Now he was in the middle of Comanche country, an area that extended west to New Mexico and east to the Dallas-Fort Worth area.

But the Sioux and Cheyenne do not rule Montana, Wyoming, and South Dakota. The only Comanches who have any power are those half-breeds whose ancestors happened to own land where oil was discovered in the early twentieth century -- people who most likely were descendents of white women and Comanche men or Comanche women and white men, in many cases children of matings that were not consensual.

Jordan remembered his trips to Mexico as a young horny Texan and Marine. He pondered if those thirty-minute relationships were consensual. But as he thought about those moral and philosophical questions, the glass usually dropped from his hand and he woke up when the coyotes started howling.

Candy did not return on the seventh day, and Jordan told the woman who owned the lake house that he was leaving. As he packed, his cell phone rang. Buck was on the other end.

"So do you want to find someplace else to get in trouble?" Jordan asked.

"Yeah, that's why I'm calling. How about I meet you at the Dallas-Fort Worth Airport?"

"Why there?" Jordan asked.

"Because it's got the most flights to South America out of Texas."

"Aren't you already in South America?"

"Used to be. But I don't have anymore friends down there now. So I'm back in the good old U.S.A. -- the great Dallas-Fort Worth Metroplex. Godawful place. Can't understand why so many people think it's a great place to live -- traffic, crime, all the things that make America great, I guess.

"But I'm looking for a friend to continue to explore South America with -- maybe Argentina or Bolivia or both. Do you think maybe you'd be that friend?"

"What makes you think I want to go to Argentina or Bolivia?"

"What else better do you have to do?"

The line was silent for a few seconds while Jordan tried to come up with an answer.

"Good point," Jordan said. "How's your Spanish?"

"It's gotten pretty good in the past few months. How's yours?"

"Oh, I figure between the two of us, we can get by. We know how to say cerveza, relaciones, and dinero. What else is there?"

"That just about covers it," Buck said.

"So, do you want to be Butch Cassidy or the Sundance Kid?"

Buck snickered through the phone and said, "Neither. I ain't planning on robbing any banks or mine payrolls. But it's still probably a good analogy for a couple of old would-be Western renegades like us."

Then Buck took a breath and said, "Unfortunately our Etta Place found a better guy to hang out with, just like the Etta a century before."

"Well, life's not a line. It's a circle," Jordan said.

"Yeah, so you say," Buck said. "Shit, maybe we won't get all the way to South America. Maybe we'll stop in Nicaragua, Costa Rica, or Panama. I understand a lot of American boomers are actually retiring in those places. After all, it's summer all year down there."

Then he paused and said, "Except, as you know, I don't particularly like summer, certainly not in hot places."

"And, as you know -- me neither. I guess we just don't fit the model. Don't want to relax all day in the sunshine. Don't have any old women or middle-aged kids to look after us as we get more creaky and cranky. But maybe we've always been odd ducks."

"Yeah, I guess so. Meet you at the airport on Saturday, Butch."

"Okay, Sundance."

The former Flash here again, dear reader. This is the end of my tale. But then a circle never ends, does it?

Printed in the United States
133867LV00001B/1/P

9 781602 642782